A
Disobedient
Girl

A Disobedient Girl

A NOVEL

Ru Freeman

ATRIA BOOKS

NEW YORK   LONDON   TORONTO   SYDNEY

ATRIA BOOKS

A Division of Simon & Schuster, Inc.
1230 Avenue of the Americas
New York, NY 10020

First Atria Books hardcover edition July 2009

ATRIA BOOKS and colophon are trademarks of Simon & Schuster, Inc.

For information about special discounts for bulk purchases, please contact Simon & Schuster Special Sales at 1-866-506-1949 or business@simonandschuster.com.

The Simon & Schuster Speakers Bureau can bring authors to your live event. For more information or to book an event, contact the Simon & Schuster Speakers Bureau at 1-866-248-3049 or visit our website at www.simonspeakers.com.

Designed by Kyoko Watanabe

Manufactured in the United States of America

10 9 8 7 6 5 4 3 2 1

Library of Congress Cataloging-in-Publication Data

Freeman, Ru.
A disobedient girl : a novel / by Ru Freeman.—1st Atria Books
hardcover ed.
    p. cm.
1. Women domestics—Fiction. 2. Rich people—Sri Lanka—Fiction. 3.
Women—Sri Lanka—Fiction. 4. Social classes—Sri Lanka—Fiction. 5.
Sri Lanka—Fiction. 6. Domestic fiction. I. Title.
    PS3606.R4455D57 2009
    813'.6—dc22

        2009013499

ISBN 978-1-4391-0195-7
ISBN 978-1-4391-2356-0 (ebook)

For my mother, my first teacher and editor, who taught me to expect more than the quietly possible out of life. And for my father, who demonstrated the worth and pleasure of breaking a few rules along the way, and whose wisdom I continue to acknowledge only after the fact.

"I am resolved of all indignities. She remains
wrapped like a flower, like the bloom
of a flower, within herself, far away.
The wind like an ogre moves
around her, not touching."

—Gamini Seneviratne, "I, the Wind,"

from *Another Selection*

· PART I ·

Latha

She loved fine things and she had no doubt that she deserved them. That is why it had not felt like stealing when she'd helped herself to one of the oval cakes that were stacked in the cabinet underneath the bathroom sink in the main house. Who would care if one went missing from the seven sitting there, awaiting their turn in the rectangular ceramic soap dish bought at Lanka Tiles to match the new pale green bathroom towels? And, since she had been right and nobody had noticed, it was now a reliable source of luxury. When one wore out, which it didn't for several months, she simply fetched herself another.

Every day, at 3:30 PM, she cleaned her face, feet, underarms, and hands at the well, using one of those cakes of *Lux,* which, despite having escaped, undetected, with thieving, not daring to smell like flowers all day long, she reserved for this ritual. Every day the soap, pink and fragranced, filled her nostrils with the idea of roses. She had seen real roses only once. That had been when the Vithanages had taken her with them on a trip to the hill country one April. She had been five or six then, her second year with them, back when her duties had been few and blissfully pleasing. The hill country, with its lush, verdant cleanliness, the ice-cold brooks, and the famous Diyaluma waterfall, at whose foot she had stood as part of the family, all their faces sprayed with mist, wet with the tears that the particular slant of the falls, airbrushed water in slow motion, invariably brought

3

on. After the falls, they had driven down for a picnic at the gardens in Hakgala, where the roses bloomed in such perfection that only their scent distinguished them from the artificial creations sold in Colombo. From that day on, roses had become a delicious prospect—a memory and a luxury blending together on her face, caressing her.

Today, as always, she felt sad as the relatively warm well water took the bubbles and the smell down the sloped pavement and evaporated both instantly between the blades of grass at her feet. She straightened up and looked off into the distance, smelling the tendrils of hair that hung long and wet down both sides of her face; she used her left hand to gather the strands nudging her right cheek, that being a more dramatic gesture, she thought, than using her right hand. This was the moment when, in her soggy state, she imagined herself into a teledrama, playing the role of the beautiful yet discarded maiden, surrounded by the soft aura of the virtuous wronged.

Next to the presence of finery, she also felt, quite strongly, that her life should unfold with a minimum of three square helpings of drama, as soul minding and body feeding as the plate of rice or bread she was given at each meal. The old well at the edge of the garden, which was used only for washing clothes and, in her case, for bathing, and which therefore she considered an extension of the spaces that belonged to her, was the perfect place to dwell on those fantasies and to populate them with characters propelled by passion, wrongdoing, and guts.

"Latha! Lathaaaaaaaaa!" That call was part of this late afternoon event too; the sound of Thara's voice calling her from the veranda, making sure that she hadn't gone without her. The maiden went the way of the soapy bubbles and Latha returned to being eleven years old again.

"*Enava,* Thara Baba!" After all this time, she still felt silly saying it. Baba. How could someone her own age be a baby? She picked up her tin bucket, the soap hidden beneath her washed underwear, and headed toward the house.

Thara met her halfway down the path.

"Can we go to *that* street again today?" she asked, linking arms with Latha.

"*Aney,* Thara Baba, I'm going to get into trouble because of you." She said it because she wanted to put a check mark in her head after the word *tried.* After all, who could fault her for being an accomplice to Thara's misdemeanors if she had *tried* to dissuade her? It was one of the first English words she had learned at school. *Try! Try! And try again!* The school principal still insisted that they chant this every morning, and though there were rumors that he sympathized with the people who wore red and marched with banners embroidered with the sickle and hammer on May Day, and that his job was a front for spreading a doctrine that encouraged his students to think themselves equal to the rich, and though all of that was considered dangerous and subversive, his message and, frankly, his possibly clandestine life resonated with Latha. She had resolved to follow her own interpretation of his creed: she might get it wrong, and she might get in trouble, but by god she would *try* to be better than she was. Next to her, Thara giggled happily; it was time for the flowers.

The flowers they picked from other people's gardens were various, and arranging them was Latha's specialty. She liked to get an assortment but favored the pastels. Rings of white vathu-suddha studded here and there with small-petaled yolk yellow araliya, her favorite flower. Sometimes, a small sprig of Ixora for a splash of red, even though the plant was considered poisonous to the mind by some who sounded like they knew these things; Soma, the old servant, for instance, with her faded clothes and neatly whittled hands that handled vegetables like pliant but precious gems, testing their firmness with a press of concave fingernails. Every now and again, if she was lucky, a fresh, new-blooming gardenia that needed nothing else, its perfume, its satin skin, its very existence enough of a reminder of highs and lows, being and death.

But lately it wasn't the flowers that Thara was after. It was the Boy. The Boy lived on the street that paralleled theirs, within the same Colombo 7 neighborhood. Thara had explained it all to Latha one day, checking off the necessary requirements on the fingers of one hand: race, religion, caste, school, looks. Of these, Thara cared about the last two. The other three were for her parents' benefit. Of course, the right address was the icing on the cake.

"Colombo Seven is best. Next is Colombo Three, Colpetty. After that . . . well, Colombo Five and then maybe, if everything else is absolutely perfect, even the money, then Colombo Six. Nothing else. Amma would never tolerate it, so why bother? Right? Right, Latha? Why bother? Might as well stick with the known crowd. I'd never go for a marriage proposal, so might as well bring home someone they can stand."

"What if the marriage proposal is better?" Latha had asked.

"How can it be? If they could find someone by themselves, would they ask a Kapuwa to do the work for them? No. Only uglets with cowcatcher teeth come calling with their mothers in tow, the matchmaker with his pointy black umbrella leading the way. Not for me. I'm going to find him for myself even if I have to grow old doing it."

Well, she had found him all right, and before her twelfth birthday, *and* living in the right kind of house to boot. Despite Latha's reservations, she had to approve of her young mistress's resolve and enterprise, and not only because Ajith came complete with a friend: Gehan. That was a bonus.

Gehan was probably destined to be one of those who would have to rely on a matchmaker to find himself a wife. Latha felt certain of that. He had none of Ajith's grace or good looks, none of that air of knowing his place in the world. He was a hanger-on, and completely ordinary. Latha was sure she had passed by him dozens of times on her treks to the stalls that bordered the cricket grounds to buy mangoes seasoned with chili and salt from the street vendors. Yes, he had been there, buying pineapples, or maybe olives. He looked like an olive eater. Her mouth watered as she imagined the taste of a boiled green olive, the vinegar and spice orchestrating its small earthquake on her tongue. She could see him spitting the seeds onto the sidewalk. Not like Ajith and Thara, or even herself; they all knew how to get rid of pits discreetly. She sighed. Well, no matter, they came as a pair, and Gehan would always be available whenever Ajith was, and she was hardly likely to find a romantic interest anywhere else, no matter how deserved that outcome would be.

"Want to try stealing today?" Thara had asked her the day they found the Boy.

"*Chee!* I can't steal!"

"Come on, it's more fun," Thara begged.

"No, baba, I can't let you do that," Latha said. "It's a sin. How can we pray with stolen flowers?"

"Why not? If everything must come to an end and die, then how is a stolen flower different from any other flower?" Thara practiced her latest coquetry, shaking her head from side to side so her shoulder-length ponytails whipped the sides of her cheeks. Latha's hair came down in waves, and she thought it was prettier than Thara's, but Mrs. Vithanage, Thara's mother, had insisted that Latha wear hers in tight plaits. Sometimes she practiced the cheek whip when nobody was home but it never looked the way it did for Thara, whose straight, silky hair brushed her face like it loved it. When Latha tried it, her hair, thick and heavy, refused to cooperate, hanging down the sides of her face and making her look like the bad women in the teledramas, the ones whom the village ostracized or husbands left their wives for. She consoled herself then by noting that they got a lot more screen time than the good women with smooth, broad foreheads who parted their hair in the middle and never changed styles.

"In fact," Thara continued, "it's a better flower to offer. It reminds us that there is evil in life, nothing can last, and we must remain unmoved by these things."

"But shouldn't we remember what the priest said about not stealing? What about the five precepts?" Latha asked, *trying* again.

"Why do you want to bring the precepts into this? We're just talking about the flowers." Thara flung up her hands. The bangles she put on in the evenings went tinkling down her thin forearms and gathered at the joints in her elbows. She cocked her arms and shook the bangles down to her wrists again. She looked funny doing that, like a chicken flapping its wings. Latha smiled just a little. They must look like sisters standing face-to-face like that, except for their feet, one set smooth and sandaled, the other ashy and slippered. And the bangles, of course. Latha didn't own any bangles. Her eyes followed the movement of Thara's arms, staying one jingle behind the narrow circles of glass. Finally Thara stopped, her fists dug into her waist, waiting for a response.

"But if we steal the flowers, then we're breaking the precepts! There is a right way to get flowers and a wrong way to do it." This was Latha's last *try*.

"There is no right and wrong, and precepts are for fools. Everything is just as it is! And we must experience things without condemning them, because if we condemn them, then we're becoming too involved. That's what I think the priest meant when he talked about it last Sunday at temple."

"I don't understand all these things." Latha shook her head and looked miserably at her empty siri-siri bag, fiddling with it and causing it to make the soft tissuey squeak that gave it its name.

Thara pushed out her lips and scratched a mosquito bite on her chin. Suddenly, she grinned. "How about this? The *flower* must remain unmoved by being stolen or being picked with permission, or even by dying! We can remember that as we recite our prayers this evening if you like," she said, her cajoling beginning to wear Latha down. "Besides, it would be quicker."

Thara was right about that bit at least. Half the time when they went flower gathering, they would have to leave because nobody was home to ask, even when there were so many blooms on some bushes that the owners would never have noticed it if they had picked a few on their way out. Besides, wouldn't they be creating merit for the owners by using their flowers for prayers? Latha squared her shoulders and nodded.

"*Hanh ehenang,*" she said, relenting.

The first three houses were easy. There were no gates and, more important, no dogs. But the fourth presented a series of problems, the largest of which was a grandmother moving around, albeit slowly, in the house. They watched her for a few minutes, hidden from view behind a short and somewhat prickly hedge.

"Hopefully she's deaf," Thara said. Latha suppressed a giggle. She felt a warm, pleasant excitement gather between her legs, like wanting to pee and never being able to pee again, both at the same time. She clutched Thara's arm.

"I'll keep watch, baba, you get the flowers," Latha said, warming to this new sensation brought on by good intentions and bad behavior.

"No, you pick them and I'll keep an eye on the old cow." Thara shoved Latha away from her and onto the gravel driveway. Latha scurried across it and pasted herself against the trunk of the araliya tree. But the very characteristics that made it so lovely to have in a garden—the low, spread-apart branches; the thick, large, moisture-rich leaves; the bunches of waxy yellow blossoms—all these ensured that it provided very little cover for an eleven-year-old girl in a bright blue, puff-sleeved dress. It was a tree meant for lovemaking, a leaning tree, not a tree for hiding from grandmothers.

"Kawda?" The voice was at once beseeching and nasty. The old lady, dressed in a housecoat of indefinite hue and cut, was at the window, shading her eyes and peering into the garden. The pee began to leak into Latha's underwear. Tears threatened to start up top. Thara was gesticulating wildly from behind the hedge, mouthing a word Latha could not understand. *Run? Come?* Maybe she was just gaping. After one last and somewhat manic series of gesticulations, Thara grimaced at Latha and stepped out from behind the bushes. She walked boldly to the front door and rang the bell. It had a tinny, high-pitched sound, entirely at odds with the dimensions of the soaring pillars and beams that made up the house, built in the style of a Walauwwa. The Boy opened the door before the bell stopped ringing and grinned at her.

Latha was just about to step out from her ineffectual hiding place when she heard the sly, teasing hiss behind her. And that was how she met Gehan.

"So how many of those flowers are stolen?"

"Naa . . . api . . . ," she said, looking somewhere off to the right of his left shoulder but instantly aware of everything about him: that his blue-checked shirt was the same color as her dress; that he wore khaki shorts and *Bata* slippers, like hers; that his hair stood up on end along the path where he had just run his hand through it, like a sculpture; that he was very brown, browner even than she became during cricket season, when she and Thara climbed the roof of their house to watch the games. One more thing: he was wiry and elon-

gated, like a reedy plant reaching for sunlight through dense shrubs; everything concentrated on the upward journey, just the barest of threads for roots.

"Don't worry, I won't tell. I'll even pick a few more for you. Look. Here, take these."

Why did he have to pick the entire bunch? She always made it a point to pick only the blooms. She couldn't stop herself: *"Aiyyo!* Don't pick the buds! You're wasting the flowers!"

"You're wasting the flowers!" he mimicked. "So what? There are at least two hundred on this tree, and tomorrow, two hundred more!"

Latha frowned at the bunch he had picked in its entirety off the tree: her favorite flowers, in all their golden sun-and-moon beauty. He wouldn't put them down but continued to hold them in his outstretched hand. He looked ridiculous: a romantic hero without the face or manner for it. Milky white sap was dripping onto his dusty slippers. There was dirt under his toenails. He shuffled his feet under her stare. She sighed and took the offering, stooping to rub the stem in the dirt to stop the bleeding.

She turned to go, then paused. "Thank you," she said, over her shoulder, pouting her mouth as she said it. He smiled and she felt happy; perhaps he had not guessed that she was a servant. She tried to ape Thara's confidence as she walked over to join her at the door.

Thara's voice brought her back to the present.

"Come, Latha! Let's go before Amma gets home!" Thara shouted as she ran to get their bags for the day's picking.

"Just give me a minute to change my dress. I'll meet you by the gate."

Thara stopped running and turned around. "Change your dress? What are you changing your dress for? That one looks fine."

"But I've been helping Soma nenda in the kitchen and it smells like curries and anyway it's wet now," she said.

"It'll dry as we walk and nobody's going to smell you after all so what's the point of changing?"

"I'll meet you by the gate," she said, and ran away before Thara could argue. She went into the storeroom where she slept, between the padlocked *haal pettiya* full of dry goods and spices and the barrel full of unhusked rice, and she put her soap away on the wooden shelf next to her mat, hiding it carefully behind an old Vesak card with a picture of the Sri Maha Bodhiya on the front. She spread her towel and wet clothes on the rack near the door. Then she climbed on a low bench and took her blue dress off the coir rope where she had hung it to air after the last time. If she was going to get in trouble, she wasn't about to let Thara bully her about her dress.

She slipped on the thin leather slippers that had once belonged to somebody, a relative of Thara's who was a schoolteacher, she imagined; they were that kind—flat, unflattering, and noisy. They were a size too big for her, and she had to grip them with her toes when she walked, but at least they were not her old rubber slippers, at least they made her feel dressed up. She checked the picture of the English princess that she had cut out of the newspaper and pasted inside one of her exercise books. Latha had taken to the princess afresh since she'd read in the accompanying article that she had been a nobody and a nanny who looked after other people's children before she decided to become a princess instead. Having confirmed that, indeed, the look she had been practicing, peering out with her chin tucked but her eyes uplifted, had been properly copied, Latha stepped out. Then she went back into the storeroom and lightly stroked the still-moist surface of her soap. She rubbed the tips of her fingers on her wrist, then rubbed her wrists together like she had seen Thara do when she wore her mother's perfume.

Now she was ready.

Biso

I have mended his slippers. Frayed, old, pinned together between the toes. This is the most that is possible. The temple bells are ringing. I pay heed, though their sweetness has been lost to me for years. I see him before the last chimes fade, picking his way through the mangrove swamps. Beyond him the sea. I would go to the water if I knew it would not humble me. Twice I tried, walking into the blue, two in one hand, one in the other, singing. But when the waves broke over us I half-drowned to save them. Dragging their confused bodies to shore until that, too, became mere play. No. No more of the hot, brined sand under our feet, no more rituals to stave off my madness. We will go to the cold green hills, to the slopes of tea and the music of waterfalls. I will make them forget.

There is a full moon tonight and the children wait, just out of sight in the kitchen behind me, still dressed in their white school uniforms, waiting to light lamps and incense around the Bo tree. I press into the splintered frame of the door as he pushes past me.

"Move, *vesi!*"

I cast my eyes down at my feet, but I stay where I am. *Whore, bitch, cunt.* Words that came calling with such fury the first time but lost their effect so soon. He looks confused but staggers indoors. I wipe his spit off the front of my blouse with the edge of my sari and raise my eyes to my children. They scamper to my side, little mice.

Outside, the air is moist, and Loku Putha leads the way. He has his father's walk, his face, his movements, the same quick eyes, the same rare smile, but he is still only nine years old. Give me two years, and with the grace of the gods he shall not become his father. My firstborn daughter stumbles over some hidden root, and he turns to catch her. He grabs her hand, steadies her, then shakes it off. He clips the side of her head with his knuckles and wipes his hand on his shirt as though she were tainted.

"Watch where you're going! *Pissi!*" he adds and looks defiantly at me.

Her face wrinkles. "Aiyya called me an idiot . . ."

"It's okay, Loku Duwa. Stay here next to me," I say, and take her hand in mine. My youngest, the baby, glances at us, then runs ahead to join her brother.

"She'll fall before we reach the temple." She sounds as if she wishes that upon her younger sister: a fall, a scream, tears, a bloody knee, a ruined evening, blame. I sigh and stroke my daughter's hair, trying to ease her older-sister conundrums, jealousies and concerns twisting together, inseparable.

The chanting of the priests floats over the sound of the sea. The smells of oil, incense, frangipani, jasmine, and lotus mix with the taste of sea salt on my tongue. It calms me. I heave another sigh, audible and long, and feel my anxieties rise up out of my body and drift away.

A boy about my son's age accosts us; he wears a banian and a pair of shorts that are too small for him. "Five cents to look after all your slippers," he says.

"That's alright, putha, we'll leave them here," I say, and stroke his head. He smiles but ducks from under my palm, moving on to other potential customers. Nobody steals slippers at temples, and yet there are people who pay to have them watched, as if they had not come to temple to meditate on the transience of their lives, on the irrationality of clinging to their possessions. We leave our slippers in a dark corner outside the temple walls and climb the thirty-three worn steps to the top. Once there, I wiggle my toes in the liquid sea sand and smile.

Despite all that has happened to me in this town, I have always loved this temple. Each full moon I have come here, alone at first, then with my firstborn, my Loku Putha, to watch him crawl on all fours at the roots of the holy Bo tree, then with both of them, my son and daughter, and now with all my children. I used to come here with Siri when the moon was not full, when the temple was likely to be empty. We would come here to light a lamp, and to reflect upon how insignificant we were, when alone, in the scheme of things, in the same way that our flowers lay, dying before our eyes at the clean, empty shrines: two flowers, two sticks of incense, two people, and all of the Buddha's teachings surrounding us in the quiet. But on Poya days like this, the moon full and low over the ocean like a lantern we ourselves had reached up to light, I came with my children to forget that lesson, to do what a mother must, to take heart in the crowds of people, in their essential goodness, in the arrays of flowers piled high and seemingly abundant with life and hope. *That is how it is when people gather together,* Siri used to tell me; *we can convince ourselves of immortality, even in a temple.* How prescient he had been, though he hadn't known it then. I have never come to temple with my husband, not even when we were first married and I asked him to accompany me. He was always uncomfortable with tranquil pursuits.

"Amma, I want to light the first lamp," Chooti Duwa says beside me, pouting in anticipation of my answer, waiting for her older siblings to preempt her with their usual cautionary words. When I say yes, her mouth and eyes open wide, letting in as much delight as her slender body can hold.

I stand aside and watch them. My son cleans out five lamps, one for each member of our family, while his sisters take note of his every movement. Chooti Duwa holds our basket of flowers; her older sister clutches our incense and candle.

"I'll pour the oil," Loku Duwa says. She takes out the old *Arrack* bottle that I had cleaned out and taken to the Mudalali to have it filled with a half-pint of coconut oil this morning. Standing on her toes, she fills these first lamps with great care.

My boy lights a match to the candle that the little one has in her hand now, then he bends down and picks her up. He holds her over rows of wrought-iron lamps, most of them already lit. Her dress is too short for her. Loku Duwa tugs at the fabric, giggling a little at the sight of her sister's exposed bottom under the scrunched-up skirt, the white knickers that I stitched the way the nuns showed me, puffing up on the side closest to her brother's body, one round buttock revealed. Together they make the kind of picture I have seen in the newspapers, the ones they put on the front page after a Poya day, to show the country that innocence has survived and will endure, to remind us that there is something worth living for when all seems lost. My little girl wriggles at the touch of her sister's fingers, and some of the wax from her candle falls onto Loku Putha's hand. He yelps in pain, but he continues to hold on to her. He reserves his frown for Loku Duwa.

"Stop it, *modaya*! You're going to make me drop her. Chooti Nangi is going to burn herself!"

Idiot. Fool. These are the words he uses to address his firstborn younger sister, never referencing their relationship with the proper term, Nangi. I sigh and move away from them and sit by the temple wall, among other women, my legs tucked sideways underneath my body, my palms together, my mouth reciting prayers by rote, mulling over my children, their respective flaws, their way forward. Do all children come into being in the same fashion? Already marked with their future, a history-to-be prewritten by their predilections? I wonder. My son, dark skinned and full of some untouchable resentment, with his backward glances and watchful spirit, had come to me that way, come out of my body full of anticipated slights, taking his independence as soon as he could walk. There was some knot in him that no amount of breast milk could console, no amount of attention suffice to untie. Then my first daughter, dreamy and sad from the start, never able to articulate what it was that she felt, never knowing, exactly. I had tried to soothe them both in all the usual ways, done my best to keep myself safe for their sake, until Siri found me and my attentions turned away from them; then I stopped trying, telling myself that it was useless, that they were who they were. Only his child, Siri's daughter, my youngest, had seemed untouched by an already-known fate; only she had seemed blessed by possibility, as if, with time and knowledge, she would become something other than she already was.

Their faces are illuminated to varying degrees as they stand be-fore the rows of lamps, first by the candle and then, when my baby reaches out and lights the first lamp, by the second flame and then the next and the next. When her brother puts her down, she runs to me and curls into my lap. I hold her close; my baby, conceived on a night like this, under the full moon, hidden by the still-wet catama-rans pulled up onshore. In everything she does, I see Siri. In the way she moves, her footsteps deliberate with pride, in the way she regards the world, her chin lifted, as though she were assessing its worth and finding it both fascinating and hospitable, in the mischief that dances in her eyes. She has kept him for me, made it impossible for people to forget him or to say that she is fatherless. I know these three children, who they are, what they desire, where they are bound, and that is the proof of my love.

Tomorrow, I will go with the dew under my feet to the plantain grove beyond the kitul trees that my father put in when my son was born. Those first plantain trees have given way to the offspring who came up around their trunks; I tended them all, felling the old to give way to the new, revisiting not just the grove but, through my care of them, my parents' lands, where I had first learned to be mindful of the growing things that sustain us all. I will cut down a frond from one of the young trees and I will walk home in the morning rain with it over my head. He will not hear me rip the leaves, or smell the steam when I hold them over the wood fire to turn their waxy green to dark. In silence I will lay them out, in silence make four mounds of still hot rice, embedded with hard, dried, salted fish, the taste of my life by the sea. Two pieces each for the girls and myself, three for my son. The orange coconut sambol, ground with the last of our dried red chilies, will stain the white. Condensation will have to provide the gravy. I will add them to the woven market bag that once belonged to my mother and that I have carried for ten years. I will slash the kurumba from our front yard with my knife, drain the sweet water into my children's plastic drink bottles. Then I will go to them. Instantly awake at my touch, rising with practiced stealth, they will follow me. When he wakes up, stinking, drunk, we will be gone . . . gone . . . gone . . .

Latha

L atha!"

"*Enava*, madam!" She always had to yell just as hard as Mrs. Vithanage in order to be heard, and she was still working on finding a way to infuse reverence into her screams. Mrs. Vithanage was becoming testy with her.

"This girl is always somewhere else. She used to hover next to me like a cat. Now I never know where she is. Latha! *Mehe vareng!*"

Latha cringed. She hated it when Mrs. Vithanage used the derogatory conjugation of verbs on her, the *vareng, palayang, geneng* that was the lot of laborers. She stopped running and began to walk. If she was going to be insulted, she was going to deserve it. Let her wait. Latha passed the driver, who stood by the family car, a sedate black *Peugeot* with white, plastic-covered interior that had arrived in the country in a fleet that had been imported by the government seven years earlier for something called the Non-Aligned Conference; she had learned about that at school because it was one of her principal's favorite topics, the conference, not the cars, which latter he had condemned bitterly. All day the driver loitered there, next to that car, even though he knew exactly when he was needed and even though that schedule never changed: take Thara to school at 7:00 AM, take Mr. Vithanage to the Ministry—whatever that was— at 8:30 AM, bring Mr. Vithanage home for lunch at 12:30 PM and return him to the Ministry after, and bring Thara home from school at 1:30 PM; on Tuesdays, take Thara to elocution lessons (where she had learned, and subsequently taught Latha to recite parts of *"The Lake Isle of Innisfree"* and *"The Song of Hiawatha"* and *"The Highwayman,"* which last was her, Latha's, favorite, what with the maiden and all) at 3:00 PM; on Wednesdays, pick up and drop off the piano teacher at 4:00 PM and 5:00 PM respectively; on Fridays, take lunch for Thara at school and wait until she finished swimming lessons to bring her back, smelling of chlorine, ravenous; and every day, bring Mr. Vithanage home at 5:30 PM. Thursday mornings he took Mrs. Vithanage to the market, with her hair in a bun.

"Latha?" the driver said as she passed, a greeting and an acknowledgment of her existence.

She stopped. "What?"

"No . . . nothing. Why in such a bad mood?" He snapped a green twig from a bush of poinsettia (there were poinsettias all along the driveway, and personally, she thought they were ugly: pale, undecided colors and too much foliage) and began to pick at his teeth, sucking bits of lunch out from behind his jaws. Disgusting. He wasn't bad-looking despite the fact that he was short, and the dark skin, but *chih*, what terrible manners. "Too much work?" he asked her, after a particularly robust, and clearly productive, suck.

She scowled. Why he insisted on talking to her as if she were an equal she had no idea. Didn't he notice that she sat in the backseat with Thara when she accompanied her on occasion? Not next to him, like the gardener did?

"I don't know why you suck your teeth like that. It's such an ugly habit."

The driver snorted. "Madam is in for trouble with you, isn't she? Sending you to school and all that. You better watch your attitude. Soon . . ."

Mr. Vithanage came onto the veranda, dabbing at the perspiration on his face with a creased brown and white checked handkerchief. She had washed and ironed it just yesterday. Washing. She hated having to do the washing, but since Mrs. Vithanage's row with Soma, the old servant, Latha was the only one left. She wished Soma would come back. In her absence Latha had become the cook, cleaner, and laundress, and while she didn't mind the ironing, she detested the washing. It made her hands sore. It made her back ache. Most of all, she had no time to pick flowers with Thara, which meant . . .

"Latha! Child, can't you hear madam calling you? What are you doing standing here? Go and see what she wants." Mr. Vithanage gestured vaguely into the house, shook his head, and stepped down to the portico.

The driver held the back car door open for him and then shut it. He leaped up the steps, picked up Mr. Vithanage's briefcase from the cane chair between the mahogany pedestal table and the matching urn with its arrangement of fake ferns the likes of which Latha had never seen in nature, and deposited it with great respect on the front seat. He got in on his side, stroked the steering wheel three times, and brought his hands together in worship. He touched the picture of the Buddha that he had cut out of a Vesak greeting card and hung from the rearview mirror with a bit of black cord, then started the car. He caught Latha's eye and held her gaze as he drove slowly down the curving driveway. Latha rearranged her body, pulling it up to its fullest height, and shouted, this time with more deference.

"Madam, I'm here. I'm coming."

Well, it couldn't last, could it? She should have known it. One day they were picking flowers and eating ice palams out of green and white striped pyramid-shaped boxes, pushing the sweet bars out with their fingers on the one side, groping for them on the other with their wet tongues—she, Thara, the Boy, and Gehan—and the next it was done. They were all ready to go when it happened.

"Thara! Latha! Come back in here. Where are you going?" Mrs. Vithanage was standing at the top of the steps on the veranda, her arms crossed. She was wearing one of her hand-loomed cotton saris with *Guippio* lace edging on her blouse. A bad sign. She was most virulently Radala bearing when she wore *Guippio* lace. Latha did not know where it came from, that lace. It was stronger than the local kind, though if she had to choose, she'd pick the latter because of the way it felt against her skin, soft and imperfect, like the work of human hands.

"To pick flowers, Amma," Thara said, her voice all girl and honey. Latha stifled her giggle.

Mrs. Vithanage frowned. "You're too old to do that. You don't need to go picking flowers anymore. Let the gardener do it."

"Amma! The gardener doesn't know how to do it. We know all the houses, and they know us!"

"Exactly. You have become common in this area. Soon they'll be talking about you like they *really* know you. Yes, no more picking flowers. Get back inside and practice the piano." Practicing the piano was Mrs. Vithanage's idea of a solid punishment, which made Latha wonder if she was actually invested in Thara's acquiring skill in playing the instrument or if all the piano lessons were merely serving some lesser role, as an excuse for Mrs. Vithanage to keep her daughter from other, more desirable, activities. This sort of banishment to the piano was becoming far too frequent to do Thara any good, since she went to it only in anger and banged furiously at the keys with no thought to the pieces she was playing.

"Latha, you go to the kitchen," Mrs. Vithanage continued. "I will tell the gardener to get the flowers from now on."

Mrs. Vithanage stared into the distance over their heads, down the driveway, past the garden, beyond the gate that was wheeled into the wall and wheeled back shut by the driver each time the car passed through. She could probably see the future too, Latha thought, with that amount of focus. She squinted her own eyes and tried to copy the look: seeing but not seeing, here but actually there.

"Amma!" Thara's voice broke Latha's concentration.

"*Kollo!*" Mrs. Vithanage's voice was strident, summoning the gardener. An end-of-discussion voice. Latha flinched.

The gardener came running from behind the poinsettias, his hedge clippers in hand. What had he been clipping? Latha was sure the gardener did nothing most of the time. He just carried his tools around, wheeling his barrow here and there as if he were engaged in something. It was always empty. Didn't anybody notice that it was always empty? Mrs. Vithanage assigned him the task as Latha and Thara listened, their heads cast down in perfect imitation of each other, their long braids—these days Mrs. Vithanage insisted that

Thara braid her hair too—hanging to the same length down their backs. Thara had new white sandals with heels. The heels clacked when she walked. Latha didn't like the sound of the clacking, only the height that the heels gave Thara, who now appeared older and more ladylike. She curled her toes in her own slippers. Maybe she could ask Mrs. Vithanage to buy some sandals for her with her pay. Better still, maybe she could ask Mrs. Vithanage to give her the money directly, instead of depositing it in the bank every month.

"Latha! Stop daydreaming! What are we going to do?"

Latha looked up. Mrs. Vithanage and the gardener had disappeared. Thara looked miserable.

"I don't know what to do. We'll let him pick the flowers, I suppose." Latha's mind was still on the white sandals as she looked—up, for now—at Thara's face.

"Not the flowers, you fool! How will I see Ajith?"

"Maybe he can come here," Latha said thoughtfully, crossing her arms in front of her. She was sure she didn't strike quite the same pose as Mrs. Vithanage. She needed a bigger bosom for that. Her arms slipped down to her waist.

"When? Amma is always here."

"Yes, but she's not in the garden, is she? They can come to the back gate, and we can hide behind the garage and talk." The plurals had slipped out, but Thara hadn't noticed. She never seemed to notice.

"But what about the driver?" Thara stood in front of her and jiggled up and down in anxiety. She looked older than Latha right then, her smooth brown skin creased around her mouth and eyes, the eyes full of worry, pleading for help.

"He won't tell," Latha said, feeling secure all of a sudden about the driver's allegiance.

"How do you know?" Thara grabbed Latha's arms and undid them, holding on.

"I don't know how I know, but I don't think he will tell."

"Amma will kill me if she finds out."

"I thought you said he was the right kind of boy. Won't she be glad that you found him by yourself?" Latha smiled.

Thara hit her playfully on her arm, then squeezed her. Latha grinned.

The next day, Thara rewarded her further with a strip of glittery gold paper from a roll, about three feet long, for which she had traded three felt pens, including red, in school. The paper rustled and glittered in their hands, and the very best part of it was that, when they rubbed it against their bodies, the gold shimmer came off on their skin and lips. Then, when they took orange star toffees and sucked on them until they were all sticky and put that on their mouths, it looked like they had lip gloss on! Fair's fair, and Latha set about assisting Thara in her quest for privacy with renewed resolve. For a time, between the fake lipstick and the constant scheming required to avoid Mrs. Vithanage, both of them were either blissfully happy or inconsolably miserable. In short, they were in heaven.

But, of course, that spell had to be followed by the biggest change of all, and after that, *everything* was different: Thara attained age.

For months, it seemed, Thara had talked of nothing else but how many girls in her school were wearing bras.

"We call them holes so the nuns don't know," she confided to Latha, sitting on the well and swinging her legs as Latha squatted beside her and scrubbed the clothes with a wedge of hard white *Sunlight* soap she had hacked off a long bar, peeling the yellow wrapper back so she left the rest unblemished. She didn't like *Sunlight* soap. It never washed things properly. She had seen something called *Sunflakes* in the stores, bright blue packets with pictures of basins full of suds, hanging down the sides of the shops from black ropes. The shopkeepers had told her that they made washing clothes easier; you just had to put a little bit into a big tub and shake the water, they said. But when Latha told Mrs. Vithanage, she had scoffed and refused to buy them. *We do things the old way in this house* is what she had said, and Latha had felt particularly outraged at the use of the *we* in that sentence, given that it was only she who did the washing. This was why she had taken to bringing a knife down to the well and making flakes out of the bars, not caring that it would be considered wasteful by Mrs. Vithanage, and rejoicing in the fact that indeed it did make it easier to wash the clothes, so long as she used the hard soap after the first soak.

"Latha! Listen to me instead of staring at those stupid clothes! We call them holes because you can't see the bra but you can see the little hole-shaped imprint on the back of the uniform where the straps come down."

Latha bunched the pile of white, box-pleated, sleeveless uniforms she was washing and beat them repeatedly on the flat stone put there for that purpose. She imagined bras inside them. She disentangled one of Mrs. Vithanage's enormous bras from a soapy pile of underwear and put it underneath a uniform, then held it up. "Like this?"

"Yes! Exactly like that!" They both laughed. "And we know that she has got her period because that's when you get the bra. First, the girl is gone for seven days from school, then when she comes back she has all new clothes. New uniform, new shoes, new ribbon in her hair, and"—she paused for effect—"the bra."

Latha considered this information, thinking about how everything in her school was different from Thara's, beginning with the gravel path, instead of paved asphalt, that led to it, and ending with this latest bit of information about seven-day absences on account of a first period. She had visited Thara's school once to pick her up after a sports meet, and Thara had walked her around the spacious grounds: the auditorium, with its dressing rooms and black curtains on either side of a curving stage for entrances and exits; the chapel, full of quiet and cool, its courtyard flooded with the voices of an after-school choir practice singing harmoniously in English about a river called the Blue Danube; even the administrative building, where the principal sat and made announcements over a sound system fed into every single classroom filled only with girls from good or rich families. Latha's school had none of that, wedged as it was behind storefronts and facing the back of a church. She learned everything in one classroom, and intervals were spent standing around chatting with other students or writing notes to be given to Gehan. Nobody had lunch boxes or drink bottles. Every once in a while some girl or boy would bring in a rupee or two and buy bright pink pori from the barefooted street boys who loitered at the entrance to the school, but that was the extent of it.

Well, what did it matter? Her principal had assured them that everybody learned the same thing, using the same government text-books, and took the same national exams, so they should not feel less than anybody else. And he was right: she and Thara studied together sometimes, and the only difference between what they learned was that Thara read it all in government textbooks that always seemed brand-new while Latha read textbooks that were always dog-eared and battered.

"Nobody in my school is absent for that long," Latha said. "We only know because they walk all grown-up, looking for boys."

"How strange," Thara said, looking genuinely puzzled. "I won-der why they don't get to take a holiday."

Latha shrugged. It seemed pointless to stay home for seven days, for her, anyway. If she stayed home, she'd only have to do more work. More laundry, more fetching and carrying, more of the driver and his stupid comments. May as well go to school. Besides, she got to see Gehan on her way to school and on her way back. He met her each morning and cycled next to her down two entire streets in the middle of her walk; a few times he'd even let her ride with him, seated on the middle bar, her legs twisted tight together and away from the pedals, her head not touching but, still, only inches from his chin, near enough to feel his breath. Too close to home and someone would tell the Vithanages. Too close to school and someone would tell the teachers. But in the middle they were invisible. That anony-mous time was what she woke up for each morning these days, for those twice-daily meetings with Gehan, whose interest in her had not wavered even after he realized that she and Thara did not share the same social status though they emerged and disappeared behind the same walls. She wished she could tell Thara, but some unspoken agreement made both Gehan and her remain quiet about their more-than-a-friend friendship.

Once, she had tried to bring it up with him. "I wonder if Thara Baba knows . . . " and she had faded off, assuming he knew what she meant. But he had taken her down another trajectory of thought, musing instead about the relative worth of the Vithanages.

"Families like hers always try to be better than they are by sur-rounding themselves with people they can bully. If you take all those people away, Thara is the same as you and me, Latha. Worse, even. How would they ever look after themselves if they didn't have somebody to order about to do it for them? I'm telling you, they are the ones the JVP is after. When they get into power, it'll be all over for people like them."

Latha had neither agreed nor disagreed; she didn't care about politics anyway. She was content simply to listen to him put the two of them on the same side of this equation and happy to join him in that space. She thought, also, that the school principal would approve of her choice had he known of it, the same way Thara was sure her mother, Mrs. Vithanage, would approve of Ajith if she knew of him. And standing next to Gehan that day, Latha had conjured up a wedding she had seen in a teledrama just that week and let it play in her head, substituting herself for the heroine and imagining the whole thing: herself decked in white, with those seven necklaces, including the gold jewelry around her forehead, jewels on her feet and over her arms, a bouquet of yellow araliya clasped in her hands, and Gehan dressed up like a nilamé, four-cornered turban and all, his thin body plumped by the forty-eight yards of cotton cloth in his costume, a glittering silver knife tucked into his belt, and proud to extend his hand and watch the kapumahaththaya tie their little fingers together while the voices of nine little girls all dressed in white half saris washed over them with their blessings.

She smiled to herself now as she remembered this, seeing those little girls all over again, hearing those first lines, *Bahoong sahassa mabinim . . . mitha sā yudanthang . . .*

Next to her, Thara sighed. "I can't wait to wear a bra."

Latha stared at her for a few moments, reluctantly letting go of her secrets so she could consider Thara's latest dilemma. "You don't have anything to put into a bra!" she said, feeling cruel, and started laughing.

"Neither do you," Thara said, tightening her lips in annoyance.

"Yes, but at least I'm not like you, Thara Baba, hankering after one. I don't want to look like this." She got up and held Mrs. Vithanage's gigantic wet bra in front of her chest with soapy hands, then popped the centers of the cups. "Thok! Thok!" she said. Thara laughed and picked up another bra. They chased each other around the well, shrieking with delight, puffing out Mrs. Vithanage's bras and taking turns deflating each other's "breasts."

But some goddess must have been watching, because just as they ran out of steam, Thara said, "I think I just got it." She said it in a quiet voice. She bent her knees open, reached under her skirt, and pulled down her panties, and sure enough, there It was: a red smudge. Thara looked up at Latha, her yellow skirt with white poodles embroidered all along the hem clutched in one hand, her white underwear still held out, as if she expected Latha to add her to the pile of laundry. She was going to cry; Latha could see it coming.

"Wait right there, baba, I'll go and tell madam," Latha said, washing her hands in a fresh bucket of water and drying them on the edge of her dress. She turned the bucket over and told Thara to sit on it. "It's a good thing this old well is still surrounded by albesia, isn't it?" she said, wanting to be helpful, comforting. "Nobody can see you through the leaves."

The next few minutes were a blur. Mrs. Vithanage came hot-footing it down to the well and covered Thara with the bedsheet that she had grabbed from the almirah. Latha liked making beds because the sheets (and towels) were done by the dhobi and the dhobi used starch and then pressed them with an iron the size of a stool and it gave them a wet-in-the-rain-burnt-in-the-sun smell. But Thara didn't seem to care about the smell. She whimpered from under the sheet, walking like she had shit smeared between her legs, stepping with her feet wide apart, hopping from one side to the other on tiptoes as if the ground was muddy.

Latha had to miss seven days of school after all because Thara had to and she couldn't see anybody but other females and her mother wasn't about to sit in a room all day long and she didn't want to see Soma, so it became Latha's task. It wasn't so bad because she got to chat and play cards with her friend, though while they did, the country went up in flames, with riots and looting and people burning in the streets, and neither of them knew about it until after it was all over because no bad news was shared with Thara or Latha during that time. And though it wasn't a happy time for anybody when they returned to school, Latha was glad that Thara had escaped having to absorb such things in the middle of becoming a Big Girl.

Mrs. Vithanage went with the driver to fetch Soma from her village, and goodness knows what she was promised because Soma came back, but she brought a certain air with her. Mrs. Vithanage made lots of telephone calls and took lots of short trips, and everything was said in hushed tones. Thara and Latha played cards, mostly 304, and Thara showed Latha the sanitary pads, which was tolerable, and then she had to take the outer wrappings off and flush the cotton down the toilet, which was not, but all in all it wasn't so bad. Even if Latha couldn't see Gehan, think about what she could tell him when she went back to school!

"What are they doing out there?" Thara asked on the third afternoon.

"Lots of telephone calls and lots of trips to the market for food," Latha said, picking up the tall, narrow bedside table that always seemed on the verge of collapsing and scraped the floor with a piercing sound if she dragged it, which, of course, she didn't, having learned through hard experience not to, and putting Thara's plate of rice in front of her.

"For whom?"

"Not for baba, clearly," Latha said, laughing at Thara's face as she surveyed her latest meal of rice with ash plantains and okra, both cooked white, gotukola mallum, and no meats. "I can smuggle some dried fish for you if you like," she offered, feeling sorry for Thara.

"No. Amma says it's bad to eat fried things and meats and chili and sweets until the seven days are over."

"Then what?"

"Then I can eat," Thara said, stuffing a ball of rice into her mouth.

"Do you have to do this every month?"

"No, you fool! This is special because it's the first time. You don't know anything, do you?"

Well, it had been only three days since Thara knew nothing either, but Latha was willing to believe in the power of blood between her legs to enlighten her too. She wondered when she would get hers. Soon, she hoped. Then, not too soon, because Mrs. Vithanage would make her stay home like this, and who would keep her company? Not Thara, that was clear. Thara would go back to school. Soma, perhaps? Latha pictured the portly, uni-breasted—that's what she and Thara called breasts like that: breasts so large they seemed to have merged like the trunks of ancient trees—old woman unfolding her mat next to hers on the floor of the storeroom instead of on the raised platform in her own room. She had a room because she was old; that's what Mrs. Vithanage had told Latha once. She was old and she had looked after Mrs. Vithanage as a girl, so she had earned the right to her room and her bed. Frankly, Latha could not imagine either of those women as girls, but particularly not Mrs. Vithanage, because what girl could turn into such a solid, feet-firmly-planted woman? A woman with so little understanding of girls? Besides, that was not a bed Soma had; it was just a plank of wood. Beds had mattresses, didn't they? And did Soma have a mattress? No, she didn't. It was better to sleep on the floor, like Latha did, and not have to be grateful for a plank of wood—that's what she thought as she lay down on the cool concrete each night, her face to the ceiling, and traced the felt definition on her body: her collarbones, her rib cage, the slope toward her belly button, the rise to the bones beneath.

On day five Thara's bleeding stopped and she asked to come out of her room to take a bath but her mother refused.

"You can't take a bath until the dhobi is here to wash you," she said, smiling kindly, Latha felt, at Thara. Mrs. Vithanage was a tall, erect woman with very good posture, and when she was kind, it made her look positively stately. Like a queen. Queen Elizabeth II, Latha thought, remembering a picture from a glossy tome called *The Book of Queens,* which Thara had shown her. Except taller, with heavier breasts and more hair. Maybe not Queen Elizabeth II. Maybe some other kind of queen. Latha ran down the list of queens in her head and forgot to be quiet and servantlike, the spoons clanging against the dishes as she cleaned up.

"I don't want a stupid dhobi washing me," Thara said, frowning again. She should stop frowning; she did it so often. It was not attractive on a face built for sweetness like Thara's; not beauty, definitely not, but sweetness, which, with the blessing of her parents' wealth and privilege, endowed it with a comforting glow. Today, for instance, thanks to all the sleeping she had done during the past five days, Thara was captivating in the way spoiled toddlers at the market managed to be captivating: just the slightest bit unkempt, a little untucked and undone, a little pouty and let's-see-what-I-can-get-away-with, but with the same sweet face. Except for that frown, which spoiled it. And the tone that brought out the Thara that, Latha had to confess, she did like better, the rebel Thara, the Thara who went out to find and keep her own boyfriend, the Thara who was more like her, like Latha.

"You can't argue about that. A dhobi must wash you. It's the tradition." Mrs. Vithanage tucked her sari pota into her waistband. She was wearing a pink sari. Pink was far too youthful a color for most ladies, but on Mrs. Vithanage it seemed just right, even this baby pink hue on soft fabric with white embossed dots all over it. Latha never got to touch the saris. They were dry-cleaned, and it was Mrs. Vithanage or Soma who folded them after a day of wear: Soma had special privileges and access *because of her history with us,* that's what Mrs. Vithanage had said when Latha had asked to fold saris once. A spoon fell from the plate to the floor as Latha continued to clean, and Thara turned toward the sound and her.

"Then let Latha wash me!" Thara wailed. "When Soma was gone she washed all our clothes, so she's as good as the dhobi."

"You should be glad I'm not getting the toilet cleaner at the public park to wash you!" Mrs. Vithanage said. Latha shrank into herself at the change in Mrs. Vithanage's voice. She tried to clear away the dishes without making a sound, but it took longer that way, and she was certain that the longer she tarried, the more likely it was that Mrs. Vithanage would find fault with her for something.

"I want Latha!" Thara howled, turning to her. "Can you bathe me, Latha?"

"*Aney,* baba, I don't think I can. Madam knows best," Latha said, gathering up as many dishes as she could, not caring about the sound now that she was in the spotlight, and backing out of the room.

On day six Mrs. Vithanage strode into the room and made the announcement that indeed Latha could substitute for the dhobi, and if Thara could stand the fact that Latha would get her favorite ruby earrings *and* the two gold bangles that she had foolishly been wearing when she got her first period, even though she had been told time and time again not to wear her gold bangles for-no-good-reason, just as the dhobi would have, she would not say one more word to persuade her otherwise.

On day seven, at 4:34 AM, Latha poured the first bowl of warm, fragrant water over Thara's head as she crouched on a stool, shivering. Before she went in, Thara had removed her jewelry and put it on top of her nightdress and left it outside the door of the bathroom. Latha had woken up at 3:00 AM and scrubbed the white tiled floors of the bathroom clean with *Vim* and disinfected it with dill water. Then she had helped Soma to boil two large pots of water and carry them into the bathroom and pour them into the two new purple basins, and she had mixed the water so it was just the right temperature. All this while Thara slept on. Mrs. Vithanage had added the right kinds of leaves and herbs and flowers that the astrologer—whom Mrs. Vithanage had visited no less than three times to make absolutely sure—had told them would assure Thara of a good marriage and fertility: kohomba for purification, saffron for beauty, and jasmine for scent and sensual pleasure, plus a sachet of bark and seeds of unclear origin for good health and the safe delivery of babies. Latha had wanted to throw in a few rampé and karapincha leaves for a touch of elusive spice, but she didn't dare.

Now, as Mrs. Vithanage waited outside, the water, sweet smelling and warm, flowed first over her friend and then over her own bare feet. Latha had never touched shampoo, so she took the opportunity to pour more than was necessary into her palm, a large, creamy pool of yellow. *Sunsilk, Egg Protein,* she read, silently. It even looked like egg yolk. She breathed in the smell of it, then regretfully turned her palms over onto Thara's head and began rubbing the cream into her hair. She had never touched Thara's hair before, either. It felt odd to be doing it now, Thara naked and vulnerable, herself clothed, albeit wet, with her day dress clenched between her knees. But they were both content to be here: Thara, her eyes closed, enjoying the sensation of strong fingers massaging her head, Latha lost in the sensory pleasures around her—the aromatic steam, the feel of silky hair in her palms, the suds falling in large, careless thuds around her—

"Only ten more minutes till you have to smash the coconut—hurry up!" Mrs. Vithanage said, rapping sharply on the door. That voice.

Thara tipped her head up and rolled her eyes at Latha. "You think if I tell her about Ajith she'll stop worrying about good marriages?"

"The coconut is for fertility," Latha said, giggling. "Soma nenda told me that."

"So silly. Like a coconut can make me have children."

"Don't you want children?"

"Not till I'm quite old. After university, after I become a lawyer, after I'm famous for working on all the big cases and people write about me in the papers, *then* I'll have children, and only sons. I'll probably be twenty-five at least," Thara said, stretching out her legs.

Latha wished she had definite plans like Thara did. Or felt definite about anything, really, other than her desire to enjoy life. Or decisive. Maybe that was the word for Thara's way of doing things. She always had a plan, she had always made up her mind, she never *tried* to do anything, she just *did*. How did she do that? Maybe Latha could practice. She picked up a bowl of water and poured it on Thara's head, making her squeal.

"Don't wash it off yet!"

She ignored her and poured another bowl. "I still need to put soap on you, and madam will shout if I don't finish this on time," she said. Thara settled down.

So. It was as easy as that. She squeezed the water out of Thara's hair, picked out the stray leaves that had got wound in it, then coiled it on top of her head in a knot. She picked up the bar of soap—*Sandalwood*, it said on the center—and began to rub it into Thara's skin. She did it in a methodical way, just like when she bathed herself: the ears, the neck, the shoulders, the armpits, then along each arm, over her chest—no breasts, definitely no breasts yet—her back with its two side-by-side birthmarks right in the middle of Thara's spine, her belly, her thighs, behind her knees, her knees over the bump of a raised scar on the right that still remained after a three-year-old tricycle accident, her soft calves, and, finally, each foot, between each set of toes, the soles of her feet. It was almost like washing herself; Thara's body was just as lean, just as tall, and their skin was the same color, like milk toffee darkened slightly with a ground spice, something used for special occasions, she thought, like nutmeg or cardamom. She held the soap out to Thara, who stood up and washed herself between her legs. She wiggled her bottom at Latha, and they both laughed, shy and nervous. Latha took the soap Thara held out and put it away, then leaned over to pour more warm water from the second basin, the rinsing one, onto Thara's body.

When she was done, Thara was so clean. So clean and so sweet smelling. Latha felt proud of her friend and of herself.

"You'll get breasts soon," she said, not knowing what else to give Thara but that hopeful promise.

Latha was just coming out of the bathroom, after having washed the floor and then the basins and leaned them against the walls to dry, when Thara—on her third try with the curved knife that Soma used for cooking, its handle held between her toes as she crouched on the floor, fingers darting over the sharp upturned blade that was used to slice the daily quota of onions and green chilies—smashed the coconut into two neat halves. Latha picked up the girl-size ruby earrings and thin bangles that had been discarded on the dirty carpet outside the bathroom door; they were soaked with the water from the coconut.

It wasn't that she expected it to be the same; of course she didn't. She went to a different school, didn't she? She went to a school where only the richest girl, a scooter-taxi driver's daughter, was dropped off, riding in her father's taxi, her father dressed in a sarong; where the teachers didn't wear beautiful clothes or even robes or veils but came traveling on crowded buses, wearing cheap nylon saris they had prettied up with scratchy, brittle, brown-tinged scalloped patterns made by holding the edges to a candle flame. She sat in a classroom where no girl was ever absent for seven days, and nobody ever looked like she had new clothes, even on the first day of school, and where their uniforms, though white, were all different, with hand-embroidered monograms ripped off pockets before they had been given away to the poor. But still, after all that fuss, Latha must have expected something, because when she did get her period, and when she told

A Disobedient Girl 33

Mrs. Vithanage and Mrs. Vithanage clucked her tongue as if she had burdened her with something and yelled out to Soma and told Soma to show her how to fold strips of cloth (torn from Mr. Vithanage's old, soft, threadbare sarongs, no less) and put them in her underwear and wash them afterward, and when there was no talk of a dhobi or a bath and certainly no talk of the kind of party that Thara had on that seventh day, a party she had not known was going to be that grand—all that time spent keeping Thara company in her seclusion—with so much gold and money and jewelry gifted by so many well-dressed people in so many cars and Thara in her new dress of orange geor-gette and lace (because the astrologer said that was the auspicious color), made specially for her, when all that happened, Latha did feel like crying. And so she went ahead and cried. And she cried more when Soma came into her room that night, even though nobody had asked her to, and laid down her mat on the floor next to her.

"Go to sleep, duwa," Soma said. "These things are like that. Now go to sleep."

Daughter. Latha wondered if Soma had a daughter. She won-dered if she had a mother, or brothers and sisters; if she did, or once had, Soma never mentioned them. Somewhere in Latha's own mem-ory was a house by the sea and a journey at dawn somewhere, but that must have been a trip taken with the Vithanages because there was no clear image in her head of parents or siblings or even a place in which she had once lived. But she remembered a sound: of big, endless water, coming to shore again and again and again, as if it was trying to claim a piece of land for itself, as if it was grasping for something that it had once owned.

Biso

It is so dark still when I wake up that at first I am afraid to move. When I stretch my legs out, I can feel the foot of my bed. On either side, the edges. Any farther and I would touch the heat that I can feel rising up from his sleeping body, wakeful and vigilant, a malignance waiting to trip me up. Outside, the sounds of creatures bidding the night farewell, and airborne things rustling awake, one feather at a time, readying themselves to take flight with the day. I ease my body over the side of the bed and feel my way on all fours to the front door.

By the time I get back with the plantain leaves, cook and pack our meals by the quieter light of a kerosene lamp, time has moved closer to light than dark. The children rise and follow me like small ghosts. At the kitchen door I motion to them, and they come, one at a time, their palms outstretched for the tooth powder I shake out from the packet of *Dantha Buktha* in my hand; one shake, two, three. I stopped buying the *SR toothpaste* that they had always used, months ago, saving every cent for our journey. They complained at first, but not too loudly; living with violence made them quiet about their own unmet needs. They stand in a row before me and brush their teeth with their index fingers the way I'd taught them to do, even my baby, her skinny body lost in the droop of the hand-me-down that serves as her nightdress, her eyes large and fixed on her older sister, mirroring her movements. Watching them, I can almost taste the sweet grit in my own mouth, almost feel the sensation of fingernails scraping the way back of my tongue. They spit, then smooth the dirt over the wetness with their bare feet. I lead them to the pot of water by the drain and rinse their mouths and feet. They take turns holding on to my shoulder, and I wipe their feet dry.

"Go and get your shoes," I whisper, and the girls scurry indoors. My son waits.

"Do I have to put on shoes?" His mouth is unsmiling.

"Yes, Loku Putha, it would be better. Otherwise, I will have to carry them, and we have so far to go. The big bag is already heavy as it is with all our things, and the second bag with the food and the drink. Go now and put them on." The set of his shoulders tells me that I am demanding a lot more than he is willing to give.

"I can't find my shoes!" Chooti Duwa says, far too loudly, coming out to the kitchen door. She is naked but for the clean underwear I left out for her, and shivering slightly from the early morning air.

"Shh. Where did you put them yesterday when we came back from temple?"

"I don't know," she says, looking left and right as if the answer will come to her if she just avoids my stare.

"If you don't find them you'll have to walk on bare feet and they'll soon be full of cuts and dirt," I say, trying to sound like I mean that. But of course when she looks up at me I relent and join the search. I find the shoes in the most obvious place: under their bed. I want to cuff her ears, scold her, but she is so happy to put them on, so grateful, that I smile and hold her face in my palms, stroke her cheek with my fingers. Such a baby still. Barely old enough to have to do all her walking herself. I wonder if I could carry her some of the way. Maybe I should make a sling with a different sari—

"You spoil her," my older one says, watching us from the bedroom door, frowning just enough to let me know she disapproves but not enough to convey any disrespect.

"She's just a baby, duwa. Let her be. She'll grow up soon enough."

"She's only three years younger than I am. She's not such a baby," she says, staring at her sister.

Loku Duwa is right, and I feel sorry. She was only one when I fell in love with Siri and two when he was murdered, and then, all the terror followed. Twenty months when the beatings began, and that was far worse than all the drinking and breaking of things that had gone before. What was it like for her when, in the ways of these parts, children began to refer to her as the daughter of the murderer, the child of the whore? What terrors my children have known. And still, how can I not favor my youngest, who has known nothing else, even when she was still inside me? At least my son had a single year when he had two happy parents, newly wed, contented with the optimism of a firstborn son. At least Loku Duwa had the comfort of having a father she could name and call her own.

"Amma, aren't we going?" my son asks, poking his head around the corner, impatient. I want to say something to my older daughter, but she has turned and walked away, my long silence enough evidence of the preference she has always suspected me of. I cannot call out to her, with some reassurance she can believe, and risk everything; not this dawn, not with so much at stake, our lives, our future. I sigh and turn to my son.

"Yes, I'm coming. Here, take Chooti Nangi and go and wait for me by the kitul tree."

"I don't want to go with Aiyya. I want to wait for you, Amma," she says, holding on to my hand and squirming against my leg like a pet scratching itself on the bark of a tree.

I separate her from my body and try to pry my fingers away from hers. "Go with him," I say.

"Come!" he says, and she looks from me to him, one set of eyes pushing her away, the other beckoning her. He smiles and extends his hand, and I am grateful.

"Come soon then, Amma," she says and goes with her brother.

Why do I want to look at him one last time, this man whom I never loved? He was my father's choice for me, an arrangement made between two old men. Of course I had convinced myself it was for the best, that this was what girls did: their fathers' bidding. A widower-father at that, how could I say no? How could I cause him any more grief? I've often wondered, though, if I was simply the last thing standing between him and my dead mother: the burden of an only child, only daughter. Why else would he have chosen this particular man for me? Why else would he have blinded himself to the flaws that surely even he must have noticed: the loud, uninhibited voice; the ugly way in which his future son-in-law had flashed his money at my father and me; the showy, tasteless saris and plastic, glass-lined serving trays he brought as gifts when he visited; even the beedi that he smoked right inside my father's house. It is hard to acknowledge it, even now, but I know I am right: I was beloved only because my mother was beloved, and without my mother, I was simply a duty he had to fulfill. And once he had, my father was done with this lifetime; he was ready to seek his wife in another. How else would my father, the sure-footed god whom I'd watched dancing on the ropes that hung over our land for twenty-three years, a toddy tapper who walked as comfortably between kitul trees, extracting sweet sap to turn into intoxicating brews, as lesser men did on pavements, how else would he fall to his death just weeks after the birth of my oldest son, except from intention? No wonder people whispered things about me: a dead father, a dead lover, and soon—they can go ahead and add this to that—a good-as-dead husband.

But he is still alive, lying there, his back turned against me. The warm-cool air of the ocean lifts the voile curtain from the window and sucks it back again: a disclosure and concealment to the outside world of our parting. I bought him that green sarong for a long-ago New Year. Strange that he still wears it. He's forgotten, I suppose, the things that aren't worth remembering in the face of things that cannot be forgiven.

My husband stirs in his sleep, restless. It is not me that he cannot forgive, it is himself; the way he suffers by comparison with a man who could make me love him in life and also in death, by comparison with me, with my better caste, my better upbringing, my dignity, my where I'm from far better than his. In a last moment of grace, with gratitude to the gods for the life I am setting out to build for my children, I cover him against a sudden chill with the sheet off my side. Then I turn my back on him.

Outside, I go ahead of my children, carrying both bags. Along the way, I consider this road I have walked almost every day since I arrived here in Matara as a bride. The shops, with their walls covered with peeling white paint and covered again with years of advertisements; there are still a few old posters from a recent visit to this area by the prime minister, sticking out from underneath the new ones advertising the first English film that is showing at the town cinema. Low to the ground, I notice one complete poster in the blue and white of her ruling party. Were I not raised to be better, I would spit as I walk by the face on that poster, on the woman on whom Siri and his friends had pinned their hopes. So many times I have tried to be grateful for the semblances of equality, for ration cards and news of nationalization and independence and self-sufficiency and the larger wealth of our island, but all that cannot erase the other picture in my mind, the way a woman like her, a mother, a widow, presided over destruction the way she did. How she withstood news of the massacres that took place that year, of the numbers of the dead that rose and rose like there would be no end, all in her name.

I am not sorry that Siri was gone before that April insurrection four years ago, only days before our Sinhala and Tamil New Year, when his daughter was born. I am only sorry that he did not live to see her, that he was not there beside me in an almost empty hospital with only a skeletal staff as people stayed home to fast and tend to their hearths and cook oil cakes and milk rice, to prepare their oldest relatives to feed the younger among them with their own fingers and to bless them, to light their fireworks at the auspicious times and to pray for peace. He was not there when I pushed her out of my body and reached over to touch her wet head as she lay there, screaming the first and sweetest song of survival. He was not there to hear that, or to share in my delight over the treasure the gods had allowed me to keep. And because of all that, too, I am not sorry to leave this place.

As soon as we reach the bus stop at the old Dutch fort, I see her: Siri's mother. She stands under the arch with its painted lions and swords and crown as she has done every day since he was killed. She is dressed in a clean white sari, her hair is combed, and she clutches her handbag to her side. I am surprised to see her so early in the morning, the sun barely risen.

"Soon he'll be here," she says to me, smiling happily.

"On which bus is he coming?" I ask her, as I always do, not willing even now to disabuse her of her insanity, to say to her, like the cruel do, that her son is dead.

"Maybe today, maybe tomorrow," she says. "It doesn't matter."

"You can come back tomorrow," I say. She nods, but then she seems to notice who we are and frowns. She stares at my children. Once or twice she has spoken to me as if she knows; she has asked about my health, or uttered those words we Buddhists cling to at such times, using them to keep ourselves from succumbing to the blows that life deals us: *What is to be done? I must have sinned in a past life. This is how it is.*

Last year, as I was returning from the dispensary, Loku Putha and Loku Duwa beside me, my little one in my arms, her legs dangling down my side, my own back arched with the effort of holding her up, Siri's mother had stopped me and asked to hold her. I had given my daughter to her, to her unknown grandmother, knowing that she knew. Right then, she knew who it was she held. She had stroked my Chooti Duwa's bandaged head, swaying from side to side, her eyes closed, hushing her though my daughter was not crying. When she gave her back to me, she asked me to promise her that I would take good care of the little one, that I would keep her close to me, promise her not to lose my daughter. Then she had looked down the road, consigning herself back to the life that had been left to her, and asked me if I thought Siri would arrive that day.

Now she looks and looks at my children, at our bags, at me. "You are leaving," she says. "You are taking them all away."

I say nothing. Perhaps she will wait for me, too, at this same place, wait in vain for her dead son, for the one he loved, for his daughter.

"Yes," she says, sighing. "I don't think he's coming today. I'll come back tomorrow." I watch her walk away, and her body gives off the scent of grief and of the curse of having endured the loss of a child. I cannot bear to watch her go, so I turn away.

"Will that āchchi come back tomorrow looking for Siri Māma?" Loku Duwa asks. Even she knows of this ritual, young though she is.

"She always comes here," my son says. "I feel sorry for her."

"Let's hurry. We need to catch our train," I tell them, not want-ing to dwell on the things I cannot change, not wanting to feel too much for her, to feel anything that would prevent me from leaving. I walk the rest of the way without looking to either side, lest some familiarity trip me and cause us to tarry too long. I do not want to miss our train.

The station is crowded when we get there. I recognize a few peo-ple from the village, and I wonder if they will tell him. Why worry about that? By the time they do, it won't matter anyway. We'll be too far gone for him to touch us. But I don't like the crowds; they make me feel like my plans are weak and ordinary. Loku Putha must have noticed my frown because he reassures me.

"It's a Poya weekend, Amma," he says. "That's why there are so many people here. But don't worry. I'll get you a seat."

"Oh," I say, relieved, remembering the visit to our temple in the light of the full moon just the night before. "I forgot. Could you go and get the tickets?" I unwrap the edge of my sari and take out two of our ten-rupee notes; six of those and a few coins are all I have managed to hide from my husband without arousing his suspicion in preparation for this trip, and almost all of it will have to be spent on the trains. I give the notes to my son, and he folds them into his palm so quickly it frightens me. It's the swift, stealthy movement of the drug dealers and pimps who frequent the beaches near the tourist hotels. I grab him by his arm. "Where did you learn to hide money like that?"

"Like what?" He grins, boyish and pleased. "Like this?" And he does it again.

"Yes."

"Don't worry, Amma, I'm just hiding it so the pickpockets won't try to take it from me." His hair sticks up in various directions, and I smooth it down. His hair has always been uncooperative, just like the boy himself.

"There are no pickpockets here. You can worry about them when we change trains in Colombo. Just go and get the tickets and be quick about it. The train will be here any minute."

He runs away from me, and I wish I could follow him, just to make sure that he knows where to go, that he won't leave me stranded with his two sisters and our bags and nothing left to do but return home. I bite my lower lip and try to find him over the heads of strangers. I want to trust him, to be confident that he can look after himself, that he will come back, but I can't. He is too young for that. Too young to be sent away for errands like this in such busy places.

"Amma, I like this sari," my Loku Duwa says, pressing her face into my waist and distracting me. "It's soft and clean." Instantly, I forget my son's youth, consider instead my older daughter's age: seven, almost eight. I stroke her head and kiss it.

"And yellow and white," Chooti Duwa adds, joining her sister and rubbing her face on my sari. My little one's eyes shine with excitement. She has never ridden a train, only counted carriages as they whipped by the shore and practiced balancing on the looping tracks that carried other people to adventures somewhere that required speedy travel. Her sister, too, is smiling.

"Amma, where are we going?" Loku Duwa asks, her fingers caressing the fabric of my sari, judging by my expression that it is safe, now, to ask me such a question.

"We're going to my mother's sister's house in the hills," I say, proud of the words: my mother's sister's house. They sound rooted and safe.

"Where are the hills?" she persists.

"Up-country, where the tea is grown."

"But you never took us there before," my little one says, her voice a perfect illustration of the innocence of the question. "How do you know it's there?"

"Oh, the hills are always there, baba, just like the sea is always there. It's people who move about."

"Like us," she says. She grins at her older sister and takes her hand. "Like us, Akki. We are moving to the hills."

"We're visiting," Loku Duwa says, looking up at me.

I return her gaze. She looks good, my older girl, in her pale yellow dress with the embroidery on the white collar that I had to pay extra to have done. Apart from the money, that had cost me another beating, but it was worth the price: with her hair combed back into the two plaits I put in and tied up in matching ribbons before we left, she looks clean, from a good family.

"We're visiting, aren't we, Amma?" she says.

"No, we're moving," I say, taking her chin in my palm, bracing for the reproach in her eyes, for the protests, but they don't come. Instead she shuffles her feet and tucks a stray hair behind her ear.

"Do you want me to hold the bag?" she asks me at last.

"No, just keep Nangi close to you. I should go and see what Aiyya is doing."

But I don't have to. When I turn around, I see him coming toward us, the tickets in hand. Just in time. The train howls around the bend, long and insistent, then comes into view, the smoke spewing from its chimney, the wheels turning slow and slower till it comes to a looming halt with a final belch: *mphghhww . . . hiss . . . hiss . . .*

We join the surge of people. My son picks up the baby, and she holds on with arms tight around his neck. I take Loku Duwa's hand. We are absorbed by the machine, and it leaves the station before we can even find seats, while we are still figuring out how to stand in its juddering belly.

Latha

She knew why she did it. She did it to *show them*.

"What do you need your money for? It's safer in the bank." That was what Mrs. Vithanage had said when she'd asked for her money. She had worked it out in her head: after ten years of paid work with them (she didn't get paid those first two years, when she was four and five and still considered a child, even by Mrs. Vithanage), and with the New Year and Christmas bonuses that she had been told she was given, she should have eleven thousand and seven hundred rupees in the bank.

"I want to buy some sandals, madam," she said, assuming the position least likely to offend Mrs. Vithanage: looking down at her feet, her hands clasped in front of her.

It was Sunday, and Mrs. Vithanage was sitting on the front veranda, having already read both the weekend papers, the *Silumina* and the *Sunday Observer,* and measured out the rice and dhal and dried spices for Soma so she could get started on cooking lunch. She was waiting for the fishmonger to come with the daily catch. She wore her morning look: authoritative yet calm, the weight of household matters heavy on her mind, but more than equal to the task.

"Are your slippers broken?" she asked, glancing at Latha, then turning away.

"No." But they were old and her feet were too big for them, and in any case, it wasn't about what she had but about what she wanted and should be allowed to buy with her own money! Besides, hadn't she waited for a whole year and a half until Thara's latest heeled sandals, with the looped clasps on the sides, had long been discarded, for there to be no chance of Mrs. Vithanage mistaking her request for a claim to equality? Even for those kinds of sandals to be out of style? Well, all right, she did have her eye on the ones that were in style now, but still.

"Then don't waste your money." Mrs. Vithanage even sounded motherly, the tone she used on Thara when she wanted unreasonable things.

Latha continued to stand, wondering if perhaps Thara could be enlisted on her behalf. Probably not; Thara barely had time for her these days, with the O/L exams looming on her horizon. She saw Ajith with her school friends now, at cricket matches and rugger matches and parties that started at 10:00 PM where they served something called punch and for which Thara left and from which she returned in good-girl dresses but to which she actually wore short red skirts and tight black tops that showed off her new breasts; all of which Latha had heard about from the otherwise-faithful driver whose sworn-to-secrecy lips could be so easily undone by her presence and conversation as he reveled in being able to give her something she truly wanted: knowledge of that after-hours world.

Frankly, Latha was tired of yearning for the things she felt should be hers, like the soap she still helped herself to, or the teaspoons of mango jam she hid on her tongue, scooped as she carried the bottle from the fridge to the breakfast table, or the milk powder she stole for her tea. She hated plain tea. She hated plain anything! And why shouldn't she? She reasoned that she had acquired tastes, and with those tastes, longings, particularly for the things that were paraded so relentlessly before her day after day on the body of her friend, Thara, the most difficult to resist being shoes. Everything else she could, by careful dressing, by pinning and tucking of hand-me-downs, contrive to present as her own, made-especially-for-her attire. But real brand-new footwear was different: it was what set the blessed apart from the unspared. Her own feet, no matter how clean, how fragranced with *Lux*, how softened with cooking oil and polished with the stone she kept for that purpose by the well, were no match for the feet that came clad in new shoes. It didn't matter that nobody else seemed to notice. What was important was that she did. *She* always looked at feet when she walked; *she* knew how to tell character from the way people presented their feet, wealth from the cut of their shoes.

Besides, she didn't want to go back to the cobbler who lived his life, it seemed, crouched into a corner between the *People's Bank* and the *General Photo* place with its glass windows full of black-and-white photographs of radiant brides. How could she? The last time she went there, her old slippers in hand, asking him to paste the sole back again, he had looked sorry for her. He had called her duwa and tried to give her some coins for sweets. Yes, she had gone to him all her life, year after year, holding one old discarded slipper or another, asking for a stitch here, a bit of gum there, a clasp maybe. They were almost friends. But no matter how kind he had always been to her, how amused she had been by his mouth with its few teeth and more betel juice, to think that a man like that, all hunched and as leathery as his wares, his tiny old backside planted in a bundle of cloth, who charged people cents—cents!—to fix their footwear, would pity her? It was too much. No, she would not go back there. From now on, she would buy her own shoes. Brand-new. In style. Today. But how?

Mr. Vithanage came into the room just as she was about to give up hope that the sandal war could be waged and won right then. He had developed some kind of chronic back pain, which, instead of making him curmudgeonly, had only made him kinder; it was as though he believed that meeting the injustice the world had dealt him with an excess of goodwill would somehow relieve him of his pain. Now he eased himself into the chair on the other side of the floor-to-ceiling doors that Latha had to open and dust each morning before leaving for school, the doors to the sitting room that was surrounded by the wraparound veranda. They looked like benign sentries: Mrs. Vithanage in her pastel yellow cotton sari, Mr. Vithanage in his worn brown sarong and white shirt. Odd how his clothes always looked old even when they were brand-new. He was the kind of person who had been born looking old and largely unthreatening.

Latha picked up the Sunday newspaper and gave it to him, her left palm holding the wrist of her right hand to signify the correct amount of decorous deference.

"I would like to buy some sandals, sir," she said, desperate enough to risk raising her eyes to Mr. Vithanage.

"Will you stop talking about the sandals? Didn't I just tell you there was no need for sandals? What is the matter with you?" Mrs. Vithanage rarely had to raise her voice to reprimand any of her servants; the tilt of her head and the slant of her eyes were quite sufficient to achieve the desired effect. But this time, the first time, really, she was loud. She sounded a little bit like Thara did when things did not go her way.

"Let the girl have sandals. What's wrong with that?" Mr. Vithanage said, but it was hopeless. He said it so mildly, disinterestedly.

"Go and tell Soma to make tea for the master," Mrs. Vithanage said, and that was that. There were no possible openings for further requests. And the very fact that she continued talking, that she knew Latha could hear her, effectively ended the argument.

"I manage the servants, and that one needs to be reined in," Latha heard her say. "All this government nonsense about sending servants to school, that's what has ruined her. It's time for that to stop. Ten years of reading and writing is good enough for her. I mean, what is this house? An orphanage? No, when this year is over, I'm going to take her out of school. She's getting too old for that anyway. Before long some betel seller will knock her up on her way there. Much better for me to pull her out of that place now so she can start learning how to cook and clean and get ready to be a proper servant."

And that was what made her do it. Be a proper servant indeed. Her math was better than Thara's, her social studies and science were better than Thara's too, and she didn't even get extra tuition like Thara did. Even her handwriting, curving with perfect *ispili* and *pāpili*, was better than Thara's. In fact, the only things Thara had that were better than Latha's were her clothes and her fancy boyfriend. And even Thara's fancy boyfriend looked at her, Latha, in *that* way. Proper servant? Ha!

It took her a while to figure out how best to go about getting her revenge, but when she did, Latha knew her plan was foolproof. Ajith came because she sent a message through Gehan: Thara wanted to meet him urgently; would he come to the back gate around 9:30 that night? A one-line plea signifying all manner of possibilities, some more dire than others.

Latha leaned on the gatepost as she waited, knowing—the way fifteen-year-old girls know these things, even those who have never had the need to put their theories to the test because there were always enough men in their worlds to let them know in subtle and not so subtle ways that they *would* be proved right if they *did* have the chance to do it—that this would be easy. And it was. All she had to do was wait for him to come, to be alone with her for a while, to be forced to make small talk with her while he waited, for their talk to be necessarily quiet, and therefore intimate, for the proximity born of that and the darkness that enveloped them to override the social norms that worked only in the dread light of day, and eventually no longer even then.

It was easy to make him forget who she was, or why it was that he had come. And so much easier than even she could have imagined for her to forget who he was and why she had wanted this, and whether it was worth the pain the first time or the longing and heartache all the other nights of that year or the fact that her days had turned into miserable drudgery now that she was not allowed to go to school, that she could not see Gehan or even get word to him to come and see her, that she had to steal Thara's textbooks and read them in secret to stop herself from losing her mind, and that at the end of it all she still did not have new sandals. The only thing that she told herself mattered was this: she became an addiction for Ajith, which meant that Thara had no boyfriend and that she wilted and waned until her B pluses turned into Cs and then into Fs and she failed her O/L exams. And Mrs. Vithanage was crushed by that.

Yes, Latha had her revenge, and she enjoyed it and held on to it for as long as she could, even afterward. After the driver found out and she had to keep him quiet, her body still and soundless as he groped her and ogled her with derision as she went about her day and there was nothing she could say to stop him; she had given that right away for a pair of shoes that she could not have.

After Soma found out and stopped talking to her, but only after she called her *vesi,* and Latha didn't know what that word meant but she knew she deserved it, the way Soma said it.

And after Gehan found out because Ajith told him.

"Gehan wasn't happy about this for some reason," he whispered to her one night, and she felt her desire fly up into the mango trees and hang there out of reach and she had to pretend the whole rest of the way, with soft, seemingly heartfelt moans, that nothing was wrong. But why should it have mattered? Because Gehan had never said he loved her, and he had never promised her anything. All he had ever said was that she was beautiful, unlike Thara, who was only pretty because of her good fortune. And he hadn't had to talk about her body or her hair or any one part of her; she had known what he meant. It was the difference she had always seen when she and Thara stood side by side, pushing against each other for a fuller look in Mrs. Vithanage's oval mirror, which tipped upward and made them seem taller: a girl of privilege could never possess the deep longings that just ripened Latha's own looks into a luminous, irresistible heat.

And even though she knew that nothing about her appearance had changed, that those longings were still there, still coursing through her blood and making her more desirable than Thara could ever be, even to this boy, Ajith, for whom she was his first love, knowing in that instant that she had lost Gehan's regard pained her from within in ways that made her no longer a child but an adult. And all the nights after with Ajith could not erase the loneliness of her walks to the small shops outside the gate for one thing or another, remembering him and feeling the lack; no bicycle beside, no teasing voice to make her feel like a girl with no chores.

And after that until the end, there was no relief from being a girl with chores that she wasn't being paid for, a girl with no new sandals, and a friend who wasn't a friend but a mistress, and a family that wasn't a family but people who owned her and ordered her about, and nothing at all but her pretty breasts and her round bottom and her misbehaving hair to help her feel any different.

Nothing and nobody could change the way things were going to be. The only person who had advocated on her behalf had been the school principal, who had walked up the driveway early one morning and asked to see Mr. Vithanage, who had already left for work, and so got Mrs. Vithanage instead.

"It's against the law to keep a child under bondage like this, without sending her to school," he had said. "Against the law!"

"Until grade eight," she had said, and refused to listen to any further arguments or chastisements, and laughed when he had compared Latha with her own daughter and asked Mrs. Vithanage if she wasn't ashamed to send a child of hers of the same age to school while depriving another, and a smart one at that, a chance to finish her education. Instead, Mrs. Vithanage had called out to Latha, herself, to bring her principal a cup of tea.

He had not drunk it. "You keep reading your textbooks," he had told Latha, pushing the cup of tea away. "You are an intelligent child, and you should not forget that. You are too good to be working for people like this. Do well in life. Somehow, do well in life." And then, he had left.

The sisters at the convent weren't unkind. They had seen everything before, heard everything before. They asked no questions of Mr. Vithanage, simply filled out columns of information in a thick binder with fine yellow paper edged in red. Her name, her age, her height, her weight, Mr. Vithanage's address, and her medical history, which was mentioned and written down as being "clean," in clear, flowing blue script, all of it pouring onto the page along the space allocated for Entry No. 1193. After he left and they settled her in, they taught her to pray, kneeling and standing, morning, noon, and night. She had tasks but not too many, just enough to be useful but not enough to be harmful to her. It was like a holiday. At first, they took her for walks in the convent gardens, to see and smell roses again. But the scent of real roses made her feel ill and the walks tired her out, so they gave up on that and taught her to sew instead.

She sewed and prayed, sewed and prayed, sitting by the window of the stone wing in which they all lived. She embroidered stacks of clothes: doll clothes, with three holes in each for a newborn's arms and head, and a ribbon to tie it on at the back. Pale green, pale yellow, pale pink, pale blue, white, like Mrs. Vithanage's saris, which she no longer saw because she was at the convent and thankful to be there after all the trouble she had caused.

"Who did this?" Mrs. Vithanage had asked when Soma told her about the early morning vomiting and the craving for pickled mangoes. "Who? Do you know, Soma?"

"Ajith, sir," Soma had said. "He's the one who did it."

"Ajith? Who the hell is Ajith?" Mr. Vithanage had demanded, the angriest she had ever seen him.

"A boy who lives down the next lane," the driver had told them, standing by and sucking his back teeth like he had always known this would happen. Disgusting.

"A Colombo Seven boy?" Oh, Latha was evil to have felt—and still feel—that momentary flash of glee at the horror in Mrs. Vithanage's voice. And when Mrs. Vithanage had yanked her out of the storeroom by her hair, her hands and body shaking with rage—was it because of the inconvenience? the shame? or because Colombo 7 was just as crass and vile as the worst of slums?—and screamed at her and asked her what she had been thinking to repay their kindness with her whoring, she had taken pride in her defiance, and in the absence of a single tear.

"I wanted a pair of sandals and you wouldn't let me have my money," she had said, which was the absolute truth. Then Mrs. Vithanage had slapped her. Once, so hard her face spun on her neck. And she still had not cried, but turned to her and said, "He was Thara's boyfriend, but he preferred me."

"Thara? Did you say *Thara*? She's madam to you. Do you understand? You filthy bitch, you—"

But Mr. Vithanage had stepped forward and taken his spluttering, weeping wife away, and yes, Latha had felt remorseful at the look he gave her: disappointed in her behavior, as if he had expected more of her than that, as if he had believed her to be capable of something higher. And she had cried then, heaving and sobbing on the mat in the storeroom because of that look and because of Gehan, but not even Soma had come to comfort her this time.

The Vithanages hadn't even told Thara the truth when she came home from school. They had blamed it all on the driver, for whom Latha had felt sorry for the first time, for having been sacrificed in the name of the Vithanage family honor that way, and for not blaming her for her role in bringing about his fall from grace.

"That's how it is," he had said bitterly to her. "They have to find someone to pile their filth on. This time it's me. Nevermind. I can always find another family, but let's see if they can find a better driver." He had looked back at the house and spat on the ground before he walked out of the gate.

As soon as they had dismissed him, they had prepared to take her to the convent. "For training," they had told their friends and relatives, who had nodded as if they believed that story though they all knew what that meant and that it had nothing to do with improving Latha's skills as a servant and everything to do with getting rid of the result of nefarious activity between Unequals and who, therefore, looked knowingly at each other.

Everybody assumed it was Mr. Vithanage who had done It. Wasn't that how it was always rumored to be in such cases? The man of the house unable to resist the seduction of the servant woman who prowled his kitchen, waiting for the moment to strike? It was the sort of story the girls in her, Latha's, school had related, and she had laughed at, about the goings-on in houses where they or their mothers worked, about how the men came after them and how, invariably, it was the servant who got blamed. About how even when somebody else—a driver or a gardener—had been responsible, the girls blamed the master of the house, knowing that he would survive the accusation but that their fellow servants could not afford to lose their jobs. So many lies that it was impossible for anybody but the two people involved to know the truth. And even if the truth was told, who could believe it?

Everybody who heard of the impending trip to the hill country and visited the Vithanages had felt sorry for Mrs. Vithanage, Latha could tell, by the way they glanced at her and then at Mrs. Vithanage and looked pointedly away when she brought them their tea. Yes, they sighed, it happened to the best of them, and by that they meant nobody else but Mr. Vithanage. And that was the real reason, Latha knew, that Mrs. Vithanage could not forgive her, and swore that she would not let her step into the Vithanage house ever again.

The convent was good for her, she supposed, in those months that they cared for her and waited for her baby to be born. But then, she hadn't known what it would feel like after: the pain, the hospital, the sterile room they left her in, the utter quiet after all that noise, the emptiness after a presence that held her so close and then let her go, taking its comfort-seeking cries with it. It was only natural that she should hold on to that silence, at least for a while, to say nothing more; her prayers inside, her hands sewing, sewing, while her breasts swelled up and hardened into a heart-blaming pain and soaked the gauze tied around them with milk again and again until at last they softened to ineffectual pliancy. Sewing as she sat at the window, looking down at cascading mountains filled with tea bushes and a scent in the air that she recollected but could not place exactly. The sound of raised voices, the sound of women and men and children, of doors shutting, and gusts from the top of a train, of perilous cliffs that hung over mists so cold and clean that she felt like her body would freeze if she breathed.

Biso

L oku Duwa says, "Colombo stinks."
    Chooti Duwa says, "Can I have a Colombo?" her eyes on a basin of freshly cut pineapple that a vendor is holding almost up to our noses; if he lifts any higher on his toes, he will either empty the basin into our laps or fall between the platform and the train.

"That's *annasi,* not Colombo," Loku Putha tells her, his eyes catching mine, laughing. "Colombo is the city. That's where our last train stopped and this train starts. My friend said that it's the biggest city in the whole world, and the only problem with it is that it's dirty. If it were clean, then it would be the best city too. My friend came here with his father for a wedding at a big hotel. The hotels are very clean, not like the city. They stayed in the hotel for two days."

"I know that's a pineapple. Can I have a pineapple?" Chooti Duwa says, clearly unable to absorb all this information about cities and hotels and weddings and focusing on the one sure thing right before her eyes, the luscious yellow wedges of fruit that take even my fancy: their careless patterns, the flecks of salt and chili on them. It is not how my mother served pineapple—we ate pineapples fresh and without spices—but I have learned to love them this way. Siri taught me, laughing at my high-caste ways and coming at me with pieces of pineapple clenched between his teeth, offering a new savor and himself too. Pineapples with salt and chili, they are the taste of memory and happiness and now, perhaps, also the taste of our future. I unwrap the end of my sari again, but my son beats me to it. How did he get money?

"I took it from him while Thāththa was still asleep," he says, his eyes nasty again, and I am sorry I asked. Well, what is to be done? A last transgression can be forgiven, after all. Soon he will be in a clean place, cool and fresh and healthy from the inside all the way out.

I have already asked him twice to get down and check the name written on the side of the train:—UDARATA MENIKE—even though I know we are on the right train. I had asked a stationmaster to point it out to us after we got down from the Matara–Colombo train along with everybody else, and the stationmaster, perhaps recognizing that I had not traveled much, or maybe seeing how distressed I was by the number of policemen on guard along the platforms, had walked us over to this train and waited until we climbed aboard. Yes, Loku Putha has told me, both times, this is our train, the *Up-Country Lady*. Already we have sat here for so long now, through lunch, when I bought a packet of cream crackers for them to eat, and afternoon tea, which I bought for them from a young boy who poured the dark, sweet water into smoky glasses from a simple tin kettle, that I feel nervous. As if he might have time to follow us, or that I might have forgotten how to be cautious and let a stranger persuade me to climb aboard the wrong train.

"Check again, Loku Putha," I say. "Please, one last time? I won't ask again."

He climbs down for a third time and chants the name of the train, slapping each carriage on its side as he walks, up and down the length of it: *"Udarata Menike!* This is our train! *Udarata Menike!* This is our train! *Udarata Menike!"* The people around us stir and peer out of the windows on the platform side, laughing, pointing at him, happy to find a way to keep their own children amused.

"Aiyya shouldn't be out there. People are laughing at him," Loku Duwa says.

"I like when Aiyya sings," Chooti Duwa says, slapping the windowpane in time to the rhythm of her brother's song.

I see a policeman accost him when my son reaches the front of the train. I don't know what he tells him, but my boy stops singing and comes back to us, walking quickly as if he regrets having wandered so far.

"What did the rālahamy say?" I ask, anxious.

Loku Putha shrugs. "Nothing. He just told me not to loiter on the platform."

I don't believe him, because he looks scared. I despise the police, for the way they stoke the fears that people have of the prospect of tragedy, for the way they always seem to collude with the worst elements of our government, for the way they disregard the murders of some people, allow thuggery to go unpunished. For letting my husband live. I try to get my son to tell me if the policeman threatened him or in some other way made him feel unsafe, but he shakes his head repeatedly.

After that bit of excitement, I put my head out of the window only to hail a man selling thambili so we can refill our bottles. It is so hot that even the one he cuts and pierces for us is warm. After I have drained the water into our bottles, the man splits the king coconut in half and we use the scoop he fashions for us from the husk to scrape out the soft flesh. That at least is sweet and filling, and the children are happy, so I try not to worry about the germs that are probably getting into their bodies, or to berate myself for not having thought to bring a spoon along for this purpose. I hope that the goodness of the thambili itself will keep them from falling sick on our journey.

The wait is impossibly long for those of us who have already traveled far to get to this station, and, after all this time, we still have to wait for an hour and a half before our train leaves. By that time Loku Duwa has vomited once, Chooti Duwa has had to go to the bathroom in the station twice, and my son has flashed his money three times, responding to the relentless vendors who ply their wares among the weary and the bored:

"*Kadalai! Kadalai! Kadalai!*" mostly for Loku Duwa, who loves roasted chickpeas or roasted anything, really.

"*Annasi! Annasi! Annasi!*" mostly for Chooti Duwa, who has eaten pineapples only in round slices, not in huge quarters like this.

"*Ice palam! Ice palam! Ice palam!*" for all of us to cool down, but especially for the little one, whose tongue is on fire from the spices on her pineapple. The children enjoy that last purchase the most, the sight of those cardboard triangular cylinders nestled in the rigiform box, the sudden cooling of the air near their knees when the vendor sets his box down and opens it, the taste of those sweet, cold blocks of flavored *Elephant House* ice.

I try to be patient with them and content, to enjoy the time between one life and another. I bring up the past so I may leave it behind, to take myself adequately into the future.

It wasn't because of the drinking that I went with Siri, though that was enough of an excuse. It was simply because he was young and I was too and he asked repeatedly. Isn't that, in the end, why any woman does anything with any man? He was a choice and he was mine to make. Of course I would choose him. What woman wouldn't? He was young and present and he had eyes that looked for me.

Siri looked for me at market when I went to meet my husband as he came off the largest boat, standing on the prow in front of his crew of men like he owned the ocean itself, broad-shouldered and square like a lump of sod, brutal and arrogant. He even looked for me when I went with my children to watch them play with the waves. He watched me when I went to the well at dawn those times when there was a water-cut and that was our only source, and he watched me when I went to temple on full-moon days. In the end I found that all I was doing was watching him watching me, and then it was not clear who had begun this game in the first place.

But more than his pursuit was the fact that he had turned away from his father's fishing trade, and that made him everything my husband was not. Other women doubled their prayers when their husbands went out to sea by the light of the moon, but I, I sang. I sang because Siri was not among those men whose boats blinked on and off on the horizon heavy with their nets and gathered on the shore in the morning to pull the *mā-dal* in, hand over fist. He stayed with me, beside me, inside me, and I did not care that my children were asleep, alone at home, or that the neighbors might come to know. He burned the fear out of me until all that was left was desire. And I took it wherever I could, whenever I could, not caring anymore what anybody thought or said or might do. Siri was like his name to me, happiness. And I, who had never known happiness as a woman, why would I say no to that?

It filled me with hope that, when he went to work, it was to a clean-kept Muslim store frequented by the students who came back to this town from the universities in Colombo and Peradeniya. He didn't earn much there, bringing plain tea and godhamba rôti stuffed with curries cooked with too much pepper to his customers, but he learned about matters that had nothing to do with the sea from the students who knew what was going on all over the country. That's where he learned about the leader of a movement who paid attention to everybody, even the lower castes, who was so intelligent he had been offered a scholarship to study medicine in the Soviet Union, and who had returned home to lead the people in revolution. He told me that this leader had united young people from everywhere—from the universities, from the unemployed, even from the military forces!

I was proud that my Siri was going to join such a man, and that he was going to help bring our lady prime minister back into power. I was proud that the leader of our movement came from my father's town, the place where I, too, had been born. How could Siri and I have known what would happen after the elections, how our Ma-thiniya would turn her back on us, how she would put his leader in prison, how the people would rise in revolt, and how they would die as the army returned to her fold? All those young people, felled in groups, falling headfirst into shallow graves.

"Biso, my Menike, someday I will be in a good position with a new government," he told me. "My campus friends have assured me of this." Dreaming with me, the sand beneath us, the skies above, and only the sound of the waves to argue against the things he told me, my husband out at sea. I believed in that future the way he did, unable to imagine that we would be wrong, unable to know that when Siri was gone that future would mean nothing to me.

Siri started to meet his university friends by the boats late at night, and too often, though that was dangerous: there were always informants, there in our South, where the plans were being drawn; the police were everywhere, and they could never be trusted, even when they claimed to be with us. I used to go there sometimes, against Siri's wishes, bringing a flask of tea as an excuse or a treat I had made with the money from the sale of the small, leftover fish my husband had no use for. I wanted to put myself in harm's way, to join them in taunting something corrupt and deadly so that my other imprudence would pale and somehow escape the notice of the gods, that Siri and I would be safe.

One of Siri's friends was a Buddhist monk, his saffron robes thrown on without care, quite unlike the priests at our local temple. Revatha Sādhu looked as though he might catch on fire himself at any moment; he was energetic and restless and moved too fast for me to imagine that he had done anything meditative in his life. I recall the thrill I felt in my spine to be in the presence of a priest without the requirement of devoutness. It was heretical, that behavior, but once we had dispensed with the usual taboos, what more was there to do or be but worse? Worse than could have been thought of me, worse than I could have imagined of myself.

They were young, even the priest, and they had opinions about everything, things I had never considered before. I listened as they shouted at one another, as they fought, and announced truces, and loved one another with a fierceness I had never seen among men. Even the sādhu, roaring right alongside them, the future almost here, their plans for things I didn't quite understand laid out, nearly complete. They didn't treat Siri differently. He was one of them. That's how he moved in their midst, contributing his thoughts, cajoling them to stop smoking or drinking, advising them about some absent girlfriend or other. I was fascinated. I sat beside him and was content to be there, like him, learning, absorbing, hiding from my real life.

But then, in one night, four of them disappeared. My Siri and three of his friends, Thilak, Priyantha, and Gamini. I think those were their names. Or maybe it wasn't them. Maybe it was some other boys, some boys whose names I hadn't caught. When Siri returned to me, limping, bleeding, all of them stopped coming to the boats and went into hiding. He grew quiet about his hopes after that. He loitered on the beach whenever he could, hoping one or another would show up, but they did not. There was only the sea, and the sea betrayed us. The sea brought a body to shore.

"Menike," Siri called to me that morning. Menike. Lady. The other half of my given name. "Menike, come down to the boats."

"Tonight? He's home tonight. I can't come," I said. I had just returned home after leaving my children at school—my son at the *Rahula Vidyalaya* and my daughter at the girls' school, *St. Mary's Convent,* where I had begged the nuns to take her without payment, persuading them by dint of my mother's education and my own association with the convent in Hambantota.

"Our sādhu's body has come to shore, bloated and full of holes."

I did not need to know more. I was familiar with the sensation of futures ending, of hopes dissolving like the froth of the waves. And because he called me, because I went to comfort him, to comfort myself, risking everything, with my husband at home to notice my leaving, to follow me, because of this, my Siri died, with a knife in his back, his life easing out of his body into me. If he could have chosen an end, I know this would have been the way for him. In my arms, beside those boats he would not step into, on that soft sand, not far from where his friends had once stood with him, convinced of success. And I am grateful, still, despite all of it, that I had one year in which I got to be a woman. Not a daughter, not a wife, not a mother.

News of his murder spread through the neighborhood like the cholera that came and went in faraway places, or the droughts we heard about on our radios. Siri's body was dragged and left in our front yard, and his parents came, weeping, to collect their dead son to the sound of curses from my husband's drunken mouth, the whole neighborhood watching, relishing my punishment. And even though they knew, his parents knew, nobody would accuse my husband. It must have been easier for them, too, to believe their son had died at the hands of the police, whom everybody despised, and for a cause that was more noble, grander, more lasting, in their minds, than love for another man's wife.

And now I remember how my husband looked this morning when I left him. How I stood and watched the rise and fall of his body, the breath leaving and entering him. I looked at him, but it was Siri I saw. The way the breath left his lips in a whistle when I walked by, so soft that only I could hear; the way the breath left his lips when we stood together in the dark; the way the breath came out of his body, all of it, leaving him behind, and me, never to return on that last night.

The train lurches forward without preamble, jerking me out of my mixed-up reverie with its passions and losses and hopelessness and pride. As we crawl sluggishly out of the station, comfortable in our relatively empty carriage, the rain begins. It looks dreary outside.

"I am glad we are not staying in Colombo," Chooti Duwa says, pronouncing the word with aplomb, now that she knows what it means.

"Good. You will like the hills."

"How big are they?"

"They are not hills, they are mountains," her brother tells her, warming to his role as the deliverer of information. "We learned about them at school. It's where all the tea in the country comes from, and the land is so good that the vegetables are bigger than any you've ever seen. And there are waterfalls."

"What are waterfalls?"

"Waterfalls are when the water in a lake is falling down from one high mountain to a smaller mountain," Loku Duwa says, trying to restore some balance to the usually shared role of knowledge-able older siblings. She has always managed to sound older than her years. It's the curse of the oldest girl in the family, I suppose. And a blessing, too, for me, for any mother, for how can one woman take all the responsibility for a family? No, there must be help, and I am glad for my older girl. I take her hand in mine and hold it. She has small hands and her fingers are short, like her father's. She is small, too, with lots of soft flesh to keep her small bones safe, not good for manual labor. Siri's daughter, on the other hand, is like him and me:

lean and strong and somehow, even at this age, peculiarly capable. I take her hand in mine too and compare my girls, tracing the lines on their palms as if I were like one of the Tamil fortune-tellers from Kataragama who pass through town, their dark green and orange cotton saris tight around them, their mouths red with betel stains, their nose rings and their baskets of potions and papyrus and twine balanced on their heads, always grateful for plain tea.

"Will the water fall on our heads if we stand under it?" Chooti Duwa asks, a baby again.

I smile. "The water in the mountains is very cold, not like the ocean. You can bathe in it, but you have to get used to it, and unless it is a very small waterfall, you don't stand right underneath it. You stand in the pool at the bottom, away from the falls, on the rocks in the river."

"I want to go to a proper school, not a Montessori school," she says, after a few moments of quiet.

"You'll be five soon and then you can go to a proper school, although in those parts it might be a mixed school."

"What is a mixed school?" Loku Duwa asks.

"Both girls and boys, not separate like our schools now," my son tells her.

"*Chee!* I don't want to go to school with boys!" Loku Duwa says.

"I don't want to go to school with girls either!" Loku Putha adds, as if he means only one girl and that would be his own sister.

I laugh. "It is not so bad. If there is a private convent, I will try to get you girls there, but if not, you will be fine. When we get to my aunt's house, I will enroll you in school with her daughter's children, your second cousins." I can share these details with them now, of relatives I had rarely mentioned before, wanting more than anything to protect them from the misery of knowing there were options we could not follow, people we could be with, trapped as we were by our reliance on their untrustworthy father. But no longer. Now, we are free.

"How old are they?" my son asks.

"She has three sons and a daughter. The oldest is thirteen; that's the girl. The boys must be nine, seven, and five."

Chooti Duwa claps her hands. "One for me!"

"He'll want to run away from you. You're such a pest," her sister says, but she's smiling and I can tell she is happy to hear there will be "one for her" as well, and an older sister at that. They notice my amusement, and their own grins broaden until I can see their teeth, crookedly perfect. My little one's smile is particularly childish, with two early gaps, which her first permanent teeth are beginning to fill.

My children, who have never been anywhere beyond our town, are excited by everything, even the long stretches of paddy on either side of the train as we approach and pass Ambepussa. When night falls, they talk loudly about the patches of forest, thrilled by the way the clumps of trees look dangerous in the dark. We are fortunate enough that I am able to show them Bible Rock and even a glimpse of Sri Pāda, both of which appear and disappear from our view like mirages in the moonlight. I consider these to be signs of blessing and bring my palms together as we pass.

I put off dinner for as long as they can stand it, hoping that sleep will follow soon after. When I finally relent, I am slightly embarrassed that our food smells so good that several passengers glance over at us. Still, I am glad we have it . . . , that the plaintain leaves have kept it from spoiling, and that we did not have to purchase buth packets from the Colombo railway station. I have never bought cooked rice from the Muslim stores, although, on occasion, to demonstrate his distaste for anything associated with me, my husband has returned home with a single packet of biryani rice and curries for himself and my mouth has watered at the fragrance. The children eat with haste and enjoyment; it is something to do, I suppose, eat, on a journey whose length I can only guess at, having learned early to think of trips such as these in terms of time, not distance. These days, even that measurement is unreliable. Timetables are for us, but it is fate that decides. Electrical outages, skipped tracks, derailments, delays—that is what we are trained to expect under our present government, nothing too bad, just enough of everything inconvenient to small people like us, people without power and wealth. Still, watching my children, their contentment, I am convinced that our journey is blessed.

I wish I had added some washed green chilies and onions to spice my own packet of rice, but I was in too great a hurry to think that far ahead. I eat my food quickly and finish before they do so I can help Chooti Duwa with hers.

"Here, hold your hands out of the train window so I can wash them," I say when they are done, and each one complies. I pour a little water on each right hand to wash the *indul* away.

"Amma, can I drink the rest of the thambili now?" Chooti Duwa asks.

"Yes, but not all of it. We still have a whole night to travel."

The small basket is no longer full. Only the almost-empty drink bottles and a packet of *Maliban* lemon puffs remain, along with the remnants of unfinished wedges of pineapple. It is very late when we get to Gampola, and there is nothing to see but the people inside the train. It is packed, and we have had to squeeze in against one another's bodies to accommodate each new group that climbs in with the same focus and effort that we ourselves must have displayed at the start of our journey. I try to keep the children from pressing too close to the windowsills, leaning too heavily against the sides. This is a cheaper compartment, and who knows what kind of illness has rested in its corners? The overhead luggage racks are jammed with bags, and ours sits between our feet. I am grateful for our arrangement, my two older ones in front of me, the little one and I across from them; at least we are together, at least we have the window. When people cough or sneeze, I motion with my eyes so the children lean out and breathe in fresher air, giving their lungs a fighting chance against whatever colds and fevers might have climbed aboard.

All along our journey there are points where solid ground seems so far below our carriage that I hold my breath, expecting some kind of punishment. Some divine blow that would put an end to me and my children. But the train passes over them again and again and it is gone, that sensation of guilt and foreboding, and I am glad. At Nawalapitiya, the train sits for what seems like a long time. I hear a rumor, confirmed by a sharp jerk of the train, that they are adding on a *pusher* for the up-country climb. We are still stopped, but at least the air is cooler now and my children can sleep.

"Can I shut this window a little?" I ask an older woman sitting next to my son. She nods and smiles at me.

"Your children must be cold," she says. She has gray hair and wears a cheap red sari. There's a smear of red in her hairline too. I wonder if she is returning from visiting relatives in Colombo or if she is on her way to visit family on the tea estates. *The tea estates are full of Tamil tea pluckers,* my mother had once told me, something in her voice conveying a criticism of them, *and they often send their children to work as servants,* she had murmured, which was what had prejudiced me, too, toward these people. But this woman looks decent. I can't picture her sending a child to slave at some house far away. Maybe my mother did not know all there was to know about these parts. She had grown up in a good home, sheltered from the world; how could she have picked up facts like that? But I don't want to think less of my mother, so I shake the thought and smile at the woman.

The older ones are fast asleep, and I have to dislodge my Chooti Duwa from my lap to shut the window. Sensing my predicament, a young man next to me holds out his arms and takes her from me. I stand at the window and try to figure out how to shut it. Our train rounds a bend, and, with my face so close to the window, I see that, in place of the forests my children had been looking at with such wonder, there are now plantations of pine and tall eucalyptus along-side the hills that I assume must be covered with tea. I am sorry that the children are asleep, and I consider stirring them awake. But they will wake up soon enough, by dawn anyway, and there will still be beautiful sights outside for them. For now, I decide that I should let them sleep. I ease the window down as far as I can. It is stuck and creaks when I move it. *Creak-creak, creak-creak.* My struggle and the sound my efforts produce have a comical effect on me, and I start giggling, my back to the other passengers. I lean against the window and laugh. It is the first time I have laughed in this way, silly, un-afraid, since Siri was murdered and so I feel the tears come through as well, along with the laughter. Behind me I hear the young man and then the Tamil woman and then others across the aisle join in the laughter.

When I get the window closed and turn around, wiping my eyes and then covering my still smiling mouth with the edge of my sari pota, I see a young girl standing by the door, watching me. She is pregnant, about five months by the look of it. Her face is long and se-rious, and though her body is swollen, she is beautiful. She seems so young to be taking on such responsibility. I am immediately sober.

"Come and sit here, duwa," I say, holding out my hand and gestur-ing to my seat. She must have just climbed aboard at the last station, for otherwise someone would have given up a seat for her already.

She steps forward through the crowds, her light blue dress soft and at odds with the garish overhead lights. She is wearing new san-dals, and her feet are clean, a well-brought-up girl. She takes my hand and eases into our small space. I help her to sit down. Someone else passes the girl's suitcase to us. It is square and has green checks on it. The young man beckons to me to take his seat. He stands up, hold-ing my sleeping girl, waits for me to sit, then lays her down gently in my arms. I thank him profusely and call him son. He blushes, and I realize that he is not that young.

"How old is she?" the girl asks, caressing my baby's arm gingerly, as if she is asking to be forgiven for touching her at all.

"Four," I say, stroking my daughter's hair, marveling at how per-fect she is, how beautifully her features sit on her small face, her upper lip sloping down like a steep hill on each side, the bottom one full and round, her lids held down by thick lashes, something definite and confident about their straightness, the way they press against the tops of her cheeks. "But she will be five soon."

Latha

H ail, Mary, full of grace, the Lord is with thee. Blessed art thou amongst women, and blessed is the fruit of thy womb: Jesus. Holy Mary, Mother of God, pray for us sinners now, and at the hour of our death. Amen."

The *Amen* always gave her pause. It reminded her of men. Our men. Or, to be more precise, her men, the ones she had known in one way or another: Mr. Vithanage, the driver, the gardener, the fishmonger, Ajith, Gehan. Okay, so the boys weren't men the way Mr. Vithanage was a man, but still, they weren't women. Now that she had Become a Woman—which was a term that appeared from nowhere and stuck to her body the minute a penis came into contact with her vagina, like an unwieldy wand—surely they had Become Men? How was it, though, that men and women became so only by bringing those parts together? What happened to those who didn't? Did they stay girls forever?

Latha stole a surreptitious look at the nuns on either side of her. Definitely not girls; no, definitely women. But how had they done it? What had touched them? She lifted her eyes, the pupils rolling upward under her soulfully lowered lids, her eyebrows arching to accommodate the move, to gaze at the figure of Christ that hung, bloodied and barely robed, above the altar. Yes, she thought, there was something decidedly attractive about Jesus: arms outstretched, eyes half-closed, the face dipping down, that meager bit of cloth over—

"Latha! Prayers are over!" It was Leela. Leela was not a nun, but she was somehow wedded to the convent in the incarnation of a devout liaison between the nuns and the laypeople. Leela sat in the parlor all day long except during mealtimes and prayers. She sat there and embroidered. She produced slim rectangular boxes of white cotton days-of-the-week handkerchiefs (which seemed a trifle excessive to Latha, for who could handle a grief requiring so many handkerchiefs?) and table linens with hand-crocheted lace edging. The table linens were always cream or white. If she ever had a home, Latha had decided, she would have orange table linens. She wondered sometimes if she should learn to crochet so she could make them herself. Then again, why bother? There was, surely, some place where people like Leela produced orange table linens.

"I'm coming," Latha said, replacing her prayer book in the wooden slat in front of her. She crossed herself three times, then unwound the rosary from her hand and put it into her pocket. She liked that rosary: it was like jewelry, smooth and pearly and pale blue. It reminded her of luxuries and new things and, of course, Mrs. Vithanage's saris. There was no escape, she had found, from the memory of Mrs. Vithanage's saris. In a way she didn't really mind that, because Mrs. Vithanage came complete with Mr. Vithanage and Thara and even Soma, and all of them came with Ajith, who, of course, came with Gehan.

"Were there any letters for me today?" Latha asked. She always asked.

"No." Leela shook her head. "But we can't say that you won't get one tomorrow, isn't that so? We can always check tomorrow."

"Yes," Latha said, acknowledging the possibility and the kindness of a friend who would utter it against all evidence to the contrary.

"I came here about eleven and a half years ago," Leela had told her one day when Latha asked, sitting next to her in the parlor, sorting through her skeins of embroidery threads. The thread had been so bright and pretty, and so little of it was allowed on each hankie. It was a crying shame!

Latha had been sitting there for weeks. The nuns had thought it would be good for her, after the baby had come and gone, leaving behind only stitches in her vagina, the sound of things ending, and the silence she would not give up. She had not spoken in almost eight months; months during which the nuns had tried to shock her into speech, bringing her news of the world outside the convent, about new political parties and assassinations of one leader or another, of a peacekeeping force from India occupying the north and bombs going off everywhere. None of it had persuaded her to break her silence. What did any of it matter to her, locked up as she was, robbed of her past life and of her baby? But that day, looking at those brilliant and colorful threads, all bound together yet coming apart with such ease, the words had just fallen out of her.

"Why did you come?" she had asked.

"For the same reason you did," Leela had said.

"I came from Colombo. That's the big city," Latha had told her and pulled in the corner of her mouth like she had seen Soma do when she returned to the house after the row with Mrs. Vithanage. It had made Soma look like she knew exactly what she was worth and not a rupee less. And now she, Latha, did too. She knew what she was worth and what fires she could play with and how much of a house she could burn down with her newfound skills. And she wasn't going to forget that, even if she got covered with soot in the process or had nothing but ashes to look at afterward or even, yes, even if she had to burn down with it.

"I used to live in a house by the sea," Leela had told her. "It had so many windows on the sea side, and a big rooftop with a balcony all around it. I used to love to go there at night and watch the lights in the harbor."

"Were you near the harbor?" Latha had asked, though she wished she hadn't as soon as the words were out of her mouth; the harbor seemed so much more important than even Colombo itself.

"No, but I could see the ships because the house had many stories. Sir and madam had a TV and a VCR, and they were the only people in the whole building with those things. We didn't have a big garden, but the rooftop was filled with potted plants with fat leaves and few blooms, and a fountain with a naked baby with a bow and arrow on it, and there were benches and everything. The people had lots of parties there with music and dancing. When they had those parties they lit candles inside big glass bowls so they wouldn't go out, from the sea breeze . . ." She had paused and looked at Latha, clearly assessing the extent of her experience, then decided to tell all. "They were *posh*. I heard their guests say that when the sir and madam were not nearby. Sometimes it sounded like an insult because they would nudge each other and laugh when they said it. But only sometimes."

That was quite a long speech from Leela, whose unthreatening, unexpectant quietness had served to lessen Latha's own, and Latha had been impressed. She'd thought about the Vithanages' house and the one real celebration she had witnessed there: Thara's coming-of-age party. The only other times they had parties were for Thara's birthday, and even then only boring dinners with chicken curry and seeni sambol and fruit salad and ice cream afterward for relatives they never saw the rest of the year. There were never any young people and certainly no music and dancing like Leela said there had been at her house.

"Were there children?" Latha had asked, hoping to score at least one point for herself.

"No, only a madam and a sir who worked all day and had parties."

"Still, must have been nice with all those parties," Latha had said, charitably.

Leela had been silent, and Latha had understood. That's what it did to you, being a woman, not a girl; it made you understand things that weren't said. She'd picked up an orange skein and offered it to Leela. "I think you should put more orange in," she had said, "orange is a happy color."

Walking back to the dining room for breakfast now, Latha wondered who had brought Leela to the convent. Had it been the madam or the sir?

"Nobody," Leela said when she asked. "I came by myself."

Latha stopped midstride. "By yourself? How did you know where to go?"

"They drove me as far as a town where they had relatives, then they took me to the station and bought me a ticket, and told me where I was going, and said the nun would meet me when I got off in Hatton."

They had reached the dining room, and Latha waited with Leela while the girl behind the counter served them their string hoppers with white potato curry and coconut sambol. They picked up their mugs of plain ginger tea and made their way to the table in the corner right near the entrance to the kitchen but overlooking the convent vegetable garden. The nuns at the center table watched her closely as she passed, and Latha took pains to look drawn and put upon. Since the delivery of her baby and her withdrawal, her silence, her fasting, her refusal to attend mass, all the things that had made them give her to Leela for care, Latha had been allowed all sorts of exceptions to the usual rules of the convent, and, quite frankly, she was enjoying them. Especially not having to look grateful for her food through each entire meal three times a day, when the meals weren't really tasty enough to be grateful for in the first place. She often wished they would stop teaching people how to sew and perhaps teach some of the girls how to cook.

"Weren't you scared to come by yourself?" she asked, when all danger of being mistaken for having recovered had passed. She looked searchingly at Leela, who was full of grace in a virginal sort of way: clear-skinned, tender, and quietly resigned. Certainly not the kind of girl Latha could picture traveling anywhere by herself.

"I was. They put me on a train, and I sat on my suitcase between the compartments by the door, because it was very crowded and I was nauseous and needed fresh air. But somewhere near Gampola, I made my way into a third-class carriage, and there I met a woman who gave me a seat. She was the kind of woman everybody wants to be good to, you know, right? The kind even rowdy teenagers on the street corners call ammé? She called me duwa. That made me feel as though things would turn out all right, and they did."

"That's nice," Latha said. "I remember going on a train once when I was a child."

"Where did you go," Leela asked, smiling a little, "when you were a child?"

"I think I went to the hill country. It was like this." Latha looked out of the window to confirm this assertion, then nodded at Leela. "That's why I don't mind it too much here."

"Why didn't you stay?"

"In the hills? I couldn't stay by myself, could I? The Vithanages brought me, and we went to those gardens with the big roses in all colors. The whole garden smelled wonderful then. I had never seen so many flowers in one place, not even on calendar pictures. I had one picture that came close, but they were tulips from a place called Holland, abroad-flowers, not from our country."

She tried to like those flowers again, the way they had dug themselves a little hole under her skin and made her yearn for their scent as a child, the way she had stolen those bars of soap just to bury her face in them again. She tried, but she couldn't. Roses now reminded her of her body, the way it had been used and twisted and turned inside out and abandoned afterward; they smelled of the bile she had emptied along the paths planted with the thorny bushes at the convent.

"What are you thinking about?" Leela asked.

"Nothing," Latha said and sighed. She looked up at Leela and wished she could add something more to her story, now that her up-country trip had petered out into a mere visit, and one leached of its magic. "Can you get me more tea?" she asked. More tea was also a perk of ailing, and Latha felt as though she was ailing right then, and honestly this time. But Leela didn't get up.

"How old are you?" she asked.

"Seventeen I think."

"You don't look seventeen. You look younger; fifteen maybe."

"No, I'm definitely seventeen," Latha said, using her pursed mouth as added evidence of maturity.

"How would you know?" Leela asked, swirling the tea in her cup, round and round and round like she was agitated.

"I counted," Latha said, majestically.

"From when?"

"I counted my birthdays."

"Birthdays?" Leela asked, real awe in her voice. "Did your family celebrate your birthdays?"

"No," Latha said, thoughtfully, "but I did. I didn't know when I was born, so I just picked a date. I chose the first of May because the school principal told us that it was the most important day of the year and he was right because it was always a holiday and we sometimes watched the JVP parades with all the red flags, because that one almost always went by our house, but when I was bigger they stopped marching in the parades and so I changed it to the first of July because I read that the princess of England, Diana, was born on that date, and I felt that suited me better because she used to be poor before she became a princess. And Thara agreed too, and she gave me old things wrapped in newspaper sometimes. Her old books and pictures torn from magazines that I would like, pictures of food, mostly, but sometimes clothes and even houses in foreign countries with big gardens full of hedges and berries and even snow!" Latha warmed to her topic and continued with pride. "Once, Thara gave me a chocolate! That's how I know."

Leela put her palm on the side of Latha's cheek and smiled. It was a smile of pity, and it irked Latha. She was about to say something irritable, but just then Leela poured her own tea into Latha's empty cup. Latha tasted it. It was not hot, but she didn't feel like pressing for a new cup; it would have been rude.

"When is your birthday?" Latha asked, hoping for the right answer, that Leela would not know either, for sure anyway.

"I don't know. I know the years pass, that is all. My people told me they got me from this convent and that's why they were sending me back. They told the nuns that I was the wrong kind for them. Odd how they didn't think that for all those years when I was doing all their work for them, cooking for their parties, washing their clothes, polishing their floors."

Latha considered this revelation and tried to imagine Leela being born at the convent and living the rest of her life here. She looked around her and took in her new home for the first time with an open heart, searching for the best of it, making it perfect for Leela.

The rooms were spare, yes, but they were clean and decent. She liked the high roofs with the immense exposed beams and, come to think of it, she even liked the chapel. It was full of colors, all over the windows, and there was something comforting about that and the sonorous sound of the masses they held there once a day and twice on Sundays. The pews, those too were not so bad when she gave it some thought. It was good, wasn't it, to slip forward from them onto the cushioned knee rest below, to feel that smooth wood beneath her elbows? Yes, she enjoyed that; it felt like sleep, the seated prayers and then the languorous slide into the kneeling prayers, when she could give herself over to all her longings while the music rose around her. Most of the nuns had good voices, and they pitched them toward heaven together, one voice rising and falling like a velvety sheet whipped over a bed. Or like the hills themselves, dipping and climbing around the convent, they sounded like that, those nuns. True, Latha didn't much like singing herself, but it was good to be at the center of it, buffeted and buoyed by the nuns' fervor. She nodded to herself; yes, Leela was fortunate to have a life unfold to the accompaniment of those voices.

Besides, the nuns kept very neat gardens, which produced sensuously corpulent vegetables that begged to be eaten: giant orange carrots, voluptuous red beets, and the long white leeks, with their masses of pale green leaves, and what about the radishes? After Latha gave up the roses, she had taken to walking there, something that only the cooks did, fondling and sniffing at the produce in silence. It had calmed her to do that, to wander within such fertility, some of the plants almost as tall as herself. Once, she had crouched there when the nuns came looking for her, worried about her recovery, her blameful silence. She had simply sat down in the black, loamy earth, her nostrils full of the aroma of healthy growing things. Afterward she had crept forward on all fours, making her way through the gardens like an animal, until she lay down, on her back, measuring her head against the rows of cabbages on either side of her face. The nuns had found her there and taken her back inside, and that's when they had handed her over to Leela for care and management.

She looked up at Leela now. So what if it might drive people like her a little crazy sometimes, the convent was good for them both. It was quiet here, and peaceful, and wholesome. Even though the sharp, cold air of the mountains came through the seemingly permeable wood and stone and made her shiver, at least it made her feel pure somehow, and untouched by all the little miseries that had visited her. And they *had* been little miseries, she told herself, nothing to really blemish her soul, no, she was quite certain about that, but at the convent there was nothing at all to tarnish her opinion of herself.

"This is a good place to come from," she told Leela and waited for a response, some recognition of her decision to affirm the convent, but there was none. Leela sat silently, looking thoughtfully at her. Latha returned her gaze for a while and then grew tired of it. She looked at Leela's dress instead. She always wore light-colored clothes. Well, that wouldn't be entirely true; she had three pastel dresses. Clothes were what people like Thara had. People like herself and Leela, they had dresses that could be counted on one hand. But anyway, Leela was quite lovely in her own, saintly way, with or without a proper wardrobe. She parted her hair in the middle, which made her long face seem quite forlorn, but it suited her. She seemed ripe for bearing the weight of unmentionable sorrows. In fact, she looked very much like the Virgin Mary, who hung around every nun's neck and hers, too.

Latha began to sing softly: *"Mother dearest, mother fairest, help us, help, we call on thee . . . virgin purest, brightest, rarest, virgin help us, help, we pray—"*

"Shh!" Leela said, putting her hand over Latha's mouth.

Latha continued to try to sing under the cool, soft hand, making Leela giggle. She brought her teeth down sharply over a fleshy rise, and Leela yelped, still laughing, and pulled her hand away. "You can't be seventeen, Latha, you are like a child!" Leela said.

Latha stopped singing. Her mouth turned down at the corners and she felt sick again. Child. She wasn't a child. She was a woman who had lost a child, and it didn't matter how old she was, that still made it impossible for her to claim to be one. Maybe Leela herself had been born here, and someone had taken her away from a mother like they had taken her own baby from her. Where had her child gone? She hadn't heard the cry of an infant inside the convent, which meant that she had been taken away altogether. If every baby here was given away, to whom had hers gone? Who was looking after her baby? They had turned Leela into a servant, hadn't they? So whose servant would her baby become? She half-rose and looked about her frantically, searching the faces of the nuns on either side of the center table. Which one of them was neglecting her baby while they sat there eating their food as though nothing evil could be traced back to them, as though they didn't spend their days tending to girls such as herself like they were fattening calves from whom they would steal everything there was to be stolen? Those clean gowns, those serene faces, all that singing. No wonder they got down on their knees so often! They were nothing but sinners!

Next to her Leela took her hand. "Sit, Latha Nangi," she said. "Finish that tea."

"I don't want any tea," she said, sinking back into her chair, the hopelessness of discovering where her child had gone descending upon her. "I want to know where they took my baby. Why won't they tell me? I've asked and asked—"

"It's no use asking." Leela interrupted her gently but quickly, as if the thought needed to be stopped before it got out of control. "Sometimes they keep them at the sister house so they can train them to be nuns, but we weren't fortunate. They didn't keep ours." She paused and then went on. "But at least our babies must have been beautiful. That's why they were adopted so quickly."

"We don't know that they have been adopted," Latha said. "If they had been adopted, they would be able to tell us that, wouldn't they?"

"Sister Angelina told me that when the babies are born, if they are beautiful and blessed, they are adopted right away. If they are not, the nuns look after them till they are old enough to become novices."

"I don't believe anything they tell us," Latha said bitterly, angry at how gullible and trusting Leela was. "You are beautiful and you were not adopted and they sent you to be a servant!"

Leela looked crestfallen, the concern gone from her eyes, confusion invading them, and Latha felt sorry for her. She pushed the cup of cold tea back to Leela, who drank it without a word of complaint.

"They took me back, Latha Nangi," she said, finally. "I had nowhere else to go and I was pregnant and they took me in and looked after me and gave me a home."

"You called me Nangi," Latha said, after a minute or two of silence. "Can I call you Akka? We could pretend we are sisters."

"If you like," Leela said, sighing, then smiling at her.

"If you like, Latha *Nangi*. You must call me Nangi to make it real."

"Yes, Latha *Nangi*." Leela giggled, sounding young all of a sudden. "I don't have any family either. And you are not so bad. You can boil kottamalli for me when I am sick, and I will make it for you when you are sick. That way we won't have to go to the infirmary and be by ourselves with Sister Francesca, who is always making us feel bad till we cry and then tells us she loves us."

Yes, Latha thought, she would like that. The nuns always said they were the Family of God, and she didn't care all that much for the God part, being a temple-going girl herself, but she could do with a family of something. Leela would be perfect for the part.

"I liked that woman on the train," Leela said absently, for all the world as if she had forgotten their conversation or her part in the sister-sister game. "She waited with me to make sure the nun came. I almost made her miss the train . . . I didn't want to be left behind by myself and there was nobody to stand with me. But she got off the train with me, leaving her children asleep in the booth where we had been sitting."

And once more Latha was back on a train heading toward roses. Once more with a family and a hill country and then, nothing else. Try as she might, nothing else.

Biso

There is something heart-stopping about the way the lights on the front end of the train curve and disappear around the edge of the cliff from where we sit in the back of it. It must be the sight of the engine leaving us behind, the sensation of derailment and doom that makes her feel like confiding. I have been listening to the station-master's melismatic chant, the repetition, save one each time, of the places we pass and move beyond: *Ula-pane, Nawala-pitiya, Wata-wala, Roz-ella, Hatton, Kota-gala, Thalawa-kele, Wata-goda, Great-Western, Nanu-oya, Ambe-wela, Patti-pola, Ohiya, Idalgas-inna, Hapu-tale, Diyata-lawa, Bandara-wela, El-la, Demo-dara, Hali-Ela, Bad-ulla* . . . and that's how he pronounces them, breaking each one into two, all except her station and mine: Hatton and Ohiya. It is like a periodic lullaby. With each town that is dropped off the list we grow closer to our destination, and farther from our sorrows. Hers and mine.

"It wasn't my fault, aunty," she says. "I don't want you to think it was my fault."

"I don't blame you," I say. "Men are like that." I pat her knee, knowing what she means and not expecting her to say anything more. Don't I have my own tale to nurse? But she goes on as if I had encouraged her, telling me that I was wrong to imagine that she was from a good family; she was no more than a servant.

"I had worked in that house since I was a child. I don't even know how old I am now. They tell me I am nineteen and an adult, but the neighbor's servant told me that I came there when I was six. I've been with them for eleven years. She says that means I must be seventeen and not an adult. But anyway, what does it matter whether I am an adult or not? They said it was my fault, so in a way it must have been my fault."

And she tells me about how she used to go up onto the rooftop at night and how, if everybody was sleeping, she would sing softly and practice the dancing she saw in the Hindi films the sir and madam liked to watch. She had learned how to turn on a television and how to play motion pictures on it through a video *eka* when nobody was home, which was very often.

"You just have to push the button and the film comes on the TV," she tells me, and I try to imagine being able to watch films anytime at all like that. There had been a radio and a record player in the house next to ours. They had bought those things with Dubai money after the husband got a job in the desert countries at a building site, and they used to fry squid with lots of chilies and invite everybody to listen to *Muwan Palessa* every week on the radio on the *Sri Lanka Guvanviduli Sevaya*. Afterward, they would play records, and I did enjoy hearing the music coming from their house all in English when I went to get my children. But one day the owners met me at the door and told me that there was a needle on the player and that my Loku Duwa had made a record get scratched by knocking it, so after that I didn't let them go to that house. I told my children it was because nobody needed that much entertainment. Those people used to boast that someday when the Japanese government built a TV station and gave the whole country TV, they would get one of those too. I imagine a TV screen must be like the film theater screen, but I can't think what it might actually look like. I suppose that is all right. I don't know how anybody could keep track of that many stories anyway.

"How did you know what to watch?" I ask her, amazed that a person as young as she is would know not only how to handle such equipment but what to watch.

She smiles at me. "I only watched the ones with the handsome actor on the cover," she says.

But the handsome actor always had a lady to love who wore bright-colored saris that showed off her shapely body, and they always danced and got caught in the rain, she tells me. She hangs her head after she says that and is quiet for a while. All the other passengers are asleep, nodding this way and that, or with their heads resting against the shoulders of friends unconsciously made. The sight of it makes me feel drowsy and happy. I feel my own eyes beginning to close.

"It was all because of the rain," the girl blurts out.

"What was because of the rain?" I ask, awake now, more curious about her story than I was before. This would be the first time I'd heard the rain blamed for a pregnancy, though, considering what I'd seen and overheard on this trip alone, maybe even that was possible.

"I went up there when it was raining one night, just to see what it feels like to be dancing and seeing a man like that, in the rain, like in the films," she says. "I took the madam's sari too. Just the sari, not anything else. It was not one of her good saris either. It wasn't raining much at first, just a drizzle. So I took off my dress and wrapped the sari around me standing right there, waiting for it to start pouring like it always does in the city, after those first large drops of rain. I waited for the big downpour, which comes like the gods are trying to wash the sins away from every crack in the pavement."

And now, I can see everything. The actor, the film, the dancing, the color, the rain. I can see her body wrapped up in blue. I don't know why it is blue, it just seems that a blue sari would look beautiful in the rain, and here she is wearing blue and it does look lovely on her. And I can see, without her having to tell me, the man who must have come upon her, and it does not matter if he lived in her house or the house next door, or even in one farther down the way from her. I just know that he sees her and wants her and she is not to blame for any of it.

"Here," I say when she has finished her story, breaking a large square of honey-coated cadju from the quarter pound of sweets I bought at the last station while my children slept, wasting some of our money on an unnecessary indulgence now that we are safely on our way and our destination that much closer.

"No, that's okay. You should save it for the children," she says, pushing my hand away gently.

"I have some more," I lie. "We'll eat this."

She takes it from me. And we sit in the carriage, and not the clanking of metal underneath the train, or the night wail of the horn far ahead of us, or the whoosh and sigh of the winds can make us feel lonely so long as we sit like that, so close that we can hear each other scrunch and bite.

When we reach Watawala, I am glad that it is night and we cannot see the pass that the train goes over, carried, it seems, on nothing but a prayer. I remember going over it as a new bride, my husband and I making the rounds of visits to all our relatives; I had felt a self-conscious pleasure, the kind generated by the ought-to-be-happy wishes of those who had put us on a lorry to go from my village in Hambantota to his in Matara after the ceremony, my beautiful teak furniture stacked neatly behind. The dressing table, the almirah, the bed my father had made especially for my mother, my smooth, heavy trunk, the oval dining table and six chairs. I remember how empty my childhood home had seemed when it was all loaded into the vehicle. Still, my father had looked delighted, so I tried to be too. For his sake. Everything, all that followed, for his sake. I remember the way the young girls giggled and the men patted my husband's back. He must have had hopes too. We had already wilted, though, a little, by the time we reached the new home two hours later; just like the coconut flowers tied to the front of the lorry had folded over, their seed-filled fronds somehow having lost the promise of vigorous fertility on the bumps and stops and in all the heat along the way.

My husband and I had reclaimed a little of that optimism on our one trip to the hills to visit my dead mother's older sister, reclaimed it exactly over this pass. Some sensation of taking a real risk, perhaps, of my needing his assurance of safety, of his pride in the ability to give it. We had held hands coyly, and when I hung my head over the window to watch how we moved over the abyss below, he had rested his chin on my shoulder and joined me. We had both looked at it, this pass. I wonder now what it was that he saw.

I see nothing now, but I can sense what is outside. Everything feels lush here, even in the darkness; the mountain air is cool, the fecund soil giving off a certain scent, like a beautiful woman with many children secure in the knowledge of more to come. I ask the girl to hold my sleeping baby while I go to stand in the open doorway of our carriage. She opens her arms with true delight, taking her from me and shushing her back to sleep, her voice instinctively pitched to soothe.

The train has emptied, a few passengers at a time, ever since we left Kandy, and by now there is nobody left to fight with over the pleasure of sitting on the steps. I lower myself to the floor and pull the folds of my sari up between my knees and tuck it underneath me; then I drape the fall over my head and around my shoulders. I hold on to the metal railing on the step and lean my head against my arm. In some places, the hills have reclaimed so much of the tracks that fronds of grass and leaves of trees I cannot identify caress my face and feet as we pass. I am amazed by their resilience, the way they have prevailed over steel and fumes and noise.

There's a little light behind me from the inside of the carriage; outside, it is pitch-black but for the moon, which is still on its first day of waning. The whole country is asleep. I sit there and wonder about the lives that are resting, what the day might bring for each one. For me. I stretch my arm out into the night, daring it to hurt me if it can. Nothing happens. My fingers brush air. We enter a tunnel, and what I had considered darkness before now feels like the first touch of dawn. It is so loud in there, the train's journey echoing repeatedly against those curved walls, that it feels as though the tunnel is angry that we have entered it at all. I draw my body in, though to save myself from what terror I cannot say. When we come out at the other end, I can see better for a while, but soon enough this relative light reclaims its former strength and once more I feel just as blind. I stretch my arm out again and again, but with less surety, and for shorter lengths of time. Eventually, I give up. I don't want to feel scared anymore. After a few minutes the moon shows again from behind the clouds.

When I return to our seats, I find that the girl has fallen asleep too, leaning against the window, my own little one's face nestled in her lap. They look like sisters, my daughter in her orange checked dress and the girl. Across from them, Loku Putha and Loku Duwa are also still asleep, supporting each other but only with their backs, their faces turned away from each other and resting flat on their seat. I touch each head and utter a blessing. The same blessing, four times. I sit next to the girl and put my feet up on the seat in front of me, forming a small barrier between the children and the rest of the occupants with my body. I listen for a while to the assurance of the tracks under this machine, the *thakas thakas* and then the pause, and again the *thakas thakas* and then the pause. It is soothing, like the feel of a mother's lap as she rocks a baby to sleep. I close my eyes.

"Nendé! Nendé! Wake up!"

"What is it? What?" I ask, rubbing the sleep out of my eyes. My feet find the floor, and I half-stand.

"No, sit, it's nothing. I just wanted to show you the dawn," she says, the girl. "Look. By the time you reach Ohiya it will be here."

Outside the darkness is relenting, but only incrementally. The girl's eyes are fixed on her reflection. It's still dark enough for that. Too dark to wake up the children; there are a few hours left of our journey. I stare at us in the glass, and then, just like her, I blurt out my own sins to a stranger.

"I had someone who loved me," I say. "He died in my arms. My husband stabbed him to death."

"Just like in the films," she says and looks interested, as if I were relating a story about somebody else, not sharing my truth.

I nod, curling my secrets back into my heart. She is nothing more than a child. I picture her holding a baby in her arms, sitting in front of a screen with colorful moving pictures. "My mother came from the hill country," I say, distracting her from the story I cannot tell with one she can understand. "And she was from a very good family. They were the sort that gave alms to the priests and made donations to the temple near their home. I never knew where, exactly; my grandparents passed away before my mother got married. She was living with her older sister in Ohiya when she met my father by chance. He had come up to the hills on pilgrimage to Sri Pāda and then to visit a cousin. They fell in love and she moved to the low country with him. That's where I was born. In the South, the real South, beyond the Benthara River."

"Where is your mother now?" she asks, not caring which part of the South I am from, not knowing these distinctions of which my father used to speak so proudly that I, too, grew straighter with that pride.

"My mother died when I was nine," I say.

I feel the old pain well up with unusual strength. Perhaps because of the way mothers hope for us, the way those hopes pursue us; it reminds us of them when we are at our lowest, a longing for a different outcome, a second chance, gnawing bitterly on our insides.

"It makes me sad to hear that," the girl says. "I don't have a mother. At least I don't remember if I did."

I look at her, but I don't comprehend what she has said; I want to reprimand her for speaking ill of her own mother. "What are you saying? Everybody has a mother, duwa," I tell her, but she only shrugs.

"I never knew her," she says. "Tell me about your mother, aunty."

"Mine died young, unexpectedly. She got sick and then she died, without any trouble at all. She never caused anybody any problems, and she never looked less than she always had. Clean, dignified, even when she died."

"What happened to you then?" the girl asks.

I sigh. Yes, what happened next. "My father sent me to be boarded at the convent where I was studying. The nuns knew my mother, so they took me in."

I do not say that I had missed the land that lay around our house, the space of it, the generous earth, the way the young paddy looked, bright green and hopeful, the rituals of each season; how I had missed helping my father the way my mother once did in tending to that land. I had never said that to the nuns, or to my father, or even admitted it to myself until now. At the time I had been glad to have been delivered to the nuns, who, though they could not compare with my mother, at least were better approximations to her than the one sad parent left to me. Something in their calm gait, their repetitive prayers, their daily observances, even the sacrament, had helped to anchor the days so that, in time, I came to feel that life had not one bliss but many.

"Were the nuns good to you?" she asks.

"Yes, they were. They treated me like a special student, teaching me a little bit more than they taught the other girls. Maybe they wanted me to become a novice, even though I was Buddhist." I hadn't gone to temple when I lived at the convent; I had prayed with those nuns. I hadn't minded that, I tell her. Wherever we kneel, we look toward the gods, after all, and what does it matter by what name they are known? And hadn't I grown up to learn the truth of it? To watch the Catholic fishermen visit the temples and the kovils as well as the churches before they set sail, the same way the Buddhist fishermen did? Kneeling and praying to every deity, asking for guidance and help from them all?

She laughs. "My sir and madam went to a Sathya Sai Baba center," she tells me. "But they also had a Buddhist shrine and sometimes went to the novena at the All Saints' Church in Borella. I have gone there with madam. I liked that church. She used to buy me candles made of melted wax. She said those were better, because other people had already prayed over them before they were melted down."

"That is the way it is with all of us, I suppose," I say. I, too, had sometimes lit candles and recited Pansil instead of the Catholic prayers while kneeling in the pews. But I had been a good novice. "The nuns were very upset when my father came one day to take me home for good. He had found a prospect for me, he told them, and he had to do his duty by his wife and marry his girl properly."

"Was he handsome, your husband?" the girl asks, fancy in her eyes.

I shake my head. "No, he was not handsome. He was quite ordinary, but big." I bulk up my arms to show her and turn my mouth down in a grimace; that makes her giggle. "Big, like this. It wouldn't have mattered, what he looked like, or that he was low caste, from the fishing village. My father was low caste too, but he was a good man and he was devoted to my mother. My husband was not like him. He had some money when he first met my father and arranged the marriage; he even owned a big boat, unlike most of the fishermen in our village. Later, he pawned most of my furniture, my mother's furniture, to buy a motor and a freezer, but he was not a good businessman. He drank. And he didn't care for me."

"Couldn't you make him love you?" she asks.

The question reminds me again of her youth, her experience limited to beautiful women and handsome actors who overcome all odds on television screens. I give up on the idea of burdening her with confidences, for how would I explain the ill will inside my husband's house? The dank misery that sullied the curtains I hung up, the way even incense could not drive out the spite that pressed down on us all?

"No," I tell her. "I could not. Some things are the way they are, there is no help for it, there is no reason, they are as they are." We are both silent for a while. "Tell me, where are you going now?" I ask, at last.

"I'm going to a convent in Hatton," she says. "They said that's where I came from. I was an orphan and I lived there. People come there for servants sometimes, I hear. Somebody came for me. When we got to Colombo, the madam's mother came to live with them for a little bit to train me, but after that I was fine. I don't remember the convent, though." She touches a mole on her neck.

"Are you going to stay there after the baby is born?"

"I don't know. The next-door servant said that sometimes girls come back after they go up-country like this, but madam said that nobody will want me now, not with my history, she said." She looks down and smoothes the fingers of one hand with the other, over and over.

She has nice hands. There is just enough space between her fingers that they look trustworthy, like they are ready for work, but neat work, like embroidery and smocking. My own hands are callused and scratched from all the sorting and drying of fish. And children, too. Children age hands somehow, even when they are not near their mothers. As if their very being requires draining what is tensile and soft from our skins. Like the way kites cut your hands, and cut and cut until you let them go and you fall away, resigned at last to simply witnessing their flight.

"I am afraid," she says, speaking to her hands; her mouth trembles.

I do not want to curse her with untruths, so I take her hand in mine and hold it. I wish I had a home to offer her, or some advice as to how she could make a life for herself, but I don't. She is an orphan; there is no place for an orphan to go to for help, except to strangers.

Latha

They had told her that nobody would ever want her again. That's what happened to little whores like her, Mrs. Vithanage had said. She had said it calmly and without acrimony, so it had sounded true. What had she meant by nobody, though, Latha wondered; did it mean no other family, or no other man? These were not the same things. One she could live with, but the other was an entirely different proposition.

She knelt in the pew and mouthed prayers as she tried to imagine life without a man. All she could see was Leela by a parlor window with her might-as-well-be-white-on-white embroidery. Sister Helen-Marie passed by to receive communion, and now Latha's picture of Leela was joined by a retinue of praying nuns in gray and white habits. No, it just would not do to live that way. There would be no hope of orange serviettes in this place. Ever. She sighed, and Sister Francesca, in the pew beside her, looked up and across at her disapprovingly. Latha sighed again, louder this time, and the two nuns in the pew in front of hers, she couldn't remember their names, tightened their shoulders and bent further into their reverence. Latha contemplated a third sigh, but prayers ended and she was relieved from having to demonstrate that her soul had not yet been saved and, what's more, that she had no intention of letting it be salvaged now and forevermore, amen. She made the sign of the cross over her chest—which was a gesture she actually liked, the grace of it, and the fact that she felt that it was she herself, not any God wherever he may be, who was doing the blessing—and stood up.

Through one of the arched doorways bordered by the dark, deep cups with their icy cold holy water, she could see Leela beckoning to her. Well, it must have been her fervent prayers that had done it, for Leela had a letter in one hand.

"Where is it from?" Latha asked, stopping by the door and helping herself to some dabs of the holy water, hoping for good news and also wanting to prolong the thrill of not knowing.

"I don't know."

"Read the envelope, Leelakka!" She had amalgamated the two words after the first couple of tries and now Leela Akka was simply Leelakka.

"I can't read."

Latha heaved that last sigh and took the letter from Leela. It was postmarked Colombo, and the writing was Thara's. "It's from Thara," she said, feeling nonplussed yet curious. What would Thara want to write to her about? In all the hours she'd spent waiting for something—a messenger, a telephone call, a letter, a visitor—she had pictured only one person: Gehan. Only he had it in him to forgive her. Mr. Vithanage did too, but he would never step beyond the requirements of his wife, and his wife required loyalty. He had been kind to Latha, once, she knew he had; somewhere in her subconscious was a memory of a chocolate he had bought for her. Not chocolate that Thara had shared with her but a whole bar, just for her. But when and why she could not remember, all the events of her life marked only by the highs and lows experienced with Thara and, later, Gehan, to all of which Mr. Vithanage was little more than a compassionate, if unimpressive, background. It was a dream, she knew, one made up of all the stories she had heard from Thara and those she had watched on TV, but she had sometimes taken it out and dwelled within it. Of course, all that remained now was just the past year, with its fury and lack of remorse and the loss that lay unmourned and pointless in the deepest part of her soul.

But despite her hope and forward-looking projections for reconciliation with Gehan, it had not come. And now here in her hands, in place of Gehan, was Thara. She had been at the convent for almost two years now and she had heard not one word from Thara. She had often wondered if Thara knew what she had done to her. But it wasn't to her, no, it wasn't, it was the Vithanages to whom she had done it, Mrs. Vithanage in particular. But was that entirely true? Sometimes, when she sat in those pews, she thought back to that time and about Ajith and Thara. How easy it had been not to care that, in punishing Mrs. Vithanage, she would lose Thara, who would, in the end, suffer the most. Or to consider how deeply Thara loved Ajith, underneath all that sassy bravado when she was not yet twelve, underneath the yearning for bras at thirteen and the duping of her mother at fourteen and the partying and dancing at fifteen. How easy to remember what she had disregarded so deliberately then: that Thara had loved Ajith through her year of misery when he couldn't bring himself to see her, content with his nightly trysts with Latha, and loved him even after her failed exams.

And now, with this letter in her hand, come so belatedly, how easy it was also to remember the pleasure Latha had got from being unseduced by Thara's boyfriend and his good looks, his little-boy smile and strong body, nothing shuffling or uncertain about his gait or his words, that upper-class cleanliness that always came with a store-bought fragrance. She had enjoyed that, hadn't she? The way she had stood there, on so many nights, letting her body feel pleasure, peak, and release without ever giving up her heart, her mind constantly on that other boy, Gehan, the one who had nothing with which to woo a girl of Thara's circumstances, or keep the friendship of someone like Ajith, neither of whom had ever paid him any real heed. Hadn't she avenged them both, herself and Gehan, for that neglect by the people closest to them? Wasn't that the real truth? And hadn't she been right? If Thara had cared, or if Ajith had, why had neither of them tried to contact her before this? No, there was only one person who could be forgiven for having stayed away, and that was Gehan.

Latha continued to examine the writing on the envelope. Thara had not said a word when she left, not one word of sympathy. She had simply stood next to her mother and waved good-bye to her father and stared and stared as Mr. Vithanage drove away with Latha in the back of a taxi, a vacant look in her eyes, hair unkempt, biting her nails as if *she* were the one who was growing an unwanted child in her belly, not Latha. Her face had not seemed to register the fact that something was being broken, a friendship, their combined history. She had just stood there! As if she, Latha, didn't exist; as if they had never been one and the same. Yes, Latha thought, she had been right to do what she had done. At least she could be certain of that.

"Open it and see what it says," Leela said.

"It's just a letter, not a present or anything like that. I'll open it later."

"When?"

"After breakfast, maybe. Don't worry, I'll tell you what it says. I'll read it aloud."

But when she did read it, Latha was glad that she was alone and that she hadn't read it aloud. It was so short and to the point: Thara was getting married and she wanted Latha to come back; she would send the driver for her. There was no reason, no excuse, no apology, not even a please; it was almost a command. As if she owned her. Still, Latha told herself, sitting on her bed and reading the words over, if nothing else, she would not have to be surrounded by nuns and embroidery. That was worth something.

Leela said she was happy for her that her madam and sir had wanted her back, though she also added various cautionary words about things, like political skirmishes, which had never worried Latha. She warned her to be careful, because the JVP leader had been killed and all the young people who had fought for him so many years ago were going to be agitating and things were bound to get bad in Colombo, and Latha needed a good house to live in, with people who wanted her. That was the only way, Leela said, that she would be safe in such a city in these bad times.

"And anyway, it isn't this way for everybody, Latha Nangi, even if nobody was fighting and there was peace in the country, not every girl gets this chance to go back and set things right. You must be grateful and not make any mistakes this time around," she said. She was sitting on Latha's bed, helping her pack her suitcase. It wasn't as if she had that much, but certainly by Leela's standards, she had enough to turn packing into an event.

Latha had washed her clothes in twos and threes over the past week, a couple of dresses here, a skirt there. The pieces of underwear in particular had to be washed well in advance so they could be dried discreetly, hung on her foldout rack, hidden between the blouses in the front rows and the convent walls behind. It didn't matter that they were all discards passed on to her from somebody else; they were just not convent-quality. It was what had brought trouble her way, the nuns had said, when she first got there and they looked through her belongings, dressing for somebody other than herself underneath her school uniforms and servant-girl dresses. They had kindly gifted her with two yards of white cotton fabric, which she had dutifully sewn into the panties of their dreams: bunched up high around the waist and ballooning like mushrooms, only to be cinched again at the tops of her thighs, which, after inspection and approval, she had sent away with the cooking girl. They had also given her, still in their pink and white boxes and plastic wrappings, two new *Angelina* bras, which were the kind Mrs. Vithanage wore; their support came entirely from concentric circles of threads, which grew ever smaller until they reached sharp points. Latha could not imagine any human breasts fitting into such contraptions, and she wasn't going to subject hers to them. She had passed them on to Leela, who accepted them with gratitude, and she had continued to wear her old underwear, hiding her sin under two slips instead of one.

Watching Leela touch these things, Latha felt her loyalty to her own notions of right and wrong waver. Her clothes looked obscene in Leela's hands. Leela was right; she should be careful of her second chance. She reached over and crammed the underwear into a siri-siri bag. "I'm not going to wear these, Leelakka, I'm just going to take them and give them to somebody else."

"That's a good idea," Leela said, smiling indulgently, "but keep something to wear home."

They continued to work quietly, sitting side by side, the cardboard suitcase open between them.

"My suitcase had green and white checks," Leela said, stroking the side of Latha's bag, "but when I knew I was going to stay, I gave it to the kitchen girl."

"How did you know you were going to stay?" Latha asked, absently, smoothing her hands over the pleats of a yellow and black dress that had belonged to one of Thara's aunts and was clearly of another era, stitched from a *Butterick* magazine pattern, the kind that were stacked in Mrs. Vithanage's house.

Mrs. Vithanage. Latha wondered why Mrs. Vithanage had decided to let her come back, knowing that everybody assumed her own husband had been responsible for the pregnancy. Latha had listened to the convent cooks talk, after her baby had been born and when she was still spending time alone in the vegetable gardens. Just like the students at her old school, the cooks had been talking about the girls who came and delivered babies under the care of the nuns. When she overheard their voices, she had stopped to listen. *They come here making all kinds of excuses, all kinds of stories, but I believe what the nuns say, it is always their own fault,* she had heard the oldest of them, a hunchbacked woman named Maggie Achchi, say. *They go to work in Colombo houses and before long they want to take their madams' place.* And even though the youngest among them, the kitchen girl, had tried to argue that perhaps it was the other way around, that perhaps it was the masters who forced themselves on their servant girls, Maggie Achchi had insisted that the girls were to blame: *If it isn't the master, then it is their own bad character. They are nothing but whores, running around with drivers and gardeners and then blaming it all on the head of the household, the good man who pays their salaries, and for what? Nothing but spite.* She had fallen silent only when Latha turned the corner and stood there, saying nothing, staring at all of them until the kitchen girl had stepped forward and led her back inside the convent. Latha felt glad to be leaving a place where everybody from the nuns to the cooks believed the worst of her, and where there was no place for the complexities of a life like hers within their limited experience of the world.

"When I stepped into this place, I felt at peace," Leela said, reminding Latha of the question she had asked. Leela had tucked her hands underneath her hips, and she was smiling. She looked young and innocent.

"How could you feel that with all these rules?" Latha asked, because Leela was clearly aching to explain. She folded the dress and laid it in the suitcase, wondering if the clothes would get crushed when she set it upright.

"Here at the convent my rules are only to do with discipline and prayers. I work, but my work is between me and my cloth and threads. Nobody can find fault with me for anything I do, not even I. The city is different. I could never go back to it." Leela looked so contented that Latha felt sad. What was wrong with her that she could not feel that same sense of peace?

She sat down next to Leela, thinking about how quiet and restful her room was, even with two people in it. At the Vithanages' her sleep had never come gently to her, finding her stretched out, clean, and hardly ever tired, like it did here. She had been used to nights coming upon her like a storm, making her curl up to ride them out, making her wake up still tired, her bones stiff from the floor. She had a bed here, and they had just given it to her the day she came; she hadn't had to be somebody's servant for most of her life to earn her bed and privacy.

She stood up and walked around the room, touching one thing and another. The brown wooden shelf over her bed with the requisite picture of Jesus and a pointy red bulb, which stayed lit through the night; the switch by the door, which was a little grimy from the many hands that had searched for it in the dark, and, beside it, the rectangular mirror, which showed her face; the rack by the window with her nightdress and the pair of socks that she wore for sleeping folded neatly over it; the simple latched cupboard, which now stood empty of all her belongings save the last.

She put her palm over her box of treasures. The box had once contained chocolates. Mr. Vithanage had got a Christmas hamper one year from somebody in the government. It was the only such delivery the family had ever received, and what excitement it had caused her and Thara! It had come full of foreign things: *Kraft* cheese in a round blue tin, black Christmas pudding in a ceramic bowl, Christmas cake wrapped in red cellophane and tied with a gold ribbon, packets of fancy tea biscuits from England, a blue tin of butter cookies separated from one another by crisp, pleated, transparent wax paper, a bottle of scotch whiskey, a bottle of rum, and the best thing of all: a wooden box packed with twelve slabs of *Kandos* cashew chocolate. In the biggest size. Her mouth watered once more at the memory of that day, the evening when all of it had been opened, the small tastes she had received when Mrs. Vithanage, obviously swept up in generosity at the sight of this feast, had sent a single plate to the kitchen with the thinnest of samplings for the servants: herself, Soma, the gardener, and the driver.

The box had been given to her by Thara. She would have liked to have the tin, but Thara had taken that for her hair clips, and so Latha had decided to prefer the box because it still, after all these years, smelled of chocolates, and the tin was just a tin as soon as the butter cookies were eaten, because it had to be washed of all the crumbs, and the local soap and city water took the scent of luxury away. Latha knew exactly what was in her box now. A yellow araliya flower pressed into silken brown delicacy from the bunch that Gehan had given her that first afternoon, a draft of the note she had written to Ajith to bring him to her that first night, the rectangular green wrapper from the cake of jasmine soap that Soma had given her when she came of age, the flat gold earrings in the shape of stars that Soma had said she arrived in and that she had never taken off until she got Thara's ruby ones, Thara's two gold bangles, which she had never actually been allowed to wear, five pictures torn from magazines that she had received as birthday presents, and the strip of gold paper Thara had given her. She heard a sniffle and turned around.

"Don't cry, Leelakka," she said, "I will send you letters from Colombo."

"There's no point writing letters to me, nangi, I can't read them, and anyway, you should go forward from here and live your life. I just feel sad because you're the first child they gave me to look after," Leela said. "I feel like I'm losing a daughter."

"Not a daughter, a sister, Leelakka! I'm too old to be your daughter." But Leela didn't laugh. She just sat and dabbed at her eyes with a handkerchief from one of her pockets. Leela's dresses always had pockets. Latha wondered whether Leela sewed her own dresses complete with pockets or whether the nuns knew she liked pockets and gave her only the old dresses that had them.

Leela heaved another sigh, and Latha tried to feel as miserable; but no tears would come, not even when she tried to imagine never being able to see Leela again, because somehow that did not seem likely. She felt as though she was simply leaving home for a new house, like a bride. And brides always came back later to visit and make people happy to see them and comment on how domestic they looked, or to have their bellies patted knowingly. She had witnessed many such visits at the Vithanages' when their nieces and nephews brought their new spouses around for personal introductions. She and Thara had always wondered what the wedding was for if the newly married couple had to "do the rounds" afterward. Maybe Thara would be busy doing that after her wedding. What would she, Latha, be doing then? Would she have to accompany Thara? She pictured herself walking beside Thara, carrying the obligatory bunches of ambul plantains and packets of *Marie* biscuits for the relatives, laughing about one thing or another, perhaps at the way an aunt wobbled, or an uncle wore his sarong tied just under his chest, like a priest who had discarded his robes and returned to the life of a layman. Yes, life was going to change for the better again.

Next to her, Leela wiped her eyes again. Latha turned back to her box, opened it, and took out the gold paper. It slipped from her fingers and unraveled, so she had to roll it back up carefully. By the time she was done she had gold-tipped fingers. She held it out to Leela.

"You can keep this to remember me, Leelakka," she said. "If you start to worry about me, you can look at it and know that I'll be shining like that somewhere in the city."

Leela blew her nose into her hankie and then wiped her eyes with the edge of her dress. She took the gold paper and unrolled a corner of it. A little glitter came off on her fingers, and she rubbed them together. More tears started to roll down her face, but they were soundless and the sight of them finally made Latha feel that she, too, was about to lose something she would miss. She knelt by the bed and put her arms around Leela, pressing her face against her chest. Leela rocked her back and forth, murmuring words that she could not make out over her head.

And the sound of Leela's voice reminded her of something. It was the voice of her mother, stern with the effort of holding back some sorrow, soothing her, reassuring her, telling her that she should go, she should go and the Buddha, the Dhamma, the Sangha, they would bless her and keep her from harm. *Thunuruvange saranai mage Duwa, Budhu saranai mage Duwa.* Yes, those had been her words, but where had she uttered those heartfelt blessings? From what television show had they come to get tangled up with Latha's real memories from her life with the Vithanages?

She pulled away from Leela, hearing Sister Angela's voice outside. Leela reached out and traced the imprint of the cross she wore on a chain where it had pressed into Latha's face.

"You will be blessed," she said, "in the name of the Father, the Son, and the Holy Spirit, amen." She smiled.

The Triple Gem; The Holy Trinity; Mr. Vithanage, Mrs. Vithanage, and Thara. Between the designs of three sets of threesomes, she should be happier. She turned away from Leela and added the rosary to her box of treasures. Then, she unpinned the bright blue medal of the Virgin Mary from her blouse and put that in there too.

Biso

The girl has opened her suitcase. Inside, I see that her belongings have come undone. I am glad that our bag is made of hard nylon, that my children's possessions are pressed tight inside so there is no chance of anything unraveling; but I feel bad for her. Things would not slide around this much if she had more to pack in her bag. She rummages inside, and I try not to look.

She pulls out a dress and hands it to me. "Here," she says, "it will fit your little one."

I refuse, push it back, and she offers it to me again. We go through the ritual a few times before I smile and accept her gift with great gratitude. I unfold it and admire the white cotton fabric, the lace edging, the bow at the back. It looks like the kind of dress a mother would have asked a tailor to make for a daughter. I used to have dresses like that too, as a child. My mother used to walk along the railway tracks with me to reach Simeon Appu, the tailor who made all the clothes for our family. I remember it well, the walk, the weight of cloth in a brown paper bag, the frayed old *Butterick* pattern books, with drawings of English girls, arranged in a rack, and the smell of the tailor's shop, like machine oil and ironing. His hands, too, pinpricked and arthritic, yet oddly soothing as he measured me for this year's new dress. But all that ended when she died. My father didn't know much about little girls. After the nuns took over, it was school uniforms most of the day, and the nuns taught me how to make those myself. I never did like sewing, though—another reason for my husband's wrath. It made him furious that I would take our children to the tailor for their clothes, saving my patience only for darning or lengthening a hem. My mother's *Singer* sewing machine with its wooden wings served as an end table most of the year, and as a magical toy the children liked to open and shut, my son doing the difficult job of reaching into its cave to bring up the heavy, curved black inside, with all its bobbing and sliding moving parts. Now, with this dress in my hands, I am reminded of all that. I feel the soft cotton between my fingers.

"It's probably a little big for her still, but by next year it'll fit," the girl says. "That's the dress I wore when I left the convent. The madam told me it was a new dress they had made for me to wear when I accompanied them home, not like the ones I had. I wore it only for special occasions and only for that first year in Colombo, to temple, or when the madam and sir had family visiting. It's still like new." She touches it fondly.

"You should keep it, duwa, to remember. Or maybe for your new baby?" I rub her stomach with the edge of the dress, but she is quiet.

"They won't let me keep the baby, nendé," she says, after a while. "The convent is for the girls, not for their babies."

"What will they do with the baby?" I ask. I am shocked, and she sees it. I look down at her belly and then at the dress that I have rolled into a ball in my lap.

"No, it's okay, don't feel bad. They treat the babies well. They take them to the sister house down the hill so we don't have to hear our babies crying, and they look after them there until they are given away."

"How do you know all this?"

"Madam told me. She said that's what happened to the children of people like me who forget their place. I know she meant to be hurtful, but it made me happy to hear that there would be a place for my child."

"Don't you want to keep your baby and look after her yourself?"

"How do you know it's a girl?" she asks and smiles at me as

though this would be a good thing. How could she think that? A daughter growing up without a mother? What would happen to a girl like that?

"I'm just guessing by the way you look," I say. "It is how I looked when I had my daughters." And then I ask the question again, unable to imagine this life she seems to have chosen. "Don't you want to keep your baby?"

"What would I do with a child?" she asks, and I wish I hadn't brought up that possibility with her; something in her quiet voice blames me for asking her to think about an option she does not have, motherless as she is herself. What *would* she do with a child? I straighten the dress out and fold it carefully. I thank her again, then bend down and find space for it in one of the side pockets of our big bag. Yes, what would she do with a child? I say to myself, and yet I cannot reconcile myself to her attitude. It seems unnatural to be that resigned, even for someone who has no knowledge of the pain of labor and delivery or the mad love that is birthed along with a baby.

Once more I take her hand, this time in both of mine. "Maybe you could come with us," I say at last. What else is there to offer than a chance to keep what belongs to her? At least I could try; try to help.

"Where are you going?" she asks, and there is a small note of hope in her words.

"I'm taking my children to my aunt's house. She lives with her daughter and son-in-law and their children, and I'm sure she will be more than happy to make space for you." I say that, but the uncertainty in my own mind must have seeped through because she asks me the one thing I do not want to think about: do they know I am coming?

"No. I didn't have time to tell them."

I say these words even though I did have time. I could have sent them a telegram, done what is usual in such cases. I know that the cryptic, expensive words typed up with full stops, the carrier ringing his bicycle bell at some odd hour, would have told them that this was urgent, and they would have understood that they could not refuse me the shelter of their home no matter what. But I had chosen to trust that they were not that different from me, even if they were from the hill country. Surely they, too, believe that only pleasant visits for several days by older relatives, grandparents, or in-laws need to be announced. Surely they do as we do in the South, surprising people by showing up unannounced, the surprise itself the only way to erase any doubt that we are welcome, a trick we play with one another, constantly unsure of our own worth. Isn't that how they, too, deprive one another of the time that could be spent anticipating? Anticipation rewinds time and plays back the bad, the small slights, the little neglects that have turned into deeply buried hurts. No, I could not risk giving them that time, any time at all. Most of all, I could not risk them sending a return telegram, alerting my husband that I was leaving or, if I had left, where it was I was going. Better that he thinks me drowned, the children too. He can wait for the sea to bring us back, one by one.

"She is my mother's sister," I add. "She will help me."

The girl squeezes my hand, and I am ashamed of what I have kept from her, of my dismissal of her because of her youth. "I'm sure they will be happy to see you," she says, and this time it is she reflecting my doubts back to me, for I can hear it somewhere behind her calm voice.

Outside, the darkness has finally lost and daybreak reaches us through the trees. Everything is visible again. The mountains and plantations still dominating the landscape, but more than that, the smaller, more intimate details of life closer at hand; the rhythms of people who live with the roar of trains with which to mark time. It reminds me of the house I have left behind, these flyby pictures of women tending small fires, half-naked children brushing teeth and waving to metal cars with blurred faces. Spaces where men are entirely absent or are only now stumbling out of thatched homes, waking to a clear day in an already-swept dirt yard, the ekel marks still visible in the back-and-forth patterns women make each dawn, which are swept away by other feet before they have cooked breakfast, these mandalas that nobody notices unless they are created by monks in saffron robes. I feel free as I am carried away, and I want to call out to them to join me; as if this compartment, which now contains only me and my children, and a young mother to be, is traveling toward a true heaven. As if there is room there for all the others like us.

"You can come with us, duwa," I say again, turning to the girl, and this time I am certain of my offer.

"The nuns will be waiting for me at the station," she says. "What will they do if I am not there?"

"What can they do? They won't know where you went, and they probably won't care. Won't they be glad not to have to tend to yet another one like you?" I don't mean it unkindly; I say it to be practical, but it has upset her. Of course she feels special. She must want to believe that the nuns would miss her if she does not get off the train at her station. That, when her baby is born, she will be unlike any other child that ever graced the world.

"They will call madam and she will be angry," she says. "She could not have children, and she would not want me to keep a child who should have been hers."

I understand now. We are both quiet. The sun has risen higher, and the scenery outside has lost its magical quality. It is just an ordinary day, dry to the touch, and we are in a passenger train going only so far. Two more stations and we will be in Hatton, where she and I will part. I feel responsible for her, and sad. I want to give her something, my first friend in our new life, a friendship restricted to a single journey. I want to ensure that the gods will look favorably upon me, too, for my kindness toward this girl. But I have nothing to give her, not even food. I fiddle with the two bangles on my wrist, but they are gold and I have two daughters . . .

"The next station will be mine," she says, disturbing my thoughts. She is regretful.

"I will get down and hand you over to the nuns," I say, "and I will give you my aunt's address, so if you need to, you can come and find us."

"*Aney* nendé, you will be blessed. I was worried about getting down alone." How grateful she is for such a simple gesture. I feel tears in my eyes, and I distract myself with the task of easing myself out from under my sleeping children. I gesture wordlessly to the girl, and she opens the bag at my feet and takes out one of my saris. Chooti Duwa stirs in her sleep but does not wake up when I lift her slowly off my lap and slide the folded cloth under her head. I open my handbag and pull out a stray scrap of paper, some receipt for a once essential purchase, and write down my aunt's name and the road on which she lives. The girl takes it from me and looks at it.

"I can't read, nendé," she tells me, not ashamed, just stating the fact.

"That's okay. Keep it. If you need to find me, you can ask someone to write a letter for you."

I watch her fold the paper and tuck it into the top of her bra. The place where we put our most precious things: love notes and money and handkerchiefs for when we cry. It makes me smile. My legs are stiff from sitting, and I sway unsteadily on my feet when I stand up. The girl holds my shoulder to balance me. She seems happier now, forward looking. She has not lost hope in the bright light of the sun, when everything is only as it is. She is still traveling toward a sanctuary.

When the train stops, I step down first with her bag, then turn and help the girl. The conductor walks by us and takes a leather purse looped on a stiff handle from a man who must be an official though he doesn't look like one in his maroon cardigan and white wool cap pulled down close to his head. A couple, one child, and an old man appear before us, one behind the other, and just as quickly pass us by. They must have got down from other carriages. Nobody climbs in.

I must have expected the station to be special, somehow, for I feel worse now than I did when the train first came into the station, the announcement still ringing in the air. It is not that it is any more desolate than the other stations we have passed, and I can imagine this very platform bustling with the pilgrims who visit Sri Pāda when it is the season for such things. It is just that the black-and-white board, with "Hatton" written in three languages, seems to offer so little to a newcomer. "4143 feet above mean sea level," I read at the very bottom of the sign, also in all three languages. Then I notice a smaller sign pasted on the glass window of the ticket booth, which appears to be closed. The names of three schools, a hospital, and *The Convent of St. Bernardine*. That at least is hopeful.

"The convent is named for a saint," I say to her, then, "*Ay mé duwa?* What's the matter?"

"There's nobody here," she says, and now she is crying.

I look up and down the platform. She is right. We are the only two standing in the cold air; we and the train, which belches almost gently, wheezing as if it needs to catch its breath after the long climb. I remember an odd bit of information that the nuns had told me in grade school: Hatton is predominantly Tamil if one counts the plantations. I hear this fact again now, uttered in their cautionary voices. I don't want to leave this girl alone. The train toots and shudders, but halfheartedly.

A man comes out of the main building carrying a green flag and walks toward the edge of the platform. He is wearing an old black coat that is short at the sleeves, and white trousers. He must be the stationmaster. The girl begins to sob audibly. I turn away from her and grab his sleeve.

"Wait!" I say, to the man. "This child is waiting for the nuns from the convent, but I cannot leave her alone."

He glances at her disinterestedly. "The train has to go. You can stay with her and catch the next one tomorrow . . ."

"My other children are asleep inside this train! Please, sir, please, could you delay for a few minutes?" I bring my palms together. "The blessings of the Buddha upon you, sir!"

"For two minutes," he says and puts the flag behind his back. The train appears to rock back on its wheels, changing its mind. He takes out a cigarette and lights it with a match, then he waves the match in the air till the flame goes out and inserts it back into the same box.

I turn away from him. "Sit here, duwa," I say and lead the girl to a smooth wooden bench. I walk the length of the entire platform, searching for some sign of life beyond the station, but find nothing. There is only what is already there: the old, low white building, the platform that stops without notice at each end, the man, the girl, the train. I come back and sit next to her, and take her hand.

"If nobody is here by the time the train leaves, you come with me," I say. "We will know then that it is what the gods wish for you."

She nods and stares at her hands. When I look up, I see my Loku Putha and Loku Duwa standing at the top of the steps that we climbed down.

"Amma, what are you doing?" Loku Putha asks.

"Amma, who is that?" Loku Duwa asks.

"Go inside and wait with Chooti Nangi," I say to my daughter, then, knowing she will not listen to me, I turn toward my son and use his name so he understands that this is important to me, "Raji . . . Putha . . ."

"I'll go," he says, looking from the girl to me, and turns to his sister. "Come."

They disappear, and I can see them inside the train, a red shirt, then the pale yellow dress, moving past the empty seats, still staring at me through the windows.

The man looks at his watch and then at me. "I have to release the train," he says. "You have to decide what you want to do. The girl can stay with me. I will be here for another hour or so. Goods train is coming, that's why. I can make sure she gets to the convent." He raises his palm before I can ask him. "She's not the first, and won't be the last."

"Come," I say to the girl, standing up. I pick up her bag. We are about to get back into the train when she appears, a nun unlike the nuns I've known, who all dressed in white. This one wears gray and her head scarf is black, and though I want to believe otherwise, she looks harmless and even apologetic. Almost maternal.

"Mr. Coorey, I'm sorry I was late," she says to the man.

"She was about to get back in," he says to her, bowing slightly, showing her the kind of respect he hadn't found for me.

The girl turns from me, though I am still holding on to her bag.

"I'll take her bag," the nun says, and I give it to her.

The girl folds into my arms and sobs.

"There's no need for that," the nun says. "You will be happy here at the convent. We will look after you well. Come now, child, we have to go."

"Wait," I say. I take off my earrings, not caring that they are gold, or that they are the only things I now have from my mother. I press them into her palms. "Keep these."

I don't know how she finds grace, in her condition, but when she falls to her knees and worships me, it is as though she is lighter than the araliya that used to fall without a sound into my open bag when I picked flowers for the temple.

"The blessings of the Triple Gem upon you, duwa," I say, touching her head with my palms. "Do not be afraid."

· PART II ·

Latha

Latha had developed a new habit: touching her ears. Whenever she felt upset, whenever things did not pan out as she hoped they would, no matter how small the disappointment—a burnt mallung, a particularly gray afternoon, a severe reprimand for some task left undone—she fingered the earrings that Leela had given her just before she got into the Vithanages' car with its new driver, who, middle-aged and round, unlike the previous one, seemed incapable of swift or threatening movements.

"Latha Nangi! Wait a little!" Leela had yelled. It was the first time Latha had ever heard that voice raised beyond the murmur she used for communication with everybody other than God, to whom she spoke with a bowed head and no words.

"I am waiting," Latha said, but mostly to herself. She didn't feel like shouting just then, particularly after she heard the new driver sigh and turn the key in the ignition, the car sound dying and leaving a singular reprimand behind along with the silence. Clearly, there were ways to compensate for age and rotundity. She watched Leela come, shuffling a little to keep her rubber slippers on her feet as she ran, hugging her pale gray cardigan to herself, her arms crossed and gripping her elbows on either side, her hips swaying. Tendrils of hair came undone in the breeze as she made her way from the dark mahogany double doors of the convent, down the front steps to the car parked well outside the circular driveway. She looked youthful and pretty. Latha tilted her head to the side, taking it in, considering.

"Take these," Leela said, when she got to her, pressing a pair of earrings into her palm. They were grown-woman earrings, heavy, intricately designed in the shape of a flower unlike any that could grow on earth: smooth and round, and full of history as they rested in her open palm.

"But these are your earrings, Leelakka," she said, "and I already have some."

"You will need these now that you are going back. Something of your own, passed down so you won't forget your older sister."

Latha laughed. "We're not really sisters, you don't have to give me your jewelry, Leelakka. And I don't need earrings to remember you by, how can I ever forget you?"

"Keep them. When that mother on the train gave them to me, they made me feel cared for and bound to her, as though she were my own family. And now that you are going away without knowing what awaits you, you should have them. Please take them."

"I'm going back to Thara. I'll be all right," Latha said, and then, because Leela stood there without saying anything more, "All right, I'll exchange mine for yours." Latha removed the ruby earrings that had once belonged to Thara, twisting the stems out of their grooved clasps, and dropped them lightly into Leela's hand. "I don't need them anymore." She felt happy saying that; it was as though she were saying farewell to one chapter of her life and embracing a new one.

"They are like earrings for a small child," Leela said, curling her fingers so the earrings sank into the careful well of her palm, creased with fortune lines and heart lines and a line of fate that was entirely pointless in lives such as theirs.

But she had been right, Leela had. Her foreboding had been the accurate measure of what awaited Latha, whose own optimism had dropped from her shoulders like a sack of jewels turned to coal when she got to the Vithanages' house.

Of course she should have known that Ajith's family would never consent to a marriage between their precious son and the daughter of a family where the *servant girl had to be sent away*. How could she ever have imagined otherwise? The Vithanages had refused to listen to the truth, or haul the real culprit out of hiding. They had thought that all the usual adjustments, the usual smoke and mirrors, sending her, Latha, away, dismissing the driver, would work. They had trusted in the invulnerability of their social status over engaging in a battle with another family of their means. In fact, they had probably thought they were protecting not simply their daughter but also that other family's son. They had been wrong. They had lost. And why should she be surprised? Hadn't she seen and heard the false narrative that was spun around her pregnancy with her own ears? First before she left the Vithanages and then at the convent? That somehow all of it would come to lay at Mr. Vithanage's blameless feet, and that in their circles that was the ultimate downfall, the one scandal that would cling to them and to their daughter like hot tar the rest of their lives?

How could she have pictured only feisty Thara and her childhood love ascending the jasmine-drenched poruwa from opposite sides, decked with smiles, all the colorful manipuri saris and smooth suits watching? She had seen all of that, all the little details, all the lies uttered by the priests about virginity and chastity and unblemished children nurtured by unsullied parents, all the drums and the decorations and the tables upon tables of luxuries seen only on such occasions, and the great rooster-topped brass oil lamps that would stay lit long after the couple had left. She had even pictured the walk up the Colombo 7 block to Ajith's house seven days later, the white cloths on the ground beneath Thara's jeweled feet, even a temple elephant dressed in bright satin in front, the fanfare that announced to anybody who cared that Thara had been proven to be above reproach thanks to a red stain on a piece of white cloth taken from their nuptial bed the morning after the first night of their honeymoon. She had annoyed the driver all the way to Colombo with her inwardly focused smiles, picturing herself in some carefully chosen hand-me-down from Thara that would allow her to look just a little better off than all the attendants who would surely come to tend to other people's children during these celebrations. She had seen herself standing just outside the gate, watching Thara arrive in her glory to step into the house from which she had stolen those first flowers, and Ajith with them. She had planned to wave at Thara, for surely Thara would catch her eye as she passed, uniting them for a moment in that shared past.

But Thara was not going to marry Ajith. She was going to marry Gehan. *Latha's* Gehan. Gehan who had once been hers but was no longer and would never be hers. Ever again. That's when the jewels turned to coal. That's when she knew that somewhere at the back of her mind her imaginings of Thara and Ajith on their wedding day had hidden her longing for a day that would belong to her and Gehan.

It was too late now to have regrets, to reconsider the magnitude of what she'd brought to pass, to hope that the gods would not have noticed or that, if they had, they would forgive her, for having been no more than a child with a child's quickness of temper, a child's inability to hide the desire for self-respect, a child's need to fight back somehow, anyhow, a child's comprehension of retribution. Too late now for her to remember that, no matter her motives, whatever cruelty had been done, some countervailing cruelty would come to attend her too. Wasn't that what she had spent so many days meditating upon, all those years ago with Thara beside her, flowers in their open palms, the scent of incense and the smell of a burning wick above their heads, the serene face of the Buddha looking down at their upturned faces?

"Amma says I'm lucky to make a match with someone like him," Thara confided to her the very night she got back there. Latha was lying on the new mat that Mrs. Vithanage had bought for her and that she had flung on the floor of the storeroom; apparently, Soma told her, her old one had been burned after she left. She had been told to sleep there, in the storeroom, but Thara had insisted that she sleep on the floor of her bedroom, and nobody argued with Thara now that she had finally stopped throwing tantrums and agreed to this latest marriage proposal.

Latha was shocked by how Thara had changed. She looked the same as she always had, the same height, the same wide-set almond eyes beneath the eyebrows that shaped upward like wings, the same curves and graces. But Thara's precociousness had turned into something harder, something that sharpened her tongue, her words falling like tiny wounds, the kind whose pain was out of proportion to their size. She had learned how to embarrass her parents, saying things that were not meant to be uttered in public; she had worn them down with her ridicule and her slights, taunting them for how they looked, for their concern, for their fallen fortunes, for their inability to change the way things had turned out. She had learned how to hide her life's disappointment: that Ajith had not chosen to rescue her from her plight, not looked for her and fought for her and turned on his parents the way she had turned on her own, if that was what it would have taken, not even when she had gone to his house herself to beg. Their servant woman had come to the door to tell her he was not home. She had learned how to hide that pain with unpredictable invective that she hurled at Mr. and Mrs. Vithanage.

That story, too, was told to Latha as she lay on the floor, culminating with Thara's revelation about her future groom. All these tales, everything that had happened to Thara during those last years, had been related, one after the other, without pause, as though this alone, to be told these stories, was the sole purpose for Latha's return.

"Do you want to marry him?" Latha asked. "He used to . . ." She paused, struggling to find the words to describe her relationship with Gehan, which had been almost more of an understanding, an expectation of each other than a relationship. Thara interrupted impatiently.

"Yes, I *know* he used to be Ajith's friend, but they are not friends anymore. Besides," she added bitterly, "who cares about what Ajith thinks? Why should it matter to him whom I marry?" And Latha knew with a jolt of shock that all the time she had lived as though they were two girls in love with two boys, she had been invisible to Thara. An add-on meant only to further her affair with Ajith, not to have one of her own with Gehan. No wonder Gehan had hidden their relationship from Thara. No wonder nobody had suspected anything when he agreed to marry her in the end. Whose idea . . . ?

"It was Gehan's idea that we get you back to come with us to the new house when we move. I told him about you, stuck in that convent after the fuss with the driver and all and how I wished you were back. So he told me to ask Amma to get you back to work in our house. He felt bad for me, that's what he said. He said that if it would make me happier, then I should just ask you to come back, he didn't mind."

"Hmmm," Latha said, feigning a yawn, sadness finally pinning her to the floor.

She wanted to examine this information privately, that his concern had been for Thara, not for her in her exile, and the fact that he had thought she would find it more pleasing to work as his servant than to stay away.

A few days later, when Gehan visited in the afternoon to go over some detail about the wedding, she experienced for the first time what would become her habit: feeling sympathy for Thara in one moment, Gehan the next. That day, she felt sorry for Thara and for Gehan, who sat next to her in his creased, dark blue trousers and white, short-sleeved shirt, looking so ordinary. For a few moments, as she brought him tea and served it, she forgot how precious that very quality had once been to her and still was, but saw instead how different he was from Ajith. She had never been fond of Ajith, but there was no disputing the fact that he was a splendid-looking man, someone beside whom a mother would walk straighter, someone women rested their eyes on when he was in their midst. She remembered how right they had looked together, Thara and Ajith, how, when they walked beside each other, their heads held high, laughing and talking, it had seemed that there was order in the world. And now here Thara sat with Gehan. And, next to Thara, with her new pouts and annoyed sighs, her hair flung first to one side of her head, then the other, he seemed completely out of his depth.

But then, later, when Latha saw him sit at the table and wait to be served and look at her only once and even then with businesslike approval, she knew that it did not matter that he had not learned to live like Thara had, in such a home, and had once scorned families like hers; he would be as Mrs. Vithanage had been, letting her wander through his house doing the work of a housekeeper, a cook, a cleaner, a laundress even, but with no concern for her welfare beyond that, or none that he would ever reveal. That's when her right hand first flew up to her ear. She moved the tips of her index and middle fingers over the earring, its carvings smooth under her touch, its solid presence a reminder of Leela. She felt Leela's own immutable strength flow out of the gold and in through her fingers and up along her arms, straightening her shoulders, emboldening her heart, and centering her body over her stubborn feet. She felt dignified.

So she cleared the plates away with an air of indifference that irked the people sitting around the table. She could feel that too. They were silent because she was neither them nor not them, and resentful because they wished she were absent but they needed her presence. Every single one of them, even Mrs. Vithanage, who scorned her, and Soma, who had welcomed her with a sort of embrace in the form of an up-down nod and a *"Have you been well?"* needed her there. That made her feel better.

Although Latha had never been to a wedding, and everything she assumed stemmed from hearsay or teledramas, in the end even she knew that Thara's wedding was grand but lacked flourish. It was an at-home wedding like the old families liked, but it was muted, like the pale blush saris of the bridesmaids. Thara had three of those: a distant second cousin of hers, Gehan's cousin, and a friend from school whom Latha couldn't remember ever having seen at the Vithanages' before. She supposed that when the mighty fell, they didn't just fall, they had to begin from scratch, and that included bridesmaids. It was clearly a silver lining to be in her predicament, with an old servant like Soma, who could forgive her, and a Leela, who loved her no matter what, and even a family like the Vithanages, who couldn't do without her.

Poor Thara, who smiled but couldn't be radiant the way brides are supposed to be. Who cried so much when she worshiped her parents that everybody could tell it had nothing to do with the bittersweet farewell, with growing up, or with trepidation about her first night with a husband but was about something else altogether. And whose groom was obviously subpar, with not even good looks to make up for his job as an advertising executive of some sort at a company so insignificant he had to describe it not by its name but with the preamble "a place called." Poor Gehan, too, whose education and professional accomplishments, his steady character, his income, could have shone so much more brightly in another, lesser family, but who was joining one in which he would never be good enough no matter what he did.

Latha overheard all the bitter remarks about Gehan as she went about her work, fetching this and carrying that for Mrs. Vithanage, her last duties in the house before she could leave with Thara for the new home. The only respite she had that day was when Gehan and Thara climbed the poruwa together and everybody grew silent and watched and nobody needed anything from her. Then Latha felt dizzy with all the mixed-up emotions that came over her. Tenderness, at the sight of her friend, who looked too young to be getting married, to be dressed up like that, with all those heavy jewels and her hair pulled back and too many sheaves of betel to be passed around, and not her, Latha, but only girls who barely knew her beside Thara to hold her bouquet and hand her a wedding ring to slip on a man's hand, the hand of a man she did not love. Tenderness, at the sight of Gehan, who had not worn the grand costume she had imagined him in once long ago but rather wore the official national dress, a simple white kurta and sarong, and so managed to look even less deserving than ever of his future wife. She stood as long as she could, the *magul bera* and flutes filling her ears, but when it came time for the tying of their little fingers, she left her post by the door and went to the old storeroom, where she sat, pretending that the sadness she felt was something outside her body, like the sack of rice in the corner, or her rolled-up mat, something that she could look at and even touch but that she could, she would, leave behind when she had to go back outside and tend to Thara.

"I hope they taught you how to cook at that convent," Mrs. Vithanage said as Latha passed by with a fresh glass of lime juice for Thara, who was being dressed in her going-away sari.

"No, madam, they didn't teach me anything," Latha said, her mouth adding the insult "They wanted me to rest." And she kept on going, knowing that today was one day she could get away without an earful, with all those people in attendance. "They said I had been through enough," she tossed over her shoulder before she nipped into the room where Thara was.

Inside the room there was dizzying color and movement. The bridesmaids were arrayed at the edge of Thara's double bed, still covered with the familiar pink and white bedding, chatting, while a collection of aunts and older relatives came and went, checking their reflections in the mirrors set up to lean along one wall. The mirrors had been ordered by Mrs. Vithanage, her kindness to all of the women who had attended weddings with her in the past and who, banished from the bedroom or hotel room of the bride, had been forced, like her, to primp themselves in front of TVs and tinted car windows. Thara sat quietly at the center of everything, resplendent in turquoise blue and gold, in front of her kidney-shaped dressing table, with its sets of curved drawers on either side and the three mirrors that could be moved to show her upper body from all directions. Three Tharas.

"Thara Baba, here's your juice," Latha said, holding out the damp glass on a small silver tray.

The real Thara glanced sideways at her from kohl-rimmed eyes without moving her head. "Where's the straw?" she asked.

"Straw?" Latha repeated, so taken aback by Thara's voice that she pronounced it *is-strow,* like the girls who didn't know how to speak their English words properly. She corrected herself. "Straw?"

"All my lipstick will come off if I drink this from the glass, you goat. Go and get a straw for me." She returned her gaze to the mirror, and the three Tharas glared at the three Lathas reflected behind her. Latha glared back. Her lipstick was all wrong. Orange was not the color for Thara to wear, particularly with that blue. She should be wearing red. Latha's eyes softened, and she was about to reach for the red tube that sat on the dressing table when someone spoke up.

"My god, you will have your hands full trying to train this one to be a proper housekeeper." It was Mr. Vithanage's sister, speaking through a mouthful of hairpins, with which she was attempting to keep Thara's floral headpiece of baby's breath and red rosebuds in place.

"Is she the one you'll be taking with you to the new house?" That was the bridesmaid who was a friend, and who sat like a pudding on the edge of the bed, her waist spilling in all directions between the embroidered bottom edge of her sari blouse and the top of her waistband. She reminded Latha of the old driver. Latha expected her to suck her back teeth. She sucked her back teeth. So disgusting.

"Yes, Latha will be coming with me to the new place."

"You are lucky to be going to a new house with madam," the aunt said, taking the last of the pins out of her vermilion mouth and speaking loudly. They always spoke loudly when they addressed servants directly; that's what Latha had learned at this wedding. As if the rest of the time the servants had been deaf to their conversations.

"You'll have to get used to calling me madam, Latha," Thara said, standing up and giggling, nervous and haughty at the same time. She turned around to face her.

Madam? Latha looked straight at her friend. Was she really going to be madam? Thara? Who could do so little without her help? She stared at Thara, seeing Gehan instead, hearing his words so long ago, telling her how people like Thara thought themselves better than people like them only because they had the power to order them about. How they could not survive without their retinue of doers. Thara's own eyes narrowed in the silent room, the other women watching this battle of wills.

"Go and get me a straw," she said, *"palayang."* The other conjugation. The one used for common servants and strays. The first time she had ever spoken to Latha with such anger, such condescension.

Latha wondered if this was how Mrs. Vithanage, too, had become the kind of woman she was. Perhaps long ago, the same kind of disappointment, a wrong turn, the wrong husband, had whittled her high spirits into derision. Thara had certainly found a way to get her through this evening. Well, Latha would too.

She dropped her eyes, then raised them again to Thara. "I'm going," she said. Then, *"Gehan* sir is waiting for you. He said to hurry up." She felt vindicated when Thara's face flushed, when the corner of her mouth dipped down, discernible only to Latha from where she stood.

And then, just as swiftly, because Thara suddenly looked like the girl who had asked Latha to help her when Mrs. Vithanage gave their flower-picking task over to the gardener, she felt bad for Thara. She felt bad for reminding her of whom she was not marrying, having spent so much time that day herself trying to overcome the same disappointment in her own heart. And so, when she returned with a straw, also on a silver tray, and found everybody fussing over their own hair and makeup while Thara sat quietly in a corner with a fan on low aimed at her midriff, which was where her perspiration always gathered, Latha swiped the correct lipstick off the counter and gave it to her friend.

"You look beautiful, Thara Baba," she said, "but this lipstick would be much better with that sari." She reached underneath her own sari pota and pulled a handkerchief out of the top of her bra. "Here, take this and wipe that other color off."

Thara gifted her with a genuine smile, the warmth spreading from her lips to her eyes, which filled up with tears.

"Everything will be all right," Latha whispered so that the others could not hear.

Thara dabbed at her mouth and then at the corners of her eyes with the handkerchief. "Do you think so?" she asked, her voice trembling.

"Yes, I am sure of it." Latha applied the new lipstick on her. "I'll be there, Thara Baba," she said, recalling Thara to the present moment. "Don't worry. What can go wrong? Think about all that happened to me, and yet here I am. I'm back and I'm fine. We'll be together, that's what matters. I will help you to cope with whatever comes our way."

Outside, the conch shell was blown, and Mrs. Vithanage came into the room as if propelled by its sound. Thara gripped Latha's wrist, her voice full of panic. "Promise me that you won't run away again, Latha; everything fell apart when you left here. If you had stayed, maybe you could have got Ajith to come back to me. If you had stayed, I would not be marrying . . . marrying . . . him. Promise me."

"I promise," Latha said, but she could not meet Thara's eyes.

Everything had fallen apart long before then, and she could not guarantee that it would not again. She was too grown-up to be sure of things. More grown-up even than she had been the morning she left Leela, new earrings in her ears.

Thara was bustled out of the room, and she went, looking back more than once, seeking reassurances from the only person in the room who could give her any, but all Latha could do was wave. Alone in the room full of nauseating fragrances, the sound of the happy commotion outside as everybody jostled for the confetti she had helped to make, cutting up shiny bits of paper night after night and bagging them into mesh cloth, tying them with ribbons, Latha reached up, this time with both hands. She walked over to the mirrors and stared at herself. She was grown up, but who was she? She turned to the first mirror: a mother with no daughter? The second mirror: a daughter with no mother? The last: a woman with no man?

"Latha Nangi," she whispered, her eyes shut. "I am Latha Nangi, and I have an older sister. My older sister gave me these earrings." Then she stepped out.

She could see the couple where they stood. Gehan's eyes washed over the room and held hers, briefly, before he lowered them and dropped to his knees, along with Thara, in respect to Mr. and Mrs. Vithanage, to touch their feet, to worship them, and to receive their blessings.

Biso

Why did you give her your earrings?" my son asks, as soon as I get back in. Even the little one is up, and they are all sticking their heads out of the window, waving to the girl and the nun on the platform the way children do. I join them, and I watch the two figures go from intimate clarity to representations to insignificance on a fading landscape as the train carries us forward and away. I do not wave.

"Why, Amma?" Loku Duwa repeats her brother's question. Chooti Duwa touches my ears with her still-a-baby-soft fingers. They feel tender and ticklish and warm from her long sleep.

"Because she needed them," I say, stroking her hair but looking at Loku Duwa.

"Why did she need them? Is she poor?" Chooti Duwa asks me.

"No, she is not poor. People do not need earrings because they are poor," I say. What I cannot say is this: a young woman needs earrings to show that she is proud to be a woman and that she has a family. Earrings are not decorations. They are a statement of legitimacy, of dignity, of self-worth. Ask any woman, and she would tell you that she would pawn everything she has before she gave up her earrings. Even her wedding band. For what is a wedding band worth except to say that a man coveted your children and wanted to claim them for his own? A wedding band can come from any man, just like children. Earrings, a real pair of earrings, come only with love. And that girl needs someone to love her, some way to feel worthy and dignified where she is going. She needs them more than I do.

"Amma, your face looks odd without earrings," Loku Duwa says. "I don't like that you don't have earrings."

"I'll borrow some when we get to my aunt's house," I tell her, my voice soothing.

"Earrings aren't important," my son says. He has always resented these female conversations that exclude him.

"Aiyya, you're just jealous because you can't wear any," Loku Duwa says and ducks her brother's palm.

"Men can wear earrings," Chooti Duwa says. "I saw men with earrings on the beach."

"Those are bad men," he says, "or they are not real men."

I still the fear in my heart. I hope that my son has never been near those men who used to come grazing for little boys like him, their skin shining pink beneath the oils they rubbed on one another lying almost naked outside our hotels. I remember how they talked to other little boys, coaxing them with round, colored sweets or chocolate in long cylinders and pyramid-shaped tubes; how well they knew the way our children craved those foreign tastes. I used to shoo those children away, pretending I was doing those men and women a favor, keeping the children from bothering them. I would have said something to them if I could, but I never wanted to get in the way of white people, who always seemed to have too much of everything, even of the good things in our own country, our best fruits and fish, our hotels, our power, doing things we wouldn't dream of doing, disregarding our customs and laws.

My son sees me watching him, and he comes over to me and grins. "Don't be troubled, Amma," he says. "I never went near those men. I got money from picking up the tennis balls and handing out towels at the *Blue Lotus Hotel*. Only those two things, you can believe me."

I believe him. What else is there to do? I am glad that we are far away, so far in the hills that no salt water can get near us with its deadly currents, tempting my children with its froth and shells, luring them into evil. I shepherd them back to our seats, but we are still in motion when we enter the longest tunnel we will go through in our journey, a full third of a mile long. All my children grab my body, pressing close to me, screaming with fake terror. I listen to the echoes of other children's voices from compartments to either side of ours. These shrieks that I have heard each time we pass through a tunnel lift my spirits. They are the sounds of childhood and innocence. When we are out of the tunnel and my children let go of me, I feel unmoored.

In our booth, the children entertain themselves by building bridges with their legs for a while, then fight over the window seats. In the end, the girls get them. Their brother makes a chair for himself with his legs, bending the left and balancing on the ankle with the shin of his right. It's uncomfortable, and I watch him switch from side to side and finally give up and persuade his baby sister to let him hold her on his lap. She pouts until he tickles her belly with his free hand and makes her wriggle and laugh. What bliss, that sound of laughter, the absence of fear.

I hear my youth in their voices, see it in their quick smiles, their delight in this new journey. I imagine that my parents must have watched me, too, that way. I had been a girl whose yearnings had been the measure of their days. On Poya, I had stood in front of our lit lamps, causelessly devout. On holidays, they had taken me to the fairs and other entertainments that came through our town and bought me thick, sweet drinks in small, ice-cold bottles from the Muslim shops, which had refrigerators. When I came home at the end of each term with a report card full of the evidence of my scholarship, it had been to the fragrance of sweet, sticky black kalu dodol studded with cashews.

I shrug. Such bliss is not meant to last. In my husband's house, my children were my real gifts: the older ones had turned fear over and over in my stomach until it molted into rage, and perhaps it was that rage, that sudden fearlessness in me, that had caught Siri's eye and brought me my youngest, the second daughter, who finally gave wings to my feet. Wings. Or rails. I am grateful for this chance, for the future, for the train that is carrying us there, its carriages full of strangers, kind to one another, kinder than anyone had been to me in my husband's village. I am grateful for its spaces, which fill up and release people, empty of fear.

There are few stations left now: seven before ours, eight after. I feel at peace in this train, in this empty car, this booth, my children all accounted for, safe, even the girl, safe with the nun. I don't want to get off. I want to keep going to Badulla. But then what? I don't know anybody in Badulla. I think about my aunt, her family, what they looked like when I last saw them, all those years ago. I picture her the same, but aged. I try to imagine what her grandchildren might look like now, but I cannot. I have received only an occasional letter, and never any photographs, which, even if they had been taken at a studio during a wedding, are too rare and too precious to send to anybody else. Only the two oldest were born when I visited as a newlywed, still enamored with my role as a grown woman and wife, and they were just four and one.

The last I had heard of them was a year ago, when another cousin passed through our village, stopping at the house, unannounced, and staying the night to drink with my husband, who was interested only in that sort of company. Before he left the next morning, he had said that they were doing well, my cousin and her children. He said that she had a job at a place called the *Farr Inn,* where she works at a desk. Her husband was still employed by the government, as a ranger in the park, he had said. Anyway, I hope they have turned out like my cousin, their mother, and not their father, who was dull and sullen. Perhaps it is the fate of women in my family to marry such men. Perhaps it is also our fate to leave them. I hope that she has not left hers, though, for where would I go then?

I am still drifting about in these scenarios, following one possibility, reversing and going down a different path, when we reach Thalawakele. The station is 4000 feet above sea level, and there is a cheerful signpost announcing the location of the *St. Claire Waterfall* and a bungalow named *St. Andrew's.* There's a photograph of it, and it looks beautiful, with terraced gardens and lavish flowers. In the picture there's a train winding its way far below, and I wonder if it is this same train we are riding on. I poke my head out and look up, but all I see is the station and the shrubbery to my left, and nothing but tea sloping away to my right. Dotted here and there down the tea-covered hillsides I can see the colorful saris of the tea pluckers, their cane baskets strapped onto their backs, their fingers flying over the bushes, somehow managing to find, at that speed, the tender, light green leaves. They look like birds to me, those women. Bright birds doing honest and useful work. I watch the tea pluckers for a long time, fascinated by their diligence and concentration. They do not seem to mind the sun, or perhaps they have no freedom to consider the inconveniences that people with time on their hands, like us, trapped inside trains, do.

The stationmaster announces that the train will be delayed for a short while until the tracks are cleared. There has been a demonstration, he says, by the plantation workers. It is clearly over now; the tea pluckers are back at work and there is nobody on the platform but two lonely policemen, who do not look agitated. I am glad that nothing disturbs them. Policemen are bad enough without them having any reason to be suspicious or feel more powerful than they already do, particularly with regard to those like us.

To pass the time, I call to my children and try to direct their attention outside. "See those tea pluckers? Without them we wouldn't be able to drink any tea anywhere in the country," I tell them.

"But this tea is green colored. This cannot be that tea. That tea is black," my Loku Duwa says.

"That's because it is dried, duwa. But when it is first plucked, it is green, like these bushes."

They talk about tea for a little while, and then my little one wants to climb out and pick tea. I tell them they can. Loku Putha jumps out first, takes his little sister in his arms, carries her across the other set of tracks, and wades into the row of bushes closest to the station. They snatch a few leaves each and come running back as though the train is about to leave. I laugh, sharing their excitement at this unexpected foray and their delight in holding real tea leaves in their palms. They taste the leaves and wrinkle their faces. I beckon to them to climb back aboard, for though they are safe there, and in no danger of being left behind, I am uneasy with the thought of them being separated from me even by that improbable possibility.

When I pull my head back in, there's a man in our car. He is sitting across the aisle from me. He looks like a government agent, formal but unimposing, straight-bodied as his job demands, but with the heavy head of someone employed at an unending task. His hair is parted carefully on the side. He must be in his thirties, perhaps only a year or two older than I am. He glances at my children and smiles at me. It is such a genuine smile that I have to return it. The train begins to move again, gathering speed. It is empty enough now for the children to sit in one booth and me to sit in the one across from them; it is as though they are traveling alone, unattended, and I am traveling with the pleasant newcomer.

"Good thing it is not raining. The train ride is not comfortable with the windows shut," he says.

"Yes, I can imagine it must not be," I say.

"Are you going home after the Poya holiday?" he asks.

The children turn around at the sound of our conversation. They all stare at him, then look over at me, waiting for my story.

"We are visiting my aunt. In Ohiya."

He nods to himself. He is from Colombo, he tells me, and stares out the window as he says that, as if he regrets the fact. Perhaps he wishes he lived out here. I feel sorry for him. He looks like the sort of man who, though competent and good, will never be happy.

"Look, Amma!" my little one says, tugging at my sleeve and pointing out her window on the opposite side, sheer amazement in her voice.

"Isn't it beautiful," I say, gazing at the white streams of water falling over the side of the green mountain, its source a mystery. "Now that is a waterfall," I add. "Remember how we talked about waterfalls when we were still in Colombo?"

"That is *St. Claire's*," says the man from behind us, and this time the children smile politely and listen as they take in the spectacle. "That waterfall is about two hundred and sixty-five feet high and is the widest waterfall in the whole country." He leans forward and describes it to us. "That is Maha Ella," he says, pointing alternately to the large and small sections of the falls. "It has three cascades. The little one is Kuda Ella. They both flow down to the Kotmale area. I have heard that the government wants to build two reservoirs there, but I hope they don't. It would ruin the beauty of these waterfalls, wouldn't it, children?"

"Yes," Loku Putha says slowly, sounding concerned, "that would be bad."

"Do you know what a reservoir is?" he asks my son. "It's a lake to collect all the water, with a dam to keep it in."

"Where would the water come from? For the lake?" Chooti Duwa asks.

"That's it. The water for the Upper Kotmale dam would come from the same river that feeds these falls, and then we wouldn't have a beautiful waterfall, would we?"

He sounds like a schoolteacher; perhaps that is why he is ill at ease, perhaps he has failed to realize some youthful dream of living in cold places, educating small children, listening to their questions, watching them change.

We gaze at the scene from our various perches. I half-listen as he continues to talk to my children, my eyes on the waterfall. It is pretty and unthreatening. The waters seem happy to be going where they are going, not like the ocean beside which I have spent my adult life, restless waters that always seemed to be flung or returning for something lost. The times when the ocean was still I had sensed as rest, a brief truce while they conspired among unseen islands and reef. I never felt safe by the sea; I am glad to be done with it.

I return to my seat and look up and out of the window again. We have passed the falls and now it is simply more of the green hills. The children go on talking about the waterfall, about what it might feel like to have the water fall upon their heads, whether it is deep at the bottom, whether the earth could crack open if the water grew strong enough, and what would happen then to the people standing below.

I sit and listen, made slightly anxious by their conjectures and how quickly they swerve from beauty to practicality to disaster and back again. "My children have never seen a waterfall," I say to the man, explaining, excusing their fertile imaginations, their comfort with the prospect of doom.

He nods and smiles. "All children are like that, isn't that so?" He sits there for a while, the smile still on his face, and then he speaks again. "Where is your village?" he asks.

I keep my silence for a long moment. Where *is* my village? Where do I live? I live on this train. I used to live in one place and I will live in another but now I live in this perfect place between the past and the future, the known and the unknown, the bad and the good.

"Are you from these parts?" he asks, prompting me to look up. There's a quality to his voice that expects truth and offers kindness in return.

"No," I say at last. "We are from the South. I was raised in Hambantota, but I lived as a wife in Matara. My father was a farmer and toddy tapper, and my mother helped him with our land; my husband was a fisherman."

He nods. "Beyond the Benthara," he says, smiling, acknowledging my pure Southern credentials.

I want him to think well of me. Of me being more than a woman caught between my father and my husband, between the distilling of alcohol and the killing of fish. "I was convent educated," I tell him. "The nuns took care of my education after my mother passed away. She was of a higher caste, from a good up-country family."

He tilts his head to one side and looks at me, but he doesn't ask for further clarification. When we stop at Great Western, he asks for permission to buy my children wrapped sweets from the lone vendor on the platform, and, as the train moves on from there, he asks me if I have family up-country.

"Yes," I tell him in response. "My mother's sister lives there."

"Then you must be going for a visit?"

"No, I'm hoping to stay there with my aunt and my cousin's family. Maybe get some work."

"What about the children's father? Is he still in Matara?"

"No," I say, and glance over at the children. They are occupied by their own conversations and do not pay heed. I say the words, my voice low and intimate: "My husband passed away."

"That is unfortunate. I am sorry to hear that. Was he ill?"

I tell him part of my story, changing what needs to be changed. When I speak of my husband, it is Siri's name I mention. I describe

Siri as he was, with all his hopes, the way he was going to be something other than a fisherman someday, the way he argued and fought with his father to stay earthbound, resisting the sea every chance he could get. I tell him about how Siri worked to organize that long-lost political campaign, about all that I had come to hear about the government, about the working classes and the strength and power we had, even small people like us, how those conversations lit something inside me. And because I have to explain this journey, the loss of Siri, I tell him something more he can believe: I say that Siri disappeared along with some university students who were his friends. He murmurs when I say that, names that year of destruction, and I nod, though Siri was already dead when the government came after his friends. I tell the man these details softly, sitting across from him on his side of the train, my head in my palm, my elbow on the window. And he sits across from me in a mirror image, and listens.

Does he believe me? I cannot tell from the expression on his face. Maybe he imagines that I am making up this history, which I have, and yet have not. Siri was the husband of my heart, and what other kind is worth mentioning to strangers?

"Your relatives must be expecting you, then?" he asks.

"No, there was no time to tell them." I repeat that untruth again, though I hadn't told them because I had wanted to feel possibility, had been scared. "They won't turn me away," I say. "They are family, after all."

"Sometimes family does not step forward the way they should," he says, as if he has learned of betrayal firsthand and more than once.

"I am not worried about that. They will help me. I don't expect to live with them forever, just for a little while, until I get the children into school and find some work."

"There isn't much work up here," he says. "But, if you find yourself unable to get anything else at the factories, you may be able to get a job at one of the bungalows."

"Doing what?" I ask, curious and interested in any information he can give me. I am determined to be self-sufficient, to look after my children on my own.

"As a domestic servant," he says. I lower my eyes and look at my hands.

He must feel ashamed for suggesting it, or be embarrassed by the look on my face, for he pulls out a piece of paper from his pocket and writes down his name and phone number in Colombo. His next words come quickly, as if he does not want to give me time to reflect on what he has just suggested. "If nothing works out, give me a call at this telephone number and perhaps I can find something better for you in Colombo, maybe working at one of the big fabric shops or at *The Joseph Fraser, The Lady Ridgeway* . . . or one of the other hospitals. I have friends there who would be willing to help out, especially an intelligent mother like you with some convent background and a pleasant manner." He smiles as he says these things, broader and broader, piling on the possibilities as though that would erase the insult.

"My children are all bright. They will do well in school. My son, he talks of becoming a lawyer. And my older girl, she says she'll study medicine and look after me. We'll be all right. They have been brought up well, like my mother raised me, not like the common people."

"I can see that," he says, his face genuinely apologetic. "You must forgive me. I was simply trying . . . It is only because I know these parts . . . Just keep the number for an emergency."

I gaze at the writing on the paper. I should be grateful for his offer, but the idea of doing anything in Colombo seems offensive. Even the word sounds all out of balance, unlike the names of the towns we have been passing and the ones yet to come, or even Hambantota and Matara. Colombo is like someone hacking out phlegm and throwing it on the pavement to lie shining in the sun till it is fried. Still, what is there to do but incline my head a little in gratitude and fold the piece of paper and place it with great reverence in the center compartment of my purse like it means something to me? He bought my children sweets. He listened to my story. Surely I owe him this bit of grace.

"Whom are you visiting?" I ask after I have gone through those motions, changing the subject to spare him from his embarrassment.

"I am going to see a friend in Pattipola. Usually, I would have driven, but I wanted to get off the road for a change, and be by myself. I was in another compartment up front, but there was some trouble there, somebody was drunk and threw up, so I moved."

We both grow quiet as the train draws into the station at Nanu Oya and then moves on. Not far from there I see the peak of Sri Pāda come into view once more, reminding me of our temple, of the pilgrimages that people make toward the divine. I imagine the slow trail of devotées climbing up to the mountain to gaze at the footprint of the Buddha. I have never had the good fortune to make that climb, though it would not have been difficult to get to Ratnapura, our city of precious gems, from the South and climb from there. I have only heard of the mystery of this journey, the coolness of the stream, which exists as though only for the relief of the pilgrims, halfway to the summit, the way the sun pierces the eastern horizon at the same moment that the sacred mountain casts its conical shadow for the fortunate few to see on the western side.

"It is said that when the sun comes up over Sri Pāda, it offers its *irasevaya* in worship to the mountain," the man says, observing my intent contemplation of the view.

"I have never been able to go," I say, "but someday I wish to take some kapuru and add it to the lamp that burns on the top of that mountain. I would like to do that in memory of my parents, and of my husband too."

"It will bring you great merit," he tells me. "I would like to do the same one day."

"Do you have children, sir?" I ask. I do not know why I added that *mahaththaya* to my words; it slipped out of my lips as though he might deserve the title.

"Yes," he says, twisting his wedding ring with the thumb of his left hand. He is married and has a daughter. He looks over at my children and points to my youngest. "About that one's age."

"She will be five, my baby; she is four now. She is what I pictured when they told me I was pregnant, so I named her for that." I think about that for a moment, remembering her arrival, how dear she seemed without the father who created her and without a father to claim her. My girl, my princess.

"One day she will grow up," he says, "just like my daughter."

"And she will still be my girl."

"Yes, you are right. They will still be our little girls." His voice is sad. It worries me a little, because he looks over at her when he says that, as if he can see her future and it is not as I have imagined it to be. So I think of the other girl, that older-daughter-in-another-time, and imagine her safe. She must be at the convent now, and I picture her being fed, being tended to, received into a house of women. It is a beautiful thought, and I delve deeper and deeper into it, my memory of the nuns I had studied with providing the images: a room of candles and prayer, of low voices, of the deep mystery of women's souls, forgiveness, comfort.

Latha

The first time they called her *that,* it was after a lunch. *Lunch* was simple and had only three curries, while *a lunch* had five and the fruits cut up in prespecified shapes for dessert. She had been sweeping the house. Again. It was the most useless of tasks in Latha's mind: this endless sweeping of the dust that crept through the doors and windows of a Colombo house. Sometimes she paused, her chin on the top of the broom, and remembered the convent: its particular coolness, the absence of dust, the crispness of it all. It made her happy to think of those spaces, but only on the good days.

On the bad days, when the memory made her feel an odd despair, she crushed the image by bringing on armies of nuns. Nun after nun after nun, their hands lifted in prayer, their skirts down to their ankles, and nothing but serenity on their countenances. Then, when she had turned the convent into a relentlessly uninspired tomb of deprivation, she rearranged her shoulders and felt happy to be in dusty Colombo. With Thara. Even if that meant *not* with Gehan, who now had no name, just a title: Sir.

"I'll ask my woman to make us some fresh lime juice," she heard Thara say.

And then, the comment from Thara's new friend from the office where she worked as a secretary, after the task had been relayed to Latha by the houseboy and she had prepared the lime juice just the way she and Thara had once enjoyed it as girls—though she had only a teaspoon or two now except on the days when she felt angry about one thing or another and made herself a glass without asking for permission to use a lime—sweet and tart in perfect complement, with just the dusting of salt and enough pulp to communicate its authenticity, and after the first sip had been taken: "Your woman must be good. From where did you get her?"

And she was still standing there! Worse, Thara had appeared not to notice. Latha had become just as invisible to Thara as she had been to Mrs. Vithanage, except for those occasions on which Thara's mother had been told of the onset of puberty or her request for those sandals or her pregnancy, except for those times. But this person, this "woman" that Thara and her friend continued to talk about, was not like the women who became women when they lay down with a man for the first time. This particular woman had no name, no past, no future, no desire or need. She had a function: servitude. To comfort herself, Latha went back to the kitchen and made herself lime juice with extra sugar, and then she squeezed more limes and made lime juice for the houseboy as well; he grinned like a monkey when she gave him the glass. A real glass, not the tin cups reserved for the servants. And though they both gulped their drinks down, his eyes big and on the lookout, his ears pricked, she felt as though they were a team, that she had an ally, little as he was.

As the days passed, Latha noticed other characteristics of this female called "my woman:" she had flaws and merits. Her flaws were an inability to make a proper sambol, or be deferential and grateful. Her merits included smelling fresh, having clean hands, and ironing like the dhobi at the laundry with the sir's creases in all the right places. And because to Gehan she was not even "my woman," she was "our woman," and because he tried hard to avoid her, steering clear of the kitchen, Latha sometimes creased the crotch of his trousers in such a way that it looked flat, like that of a woman's. She contemplated doing the same to his underwear but felt that might require a further insult. She held that in reserve, for the future.

Thara's new home was an upstairs-downstairs, modern affair, with three bedrooms and a bathroom on the upper floor and a dining room, living room, and wraparound veranda below. It even had an attached garage, unlike at the Vithanages', where the car had to remain parked outside, and a servant's room for Latha. The houseboy slept in the kitchen and stored his mat under the hāl pettiya, which sometimes meant that Latha had to come and spray a flying cockroach that had crawled into his mat with *Baygon* and wait until it squirmed itself to death so the houseboy could stop whimpering and go to sleep. There was a garden, but they did not have a gardener. Watering the plants and sweeping the outside was part of the houseboy's job, and not one he did very well, considering that the ekel broom was twice his height and he kept being distracted by everything that was going on outside the parapet walls that enclosed their property, particularly the vendors, at whom he stared as though they were magicians or puppeteers come especially to entertain him.

The transition to this house had not been without its moments of camaraderie. When they went shopping for the curtains, for instance, and Latha guided Thara away from the cream to the green and from there to the green and orange ones. Well, mostly orange, with a thin green stripe that you could see only if you got really close. Or when they went from the curtain place to the store for table linens, which Thara had thought should be white and Latha had told her should match the curtains, and couldn't they be orange?

"You're going to make my house into a Thambi house!" Thara said at the *Lanka Handloom Emporium,* where the saleslady had laid out the options on top of the glass case that contained jeweled ebony elephants and sterling silver teaspoons made for disuse.

"It's not the Muslims, it's the Tamils who like orange and green," Latha countered. She dropped the "Thara Madam" when they were together alone, and Thara seemed not to mind.

"*Anh?* So you think Amma would like my house to look like a Tamil house?"

"Why care what Amma thinks? Isn't this your house, after all? You should decorate it any way you like. You're the mistress of this household; she can be the mistress of hers. I say we should pick orange."

"Your sister is right, madam," the saleslady said, glancing from one to the other and holding up the swatch from the curtain shop next to the table linens.

And Thara laughed and corrected her and told her they weren't sisters, but when the saleslady apologized and referred to Latha as friend, Thara let it pass. And that was a good time, wasn't it? To be able to be friends again? Latha thought so, particularly since Thara compromised and got six green serviettes and six orange serviettes, and Latha relented and confirmed that white *Noritake* dinnerware was classy. Even though she secretly thought the creeping green vine along the edges might make a meal appear unappetizing.

And afterward, after they had selected the woven table mats—which Latha felt were not very classy and Thara had insisted were old-fashioned and therefore *were* classy—and the glasses in all those different sizes for purposes that had never been apparent in the time Latha had spent at the Vithanages', but that she assumed must have been because she was uninvolved in those operations, Soma being the head servant there, Thara had taken her to *Green Cabin*. They had sent some food and drink to the driver (who had done all the carrying) and then sat together at a table. Thara had bought soft, creamy Chinese rolls, with their crisp brown outer skins, and pastries with bacon and eggs, and éclairs full of chocolate. And they had eaten and chatted about the wedding and the house and what fun it was to buy things and be out in the world and drink enormous glasses of fresh golden mango juice thick with the taste of Jaffna mangoes (for Thara) and excessively sweet pink faluda piled high with bits of square-shaped red and green jelly and black kasa-kasa seeds that slid about her tongue like tadpoles (for Latha), whose relative merits they could compare.

But after the first few months they had nothing more to buy. The house was decorated, the furniture delivered and arranged, the paintings hung in the bedrooms. Now there was nothing to do but live, and the sort of living that happened at Thara's house, the Pereras' house as it was referred to, that being Gehan's last name, was not that different from the living that had gone on at the Vithanages'. It was routine and boring, and only the pace was faster.

Thara began working for the office of a dealer in *American Standard* sanitary ware. Bathtubs and washbasins and things like that, but mostly the washbasins because, Thara pointed out, but only to

Latha, the Americans were crazy—very few people could afford the tubs or wanted to sit around in warm water when the temperature was consistently ninety degrees. The company also sold bidets, but those came from England and Japan. There were three other people in the office, two married girls and one unmarried man, of whom Thara liked only the younger of the married girls, who turned out to be the one who came to that first lunch. The days at the office were dull, with few purchases, fewer visitors, and too much bookkeeping. She might even quit and find something else, or go to the Institute of Chartered and Management Accountancy, which was what a lot of her friends did while waiting to get married. If she hadn't dropped out after one year of trying the advanced level classes, she might have tried to get into law college like she had always hoped to do. But her parents had wanted her to settle down, and who cared about all this now? She hadn't been able to study anyway, not after the whole drama of Ajith. All these things Thara told her, but only on the evenings when Gehan was late coming home.

On the nights that Gehan was home, Latha stayed in the kitchen and pantry area, allowing the houseboy to do the table setting and the running back and forth for more water, which he invariably spilled, being some indistinguishable and equally hampered age between seven and nine years when little tasks such as these could never be completed successfully. When they finished dinner, Thara and Gehan held hands and watched TV or went upstairs to their bedroom and read books. Sometimes they shut the door to their room, which meant only one thing. When that happened Latha sat in the pilikanna at the back of the house with the houseboy and taught him to read, fiddling and fiddling with her earrings, longing for something to happen in her life to change its course and take her far away from Thara.

She wrote to Leela and prayed that somebody would read the letters to her, though, knowing Leela, Latha could just as easily see her tucking them unopened under her coir mattress, afraid of the imagined sacrilegiousness of the contents and of revealing to the nuns her own participation in such a friendship. Latha waited all that first year for word from Leela, but none came. It was as if she, too, had disappeared into the hills that came to Latha like a dream now. When she wrote, she imagined the good things before her: those colorful vegetables, the rest she had enjoyed, Leela and her embroidery, the hymns, which she now hummed as she cooked, and the stories they had made up together. Somehow, those days, that time in the mountains, seemed, in retrospect, full of potential. It was unlike her present, with its roster of duties, which came at her without deviation.

It did not matter that she had been elevated to the status that Soma had enjoyed, that she had a bed, and not a mat.

It did not matter that Mr. Vithanage had given her a lump sum when she moved into Thara's house, pressing it into her hands in Thara's presence so there was no mistaking his intent. The sum, though large, was not equal to what they owed her, but she had used it to purchase bedsheets and two towels in navy blue and white.

It did not matter that Thara had provided the personal introduction and the guarantor's signature needed to open an account at the brand-new *HKS Bank* in her own name with the rest of that money.

It did not matter that she received her salary from Gehan himself in an envelope he left on the kitchen table on the last day of each month, and that she sensed something soften in him in that gesture, to leave the money for her to find rather than give it to her directly and affirm their relationship as master and servant, to allow the transaction to be one of service but not necessary hierarchical. Or as if he were ashamed that they had set themselves up with this arrangement.

It did not matter that the houseboy scurried about under her watchful eye and did her bidding, or tagged along to carry the vegetables she purchased from the Sunday market in Jawatte.

And it did not even matter that if she bought the houseboy a yogurt with her own money he ate it slowly, as if it were a delicacy; and that watching him she would pretend that the baby she had given birth to had been a boy and this was he. This was not that baby, and that baby was not Gehan's; it had been Ajith's, so what did it matter to her where she or he was, except that it did. It did, it did, and that fact came back to her and punched her repeatedly in her flat stomach just when she least expected it to. Until, one day, it stopped.

Because of the sound of Thara vomiting in the morning and

looking wan in the evening and drinking nothing but that lime juice and finally saying it aloud: "Latha, I'm going to have a baby." And those seven words became a kind of chariot that carried Latha's lost newborn away, left it to fend for itself in the green hills, and then came back to this present, full of promise in the form of an infant she would be permitted to love, to watch grow.

Thara's pregnancy was different from how Latha's had unfolded at the convent. Whereas she had been taken for quiet, contemplative walks—at least externally; internally she had been roiling with the bitter notes of her eviction from the Vithanages' home and her arrival in that place of silence and abstention—Thara went for endless checkups at the unexpectedly quiet *Joseph Fraser Hospital* or lay around in bed all day. Whereas Latha had engaged her hands in making those baby clothes that nobody had told her she would never be allowed to put on her newborn, Thara shopped for stuff. Whereas Latha had gained weight slowly with the nutritious meals that had been made especially for her, a skill and prescience in the celibate nuns' ministrations that Latha had marveled at even in her state, Thara expanded, it seemed, by the day.

"You must not eat so much," Latha told her one afternoon, watching Thara consume a second heaping plateful of rice. Thara's cheeks had puffed out, and, along with her swollen fingers and feet, they made her resemble her mother more each day.

"I have to eat for two, that's what the books say," Thara responded, packing well-mixed rice and curries into the puffed belly of a papadam. It finally burst, and they both laughed.

"That's what's going to happen to you if you keep eating like that," Latha told her.

"What do you know about anything?" Thara said, still giggling, poking at her papadam.

Latha said nothing. Thara stopped laughing. She pushed the papadam to the corner of her plate and played with the murunga, splitting them with her index finger and then scraping the flesh out with the side of her thumb. Not eating any of it.

"What was it like when you . . . when you . . . had that baby?" she asked finally.

"Like nothing," Latha said. "The nuns took me to the expecting room, that's what they called it, and I had a comfortable bed where everything smelled clean. There was an older girl who tended to me there and brought me food." She stopped and began to clear the table, remembering Leela's face, her competent hands, the insistent voice that had coaxed food into her, and later, most of all, Leela's soothing quiet, which had put an end to her own silence.

Thara put her free hand on Latha's arm. "Did you have the baby at the convent?"

"No, they took me to the hospital."

"What was the hospital like?"

Why was Thara asking these questions now, after more than two years of no letters, after her return, after all the chats about her wedding, the moving, the decorating, the announcement of her pregnancy, after all that, why only now? Yes, Thara hadn't cared for a long time. Latha was under no obligation to confide. She felt angry.

"Are you done with the fruits?" she asked, and when Thara did not reply, she said, "I'm taking these away." She put one hand on the plate of salt-and-pepper-flecked sliced pineapple, looking straight at Thara the way she did when she wanted to threaten her with something— stubbornness, disobedience, insolence, pride, one of those things.

But Thara did not flinch. "I'm done with the fruits. What was the hospital like?"

"I didn't like it. It was cold and hard," Latha said. But after she had said that, the rest came back and she could not stop herself, so she tried to make it brief and factual. "I was high off the ground and I felt lonely and I shivered all the time and it didn't feel safe. The doctor barely looked at me, and the nurses had masks over their faces so all I could see was their eyes, and none of their eyes were kind. And when . . . when they took the baby from me . . ." And there she stopped, feeling the sadness untying itself easily, like it had been waiting for this moment, funneling up through her body, reaching her heart, her voice, her eyes.

"Sit, Latha, sit here," Thara said, standing up and guiding her to a chair at the dining table. It was the first time Latha had ever sat at a real dining table in a respectable house. She felt awkward.

The houseboy peeped around the door leading to the dining room from the kitchen, and Thara shooed him away. She poured some water for Latha and then held out a serviette. It was orange, but Thara had used it to dry her hands after she had washed her fingers in the bowl of water next to her and so the cloth was already damp and had *indul* on it from the curries, and the chili got in Latha's nose and made her sneeze six times in a row, as she did whenever she started sneezing. She giggled nervously and peered at Thara, who stood watching her.

"They took my baby from me," Latha said, this time with no tears, "and I never knew what happened to her."

"You had a baby girl?" Thara asked, and there was a sweet reverence in her voice, as if she, too, would want a daughter.

"A daughter, yes, but they didn't call her that. They called her 'the infant' and never spoke to me about her or answered my questions. They just left me there. It was still and silent, and much later, it seemed, a nurse came by to clean me up. She was older and she asked me my name, but I didn't say. I didn't talk after that for a long time."

She looked up at Thara, who said nothing. She stood, one hand on her belly, one on the edge of Latha's chair. She seemed far away, probably in a place of romantic imaginings about daughters, lost and found. Then, just as Latha was about to stand up, Thara reached out and stroked her shoulder.

"We're having a baby now, Latha," she said. "Don't worry about it any more. Forget the past. There will be a new baby in this house, and you can share."

Latha nodded, but she knew that sharing willingly was a concept that did not apply to the living beings that spring out of a woman's body. Thara was talking about things she did not understand. But she would. And what would happen then?

Biso

After we pass Ambewela, the landscape gives way to dense forest. I miss the open hills of tea, but the children welcome the change, their eyes watchful for what is new. It is still relatively early in the morning when we reach Pattipola, at the very least, and the children have not tired of their mountains and the cold air. Between stations, I let them sit on the steps, Chooti Duwa in my lap, my boy and Loku Duwa next to me, my arm stretching across their chests to the opposite side so I can keep them out of danger. I imagine that this immersion in the chilly gusts of wind that catch their hair and make their eyes fill up clear and constantly, the way they do only sitting on the steps of a train climbing up the hills, will cleanse their lungs of all the grime accumulated in Colombo during our trip and the stench of fish before then and even the uglier, psychological dirt that stains their insides. When we get up and go inside, the gentleman is preparing to leave.

"I will be in Pattipola for a week," he says as he gathers his belongings, and then, I must go back to Colombo." He sighs.

I don't know what else to do but thank him for the sweets, which seems insufficient, even though he has not done anything further for me. Something tells me gratitude is called for. Then I remember the number. "Thank you for giving me your phone number, sir. I will keep it safe."

"You are a good mother, Biso," he tells me. "Your children should be proud of a mother like you." He looks over at them, but only the littlest hears him, so he speaks to her. "Look after your mother, little daughter." Her brother and sister continue to hang out the window, looking up and down the platform, pointing to odd fruits on the thorny bushes in pots beside the station walls. There is only one vendor here, a child about my son's age, selling *Uswatte* chewing gum and *Delta* toffees, and even he appears to have got off the train. The toffees are in the center of a white basin, with the packs of gum stuck like a bordering wall all along the sides. My mouth waters and I am distracted.

"You are a good mother," he repeats, talking as if only to himself.

I turn away from the sight of the sweets. "It is kind of you to say so, sir; they are good children."

"Yes, I can see that," he says. Then he reaches into his pocket and pulls out his purse. He hands me three crisp two-rupee notes. "Give these to your children to keep for an emergency," he says. I shiver a little, feeling the cold. I'm not a beggar, and I don't need money from strangers. I say nothing. I pull the fall of my sari over my other shoulder and tuck it into my waistband, busying myself so as to avoid his eyes.

"Just something to buy *Panadol* or a sticking plaster for a wound or some pori . . . something if they need it," he says, noticing my distress. "It's only what I give my little girl once a month. Here, please take it."

I take the money and hold it in my hand, wanting to hide it but not wanting to offend him. Besides, the notes are new, and if I fold them I'd have to use them. I have always liked to save new things, at least for a little while. Bright rupee coins, unopened bars of soap, and new money. Even though I do not want it, the smell of it tempts me. I look away.

"Can I smell the money, Amma?" Chooti Duwa asks, and her voice seems out of place in the midst of this adult interaction. I smile at the way she has picked up my habits, and he laughs, relieved, perhaps, of his embarrassment.

"Yes," I say and give her one of the notes. She sniffs at it, her eyes shut. She does not open them even when he pats her head. He nods in my direction and gets off the train.

"He's leaving!" my son says, turning around to me. "That gentleman who was talking to you has got off the train. Look!"

So I look just to please him. How strange it is that a man so young should look so tired even in such well-made attire, nice khaki trousers, and respectable dark brown shirt, and with such a light bag to carry. I wonder what had made him want to offer me his help when, by the look of him, the stooped conduct of his life so apparent in his gait, it is I who am the stronger of us two strangers. Perhaps it was nothing more than chivalry: I am a woman with children, he is a man. When Loku Duwa announces that we are now all alone, it feels more frightening than it had before Thalawakele, when he had walked into our compartment and joined me. To comfort myself, I explain the station sign to Chooti Duwa, who has opened her eyes, drunk with the smell of new money, which she gives back to me for safekeeping. Pattipola is the highest station in the whole country, I tell her, and its summit is at 6,226 feet. Of course she does not know what that means.

"As tall as the Colombo buildings?"

"Taller," I say, holding her close as the train begins to move again, and frowning at my son, who, I can tell, is about to call her stupid. "So tall that they don't need those big buildings up here. They just climb the mountains when they want to see far away."

"What do they see in Colombo?" she asks me.

"More buildings," her brother says, his voice full of condescension toward the city he has passed through only this once, all of a sudden sounding like he had always lived here, among these greens and brights and close skies. Before I can consider the change in my son, or my uncertainty about our safety now that my last adult companion has left us, we enter another tunnel and are plunged into darkness. The train seems to veer suddenly around a corner, and I feel terrified that we might crash into the side of the mountain. My children squeal with delight, and this time there are far fewer voices to echo theirs. Someone yells out that there are bats in the tunnel, and another voice, male, says that when we come out at the other end we will be in the dry zone of our country. I do not believe him, but when we emerge into daylight again, the air seems different, less cold, and the foliage is not as dense as it had been approaching Pattipola from the other side.

It feels like an omen to me, this darkness that we have gone through only to arrive in a climate less refreshing than the one we had climbed toward from the moment we left Colombo. I shake these thoughts and try to reclaim my equanimity; it is foolish of me to give in to such imaginings simply because I have taken leave of a stranger. I give the other two children their two-rupee notes. Loku Duwa opens our bag and puts hers away inside a math textbook I hadn't noticed she had tucked in there. My son folds his in half and puts it into the pocket of his shirt, away from the other, contaminated, money in his trousers, and again I rejoice at the progress I have made since we left Matara.

But it is as if the train wishes to prove me wrong, or some deity is offended by my pride, because just as I reach forward to gather my three children to me in an embrace of gratitude, we are flung away from one another: they against the seat opposite mine, and I to the floor. Loku Duwa begins to cry, so quickly that it is almost as though her crying caused the train to pitch and stop. Her forehead has a small cut from where her head hit the edge of the window, and, when she brings her fingers to it and then sees the blood, she starts screaming. There are shouts up and down the train, loud from the adjoining carriages, fainter in the distant ones. I get up and tend to her: we have no more water, so I pour some thambili water from one of the bottles onto the edge of my sari pota and wipe the wound; I bunch up another corner of my sari and blow several times into it, then press the warm fabric to her head, soothing her, telling her that it is only a scratch. She continues to cry and I try to placate her further; I rub the tips of my middle and index fingers in the center of the palm of my other hand until I can feel the heat and press my fingers, too, to her forehead.

My son has his arms around the little one, who seems oddly at ease in the midst of the chaos around us. She smiles at her brother and snuggles deeper into his body, as if her thoughts are only on enjoying the rare pleasure of being in his good graces.

"Amma, what has happened?" he asks me.

"I don't know," I say, and then, because he is looking to me for further explanation, "but there must be someone around who can tell me. It won't take long to find out. Can you look after your sisters until I go and see?"

He nods. I dislodge Loku Duwa from my body and settle her into the seat, her head to one side, resting on the outer edge of the window. She pouts, and so I take one of my son's banians from our bag, blow, again, on a corner several times so that it is warm and moist, and give it to her.

"Here," I say, "hold this to your head, my pet, and it won't feel so bad." Then, with another glance at my boy to confirm that he is now in charge, I leave before she can plead with me to stay.

When I get to the steps we had been sitting on earlier, I see that we are between stations. There is no platform to stand on. There is a man about my age on the opposite set of steps. I decide to be safe and refer to him as a younger brother.

"Do you know what is going on, malli?" I ask.

He looks back and down at me, taking in my age, verifying that I am indeed older than he is or, perhaps, my status; I am better dressed than he is; we are clearly not of the same class. My feet are clean, shod; his are cracked and bare of coverings. "No," he says, slowly, drawing his lips down and shaking his head, disappointed that he lacks the necessary information. "I was just wondering if I should get down and see."

"Is there room to walk on this side?" I ask, not wanting to get any closer to him but just as curious about our derailment.

He peers down. "Yes, there's a little bit of space to walk on."

"I will come with you," I say, then I add, "I told my children that I would find out what is going on." This seems to reassure him, that I have children, for he agrees.

"All right then, let's go and see."

He steps down and respectfully holds on to my upper arm to help me navigate the steps. We walk, one behind the other, clinging to bushes in places so that we don't have to step on the tracks, which seem somehow more dangerous than they do when hidden by the steep sides of a station platform. A couple of people join us, stepping down from their carriages when they see that it is possible to walk. I am the only woman in the group. Once or twice I look back and see my son watching us from the window, the front half of his body starkly bright with the red of his shirt against the dull brown and black of the train, and I wave to reassure him. The front of the train is around a corner, and I wonder if, when I cannot see my Loku Putha anymore, I should go back. But I tell myself that the train is almost empty, that my children are safe. I can always step back into one of the carriages near me should the train begin to move.

"Sometimes these factory workers tie things to the tracks," someone says.

"For a strike," says another.

"I thought the strike was in Thalawakele," I say. "How many strikes do they have?"

They all laugh, and the young man in front of me says, "No, Akka, it's all tea country here. When they strike, they strike up and down this whole area."

"How long do you think the delay will be, then?" I ask, feeling a little ashamed of my lack of worldliness, yet not wanting to add that I haven't seen any tea plantations for a while and that perhaps it is they who are misinformed.

"An hour or two maybe," a man says behind me.

Two hours. That means that it will be late morning when we get to Ohiya. I sigh. If we begin walking right away when we get off the train in Ohiya, and making allowance for my little one, who I know will need many rests, we will not be at my aunt's house until long after lunch. Maybe there's a bus now. I am still dwelling on these calculations when I make the turn, and at first I don't realize that what I am seeing is what it is. There are still several carriages ahead of us, but right next to where we stand are four bodies lying on the tracks. A woman, a man, and two children. I feel my body grow cold and weak, and the man I had spoken to, who had been walking in front of me, turns and catches me as I sink to the ground. There are voices all around. The engine driver—I assume it is the engine driver—shouts at us to leave the scene, but he does so half-distractedly and none of us move.

"Let's go back to your carriage," the man says next to me, half-carrying me now.

I am on my knees, and I cannot tear my eyes away from them. There are ropes mixed up with the bodies, and the woman and her children have mangled middles. I can see where the train wheels ran over them. The fabric on their clothes is ground into the train tracks, and pulled away from the tops and bottoms of their bodies. Their forearms and wrists lie on the tops of their thighs as though their hands had been clawing at their own flesh. I cannot see their faces, which are beyond my line of vision, there under the train. The boy wears shorts, and his thin legs are bent at the knees and spread apart as if he had been flailing. The girl's legs are straight out and together as though she had been asleep. They must be seven or eight years old. The woman's sari is white and her feet are bare, like her children's. She wears it the Kandyan way, the osariya, the respectable way. A good woman. I realize they are all wearing white, as though they had been at or were going to a funeral, or to temple. I cannot see their faces. Yes, I can, I can. Just one face, only the man's.

The man's body is untouched. It lies on its belly. It rests between two cross planks as though it were on a bed. It is well dressed, also in white: starched, pressed trousers, and a white shirt. The shirt has been pulled out of his trousers, and, above his shoulders, the white collar is soaked in blood. The tracks and line are rust red between his torso and his head, which lies, faceup and close to the steel rail, as if it just fell off him, like a dead, dried flower without the energy to scatter. His hair is parted on the side, and it is smooth and oiled. He has clear skin and a thin mustache. His eyes are shut, his mouth open, as though he were breathing through it as he waited for our train. His head, his body, these things look peaceful, and suddenly I know that he did this to his family. He tied them to these tracks. But why had they not struggled? Why had they not run? Did he trick them? Did he tell them it was just a game? How could she not have known? How could she have let him? I turn my face a little, and I see four sets of shoes arranged in a row by the grass near the track. There are four half-drunk bottles of *Portello* there, and the remains of some meal. He poisoned them. He poisoned them first. I feel relief wash over me, the blood return to my limbs. As if it matters that they were already dying, unable to fight, or if they were already dead, or anything.

I cannot stop myself from swaying and murmuring prayers, asking the gods what has happened here, talking to the dead woman, calling her nangi, sister, younger sister, talking to all of them as though they can hear me. I must have aged right there on my knees before those bodies, because the man calls me mother. "Ammé," he says, "Ammé, let me help you back to the carriage. Your children will be worried."

My children. I get up and shake his arm off me. I start to run, tripping and crying as I fight through the bushes that helped my walk before but now seem to pull and tear at my hair and skin and hold me back. The man catches up with me and grabs my arm.

"Let me go!" I yell, again and again. "Let me go! Let me go! I must get back to my children!"

"Ammé, get into the train and you can walk through it safely," he says. He has to say it twice before I even understand. "Ammé, get into the train. It's safer to walk through the train."

Up ahead I see my son again, still looking out the window, waiting for me to return. I stop running and allow the man to help me into the carriage. He gets in behind me and walks with me. When we reach the first lavatory, he taps me on the shoulder.

"You should stop and clean your face," he says, "before you go back to them."

I go in, not caring about the stench, and sob over the sink. I sob as I never did for Siri. I had not cried then, not one tear. I had held it in so that the man who killed him would not have the satisfaction of seeing how broken I was. No, I had lain there, my arms around his dying body, the blood from his wounds flowing into me along with his passion, his body shuddering until there was nothing left except the blood that came over his body and included me in its embrace. I had stayed like that until he slipped out of me, and then I had stood. I had walked into the ocean and let the salt water wash my skin, the churning sands scrubbing my exterior of his blood even as the night air hardened my pain into a fist inside my chest. I came out of the sea, dripping, and went home. I walked by the drunken murderer sitting on the front steps and changed into the white sari I had bought to mourn my father. Then I took my two older children and walked to the temple to light a single lamp. And all that time, not one tear. Not one until now, when I have been reminded of what I once had, what I miss, that feeling of safety.

I rinse my hands in the trickle of water that drips from the faucet. There is no soap. Finally I wash my face and dry it on the edge of my sari, not understanding why it is already damp till I remember my daughter's wound. I begin to cry again, this time for my children, the things that I cannot keep from them, and I cry until I realize I need to relieve myself, so I squat over the toilet and urinate, my sari gathered up to my waist in my arms. Then I wash my hands again, my face again, and again wipe myself with the edges of my wet sari.

When I come out, the man is still waiting.

"They say it is the most painless way to die," he tells me. "They say that you are hypnotized by the train as it comes closer and closer, and then it's over."

"It was painless for him," I say, and my voice sounds odd to me. Deep and full of the bitterness I had shed with each station on this journey. "He poisoned them."

"How do you know?" he asks, his brow furrowed.

"They ate and drank before they died, that's how I know."

I want to say more, but the train begins to roll backward slowly, and I have to catch myself before I fall.

We walk silently to where my children are waiting.

"Amma! What took so long?" my daughter asks, reproach in her eyes as she hands me the now cold banian.

I take it, open it out, find a dry area, bunch it up, blow on it, and give it back to her wordlessly. The blowing calms me.

"I heard them say there was an accident," my son says, searching my face.

"Some . . . some trees . . . some trees had fallen across the track," I say, sinking into my seat. "The railway workers are removing them. It will take some time."

"So we have to wait here *again?*" the little one says, her voice disbelieving. "But there aren't even tea leaves for us to pluck!"

I see a vendor approaching us through the train, a basin of sweets on his head, a basket of mangoes in his hand. I stop him.

"Why don't you buy some mangoes or sweets with your new money?" I say.

I help Chooti Duwa to buy a chocolate-flavored lollipop and a mango; Loku Putha buys a bar of *Cracker Jack,* and Loku Duwa buys a bag of toffees. The vendor gives each of them their change separately, and they put the coins away in places that seem safe to them.

I wipe my face with the now abandoned banian, then lay it on the seat next to me to dry. There is hardly any blood on it. My child's wound is a mere scratch.

Latha

Latha!" Gehan yelled. "Go and attend to Nona." And then he got in the car and was driven to work as if it were no problem at all that his wife was crying and bleeding.

According to Gehan, Thara didn't fall; she cut herself with a blade. Latha heard him saying that as she stood, just out of sight, and waited for him to leave. What Gehan thought about Thara and her motivations had deteriorated steadily over the first three years of their marriage, and now, right on the eve of the first birthday of their second baby daughter, it seemed that he had reached a new low. Latha shook her head as she went into the bedroom where Thara was. She was half-propped on her pillows, holding one of Gehan's banians to her head.

"Give me that," Latha said. She took the banian, found the blood-stains on it, and spat all over them as Thara watched.

"*Chee!* What are you doing?" Thara asked, some disgust creeping into her voice, which Latha felt was out of order considering the source of the stains.

"Getting the stains out. Otherwise I will have to use salt, and it's not good to waste salt. If we waste salt, we'll waste money. Soma nenda taught me that."

"Oh," Thara said, affirming Soma's knowledge about such things. "Has that *para balla* left?"

Latha bit her lip. She hated the way Gehan treated Thara, and not only because it was an extension of the way he treated her, with an absence of recognition. But she felt that way only when she thought of him as Thara's husband, someone responsible for her happiness. Other times, she silently took his side.

When she watched him with Madhavi, for instance, and her heart melted at the way he held the baby or took her from Latha's own arms, and she could almost feel that the tenderness with which he surrounded his daughter was extended to her, too. Then she would feel as though he was willing to share the same space with her so long as their affection was directed outward, away from each other and toward the treasures only a baby could bring: a stray curl, a fist unfurled in sleep, toes gripping the feet of a father as he held her outstretched arms and seesawed her up and down every evening after work. Or when she listened to Gehan singing in a voice he had revealed he possessed only when he had a daughter to soothe. Latha would hold the mosquito net aside while he bent down and laid his daughter down to sleep and covered her with her cotton blanket, all the while singing the last lullaby of the night, *"Bilindā Nalave Ukule."* Thinking about that lullaby, that first verse dedicated, ironically, to the love of a mother for her child, Latha would find it difficult to forgive Thara for the way she held herself away from her baby, and she would choose, instead, to let her sympathies rest, unchecked, unexamined, with Gehan. She would remember him as he had once been to her, someone who had treated her with respect and who had, she was certain of this, loved her, and she would feel resentful of Thara's remarks. Like now. Yes, he wasn't from the right family and he didn't have all the right connections and credentials the way Ajith had, and he wasn't even good-looking, but that didn't make him a stray dog. Or if it did, and Thara was his wife, she was nothing more than a stray—

"Latha! I asked you if he's left!"

"Yes! the car is gone! Why? Didn't you hear it drive away?" Either Thara didn't notice or she was too self-absorbed to care about Latha's tone of voice this morning.

"The bastard has the nerve to say that I cut my own face with a blade. Why would I do something so stupid? If I wanted to cut anything, I would have cut his! Maybe it would be an improvement!"

Latha thought that, post-marriage, her friend had grown from the twinkling stars implied by the first part of her name, Thara, into the virulence of her full name, Tharindra: terrible goddess of the universe. Wasn't this one example? This kind of remark that she threw around so easily, as if she were not even speaking about a human being? As if a human being wasn't listening to her? Sometimes it sickened Latha.

"The baby is crying. Shall I bring her to you?" Latha asked, her voice crisp.

"Babies, babies, nothing but babies. Look at me, Latha!" Thara rose from the bed, strode to the mirror, and ripped off her skirt and blouse. She threw them on the floor and stood there in her underwear, staring at her reflection. After a few seconds she began a fresh bout of tears. "Just look at me! Look at how you are and then look at this!"

Latha could not see anything the matter with Thara. Yes, she was a little plumper than she had once been, but she had always been curvier than Latha. The only differences now were the scars from the cesareans. All right, there was more undulation to the surface of her skin around her lower belly. But neither of these things diminished the fact that she was a pretty woman in the traditional way: oval faced, rounded in all the right places, and with that air of clean sweetness that came with privilege.

"There's nothing wrong with you, baba," Latha said, reverting to the soothing childhood moniker that Thara loved to hear. "You look just the way you always did. You're a mother now, that's all."

"But why don't *you* have all this?" Thara wailed, grabbing hunks of flesh from the sides of her waist.

"I only had one baby," Latha said, amazed at how those words came so easily to her now, no regret, no attachment. She tried to add something, a few more words of comfort, but the baby began to scream at the top of her lungs and she shrugged. "I'm going to get Chooti Baba," she said to Thara's reflection, shaking her head at the sight of her friend, her palms clapped over her ears.

✦ ✦ ✦

How it all got to be this bad so fast, Latha could not imagine. The first year had seemed so perfect for them all. Thara had her lunches, which, though they came with the usual disparaging remarks from her friends, Latha learned to steel herself for by squeezing the lime juice for herself and the houseboy—and on particularly bad days, the day driver too—in advance. Every couple of months they had dinners for Gehan's friends from work. Latha liked the dinners because Thara cooked the desserts she had learned to make at her pre-wedding cookery class, which meant they got to spend the whole Saturday together in the kitchen, she with her buriyanis and seeni sambols that she had perfected with each new try, and Thara with her pineapple fluffs and trifles and fruit salads with custard, laughing and joking and tasting dry ingredients and cooked food all day long. During cricket season, Gehan and Thara went to matches at the SSC and the Oval, and Latha and the houseboy watched the games on TV. And on Poya days they went to temple together—Gehan, Thara, the houseboy, and Latha—dressed in white, standing in a row, no differences apparent in their status or circumstances, their heads bowed together, the fragrance of thousands of lotuses and nā mal and delicate araliya flowers in all their shades of color—yellow, white, pink, dark red—transporting both women back to their youth.

The only lows that whole time had been during Thara's unruly—and frankly, in Latha's mind, overly indulged—first pregnancy. Still, even that had taken the usual course to celebration when the baby arrived, except for the sacking of the old houseboy, who was discovered tasting the milk from the baby's bottle.

"I was trying to check for the right heat for the baby!" he wailed as Thara screamed at him and sent him to pack his bags and called Gehan's mother to report this crime, clearly deriving great satisfaction from the act, given that the houseboy had come from "his side."

Of course, the baby had become the highlight of everything for Latha. Nothing could change that; not even bad news. Not all the celebrations after the departure of the Indian soldiers, whom all the fighting factions had joined together to drive out, shouting from one loudspeaker or another, screaming from the radios and TVs that she heard in the shops and the neighbors' houses as she walked by. Not any of the other agitation going on in the country, with the communists from the South and the terrorists from the North and a corrupt government. Not the kidnappings and disappearances and curfews here, there, and everywhere that seemed to worry everybody, even Thara. None of it could touch Latha. Her world was lit like a Vesak pandal by Madhavi from the minute she was born. From that moment Latha knew, not knowing why, how to love a baby just so: madly when she was freshly washed, powdered, and oiled, and ready for the morning; gently when she was full-bellied and sleepy; tenderly when she had hurt herself; and secretly, behind a veil of steady nerves, when she was a stinking, mewling, parasitic and decidedly ugly blob of flesh. Thara, too, loved her baby daughter, but it was a tolerant love, vaguely distant, cautious and self-aware, like that of a visitor.

"We're going to name her Madhavi," Thara had told Latha after the astrologer had been consulted. "Amma wanted me to name her Ruby, like her grandmother, but I prefer Madhavi. It means a sweet, intoxicating drink."

"It's a better name," Latha said, "Madhavi. It sounds like a song. It suits our baby, too. She seems so good tempered."

"Gehan wanted Madhuvahini, which means 'carrying sweetness,' like a river, but I don't believe in big fat names for small babies."

"Madhavi is better," Latha said again, trying not to notice how uncomfortable the baby looked in Thara's arms, and then blurting out, "Here, hold her like this."

"She spat on me! Could you take her?" And there was the new baby in her arms.

And before long Madhavi, the new baba to Latha, was thrust so repeatedly into her arms that all Thara had to do was hold her daughter to nurse her. And sometimes take her from Latha to pass her to Gehan when he came home from work. By the time Madhayanthi arrived, barely two years later, full even as an infant with the promise of her name, with her pouting mouth and long-lashed eyes all stretched and doelike, Madhavi had already become a kitchen child who toddled behind Latha, mispronouncing her name, calling her "Thatha!" "Thatha!" "Thatha!"

Of course, Gehan assumed she had learned how to call for her father and didn't seem to notice, scoffed Thara, that the two syllables were far too short to be mistaken for "Thāththa." It didn't matter to Latha either way, because Madhavi needed her so much of the time that it was quite clear to which member of the family she was referring.

Soon she was gifted, by Gehan no less, with a newly procured houseboy, to help her out. Which, at first, wasn't any help at all since, all of five years old—because Gehan's mother had said it was better to *start them young*—and with a type of retardation that was unexplained to her, the boy knew nothing and she had to spend time teaching him simple cookery while all of them ate bought food, which brought its own share of ridicule from the usual quarter, Mrs. Perera, Gehan's mother. Nonetheless, Latha liked the new boy, who came from the estates, they told her, just like the other one. The only difference was that he was Tamil, wiry, dark brown, and moist eyed, a baby himself, except by comparison with the plumped, pampered ones in pink and cream frills whom he, too, had to tend.

The only sore spot had come over the handling of the nappies. They had to be washed by hand, and Latha had to do it. She wouldn't have minded it, really, except that she got tired of the armies of visitors who all inquired, and who were all assured, that the baby wore cloth diapers and that they were hand washed.

"By hand, yes, Badra Aunty"—or Srimathi Nenda or some other version of aunt—"only by hand."

To which Badra Aunty or Srimathi Nenda or whatever other garden variety of woman between the age of forty and sixty-five who was visiting at the time would intone: "Because these days there are disposable things available and those are very bad, *vereeeey* bad for the baby. You must never bring them into the house."

"My god," Thara would say. "I'm not like those mothers who put their babies in disposable things." Which would have been all right, but she always added, every single time, "I boil the nappies afterward and then even add nappy disinfectant and boil again and then, after they are dried in the full sun, I won't put them on the baby unless I have ironed them!"

And the older women would beam, their congratulations and ap-

proval breaking over the liar before them in great waves while Latha
stewed and fumed in the background and fought the urge to storm
in and set the record straight. Which perhaps accounted for the reason why, when Thara scoffed at her mother's attempts to stick with
tradition and proven practice and tie the long gauze towels around
her belly to tighten her uterus and restore her former shape, Latha
supported Thara and unpinned the wraps herself.

"Silly old wives' tales. If these things work, then why does *she*
have a belly?" Thara complained.

"Hmmm," Latha said, the pins stuck in her mouth, saving her
from actually having to utter lies herself.

"Don't you think? You have a flat belly, and you had a baby, after
all," she said, after the pins were gone.

"That's the thing," Latha said, agreeing, about the flat belly and
the baby, and comforting herself with those two truths, burying the
memory of the nuns and the taut wraps that had helped her to regain
her shape in those hills.

Once the houseboy was more or less trained to do the bare minimum and sometimes a little more with frequent supervision, Latha
returned to the far more entertaining task of pushing Madhavi up
and down the driveway of their house in her pretty covered pram that
had come from England and once belonged to Thara's grandmother.
After a year of that, she started taking Madhavi for walks to the end
of the road, and a few months later to the Independence Square
Park, but only after Madhavi had eaten her fruit and been freshly
dressed for the evening, and only after she herself had taken a body
wash under the headless shower spout in the servants' bathroom and
put on a clean dress and a matching pair of sandals from the many
she now bought with her own money whenever she pleased.

And that was what she was doing when she met Ajith.

"Latha?" She heard the voice beside her and froze. Madhavi too
turned her head to stare at the man seated on the stone bench. What
had it been now? Five years? Six?

"Latha! It *is* you!"

She didn't say anything at first. Time didn't seem to have touched
him. There he stood, broad-chested, straight and sure of himself. Still

in one of his shirts with the man on a horse embroidered in white over his pocket, still with his clean feet settling easily into fine leather sandals. Still nothing like Gehan.

He didn't look that different from the last time she had seen him, at the back gate of the Vithanages' house, underneath the mango tree that hardly produced any fruit anymore but stood there anyway, providing its helpful shade. She had gone there to tell him about the pregnancy, now that the whole story was out. She had moved her shoulders out, first one side, then the other, to show him the half-moon-shaped scratches along her upper arms. For a moment she had even slipped back into her teledrama role as the wronged woman, the one who would be avenged by a man, any man, because all men loved her, even other women's men.

"Mrs. Vithanage," she had said.

"What for?" he had asked, his palm stroking her right arm and shifting almost instantly from the gentleness of concern to the pressure of desire.

"Because they found out I am pregnant."

He had laughed. And although, afterward, he had said he would help her, find a friend, ask somebody, borrow money, a whole list of things, she had known he would not. It was just a story he could tell his friends, about the girl he had made pregnant when he was still waiting for the results of his university entrance exams. Some girl whose name he would probably not even tell them, pretending that he was protecting her honor that way. He had stayed only long enough for all the usual things, and then left for good without a backward glance, leaving her to stand by herself with the realization that no, she was not in a teledrama, she was no heroine, and all her blunders were her own to sort out, nobody would fight for her.

"This is not my baby," she said at last. "This is Gehan's . . . Thara's baby."

He crossed his arms in front of his chest, and something inside him seemed to slump. He started to say something, then stopped and stood there nodding at her, gazing at Madhavi.

"I heard that they got married," he said finally, "a year or so ago, right?"

"Three years ago," Latha said. "They're expecting another baby any day now." Madhavi began to hurl herself forward in the pram, making it jerk back and forth. Latha bent down to her. "We'll go soon, baba, stop doing that, you'll fall out."

He shifted his weight from foot to foot, as if trying to find something to say that would make her listen for a little longer. "I was abroad," he blurted. "My parents sent me to America to go to university there," he said. "To Michigan," he added, after a pause, "a place called Michigan."

"Michigan," she repeated and nodded.

"It's a cold part of America."

A car pulled up not far from where they were standing, and two young girls got out. Ajith glanced over at them, and Latha seized the distraction to try to get away.

"I have to take the baby back home now," she said, trying to seem regretful.

"Have things been well for you, Latha?" he said, turning back to her and staring at her face with eyes that, precisely because he was so clearly not looking at her body, were doing just that. Latha nodded again. She could have been polite, asked the same question of him, but she had no interest in him, his body, his story, or making him feel good about any of it. He hadn't even asked about the child she had borne. It was as it had always been; she was a means to an end, no more, no less. The thought must have shown on her face because he sounded awkward when he began speaking again. Good.

"I used to come here to run when I was home for holidays, Latha, but this is the first time I've visited since I came back for good. I am back for good now. I'm at the Central Bank . . . my father got me a job there."

"That's good, isn't it? I'm happy to hear that." She didn't even try to make it sound like she meant it. Looking at him objectively, she thought how well he suited Thara. The two of them, something they called decency dripping off their shoulders like magic capes, the weight of their upper-class families almost a visible backdrop to their movements no matter what they did. How right Thara had been to choose another like herself, and how unlucky to have misjudged his character.

In the end, coming from the "right family" had been his undoing. No, on second thought, they were not the same, Thara and Ajith, Latha thought. Thara had fought off her parents and turned down all the proposals, one after another, gone to Ajith's house to plead with him, and finally chosen the one who had been closest to Ajith, marrying not Gehan but his association with the one she had loved since she was eleven years old. Was it love? Perhaps, or not. Perhaps it was just habit, or want. Ajith was the one she had chosen, the one she had wanted, and maybe Thara, who had been told so relentlessly that the most important choice, her husband, would not be hers to make, had wanted to force her parents to learn otherwise. But Ajith had listened to his parents, let them send him to this cold place he talked about, and come back to his good job carrying nothing but guilt. Latha turned the pram around to go back the way she had come. She didn't want to be reminded of the past. Didn't she live with it every day?

"Latha, wait. Tell me, are you keeping well? Do you need any help or anything?" he asked.

"I work for the Pereras now. I'm not at the Vithanages'," she said.

"How is Gehan?"

She shrugged. "He's the same, I suppose."

"And how is . . . how is Thara, Latha?" He touched the top of her shoulder. "Can you tell me?"

She glanced down at his hand and waited until he dropped it. "Different," she said and felt oddly pleased to be able to leave him standing there, staring after her, wondering what she meant. The real *para balla,* she thought to herself. He's the one who deserved to be called that, not Gehan.

She didn't decide to tell Thara until the day of Madhayanthi's first birthday party, a whole year later. That was on the eighth of September, and the last of the monsoon rains were threatening the skies even as the birthday cake was cut, but they held off until the last furious guests, the two sets of grandparents, had left. And the only reason she did it was because that was the day Gehan and Thara had their ugliest fight.

It began because, at the party, Mrs. Vithanage made a disparaging remark about the fact that they never seemed to see their daughter and son-in-law at the big house anymore.

"It's as if you live in the outstations! I mean after all, we are just around the corner from you, and surely you could visit more often." Mrs. Vithanage was laid out in the reclining armchair at the end of the side veranda, one of two such chairs Thara had been given by the old couple when she got married. Latha liked those chairs. They were smooth to the touch from the years that separated them from their former life as magnificent teak trees on the family estate, which Latha had visited with Thara when they were girls, playing in the dark green paddy fields, eating raw mangoes and raw wood apple with vinegar and chili and salt until the kahata made them hoarse, all the while studiously avoiding eye contact with any of the laborers, the coconut pluckers and paddy farmers, with their bare upper bodies and servile manners that Mrs. Vithanage had pointed out to them, as a warning.

"Maybe you should visit us," Gehan said, smiling just a little.

"Children should be visiting the parents, not the other way around," Mrs. Vithanage said, preceding her words with the slightest of wheezes; she could have been beginning an attack of asthma, but Latha knew from long experience that it was more likely to have been an intended adjective. "That's how it was in the *old* days."

"We barely have time to manage the simple things, let alone go visiting various people. The old days are gone," Gehan said, the modifier leaving his expression and a dark glare coming into its own.

"Hmmm. That much is certainly clear to us all," Mrs. Vithanage said. She could never let things go. "We can see that things are not the way they used to be. Particularly when parents are referred to as 'various people.'"

Of course Mrs. Perera, who was within earshot, had to leap to her son's defense; this was the moment that every mother of a son waited for, particularly those whose offspring had married up, and she was clearly relieved that it had finally arrived.

"My son is very busy, working morning, noon, and night to support the wife and the children," she said. "If the wife was working, then perhaps he would have more free time and they could do all these visits. Otherwise, at this rate, with one person doing all the work . . ."

The trail-off was the biggest insult of all, and Latha braced herself on Mrs. Perera's behalf. Not because there was any love lost between herself and Gehan's mother but because Thara's marriage down, on top of her own to Mr. Vithanage, whose caste was one step lower already, was the sort of inward-burrowing humiliation that lurked just behind the throat of someone like Mrs. Vithanage. An internal hemorrhage that made everything she said sound like a gurgle until the day it could all come spilling out. At that moment, this moment, she could be free from its malignance because after she said What Needed to Be Said, and People Were Put in Their Places, her daughter, and therefore herself and her family, would be restored to their former status as people not to be trifled with. So, Latha waited.

"If Gehan had a proper job in the government, like Thara's father, then perhaps he could afford a wife from Thara's background. After all, she is not accustomed to this kind of life. She comes from a different sort of family." Mrs. Vithanage stood up and yelled for Latha as if she, Mrs. Vithanage, was the real mistress of the house. "Latha! Come and clear this table!" Then she turned and fixed Mrs. Perera with the full force of her Kandyan stare. "A *very* different sort of family."

Mrs. Perera rose to her feet. Latha had to agree that, when they stood up together, Mrs. Vithanage was at an advantage. But, not having the curse of the Kandyan Govigama caste Buddhist (or the KGB, as Gehan called it), Mrs. Perera had never had to be concerned with what people might think. So what she lacked in height she had in lungs. And lungs were heavy artillery in a Colombo 7 neighborhood.

First, she snorted. Then, she spat. Even Latha considered that beyond the pale and rushed forward to wipe the floor with a serviette she grabbed off the table. She also made a last-ditch effort to save Mrs. Vithanage, but only because she saw Mr. Vithanage approaching from the garden and she wanted to protect him from hearing the vitriol she knew was coming.

"Perera Nona, can I get you some passion fruit juice?" she asked.

But the moment she said it, she regretted her words, because Mrs. Perera spat again, this time in her direction and called her what Soma had, six years ago: whore.

"*Vesi!* I cannot believe you are here in my son's house, looking after him and my two innocent grandchildren!"

"She's here, like all the other servants, including the driver who takes that son of yours to work, because we pay them. Otherwise I can't imagine *what* my poor Thara would be forced to do in this house that we bought for them," Mrs. Vithanage said, snorting in turn. This was the only time she had ever defended Latha, however backhandedly and, come to think of it, falsely, Latha thought, since it was Gehan himself who paid her salary.

Mrs. Perera turned to Mrs. Vithanage, and her voice rose and shrieked at such a pitch that Latha was sure she could be heard three houses away in every direction.

"It was an act of charity on the part of my family to let Gehan marry into yours. Into a family where the master of the house was fucking the servant girl, who was young enough to be his child. Who knows? Maybe that is *why* you want to keep her so close. Maybe she *is* his child from some other woman up in the estates where she came from. I heard it was he who brought the little bitch into the house in the first place."

Latha didn't know what possessed her. Later she told herself it must have been the look on Mr. Vithanage's face as he reached the top step just in time to hear this speech, and the way his eyes flew to her face and then looked down at his shoes. She didn't know if it was because she believed what Mrs. Perera had just said, or whether it was the memories that came back to her in quick flashes and then were gone: a memory of that just-for-her bar of a *Kandos Cracker Jack* chocolate, and the voices. The voice of a woman telling her that she was an orphan, and then Mr. Vithanage's voice saying, *Come, daughter, come*; and the voices of nuns soothing her and promising her things even though she wasn't afraid at all of Mr. Vithanage.

Whatever it was that made her do it, this much was clear: it felt good. She spat right back at Mrs. Perera, and not away from her, in her face. And then, just because that felt so perfect, she slapped her.

So Mrs. Perera shrieked, and Mrs. Vithanage said it served Mrs. Perera right that she was slapped by a servant woman, and Mr. Perera and Mr. Vithanage bundled their respective wives into their respective vehicles and sent their respective drivers back for their wives' handbags and the party was well and truly over because Madhayanthi screamed and screamed and wouldn't stop until Latha went and picked her up and took her to the kitchen. And after she had helped her out of the absurdly puffy pink nylon dress that Mrs. Vithanage had given her for her birthday even though it was scratchy and hot, and taken off the squeaky shoes that Mrs. Perera had given her even though she wasn't walking yet, and filled a basin on the back porch and brought Madhavi and put both girls in there to play, Madhayanthi stopped her crying, and Latha was resolved.

She was resolved, but her resolution only grew as she listened to Thara defend her when Gehan told her they had to get rid of Latha or else his mother would never visit them again.

"Good, I hate your mother," Thara said and screamed, twice, as Gehan's hand fell first on one side of her face and then on the other. She screamed and then she started yelling at Gehan and that was the end of Thara's former life as an upper-class, Colombo 7, KGB princess. She was now most definitely not a Vithanage; she was a Perera. And the more she said to Gehan, the further she stepped from her blessed childhood and the angrier she got until at last she hurled words so crass and raw at him that even he, an ordinary Perera, backed away from her and left the house.

Latha, listening in the kitchen, put the kettle on to boil even though nobody had asked for tea. As the water warmed, she peeled and sliced a bit of ginger. She could feel a long night coming, a night of acrimony and tears and regret, and it all felt oddly familiar to her. Thara's words, Gehan's slaps, even the determined thud of the rain that finally let go all over Colombo, but most especially, it seemed to Latha, over this particularly sad home. There was a known quality to the evening, an inevitable end to anything vaguely connected to happiness. Maybe that was how it was with women, she thought, whatever their status; eventually their men would be found unworthy.

Biso

The children are hungry; they have not had any breakfast other than the slices of mango and sweets that they have shared with one another, haggling and bartering until I almost intervened. I yearn for a cup of ginger tea, sweet and strong, but for now I am glad that my children have something to occupy themselves with; it lets me disappear, leaving just the ever-watchful eyes and ears of a mother on guard. I sit quietly and retreat inside my head.

I take out the images of the family still under the train and examine them, one by one. I go over the details of their white clothing, the condition of their feet, clean but for a dusting of dirt, their food. It must have been breakfast, this early. The children would have been happy to be given *Portello* for no good reason that they could see. It was because they were good at temple, he may have said. That's where they must have spent the previous day, observing Sil, attending an all-night Pirith for an almsgiving, perhaps, that coincided with a Poya day, then staying for some other observance afterward. I imagine the moon bright and full of benign peace as it floated over the temple where they must have sat, close along the boundary walls with the other devotees. I remember our own visit to the temple, and so this temple becomes that temple. Their story, ours. But for the father in theirs, the absence of one in ours.

My last visit to the temple, just two nights ago, was full of concern and fear, but our lives have turned out differently. Here I am, my children beside me. And there they were, that woman and her children, after all the peace of their devout meditations, the bliss of that meal together, and all for what? To be dragged and tied down, to be lying split apart, their insides out like forked eggs, to be so irreversibly over.

What does my escape mean in the face of such endings?

"Amma, I'm hungry, Amma, Amma." Chooti Duwa taps my chest with the flat of her palm. She looks tired and dehydrated, and the word, *badagini,* sounds more appropriate than it ever has before; she looks as though her stomach is smoldering with hunger.

"Me too. I'm also hungry." Loku Duwa looks positively robust by comparison.

"What can we eat?" my son asks.

What indeed. I don't recall any vendors on the train other than the man with the fruit and sweets.

"Putha, could you ask that uncle who took me to see the . . . accident . . . if he knows how much longer we'll have to wait?"

"Where is he?"

"He should be just around the corner, standing on those steps." I gesture with my head. He goes, and comes back almost immediately.

"He doesn't know, but he says that he saw an ambulance come and go. Why would they need an ambulance?"

"Somebody must have been sick on the train," I say.

He frowns a little and glances over at Loku Duwa. She frowns in response, but hers is more perplexity, less accusation. "Is it the driver? Is the driver dead?"

"Nobody is dead! Don't say things like that. It's inauspicious!" I spit three times out the window to take away the curse of his statement. "Nobody's dead," I say again, very firmly. My agitation has rubbed my body free from the heaviness that descended upon it the moment I sat down. I get up. I feel energetic and determined. "I will go and find something for you to eat," I say.

When I look back from halfway down the compartment, they are all staring after me, their faces curious and worried. I smile and send them an eyes-squeezed-shut-puckered-mouth embrace, and the girls giggle. Even my boy smiles a little. I used to do that when I dropped them at school. We used to call it the pinch-and-kiss kind of love; our name for it. What we women do to babies, gathering the soft folds of skin on plump cheeks and backsides and thighs and squeezing, just a little harder than we should, then kissing them; because really what they make us want most is to swallow them whole and keep them very, very safe. So, from afar, I convey that desire with my eyes and mouth, and their smiles reward me. I keep standing there for a few moments, enjoying the sight of that trust. I cannot put them back into my body, but they know I will keep them safe. I smile back at them, then turn away to go on with my search. Food. Where will I find food in this nearly empty train?

In the third carriage away from the back of the train, I come upon a vendor, squatting by an empty seat, dozing over his wares. Strange how even in a carriage full of vacant seats, he chooses the floor, content with where he belongs. He is one of those men who grow old fast, then stay that way until they pass. He could be fifty-five; he could be seventy-five. The hair on his unshaven chin and on his head is a mix of black and gray. I can tell from the way his mouth caves in just a little that he doesn't have all his teeth. His gray sarong is tucked carefully between his legs, and he wears tennis shoes with no socks. The stripes on his green, long-sleeved shirt are faded; he has wrapped a woolly length of brown cloth around his neck. I stand for a long time, staring at him, lost in the memory of my own father. A similar man but cleaner, distinguished in his own fashion, particularly when my mother was alive.

People always told me what a decent family we were, how my mother must have good blood, because she was quiet. She had the qualities that set her apart in our village: the pastel-colored osariya she put on every morning as soon as she rose, the pleats and fall neat, her unhurried walk, her soft voice, the way she knew how to be present and absent in the same moment. On the rare occasions when one of my father's friends visited, my mother cooked simple but well-balanced meals, served them unobtrusively, and attended to their conversations, but never participated, not that I can recall. And yet, she made all the decisions. My father gave her his earnings to spend as she thought best; he asked her for money when he wanted it. Sometimes she would persuade him that he did not need what he said he did. And he would cajole and she would remain firm but there were no arguments. What my mother said was respected. I assumed that was what marriage was, providing and obedience on the part of the husband, good conduct and power on the part of the wife.

Was that what my mother wanted from her life? I wonder now. She had not married within her caste, or among her people, but she had always seemed content, almost willfully so. She was gracious, and did what was right. Was that her choice or her upbringing or her circumstance? I had never asked her these questions, if her life was unfolding as she had imagined it would, if what was, was as her own mother may have imagined for her. I had simply assumed that all was as it should have been, with myself in the center of her life, my father's life, I their sole delight, their sole hope. How easily I had stepped away from the path that my mother had walked. How swiftly I had turned from that model of duty to desire, from caring about others to caring for myself. Would she have approved?

I wipe my eyes. I hadn't thought about my mother's quiet admonishments, her expectations of me, to be good, to do right, to live without shame, for a long time. I had taught myself to stand alone after she died, and continued to live that way after I was disabused of my childhood ideas of matrimony. And now, here she is on my mind, carried to me on the wings of my memory of my father. I realize that my journey up-country is a journey toward her, toward whatever grace she hailed from, a hope held tight to my chest that in these cold mountains there will be some refuge for me.

A child brushes past me in the narrow corridor, and I remember why I am here. The vendor has some kind of bread-roll sandwiches in his basin and a small pile of hard issa vadai. A few flies have found their way under the plastic covering. I tap the basket to get rid of them, and he is startled awake.

"Madam . . . ," he says.

It's the first time I have been addressed this way. Even the schoolteachers never called me that. They never called me anything but Mrs. Not even a real name after that. Just Mrs. I smile at him.

"I was wondering if you were still selling these," I say, pointing to his basket. Two flies have returned, and he shoos them away with exasperation and a click of his tongue, as if this were unheard of: flies on a train! On unsealed food, no less! I want to laugh, so I just tuck my upper lip in and wait. He looks up and sees my expression.

"Yes, these flies. They get in everything, madam, no matter how hard I try! Even up-country. In Colombo you can expect such things, but here?" And he pulls down the corners of his mouth and looks disappointedly out the window. I follow his gaze. It is true. There is something about beautiful places like this where ordinary displeasures have no place. Or shouldn't. Ordinary things, like flies, and hunger, certainly not murder; some perpetual serenity ought to attend.

I nod in agreement. "*Eka thamai . . . ,*" I say, and he smiles.

"How many do you want, madam?" he asks, recalling me to the task. "These egg ones are twenty-five cents. They have green chilies. If you like I can give you plain ones with no chilies for twenty cents. I also have sambol ones; those are only ten cents."

"Three . . . four," I say, feeling hungry now. Hungry and determinedly alive. "The egg ones."

He shakes his head sideways at me. "One rupee then, madam." He wraps them in newspaper and gives them to me. I thank him and am already three steps away when he starts talking again.

"It's a terrible thing that happened, isn't it?" he says behind me, and I stop and turn to face him. "Did you hear, madam? About the accident? Whole family." He clucks his tongue, slack lips reaching down on either side. "Apparently the woman was having an affair with her husband's brother. Their uncle. Can you imagine? When the husband confronted her, she poisoned him and the children. They say she tied them all to the train tracks. At the last minute, must have felt bad, she flung herself under the train!"

And he spits in disgust. It is as if he is spitting at me.

I feel it evaporate, that comparison I had made so recently between this man and my father, my honorable father, who loved his wife and cared for his daughter and did the best he could. "Did you see them?" I ask.

"No, no, what to see? But I heard them talking. They said that's what the conductor told them when they asked."

"I saw them," I say, and my voice has recovered its former strength. "She was tied to the track along with the children. He had put poison in their drinks. He had taken their shoes off. He had tied his wife and children to the tracks. They were split open. It is *he* who did it. *He* killed them. She was just a young girl. They were little children."

He stares at me, confused by the anger that rises from my body, but he says something else, something unconnected to his lies. "Madam saw? Madam went to see the accident?"

"A mother would never do such a thing to her children."

"They let you see the bodies?"

His words have made me so angry that my hands are shaking. I put the parcel of buns back in his basket and I walk away. I don't need his poisonous food. Better that my children starve than that they eat the food of a fool, an ignorant, stupid man who will believe the worst a person can say about a woman they don't know.

When I reach our compartment, the children look up at me, eyes expectant. I shrug my shoulders and feel a keen twinge in my heart at their crestfallen faces. Still, I won't go back. Not even for my precious rupee. They leave me alone, the children, sensing my distress, and again I feel that prick inside me, for all the times they had to practice this art of becoming invisible because of my husband, because of me. I make an attempt to reach out to them, stroking their heads one by one, but they are unmoved. They glance back but turn just as swiftly to their own conversations, the sights outside the window, the hunger in their bellies reminding them to leave me behind and alone. I take a sip of the little thambili we have left and imagine what stories are being told of me in the village.

Everybody knew, of course. I wasn't the only woman there who had a lover, but I was the first who didn't care what people said, who didn't try to hide how I felt. I walked just as straight as I ever did, and I went to every public gathering that was held. To school, to meet the teachers, to market, to the well, to temple, and to observe Sil, to the Avurudhu festivals and to the weddings and funerals that took place during that year. I met Siri's eyes in the presence of other people; I smiled at him. When my husband was at sea, we even stood together as though we were the real family. They didn't like that, those women, but they admired me for doing it, even wanted to be friends with me, letting the power I so clearly felt creep into their bones too. The people who hated me for it were the men. No wonder they goaded my husband the way they did. They didn't want me to contaminate their women, that's what they said. Those men wanted lovers to remain sordid, affairs to be conducted underground, like their own with women at brothels and taverns and with the wives of their friends.

They called me a slut in my hearing. They muttered vile epithets under their breath when I walked by. They even tried to keep their children from mine. But I was too full of the beauty of what I loved for the children to stay away; they were perpetually in my house. They came with their mothers. What could those men do but try to end it all? And still, it was I who won. My round belly and lifted chin, the lack of any traces of sadness on my face even after all that blood and mayhem, and later the baby herself, so perfect, so innocent, so beautiful, these were my weapons. And while I wielded those weapons, I robbed them of their filthy words.

I wonder what they call me now. The usual slurs, but what more? The conductor had done so much damage to that woman in a matter of minutes. What other despicable history have they constructed about me in these past two days? I try to imagine it, but I cannot conceive of my life as anything less than it has been.

And here's the vendor before me as if in answer to my dilemma. "*Samawenna,* madam," he says, bending from his upper shoulders, his hunch accentuating the apology. "I'm an old man. I believe what people tell me." He holds out the package of food to me. "Here, your children must be hungry. It's close to eleven now."

He has left his basket unattended to look for me, and that touches my heart. The children look from his face to mine, waiting for permission. I nod.

Latha

For months after that fight, Thara did nothing but eat, Christmas and New Year and then the Sinhala New Year coming and going in a blur of food, food, and more food. She was constantly hungry. She ate mountains of string hoppers from the carryout joint on Jawatte, sending the driver out for three bundles all for herself. Every morning Latha had to boil eggs and make white curry and sambol for her strings. She ate fruits and *Chicken in a Biskit* from the boxes that had been bought for Madhavi as snacks and huge piles of rice and curries for lunch. In the evening the houseboy had to go and buy the vegetable rôti hot-hot from the saiwar kadé all the way near the cricket grounds so she could have them with tea. She demanded steamed bread every night for dinner, still warm from the bakery, and devoured at least half a loaf at each sitting. She did not serve Gehan, nor did she wait for him. She ate alone. And in that time, her voluptuous curves turned into matronly spreads.

Latha, the guilt of those unpinned belly wraps still prickling her conscience, felt duty bound to stop Thara's descent. Not only that, she had her own guilt to nurse. On the one hand, she felt vindicated by Thara's defense of her, of Gehan having clearly lost the battle to evict her from their home. That served him right, she thought, because in all his dealings with her, he had not given her any indication, not once, that he remembered their past. It served him right, then, to know that Thara cared more about her than she did about his feelings or the visits of his mother. On the other hand, she felt it only right that she repay Thara with some tangible gift, something to replace the regard she had lost from her husband at least in part on her, Latha's, account.

But in the end, she had to postpone her intervention because not long after the New Year, an opposition political leader, a relative of the Vithanages, was murdered at a rally and even Thara was moved to action and went to protest and mourn and came back haggard and shocked after the funeral procession, in which she was participating, was teargassed by the police. That meant that Latha had to spend days listening to her, comforting her, and agreeing with her that the whole country was a disaster because of the corrupt president and finding creative ways *not* to agree with her that the reason for his corruption was his fisher caste. Mercifully, he was killed too, just a week later, because by that time Latha had no more excuses left and felt that soon she would have to say yes, yes, his caste was the reason for his deviant and morally repugnant behavior, and she didn't want to do that. And although that second period of bedlam also had the effect of giving Thara reason to fret and fume, at the very least she seemed to gather in strength every time she could say, *"Bloody low-caste bastard, he had it coming,"* which she did quite regularly, particularly when Gehan was within earshot. And by the time things had died down and even Thara had stopped passing on all the ugly rumors and crude remarks about the dead man to her friends on the telephone and Gehan seemed no longer to care what she said about any caste at all, Latha was glad to be able to offer Thara something more uplifting than the timely death of her love-to-hate president.

Latha had known how things would play out when she told Thara about her meeting with Ajith. Of course she would want to know everything, all the details, from that logo on his shirt pocket to the leather of his sandals, the still-the-same questions that would come tumbling out of her unloved body and heart. What Latha hadn't anticipated were her own feelings: the strength of her motivation to help Thara, to effect her happiness. All she needed to see was the light unfurling inside her friend, from an ember so well hidden that it barely gave out any warmth at all until her mention of Ajith ignited it and warmed Thara from inside so she shone, from her eyes, from the suddenly girlish corners of her mouth, from the very tips of her fingers as they grabbed Latha's hands and squeezed them with excitement. It made Latha feel young again, too, and important in that youthfulness, a sensation so different and so satiating and quite unlike the responsibility, and therefore importance, she had as the de facto manager of a household. Yes, there was no reason to resist the tug of Thara's call for help. Who could be harmed?

She gave Thara an ultimatum: two months to make up for the damage she had done to her own body and mind, and then she would do it: she would get Ajith back for her. And when the months had passed and Thara had adhered to Latha's prescriptions for the entirety of it, all of it, including nothing but fruits and a single pol rôti and tea for breakfast, one cup of rice and only vegetable curries for lunch, and thambung hodi and plain bread without even *Astra* margarine for dinner, Latha did it. She strapped Madhayanthi into Madhavi's old pram, took Madhavi by the hand, and—dressed in the new green midi-skirt she had asked Thara's tailor's assistant to stitch for her, and the recently donated hand-me-down black cotton blouse from Thara, and her new open-toed sandals with a heel on them— she went back to the Independence Square Park for a walk.

Ajith was there, as he had been nearly every evening for the past year or so, and this time, unlike all those other evenings, Latha stopped in front of him without being asked. And he must have known that she finally had the news he'd been hoping for, because he stood up and there was a mixture of gladness and hope in his face that touched Latha, albeit fleetingly, and made her believe that even he could change.

"She wants to see you" is what Latha told him, requesting discretion with a glance toward each of the children.

"When? Where? I can come anywhere she wants," he said.

Latha unstrapped Madhayanthi and told Madhavi to take her sister to the rectangular ponds where the fountains were lit by colored lights. "Go and watch the water, my little pets," she said, "but don't lean over the sides. Madhavi Baba, look after your nangi, okay? I will watch from here. Hold her hand and go."

"Latha, come with us," Madhavi said, tugging at her hand, her eyes wide and clear as she looked up at Latha, though not with much expectation. "Latha, you have to stay with us. We're too small to go alone."

"I have to talk to this nice uncle, baba. Go, I will be right here," she said, unclasping the fingers that held hers, one by one, and then giving the whole hand a last kiss of apology. "Don't worry. I'll be watching."

"He's not a nice uncle, he's a bad uncle," Madhavi said, not looking at either of them; she took Madhayanthi's hand and walked away.

"Walk slowly, petiyo," Latha called after Madhavi. "Nangi can't walk that fast!"

Ajith laughed. "What a precocious child! Just like Thara!"

Of course he had it wrong. Madhavi was like her father; she objected to Ajith for reasons that were innocent in their clarity: he was preventing Latha from taking care of them. It was Madhayanthi who would be like Thara, that much was clear even now, when all she could say was "Amma," "Thāththa," "Latha," "Kolla," and, of course, "no," "can't," and "won't."

"Madhavi Baba is right," Latha said, frowning at Ajith, "but her mother thinks differently, so that's why I'm here talking to you. Thara Madam said she would meet you on Saturday at the Plaza in the coffee shop downstairs. She said nobody goes there anymore and Gehan and his friends will all be at the cricket match."

"What time?"

"In the morning, at about ten thirty," Latha said and, her work done, began to walk toward the children.

"I am in your debt, Latha . . . ," he said, his voice following her.

Latha shook her head. "You are indebted to her, not to me," she said over her shoulder.

"I just want to say—"

"For what purpose, to say anything after all this time?" Latha said, turning around fully and facing him to deliver her reprimand and to preempt the easy apology she knew was on his tongue, waiting to deliver him from his guilt. No, it was better that it be stopped before it could be uttered; apologies like his only passed over the insult of the original injury. She walked on, frowning now. There was something more she had wanted to say, but it hovered just out of reach of her vocal cords.

At the fountain, she watched the children for a while. She had dressed the girls especially well, matching their ribbons to their dresses, puffing up their cotton skirts. She took care with them every day, indeed, all day long; she wanted them to look the part of good children from a decent family, of course she did. But more than that, she wanted to teach them to care about how they looked, how they appeared to the world. She wanted them to learn the value of such things early, before they became corrupted by Thara's haphazard way of dressing, her mood sending her out either dressed to the nines or thrown together like the half-breed Lansi girls, careless and unkempt. No, that would never do for her girls. They had to learn that mood had nothing to do with presentation and that presentation was the foundation of everything.

There were many children near the fountain, and some, like her girls, clad as they were, stood out from the others. There was that air of goodness about them, the inner quiet that stemmed from the things they never had to miss in their lives, like three meals a day and school supplies and places to go to on holidays. Yes, an air of charity and calm well-being; but even she could see the most minuscule breach in the way Madhavi tugged her younger sister's hand just a little too firmly, in the slightly more frequent irritations that seemed to plague Madhayanthi. Latha tilted her head a little, remembering that same resentfully concerned feel of an older sibling's hand on her own. But when had that happened? Or where? There was only Leelakka to think of, and she had treated her with such gentleness. Latha could not have annoyed her if she had devoted herself to the task, and Leelakka would never have touched her roughly. Who, then, had held her hand that way?

Latha shook her head free from that faint thread of memory and sighed. It was nonsense, the stuff she made up to convince herself that she knew how to raise children. There was only this, these children, almost hers, hers, really. She should do more to keep them from the new miseries that had come to call with that one furious airing of all grievances between the Vithanages and the Pereras. So brief and vicious, as if both sides had known this would be their one chance. Yes, she should keep the kitchen free from penance and unhappiness for her girls. And then she remembered what she had meant to add. She looked back and was glad to see Ajith still standing by the stone foundation of the pillared monument to the country's independence.

"*Poddak inna,* Madhavi baba. Watch nangi for a little. I will go and come soon." She crossed the short distance to Ajith and spoke without preamble.

"You be good to Thara Madam," she said, "because she doesn't know whose baby I had, and I won't tell her unless I have to," and she stared at him until he dropped his gaze. "Do you understand?"

He looked up at her. "I understand. My fate is in your hands." He made a gesture with his right hand as he said that, waving his fist and opening it out, palm upward like he was begging for something.

"Her happiness is in yours. This time at least, don't forget that."

He didn't even have the decency to look ashamed. All he said was "You are in charge," and there was a trace of bitterness in his voice.

"Only if I have to be," she said. "If you make her unhappy one time, just one time, I won't hesitate."

"I wonder what that would do to her relationship with you," he said, and there was a cruel gleam in his eyes. "I wonder where you would go. Back to the estates?"

"I won't hesitate," she repeated and returned to the girls. Again, she watched them, but what she saw was herself and Thara, not that much older than Madhavi, five years old, perhaps, and playing at this same fountain, together. They had been brought here only once or twice; the Vithanages thought the whole place was a little vulgar— all those half-dressed joggers and couples fondling each other under umbrellas—except when it was used for state funerals for a national leader called N. M. Perera, whom she did not know but was told had been important enough to lie there in state when he died. But on those rare occasions, she remembered that she and Thara had stretched their arms out to each other, across the falling, colored water, and that they had been so young that they had had to reach out of their legs to touch each other, getting their dresses wet in the process. Their fingers had caressed and grasped, and they'd held on because, if they didn't, they had known, something bad would happen. And the bad they had imagined then was falling in, or falling away, nothing more.

Despite her having brought them about, even Latha was taken aback by how swiftly the new arrangements took root and held. There was a new script, and all three of them got comfortable with it as if they had always known that this was how things would go for them: Thara and Ajith as old lovers turned new, and Latha as the go-between, communicating times, dates, and places to Ajith, and delays, postponements, and cancellations to Thara. During that month of December, the two met so frequently that Latha was afraid they would be seen by some mutual acquaintance, or a relative, or a friend of a neighbor, and all would be lost. But it was Christmas season, and everybody was caught up in the madness of shiny things and love cake sold by the pound even on street corners in Nugegoda and Wellawatte, where Latha sometimes went with Thara. Nobody had time for idle people watching, and Thara and Ajith reaped the fruit of their negligence. They met at bus stops and parks and under umbrellas on the Mount Lavinia beach, at the last remaining cafés inside the formerly impressive plaza, and once even on a train, which they rode all along the seashore somewhere toward the South and back between the time Gehan left for work and the hour of his return.

"We went to Matara on the train," Thara said, coming back with hair sticky from the salt spray and sweat of public transport, but flushed with pride as if she had conquered some new territory, which, in a way, Latha thought, she had. "We didn't even get down to the water when we got there, even though the beaches looked so nice. We decided to go back another time. To spend the day."

"When?" Latha asked, alarmed at the thought of lying to Gehan about an overnight absence.

"I don't know when, but someday. I think if we got up early and went then we could be back before dark, or maybe even a little later. You can say I went to dinner with someone; Mahaththaya will believe anything you tell him about me," Thara said, laughing at her gullible husband, which made Latha regret her culpability in getting Thara started down this road in the first place. Now, the more she lied to Gehan, the more she sympathized with him, seeing not the set of his features against any intimacy with her but rather his solid loyalty to Thara, his wife.

After the first rush, though, and to Latha's relief, they settled into a calmer routine of meeting once a week, sometimes only once every two weeks. Either way, Thara was blissfully happy, and though Latha hoped that Thara's newfound elation would infect her with some deeper maternal feeling toward her children, so far, nearly a year later, there had been no evidence of that. Thara's happiness was invested only in herself, and so, while Madhavi was at the Montessori school, Latha's job became to carry Madhayanthi around and accompany Thara to *Janet's* beauty salon for manicures and pedicures and threading her eyebrows, and on shopping trips to *Daffy's* and *NeXt* and the glass monstrosity called the *Palace of Fashion,* which had no dressing rooms and only male attendants, who in appearance and size and demeanor (not to mention their dull green uniforms), looked like an army of emaciated, heads-cast-down robots. Everybody in town shopped there, including foreigners, because of the prices. It was the great equalizer. It seemed only fitting, therefore, that they would meet Gehan's mother there, for the first time since the fight.

"Āchchi!" Madhayanthi said, taking her fingers out of her mouth to point excitedly at Mrs. Perera, who, dressed in a dark gray and blue sari, was taking the stairs up to the floor they were on, stopping every third step to catch her breath.

Mrs. Perera looked up and caught sight of them. Her mouth pursed and she looked away, holding on to the railing and not moving any farther.

"Āchcheee!" Madhayanthi yelled and tried to leap out of Latha's arms.

"Chooti Baba, you will fall! Here, I'll put you down, and we can go and see Āchchi," Latha said, not knowing what else to do in such a public place. She put Madhayanthi down, and the child toddled a little ways, still holding on to Latha's fingers.

"We're not going down to that Padhu woman," Thara said.

Latha did not think that the Pereras were Padhu, or Karā or Berava or any other caste that she had heard mentioned with this same bite by Mrs. Vithanage and now Thara, only that Mrs. Perera had spat at her, and dishonored Mr. Vithanage, and that these two things made her a worthless human being. Thara abandoned Latha. One second she was next to her, the next she was absorbed by the crowds and sucked into the Women's Dresses section. Latha would have liked to follow, but Madhayanthi was tugging at her hand.

"Come, Latha! Come!" she was saying, her eyes on the grand-mother she and her sister were taken to see, religiously, every other Saturday by her father (which meant, usually, that Thara was free to see Ajith and Latha free to drink lime juice with the houseboy). She clung to and pulled at Latha's fingers.

What could Latha do? She picked up the child and started walk-ing down the steps, protecting Madhayanthi from the elbows and bags and umbrellas of the other shoppers. Mrs. Perera was waiting.

"Come here, darling!" she said, opening her arms to Madhayan-thi, who leaped out of Latha's arms and into the soft folds of the older woman. Latha felt considerably irritated by this. Madhavi would never have done such a thing, she said to herself; she had sec-ond sight. She knew what was what, that little girl. Not wanting to participate in their affection-filled meeting, she held on to the rail-ing and looked around at the shoppers while Mrs. Perera cooed and cuddled Madhayanthi.

From where she stood on the curve of the wide spiral staircase, Latha could see hundreds of black heads, dotted here and there by colored ones from abroad. Red, yellow, light brown, even painted heads. One looked up at her: a brown-haired man with dark eyes; his smile was so wide she was sure it was meant for someone he was well acquainted with. She looked around her, then glanced back at the man. He was still smiling, and this time he waved. Mrs. Perera must have been watching because she muttered something about *Rodi* whores who were just the type to lick the arses of the *Suddhas,* and about mistresses who allowed their servants to dress like the lady of the house. Out of spite, Latha let an initial no-teeth smile blossom into her chin-dimpling, three-cornered grin at the man. Gehan had once commented upon that smile, and how endearing it was to him. But she had been just a girl then, and thought her smile was controlled by him, not naturally hers. Now, she knew better. She smiled, and then she waved, surreptitiously, with her arms still at her sides, so Mrs. Perera wouldn't see it. The man laughed and gestured for her to come downstairs. No, she said, with her head, but smiled again.

Latha looked away from him to see if Mrs. Perera had noticed. She had not. She continued to talk to Madhayanthi at her side. When she looked down again, Latha was disappointed to see that the man had disappeared. It had given her a quick thrill, that look of appreciation, even from a foreign man. Of course other men looked at her, but that was different. Those men belonged to the group Mrs. Vithanage disparagingly referred to as the Servant Class. They were hired help, drivers, day laborers, vendors at the butcher shops and markets where she went to buy provisions with the houseboy. Gehan had been her sole exception; the only equal, in her mind, who had paid her any sustained attention, who had known her for more than what she did for room and board. And Ajith, she didn't know what it was that he had told himself, but over the years she had a story to fit that year of madness, one that excused him as best as she could, if for no other reason than that Thara saw something in him to love: he had wanted to know a woman sexually and she had been vengeful enough to be that girl. The simple truth was that they had both been too young to think about each other.

Now, Gehan's friends—never Gehan—would look her up and down when she poured water for them, served them a cup of tea, or cleared the dishes, but those looks never rose to the level of true admiration. They were the disappointed if-only variety; if only she wasn't a mere servant. The admiring kind was what she had once got from Gehan and, fleeting though it might have been, from the foreigner. She straightened up, happy that she had stuck to her guns when it came to her attire. No wonder the foreigner had given wing to his approval of her, of her motherhood. She would never dress like a servant.

She could spot servants from a mile away. There were several right here: they wore shabby clothes that were clearly hand-me-downs or, if they were new, in a cut that simply aped a current style but did not suit them: ankle-grazing dresses on short, stubby women, tight printed T-shirts on chesty ones in colors not picked up by their skirts; they wore *Bata* slippers or sandals that did not match their clothing; their hair was bunched together and frizzy; they didn't smell fresh like she did; there was no mistaking the servility in their manner. Latha smiled to herself, feeling particularly lovely in her calf-length denim skirt, the pin-tucked white cotton blouse, her brown sandals. She felt the soft edges of her hair hanging long and loose down her back, and readjusted the coconut-shell hair grip with its matching pin, which kept the front from falling over her face. She touched her earlobes. She looked regally around at the crowds, thinking of Leelakka, how she had promised her that she would shine again when she was back in the city. Somewhere in the future there was a life beyond all this for her. She was absolutely certain of that.

Mrs. Perera broke into her daydream.

"Let's go and find this poor child's mother. God knows what *she* is up to."

"Thara Madam is shopping for clothes in the women's section. I can take Chooti Baba to her," Latha said, knowing that Thara had no intention of making this pleasant for anybody, even in the presence of her daughter.

Mrs. Perera snorted. "Clothes? What for? In my day we stopped shopping for clothes after we got married. After that we only shopped for our husbands and children and the servants at New Year. But what can you expect from her type . . ." And she blew another audible gust of air out of her nose.

"Thara Madam has very important functions to go to," Latha said. "She has to be properly dressed for these things, that's why."

"Functions? How can she have functions now that she doesn't even work?" Mrs. Perera said. All her comments were to the air on either side of Latha's head, not directly to her. It was as though Latha was a visible apparition sent to save her from the embarrassment of talking loudly to herself.

"Thara Madam is a secretary now at the Old Girls' Club at her school, and she is an important lady at the Colombo Tennis Club and at the Lionel Theater, too," Latha told her, trying to make those activities sound as dignified as she could. She wished she knew what duties were attached to such memberships. She made a mental note to ask Thara when they got back in the car.

Mrs. Perera sniffed. "Darling, go with the woman to Amma, okay?"

"Āchchi come," Madhayanthi said, taking one hand in each of hers, Latha's in her left, Mrs. Perera's in her right. Latha was glad that Madhayanthi's vocabulary presented slim pickings for the child; even these monosyllabic words created such emotional quagmires for the adults in her life.

"Āchchi has to go, darling. I have to get a nice present for Seeya. You go with the woman," Mrs. Perera said and tried to move down the staircase. Madhayanthi's mouth turned down. Latha panicked. Unlike Madhavi, who had inherited Gehan's equanimity and careful grace, or those aspects that he had possessed as a teenage boy who had befriended and loved a servant girl, Madhayanthi was fully equipped with Thara's sense of entitlement, as well as the wiles to ensure that things turned out her way.

"Chooti Baba," Latha said, her voice syrupy, all treacle, singsong, up and down, the whole works, "Āchchi has to go and buy you a big teddy bear from downstairs so next time when you go to visit her you'll have a surprise, so we must let her go now, okay?"

Madhayanthi, her head hanging down, bit her finger, then let her eyelids open to reveal a mischievous delight. "Baba go Latha," she said, letting go of Mrs. Perera.

Latha felt glad at the look on Mrs. Perera's face. It was written, clear as day: drama had been averted, as had confrontations, thus thwarting what might have been a solid victory for Mrs. Perera, and in a public place; not only that but now she had to buy a big, no, *beeeg!* teddy bear. It was perfect. Latha hid her smile as she walked up the stairway, glad also to be walking up, and therefore turning her rear to Mrs. Perera, who was, as she had expected, standing there, waiting for them to be out of sight before continuing her own journey up to the third or fourth floor. Latha crossed her feet in front of her as she climbed like she had seen women do on television ads, ensuring the widest sway to her bottom.

Latha hoped that Thara had not strayed too far. It was madness trying to locate anybody in the chaos of the *Palace*. The only hope was that kindred spirits would find themselves drawn to the same fare. She found herself heading toward the pretty sets of underwear vulgarly displayed for all to see on a wall of racks. There were several men idling within sight. Perverts. She tried to examine the various bras without them being able to derive any pleasure from seeing which ones drew her attention. Madhayanthi stood beside her and pulled at the panties that were at her level.

The colors! If she could, Latha thought, she would exchange all her underwear for the ones on these walls; but the prices, even on sale at a bargain shop like this, were still too high for her. Seventy-five rupees for a pair of panties, 125 for a bra, or 175 for a set. Perhaps she could afford one this time. She chewed on her lip and debated between a deep purple set and a pale blue one. The purple had a plunging center and hooked in the middle, a version of the bra that she had never experienced, though she had observed on a number of occasions how that model accentuated Thara's cleavage. The pale blue made her feel virginal and holy, and she couldn't put her finger on that until she remembered Leelakka and her chaste life conducted entirely robed in a shade of that color. Of course, having remembered that, she could hardly buy the blue; she'd feel like she was committing some sort of sibling-related sacrilege. She extracted the purple set in a size that seemed about right—at the Palace the only recourse was to duck behind a friend or preferably a group of friends when it came to trying on things like bras—and turned to go on with her search.

There behind her was the man with the dark brown hair who had waved at her.

"Hello," he said, before she could even wonder about his presence. "I came looking for you."

How bold. And not on the fringes, like those other men with their trousers held up with huge belted buckles over their small waists, but in blue jeans and an untucked cotton shirt right inside the women's underwear section! Still, he seemed entirely unaffected by the wares that surrounded them on all sides. He could have been at a fruit stand, or a Sunday market with lots of leafy greens that he might say were good for one's health. He looked like the healthy sort. She imagined that he might drink thambili each morning and have ambul plantains and definitely did not smoke. Yet there had to be a vice in which he indulged himself; every man did. All this passed through Latha's head, along with the fact that his eyes, though dark, were not black as she'd assumed, but a blue so deep they looked like the *Gentian Violet* that turned purple over cuts and bruises.

"My name is Daniel," he said. And he stretched out his hand.

Well, what was she supposed to do? In one hand she held Madhayanthi close to her, in the other a set of lacy purple underwear. He finally looked down and saw both the child and the garments.

"Oh," he said and laughed. What an oddly happy man. He had so much to smile about. She wondered what he did with his time that he seemed so easily given to merriment. "Is this your daughter?" He talked like the men on the *ITN* program called *Sesame Street,* which came on at 5:00 PM on Tuesdays at home, so that meant he was probably American. Maybe it was being American. All the American people on that TV program seemed happy too. And usually without any cause that she could figure out, even though she watched it every week with the children.

"No," she said, correcting his mistake, her heart beating fast, "not my daughter." She said the words but drew Madhayanthi closer to her as she spoke as if to belie the fact.

"Oh," he said, and smiled again, then reached over and patted Madhayanthi's head. "She is a cute kid."

"Cute kid," she repeated and nodded. "My friend's daughter," she added.

"You shopping with your friend?" he asked and glanced about, over her shoulder, behind him, as if his gestures would help translate the question for her. She almost smiled.

"Yes." She found herself looking everywhere but at this man who seemed to think nothing of staring straight at her face as though they were lovers. It was not that she disliked the implication of such intimacy; far from it. She felt giddy at this confirmation of her appearance. It was just that it seemed inappropriate in the presence of a small child and with a purple bra and panties in her hand, not to mention the bulging assortment of other bras and panties arrayed about them in all the colors of the rainbow.

"What's your name?" he asked.

"My name is Latha," she said.

"Oh, Latha means 'girl'!" he said and laughed again. "See? I'm learning Sinhala and I'm quite good at it."

She doubted that. He probably added *ekak* to the ends of his English words and deluded himself into thinking he spoke the language because everybody understood. That's what Thara had told her the Americans at her old job used to do when she still worked among all that bathtub equipment that nobody wanted to buy in their hot country.

"Girl *ekak*," he said. "See? A girl!" He raised his eyebrows, waiting for applause.

"That means one of a girl," she said. "To say 'a girl,' or 'girl child,' you have to say *lathava,* or *kellek,* or *gehenu lamayek.* That is most respectful, especially if you don't know the girl." She felt pleased with herself. Some of the men outside their area were staring at her, some women too. She was talking with a foreigner as if she did this every day, not as if this was her first time.

"Girl child! You look like a girl child," he said, nodding enthusiastically and raising his eyebrows again. They were bushy and dark and very expressive.

She smiled, no teeth. She wasn't a girl child, no matter what her name implied.

He shook his head. "See? I have even learned how to do that thing people do here, saying yes like you're saying no. This is it, right?"

Latha stared at him. Instead of the delicate side-to-side move that could convey everything from "Yes, I'll do it" to "Oh, I understand," he looked like a man with an elastic neck, his face thrusting in all directions as though he was possessed. She laughed out loud, then stopped. A smile escaped.

"You have a beautiful smile."

Her smile broadened into the grin she knew he was waiting for, staring at her mouth. She was rewarded by that laugh again. She sighed. This was all very well, and it had been nice to be singled out in this way by a respectable man, albeit a foreign one, but she had to get back to Thara. Odd that they hadn't found each other in this section. She had been sure Thara would be there.

"I have to go now," she said.

"Oh, that's too bad," he said, and his mouth turned down even though he did not look sad.

Well, what did he expect? That she would pick up a small child and walk out with him into the burning sunlight? Perhaps go off to *Gillo's* in a scooter taxi for an ice cream sundae that cost three quarters of her monthly salary? That's what Thara and Ajith did sometimes. They went to *Gillo's* and ate things called pizza and sundaes that Thara swore were the best food she'd ever tasted, which was absurd because how could anything taste good at that price?

"I could take you to *Gillo's*," he said, cocking his head.

"I must find my friend now," she said. "I must go." But she didn't know how to take leave of a foreigner. It seemed unlikely that he would understand the meaning of the glances, the backward looks, the hidden smiles that were her native language and worked on local men like Gehan. That made her feel crestfallen. Not that he didn't understand, this man called Daniel, but that Gehan had once treasured those moments of parting with her and now barely looked at her at all. His voice made her look up again.

"Don't look sad," the foreign man was saying. He took out a smooth brown purse from his pocket and extracted a card. "Here, this is my number. Call me anytime and I will come and meet you." He reached for her hand and she dropped the underwear. He closed her fingers over the card, then squeezed her fist in both of his palms. He had big, warm hands. She had never been in the presence of such enormous hands, let alone been held by them. Her own hand felt protected and threatened at the same time. And her skin! How dark she was!

"Anywhere at all," he added and was gone.

Latha stooped and picked up the underwear, gave it to Madhayan-thi to hold. Then she looked down at the card: *Daniel Katzen-Jones, Public Relations Specialist, WB Asia. 581914.*

Biso

My head hurts. I reach into my handbag for a *Disprin,* but my fingers find the piece of paper from the gentleman instead. I unfurl it: *"Don Mohan Victor Vithanage."* I wish he were still sitting here, on this train, across from me. I don't need his help, just his presence. He had a solid presence, that gentleman, tired though he seemed, and solidity is what I need now. The events of the past hour or two have shaken my faith in our future, my children's and mine. How can this mass murder, the suicide, these things, be anything but bad omens? But what message they carry for me I cannot discern. I unfurl and close, unfurl and close the paper. I wonder if we would be safer if I asked Mr. Vithanage for help. There is his phone number: *"871101."* But what would I say? I rub my fingers over the numbers, wondering how long it will take for him to reach Colombo after he finishes his visits. I don't remember what he said. Was he leaving for home in a week or two weeks? Two weeks, I think he said that. I feel even more anxious. Why hadn't I paid attention? A woman alone, with three children to look after, I should have listened to his offer when he made it, if for no reason than to reserve that option for another day.

"Amma, what is that?" Chooti Duwa asks, next to me, touching the paper. Loku Putha turns his attention to us at the sound of her voice, or perhaps my silence, and finally all three are staring at me. They can tell that I am not as sure as I was when we left. I can see it in their eyes: they have withdrawn some of their faith in my promise of change, of a better life. They may even welcome the intervention of someone more confident, more capable than I probably seem to them now.

"What is that?" my son asks this time.

"The gentleman gave me his phone number in case we needed help," I say. I watch his eyes narrow, so slightly, some memory of Siri filling them up, making him judge me for the past, for making it impossible for him to love his own father, for this present; so I add, "But I told him we don't need any help. We'll be at my aunt's soon."

They turn away from me, one by one, and I tuck the piece of paper into my sari blouse, inside my bra, hiding it from them. Having uttered the words, I am suddenly surer of it: yes, we will be all right.

But not yet.

The train has been creeping through a tunnel as if in mournful regret, or in anticipation of further tragedies. It has seemed tired, and, as a result, the few passengers left seem weary too. Maybe the slowness of the train prompted them to pick it as a possible candidate, or maybe they had simply been waiting for it. The train is stopped, and it fills from end to end with police. I have never seen so many in one place. And I have never seen any who look quite as grim and ruthless as these.

"Get up! Get up! Everybody out of the train!"

And once again, I am back on the shores of Matara, the salt air and the dark skies, the night lit by a single kerosene lamp, listening to Siri talk, his friends talk. I am standing on the fringes of their impassioned circle and letting their words enter my body through each willing pore of my skin, learning their fear, repeating it, memorizing it by heart. I can see again the welts on Siri's back and on the undersides of his knees, his calves, where the police had beaten him. For nothing. He had done nothing and they had beaten him, screaming, he told me, screaming so loud and asking questions for which he had no answers. It was the police who turned him quiet, who put a stop to those meetings by the boats, who took his friends from him, who ended the life of the one priest I had felt was not better than I was but simply a human like me, searching for some closer truth.

"Amma! What is happening?" My little one asks me this, but I am too frightened to think, to answer. All I want is to get off the train with my children. Together. Having lived through these past years, having attended the funerals I have, the ones with and without a body to mourn, I know not to get in the way of the police. Sensing my distress, Loku Putha steps forward.

"Let's get down," he says. "We'll find out after we get down!" He hustles Chooti Duwa in front of him. Loku Duwa follows in her usual manner, neither concerned nor unperturbed but something in between, perpetually waiting to be told which emotion to express.

I bend down to pick up our bags, but a policeman raps a baton on the handle of the larger one. "Leave it." And then, maybe because I look sufficiently harmless or perhaps deserving of a little respect, his voice softens and he says, "We're checking the train. We need to check all the bags. There's a rumor of a bomb."

I am so taken aback that I forget my caution and engage him instead. "On this train?" I ask, amazed. "A bomb? Why would someone put a bomb on this train?"

"Hurry up and get down," he says, and I am surprised at the sudden change in his tone. So harsh and inconsiderate, this man who could be a brother or a cousin. He averts his gaze and glances at someone behind me. I look back as I follow the children and see a man with many medals and a grand hat, some superior officer, staring at us. I shake my head sideways in understanding and agreement and conciliation, whatever it is they want from me, I make sure all three are apparent in that one gesture. I hurry down the aisle between the seats. My Loku Putha is waiting to help me get down off the train. I don't need his help, and his offer makes me feel old, and sad.

I hesitate for a moment on the lowest rung, contemplating the scene. There is nowhere to stand, really, but the slight rise of green beside the tracks and the soft red earth of the hill, which seems about to reclaim its connection to the rest of the earth across the railway lines. If no trains passed in a week, it seems, the two sides would merge and be one again, a steel track running inside the heart of the mountain, unused.

Outside, I linger apart from the others who have dismounted. There are about twenty to thirty of us left now, including our family. We all move with the same slow manner of disbelieving mourners. But I feel different from them. For one thing, I'm the only woman in a Kandyan sari; the others all wear theirs like the women on the estates. There are only two other children: the one who had pushed past me that time when I went searching for food and an infant in the arms of a small, newly rounded woman. Her husband hovers close, a rattan basket, filled with baby-related things that the police have not taken from him, in his hand. I suppose they decided that nobody would plant a bomb near a young family like that.

Someone must have given us directions to move on, because now I see that there is some movement toward the front of the train. "Come," I say to the children, "we should start walking along with the rest."

"Amma, I heard that man say that there's a bomb on the train," my son says to me.

"Which man?" I ask, buying time. I breathe slowly, trying to still the thudding of my heart.

He points to the man who had helped me earlier, the one with whom I'd walked toward those bodies, not knowing, and who had helped me back to my children afterward. "That one." He is a little farther along the straggling line that has formed and that we are yet to join.

Loku Duwa asks, "Will our train blow up? How will we get to their house then?"

The little one starts to cry and curls herself into the fall of my sari. I unwrap her and pick her up. She is so light in my arms still. She tucks her face into my neck and lies there, and there is no sound, but I feel the tears slide down my neck. I stroke her hair and kiss her, breathing in the smell of *Pears* baby soap, coconut oil, and an assortment of sweet things: pineapple, bombai mutai, chocolate, and bread.

I coat my voice with the ineffable calm that they need from me now. "They think someone may have left a bomb on the train and got off, but that doesn't mean there is one. They just have to check, that is all."

"How do they know?" Loku Duwa asks.

"Someone gave them a tip," says her brother. "That's what he said."

Chooti Duwa perks up in my arms and wriggles to be set free. I let her go, reluctant to lose the weight of her, those perfumes.

"Aiyya, what's a tip?" she asks.

"When someone tells the police about something bad before it happens," he says, "that's what they call a tip."

She mouths the new word over and over, rocking back and forth on her feet, seemingly unconcerned with the subject of the tip, the bomb, more enamored now with the notion of secrets. How quickly young children reset their realities. And how quickly they lose the ability to do that. My son, I can tell, has almost given up the habit entirely, and again I feel sad. For not having been wiser, stronger, more courageous, for not having made this same choice when he was still not old enough to understand. Surely it was just as possible then as it is now. What had I waited for? I had always known that there would be no change in our circumstances. Not before Siri, but especially not after, and even less so with his death. And still, I had waited. The first year I was preoccupied with tending to my pregnancy, the free will that she, my unborn daughter, represented to me. Then, I had to keep her safe until she was strong enough to walk, to speak to me. But why had I continued to wait, even after that?

I shake my head at my own foolishness. I had waited until the last fight. The one where he threatened to kill me in my sleep and send my bastard child—that's what he'd called her—to the hotel owner's house to be a servant. Those coarse hands gripping my arms, pinching the skin, that voice, slurred with drink and hatred in my ear.

"You know, that large house, with so many people for her to cook and clean for? Where they would beat her, like this, like this, like this . . . you hear me?"

I had resisted shouting because I never wanted to wake my children up. I always tried to keep it quiet so they would think it was not so bad, only bad enough to wake up, not so bad that they had to come and see, see this, the ripping and tearing, the struggles, the flailings, the arms over my face, the feet kicking.

"That place . . . where when she is old enough, you know what they will do to her. What they always do to all the girls who come to work there . . ."

And I had screamed then and not stopped despite the beating, despite the fists on my face, despite the glimpses I had of my children appearing and disappearing at the doorway, their fearful faces, their impotent presence. I had screamed until she flew into the room propelled by her love for me, some instinct, also, for her own survival, her fingers clawing at the beast, screaming in her little girl voice, *Get off my mother! Get off her!* and all the rest of the words I don't know where she had heard or learned or known to keep hidden until then. Those words just before I saw it: the sight of her body hurled so effortlessly across the room, the sound of it hitting the wall, her silence.

Why had I waited for that? Hadn't I known it would come? He had watched me without expression when I picked her up off the floor and ran all the way to the dispensary, not caring how I looked, not caring that my older children trailed behind, my Loku Duwa whimpering now and again. As soon as her stitches were taken out, we would leave, I had told them. But I had waited longer, waited for her hair to grow back, for the scar to heal and become a smooth ridge under my searching fingers, my guilt looking for it on her head each night until she learned to fall asleep to that touch, for her birthday to draw near and then pass. For a final visit to our temple . . .

My son's voice again. "Amma, look! They're taking all the bags . . ." And then, there's an explosion. A sound that is a boom more than an eruption, held in and made doubly loud by the echoing hills. Once more I am surrounded by screaming people, and I can't tell which came first, the screams or the blast. I scoop up my Chooti Duwa, and we start running now, behind the others who have a head start on us, along the tracks toward the front engine. I look back and see the center of the train shatter outward, almost like fireworks, colored chips flying everywhere. I picture lettered metal wedging itself into that yielding earth. I picture scars left. And twisted seats and dead bodies. But no, there can be no dead bodies; we all got off the train! A sudden happiness darts across my chest. All this passes so quickly through my mind, in the time it takes to catch up to the other passengers, to keep pace until we arrive in the blessed openness beyond the engine, to the train tracks, which afford us all a clean platform for our feet.

The police run toward the center of the train, to the shattered tracks and debris from the innards of the crushed compartments. Through the smoke I see them carry a few people out; they seem to be alive, still. I shade my eyes and try to focus on the activity, but nothing more is clear. Just that there are injured people, that the train is spewing smoke and now, suddenly, as if in a rage of its own, gusts of fire. The policemen step away from the train, blown back by the heat and intensity of the flames. The captain in the hat with all those badges shouts something, and two policemen run part of the way toward us, waving their arms and yelling. I can't hear the words, but I join the crowd when everybody turns and continues their journey farther down the track and away from the front of the train, too, where we had gathered.

Nobody seems to know what we should do, but eventually our steps become slower until we're simply shifting from foot to foot, looking back at the train. I listen to the outraged hiss of water touching fire as the policemen pass buckets of water to one another down an oddly, given the circumstances, orderly line stretching from the blast site back along the train and over the hill to some unseen spring. I picture a hose such as I had seen along the tracks in some places, reaching down through time-thickened trunks of tall trees and low bushes to spill clear and icy mountain water onto flat slabs of rock where travelers perch to catch it, their skirts, saris, and sarongs clenched between their knees. I feel thirsty. Unbearably thirsty. I swallow spit, but it is thick and unsatisfactory.

Around me, the crowd is settling. We look at one another and then away, eavesdrop on discussions, contribute a word or two, and slowly become united in the way people do at scenes such as this: bomb blasts, accidents, a hanging suicide in the village. We become a joint entity, a single family. There is a sort of solace in these measures we take; someone holds her baby for a moment to relieve the new mother when the father walks away for a brief absence and returns with a sheepish smile, which tells us all that somewhere in that sun-dried grass along the track is a patch of wet grass. Other men nod and smile at him, then drift away themselves. The older women exchange glances that communicate their feelings about relieving themselves in public, perhaps their wish that they could, too. I join them in the quick succor we gain from strangers, in our trust that when disaster strikes, we are all family. Someone brings out a packet of *Marie* biscuits and passes it around. Again, the older women decline, and the young people eat. My children are delighted, and, noticing their smiles, the man who helped me before gives his two biscuits to my girls.

"Putha," I say, "do you know what will happen now, son?"

He shrugs. "No. I think the police will get our names down and then we'll have to wait and see what they want us to do. The tracks are going to be blocked, so there won't be any other trains coming this way for the rest of the day. By tomorrow morning, probably. Sometimes they use the same track to run the trains both ways, but I don't know if they will do that this time, with the bomb—"

"Then how will I . . . how will we get out of here?" I ask, panic setting in.

"Don't give it too much thought. They will tell us what to do," he says, gesturing with his head at the police. But then he looks at each of my children, and he purses his mouth, contemplating my predicament; his lack of hope is palpable.

I turn to the train. It looks like a stopped animal, a wounded one. If it could, I imagine that it would be screaming some discordant howl aimed down the tracks toward where we stand. I half-wish that I could make that sound on its behalf, this train that had been my hope. My fingers, fiddling with the back of my neck, brush against my earlobes, and the absence of my earrings reminds me of the pregnant girl. How simple that moment had been, in retrospect: a meeting, our conversations, the exchanging of confidences, a brief wait, an arrival, and then that parting. How gracious and perfect. I had thought it monstrous that a pregnant woman, just recently a child herself, had to be delivered to a nun, had to go, motherless and afraid, trusting in the grace of a half-woman. And yet I would exchange the rest of my journey to walk within the comfort of that woman's care, my children and I, headed somewhere clean and quiet and peaceful. Hatton. Almost seven stations before this. How would we ever get there? Certainly not by train. I sigh. I reach into my blouse and look at the paper with the name and number on it, the only thing I have from the train. Pattipola, surely, is not that far off by road, barely a single station. Perhaps I can find the gentleman there. But where would I look for him? The number I have is for a home in Colombo, and he won't be there for another two weeks. Family is better, surely. I look down the opposite side of the tracks, away from the train, pointing myself in the direction in which I should be going, toward my aunt's house.

A policeman comes over to us with a notebook and fountain pen. "I need to take down your names and addresses," he says, and he sounds as though he is in control. Immediately everybody clusters around him and asks questions. Some of the men demand answers. "Back away!" he yells, finally. "One at a time. I can't do this if all of you talk at once."

They all move away, and, as should be the order of things, the young mother comes first, followed by the oldest men and women. I count myself among that latter group though my hair is untouched by gray, and I am not yet thirty years of age. I ignore the sideways glances that judge me as an upstart, an opportunist, for clutching my three children to me as I step forward and claim the rare perks of age, for surely I have earned the additional years through the hardships I have endured. Those waiting their turn murmur to one another about the strikes and the political disquiet they have all experienced in their lives. As usual, the most bitter remarks are reserved for the government, which has neglected the railways.

"Name?" the policeman asks brusquely when I get to the front.

"Dissanayake Appuhamilage Biso Menike," I say, "but I'm known as Biso."

"Is that your married name?"

"No, rālahamy, that is my given name." I hope the deferential title will save me from having to say more, but I am wrong.

"What is your *current* name? That is what we need." His impatience is like a slap.

"Biso. The children's father's name was Samarakoon. Daya Samarakoon."

"Then your married name was Biso Menike Samarakoon. All right," he says, shaking his head from side to side, accepting this answer and expressing his sympathy at the same time. Next to my name he writes, within brackets, "husband, Daya Samarakoon, deceased." I am glad that even my son is too short to see what has been written. But I smile and give the rest of my responses with speed and accuracy: my children's names, and then my aunt's address as my own.

Latha

At first, Latha was amused by Daniel's fascination with her stories of her family. She was an orphan who could not vouch for any reality that had ever contained a mother or a father; she had a sister she told him was at a convent she had visited only once and wouldn't be able to find again on her own; she had another sister with whom she lived, but she would not say where. Besides these unusual declarations, she had other, more practical, limitations on what she could give him: she decided when she could see him, she would not accompany him to public places, and she could never stay the night. She chalked it up to his nationality that he could tolerate these restrictions. No local man would have; jealousy would have outed her lies, the questions would have been relentless. Daniel was truly fond of her, she thought. That, or Daniel felt no jealousy, which was not a possibility she truly wished to entertain, since it reflected not so much on him but on her own desirability.

She sometimes wondered if she should tell him how her life beat a path bordered by the doings of the Vithanages and the Pereras, but he never inspired her to go that far. Far enough to risk losing this chance to be someone unfettered from her present circumstances. Furthermore, the more captivated he became with the mystery that she seemed to be, the less likely it was that she would ever tell him the truth. His lack of probing wasn't a burden to Latha. He was a good host, a happy lover, and he made her forget that she was still a servant and, worse, that she was Gehan's servant. And, it was particularly disarming to make herself comfortable in a house that had no servants at all.

"They had a servant all lined up for me when I got here," he had told her the first time she came, apologizing for the rather weak tea he brewed for her, and repeating everything many times, and slowly, so she could understand. "But that was very awkward for me, so I told them that I didn't want her. Then they brought a man, but that was just as bad. So, finally, they let me be. Now I just have the driver, and he doesn't stay here. I have the place all to myself."

He had spread his arms wide and turned around in a slow circle as if inviting the room to dispute his claim. Latha had said nothing, only crossed her legs the way she had seen Thara and her friends do, trying to feel comfortable in the brocade-covered, cushioned chair into which she had sunk, hoping that she looked appropriately delighted with his choice to fend for himself in the domestic arena. It had been hard to both concentrate on creating the right impression and stop wondering if he could tell that she looked out of place among his furnishings.

But her fears had disappeared more quickly than she could have imagined. She grew to like the thick curtains that shut out the sun, and the array of soft-bulbed lamps that made the interior glow in a way that changed time so that sometimes she was surprised that it was one or two o'clock in the afternoon when she opened the doors to go back home, not late at night. It was magical and so unlike the naked sixty-watt bulb that swung from a single rope in the middle of her room; she resolved to get herself a lamp someday, something to re-create the particular lack of urgency of Daniel's rooms. She enjoyed gazing at the huge black-and-white photographs of foreign places in the hallways. She liked to touch the cold stone of the sculptures he had sprinkled throughout his house, some mounted on steel posts, some leaning against bookshelves and, in some cases, books, which she forgave, though it meant that the books were clearly never read, and that seemed like a waste of money and space, because they were so beautiful.

But among the things she learned to like, there was one thing about Daniel's home that she loved: its colors. He had bright tapestries that hung from the ceiling to the floor in his bedroom and behind the settees in his living room. And his bed was a mattress with dark blue coverings centered over a brilliant orange carpet that looked like it was on fire when he turned the lamps on. She liked to lie there by herself, letting the color enter her body and light her up.

On those days that she was allowed to be alone in that bed, which usually happened only when Daniel made phone calls abroad and typed on something called a computer, when she could gather those colors inside her, she left him and went home in great spirits. She would stop to buy chocolates for the children, including the house-boy, who came running to her and always reached her before her girls but who always stopped short and put his hands behind his back though she could tell that he, too, wanted to dig through her bag the way they did, looking for treats. Sometimes, she would hide an extra sweet for him, young as he was, just eight years old, just so she could watch his delight. She would feel virtuous and motherly, and that feeling would erase any doubts she had about conducting her secret life and lying to Thara, and keeping the truth from Daniel.

The first time she dialed the number for Daniel had been after Thara and Gehan had fought about what to do over New Year. Thara had refused to go to his parents' house for kiributh for the Sinhala and Tamil New Year. Why this should have caused the old wound to be opened afresh, Latha could not say. After all, they had not visited the previous years either. But perhaps, she had told herself, it was because so much time had passed since the original fight that Gehan thought Thara should forget about it. Which wasn't like him, clearly, given the fact that he had gone from being her boy-who-was-more-than-a-friend to treating her as a servant over one, albeit egregious sin, and had never once, by look or word or deed, indicated that the future might contain even a fleeting reference to their romantic past.

"My whole year will be ruined if I step into that house to begin it," Thara had said at the dining table, and Latha had agreed with the houseboy, whom she had brought up to speed on the long list of disagreements between the Vithanages and the Pereras, that this was reasonable, given the history. They did this often, she and the house-boy; they conducted a parallel commentary to the conversations at the dining table or lack thereof. It helped them both, particularly Latha, to feel as though they were in control of things.

"Then I will take my children and go without you," Gehan had said, also quietly, which Latha knew to read as a sign of an impending fight. She had uttered a few prayers to an assortment of deities, both Buddhist and Catholic.

Thara had tossed her hair and poured herself a glass of water from the glass decanter, then poured it back in. "No bloody way," she had said. "I'm going to take the children and go to *my* parents' house like we have always done. That's where the New Year begins, particularly now that they don't visit this place after all the insults they suffered—"

"Okay, then if I have to go to your parents' house, we will all go to mine afterward," Gehan had said, cutting into the speech that Thara was always ready to deliver and was never allowed to finish.

"Nobody invited you to come along. You might think you're wanted because they are too decent to be rude to you when you go, but personally I don't think my parents wanted to see you step into their house ever again after all that was said by that foolish bloody woman that you call a mother," Thara had said.

And, listening from the kitchen, Latha had struck her own fore-head with the heel of her palm and pursed her mouth, knowing what was going to follow that remark. From the scraping of the chairs she had been able to tell that Thara had stood up and Gehan had followed suit. She had hurried to the dining room, where the conflagration was about to start, and hustled the girls away into the kitchen, where she had told them they could help her cook lunch—even though they had just finished breakfast—and followed this statement up by emp-tying a nebiliya full of coconut she had scraped for a sambol into the blender with a cup of water and pressing the button. By the time the girls had tired of watching the blender turn the gray water to a thick milky white, the slapping, scratching, and screaming had been over.

Latha had developed a keen intuition about when, exactly, she should get her babies away from their fighting parents. She often imagined that it would be far better if she left Thara's house with them. Once, she almost had. The idea had come to her one evening when she accompanied the girls and the houseboy, who, but for his dirty feet, was like an older brother to Madhavi and Madhayanthi, to Galle Face. They had eaten kadala and ice palams, and she had even paid for horse rides for all three of them, the driver looking on from the vehicle parked along the edge of the green. The ocean had seemed so serene to her, so soothing with its comings and goings, the long, expected tosses and turns it made over and over again; it had mesmerized her. For days after that, she had thought that if she could make it toward the South, where the ocean was surely even better, there would be a place for her, a home where the girls could be kept happy far away from their inattentive parents, each of them wound up in a cycle of bitterness and cries of unfair. She could get work in a hotel where the foreigners would find her charming just as the man in the store had, and she could take the girls for long walks at dawn where they would pick up beautiful shells and buy new fish from the fishermen who worked by night. Her girls could be happy.

And so, one afternoon, just to take a closer look, she had taken the girls and the houseboy to the railway station and got on a train, telling them they were going to see a cleaner ocean, somewhere near Matara, which was the place that Thara had mentioned to her, the place she had said she wanted to visit again with Ajith. But they had got off long before then, somewhere not far out from Mount Lavinia, because the girls had wanted to. When they got to the beach there, Latha had realized the absurdity of her plan.

The ocean had been gray and choppy, though the beach was sandy. At first Latha had watched the children play together as they never did at home, the dancing salt water erasing the distinctions between them just as smoothly as it took away their footprints. The three children had lengthened out from the rounder, softer babies she had tended: two girls and a sun-soaked brother, darkened the way boys ought to be. She had liked the way they held each other's hands as they went toward and fled from the little waves that came ashore where they stood, far from the crashing swells farther away. They had paddled in the water for an hour or so, picked up a few stray shells that had been overlooked by the collectors who had scoured the beach before the sun rose, and eaten some pineapple in big chunks. But then, as they grew bored, the girls had become irritable and clung to her skirts, and the houseboy had kept asking when they were going back home.

"Latha, I'm hot, and I don't like all the people staring at us," Madhayanthi had said in her complaining voice. "I don't like foreigners either."

"Latha, are we lost?" Madhavi had asked.

And the houseboy, with his "Madam will be waiting," and his "Mahaththaya will be worried," and his "Don't the babas have music lessons today?" had finally taken his toll, and even Latha had wondered what on earth she had been thinking. So they had caught a train back to the station in Colombo and ridden a scooter taxi home. When they reached the house, she had told the girls to keep the whole thing a secret, bribing them with chewing gum and spoonfuls of sugar, scolding herself again and again as their stomachs turned that night, holding them as they threw up bits of pineapple at the tail end of the rice and curry dinner she had forced them to eat. Then she had returned to the job she knew how to do: creating a refuge for her girls inside Thara's home, just out of reach of either parent.

The only thing she had not been able to spare them from this time was the slamming of the front door and the sound of their mother sobbing. So she had made a glass of lime juice, told the houseboy to let the children eat as much sukiri as they wanted, and taken the drink to Thara. Then she had sat on the floor and massaged Thara's feet while she wept at what life had dealt her, called Gehan every foul name she could think of, and waxed lyrical about how different things would have been with Ajith.

Latha had sat there listening, wondering for the umpteenth time what it was that Thara and Ajith saw in each other. Besides his looks, obviously he had a job that allowed him to pay for the expensive trinkets and perfumes he bought for Thara. But there had to be something else, she thought, because those things were available from any similar man. What made Ajith special? He had no particular sexual expertise that she, Latha, could attest to anyway, so it couldn't be that, unless he had learned something besides banking in that cold part of America to which he had been banished by his parents. She concluded, again, that it had to be nothing more than the fact that Ajith reminded Thara of her resolute past, the way she had once ordered life to suit her, picking everything from flowers to her future husband with a quixotic sparkle in her eye. Perhaps Ajith made her feel that she was still the same girl who had once had her entire future planned, who had predicted her name in headlines at the age of thirteen. And perhaps what he loved was the part of her that had remained that girl, with that nerve and those plans.

And while she had sat there and wondered about Thara, and whether she had, in fact, reclaimed that girlish past with Ajith, Latha had begun to entertain the possibility that perhaps she could do the same. So when Thara had ended her monologue about Gehan and how reprehensible he was, and given Latha the key to the lock on the telephone and made the inevitable request that she call Ajith and tell him she needed to see him right away, Latha had dialed Daniel's number instead.

She had arranged to meet with him, then returned to tell Thara that there was no answer from Ajith's phone, which was really his parents' phone. And though that had meant more wailing and massaging, she had felt better about it all, knowing that there was something good waiting for her even if only in the short term, though what that was she hadn't been able to say, never having had a conversation with Daniel outside of the one in the lingerie section of the *Palace of Fashion*. She hoped that, whatever it was, it would be good, stilling the misgiving that had quickened her heart momentarily when Daniel answered the phone and had to be reminded who she was and where they had met.

"Who is this?" he had asked, sounding as though he was very busy.

"Latha, I am Latha. You met me in the *Palace of Fashion*—"

"Where?"

"The *Palace* . . . You gave me a card and told me to call anytime. You said girl *ekak*. A girl. I'm Latha—"

"Yes, of course!" he had said and laughed, his voice growing warm and louder, as if he had brought his mouth closer to the tele-

phone, as if he had abandoned whatever it was he had been doing
to make him so irritated when he answered the phone. He was a
foreigner, after all, and it must be difficult for them to remember all
the native people they met, she had reasoned, though she had imagined herself to be rather more memorable than the usual well-met
woman. "Are you still there?" he'd asked.

"Yes. I am here."

"Good, good. I can't hear you very well," he had said.

"Thank you," she had whispered, not wanting Thara to hear. She
couldn't think of anything else to say now that she had done the
work of calling him like he had asked her to. It was his turn to offer
himself to her.

"No, thank *you* for calling me! I remember you. The girl with the
long hair and the very pretty smile," he had said. "I remember you.
Latha. I'm glad you called."

Finally, after too many rounds of telling her what she looked like,
which she didn't need to hear since she already had a pretty good
idea, he had suggested they meet, and talked about when and where,
which was far more useful.

And when Daniel had welcomed her into his home whenever she
could go there as if she were, indeed, just another girl with a family
and a respectable history to justify the lift of her chin and the straightness of her walk, she had been delighted. It was as easy for her as it was
for Thara, she thought; they could both go back in time. And if her
own version of that past was not quite true—she could not go back
to Gehan—she could at least go back to her girlhood fantasies of the
hardscrabble gains reserved for difficult women like herself. Women
who were not ordinary but whose presence in the world was more
affirming of its vitality, and also more entertaining, to her imaginary
audience, than that of legions of virtuous bores in the form of women
who never asked why and always chose the known over the unknown.
Yes, she could go back. How easy then to pretend that, indeed, she was
that girl. That girl with a real home and a real family and a real life,
which she sometimes left behind to be with him because she could.

It was not hard to arrange those brief yet soul-sustaining meetings. Madhavi and Madhayanthi were both at the Girls' Preparatory

School now, which released Latha from her duties at least during the mornings and sometimes, on the days when they went to ballet or swimming, in the afternoons. Yes, she did think it was odd to squeeze their sweet bodies into tight, scratchy costumes and even tighter shoes, but so long as they did not complain when she had to get them ready, she was willing to keep her thoughts to herself. She did not have strong opinions about swimming, though, which, she felt, might someday save their lives should they ever have to go somewhere in a boat. Besides, both activities allowed her to vary her meetings with Daniel so that, at least by time of day or day of the week, she could imagine that spontaneity was possible in an otherwise routine arrangement: greet him with a smile, accept the offer of tea, use the bathroom to freshen up while he poured it, listen to him talk about life in America, which she liked, and sometimes about government officials and garment factories in her own country, which she didn't, stand up to put the cup away and protest a little when he offered to do it for her, and then let him lead her to the bedroom.

The only thing that diminished these meetings was the fact that after their first time, when he asked her all those questions and listened patiently to the answers she had to repeat many times, with lots of nervous laughter due to the sparseness of her vocabulary and her pronunciation, he didn't seem that interested in what she had to say unless she recited scraps of the poetry that Thara had taught her when they were both girls, and then he was thoroughly amused.

Still, he seemed content enough with her occasional visits and, she felt, the quick and unnecessarily tumultuous rolling around in his bedroom, which clearly constituted lovemaking in his book. In that way, he reminded her of Ajith; never really looking at her while he ransacked her clothing and body at top speed, as if he were about to be caught or merely easing an itch. She had never had the opportunity to consummate her feelings for Gehan, and their physical contact had been limited to the merest of touches, yet those had been more passionate and lasting than anything she had experienced with either of these two men who had familiarized themselves with her body.

She treated her visits as little respites from the diurnal grind, opportunities to experience some sensual pleasure, for, despite the brevity, she did like the aftermath of the activities in which she engaged with Daniel, and a furthering of her own education about the world. And eventually his habit of comparing the colors of their skins (he especially liked to line up their forearms, white brown white brown, or sometimes their legs, white brown brown white) became irrelevant to her enjoyment of those other things, particularly the learning.

"Do you not want to go back to your country?" she asked him one day, sitting on the floor and looking through a book of photographs by someone called Ansel Adams, one out of a stack of photography books he had under the long, low table where they usually drank their tea. The pictures showed a large and empty land, unpopulated by the kinds of crowds that she battled every time she went shopping or marketing.

"That's not my country," he said.

She flipped to the back and slowly read the details in the short paragraph explaining the contents of the book, trying to find in the words she did not quite understand some clue as to why his assertion might be true. Then she looked up at him. He was sitting with his legs outstretched, his fingers clasped together over his chest. Like a corpse, she thought. She wondered whether Americans buried their dead or held funerals. She wanted to find out but didn't want to jump around from topic to topic. He accused her of doing this sometimes, not unkindly but as if he observed her closely, which made it feel as though he was criticizing this mental twitch. "This book says this is America. On the back. Look."

He took the book from her and flipped the pages with one hand, like a deck of cards, not even opening it fully. "This is Ansel Adams's America," he said, "not mine." Then he laughed. He still laughed more than anybody she knew.

She shook her head. How many could there be? Maybe Americans owned parts of their country. She thought about the pictures in the book. It made sense. Such a big country and so few people; each person could have a large piece of it. But then he confused her again.

"My city, New York, is full of people. There's people everywhere all day and all night long. And when I go out of the city, there are fewer people, but I can't see them because they all live by themselves in big houses. Big," he nodded. "Lots of bathrooms," he laughed, "yeah, lots of those. And we are all very rich. That is why I'm here. I prefer to be in a place where people are not rich and where every-thing is connected"—he unclasped his fingers, spread his arms out, and then brought them back together again so his fingers laced into a fist—"like this. Tight."

Latha sighed. She thought people were quite rich in her country, but perhaps he had some other yardstick. And she for one could do with a little less tightness. She could do with some freedom. Maybe he would find her country to be just as stifling soon enough. He had not been here very long after all, just a year and most of that spent moving in, settling down, getting familiar with whatever work he did. And she was the only gateway she could see him moving through to gain that understanding; everything else he did, he seemed to do with people from other countries, so how could he tell?

"What's the matter?" he asked. "You look disappointed."

"No, no, I'm not disappointed," she said, gagging a little over that long word, and smiled to prove it.

"Why doesn't your sister want you to go out at night?" he asked her, then, "Surely you are old enough to decide." He did that every now and again, asked her some old question in different ways.

"No, no. Girls who are not married don't go out at night in our country," she said, wondering all over again if he was really as gull-ible as he seemed. "That's why."

He laughed out loud at that. "Well, that must just be a rule for respectable unmarried girls, my Latha-girl," he said. "Because I have seen quite a few unmarried girls around way past midnight at the dance clubs."

So, of course she wanted to know what a dance club was, but how could she ask? She imagined it was like the parties that Thara had gone to as a teenager, to meet Ajith, and it made her a little wary of hanging around a man who went to such places so often and with unrespectable girls. She wished, fleetingly, that she could stay the night, if not actually visit a dance club, at least place herself into that time of day in his mind. Not because she was jealous, she wasn't; it simply irritated her that there were women—not girls, like he said—who could be where she couldn't be. That even after all she had done to escape the gilded cage of Thara's house, with its little birds and their sweet music, and even risen a bit above the ordinary with her foreigner, there was so much more territory to be conquered. But she couldn't stay the night, so she let it go.

Well, some god must have felt sorry for her and wanted to give her a way to correct that imbalance in her experience, a way to feel that, despite her lack of familiarity with dance clubs, she could break another rule or two, because that was the same evening Gehan finally looked her full in the face again.

It happened because he and Thara were going out to a cocktail party, and since Thara had seen Ajith that morning, and was therefore in a generous mood, she wanted to wear a turquoise blue sari that matched Gehan's tie.

"Latha! Go and get my turquoise shoes!" she yelled.

When Latha came into the bedroom, Thara was standing in her sari blouse and matching underskirt, tying the patiya for her pleats around her waist, and Gehan was already knotting his tie. Latha knelt on the floor and pulled out the first row of boxes. The shoes were not in any of them. She had to lie on the floor to reach farther and retrieve the next row. And in the third box from the right was the pair of turquoise shoes and, looped through the heels and straps, a coiled karawala. Thara must have been looking over her shoulder because she screamed, a high-pitched and bone-scratching sound that startled the snake and Latha. Gehan swore at Thara to stop screaming. The children came running, along with the houseboy. Somewhere Latha could hear a pounding on the front door. It must be the driver, she thought. All this in the split second it took for the krait to raise its head and seem to look right at her, its long black body tensing, the white rings seeming to rock back and forth in slow motion, and the instinct that made her slam the box shut and grip it at both ends and hold it steady despite the desperate movements inside.

She stood up with the box, and that was when she noticed that

Gehan was looking at her as if time had moved backward and they were on their way to their respective schools again. He was looking at her as though she were somebody worthy of attention and respect. So she continued to stand there and enjoy the exquisite moment: the memory of the past, herself and Gehan within one pair of parentheses, with the warped and bittersweet present of Thara and the girls and the houseboy outside that space, and all of time suspended because in her hands she held a box that was alive with the writhing of one of the most poisonous snakes in the country. It was heavenly, and she was filled with gratitude that it had come, and that she had been the one to discover it.

Of course, it ended almost as soon as she could name the scene and her emotions. Gehan's fingers dropped from his necktie to his sides, taking his glance with them, Thara declared it a bad omen and refused to go to the party, and the girls had to be sent to watch TV so Latha and the houseboy and the driver (she was right, it *had* been the driver hammering on the door) could dispose of the snake.

The driver got the fire started in the garden, almost at the edge of the back wall, the houseboy got the can of kerosene oil, and then the two of them tied the box with rope, round and round and round until they could be assured that the snake could not escape. Latha stood with it in her hands, following the slow movements of the snake, imagining it coiling and uncoiling itself inside the small space that had been its refuge, unaware of the preparations. Then the houseboy, talking nonstop in his slow, dim-witted manner, the words full of lisps and too much tongue, doused the box with kerosene and the oil poured over Latha's hands and it took her days to get the stench off her skin, and even longer to erase the way it felt, the snake, now disabused of its innocence, thrashing madly in the box when the kerosene touched its body. Finally she handed the box to the driver, who tossed it into the flames, because even though they told her she should do it, she could not. And when he did it, it was awful. The stench of flame and kerosene and burning leather. They watched, all three of them, and she wanted to believe that the movement she saw in the fire was the snake escaping, but she knew better. So she wiped her face and blew her nose and washed her hands and washed them and washed them and held on to one fact: that after all the years that had passed, eleven to be precise, she had touched Gehan's heart again.

She should have been glad for Thara for what followed, but she wasn't, because Gehan turned that moment into renewed attention to his wife and marriage, which meant that now Thara had both Ajith, whom she loved, and Gehan, whom she did not, and all Latha had was the houseboy, the children, and Daniel. And moreover, Gehan announced, after a few weeks of devoted attention to Thara, which she clearly found stifling but in which he persisted, that the family was going to take a vacation at *Kandalama*—a place that sounded so exotic Latha knew Thara would never be the same after going there—and that the trip did not include servants.

Latha knew she had not imagined the meaning of that moment when Gehan had acknowledged her, or the fact that he, too, had remembered that once they had hoped to be more than they had become to each other. The only way she could make sense of what he chose to do afterward, being so firmly and pointedly affectionate to Thara, planning this trip, running away, was by realizing fully that Gehan was only trying his best to be loyal to the woman he had married, and perhaps there was no other reason than that for the way in which he had conducted himself, aloof and far from her, all these years, and surely there was some redeeming grace in knowing that.

Still, it did not erase how she felt, abandoned yet again, and so, after they left, packed into the car like plantains with their fancy luggage in the way back and the grinning driver, who had driver accommodations lined up, she told the houseboy that she was going to visit relatives and, not trusting him with the stove, told him to eat nothing but bread, butter, and the eggs she had already boiled for him, packed a bag with a few things, and got ready to go.

"Daniel? This is Latha. I can come and stay in the night," she told him. She felt dangerous and worldly, and as if she, like Gehan, was staying true to the life that they were being forced to live by finding a way to make it tolerable. But though Daniel seemed thoroughly pleased, she didn't feel good inside, because however well he treated her, and he did treat her well, he was not Gehan. He was like Ajith, only foreign.

Biso

I quiet the fleeting sense of shame I feel for having lied about my
status. It is easy to do; now that he believes my husband is dead,
the policeman is particularly considerate of me. And why shouldn't
I exploit that? This is the first time I have had that experience with
someone in a uniform like his, with that kind of power, and I am
alone with three children, a smoldering train blocking my way backward or forward. Secure in the knowledge of preferential treatment,
I walk away from the crowd, trying to make myself inconspicuous
so as not to rouse their ire any further than I already have. There
is a noisy disarray to their voices, now that hierarchies have to be
negotiated.

I gather the children close to me in a footprint of shade offered by
a small bush scrambling out of the earth over our heads. Removed
from the breezes that blow through open windows in a moving train,
and with our subsequent agitations, we have all grown sweaty and
uncomfortable. The heat from the burning train is unbearable. I
fan the children with the end of my sari, but they are too wilted to
benefit from my efforts. Their hairlines are damp with perspiration,
and, with their eyes squinting beneath childlike frowns against the
sun and their mouths pushing up toward their noses with fatigue,
they are the picture of discontent. Our feet are dusty, and we look
bedraggled. I gaze up at the sky and wonder if there is any hope of
rain before I realize that, but for cleanliness and refreshment, rain

would be an additional inconvenience in our present state. I wish that I could recover our bags, for if I could, I would be able to take out a sari and construct some sort of shade for the children.

"Raji, my Loku Putha, could you look after your sisters while I go and get our bags?" I wait for his nod before I set off toward the train.

"Where are you going?" the policeman asks when I pass him.

"I'm going to try to find our bags, rālahamy," I tell him.

"The bags are still being examined. There may be more bombs. They won't let you touch them. Wait until the examination is over, and then you can get your bags."

"When do you think it will be over, sir?"

He sighs in exasperation. "Do you see that?" He gestures toward the smoking train, the chaos from which we are shielded if only by distance. "They are still trying to put the fire out and get the injured people to the hospital. Be grateful that you are not lying there with the dead and wounded."

I feel chastened. I walk quietly to the back of the crowd, which has now swelled to accommodate the people from around here who have joined us to listen in and report back to their neighbors. I squeeze my way past them, imagining the story percolating through the hills and being handed away like a sin with each fresh cup of tea. The children are waiting for me.

"*Mata choo barai,*" my little one says when I reach them. Indeed, clutching herself between her legs, she personifies her need, the urine heavy inside her.

The policeman is still writing down the names and addresses of the other people; he has a long way to go. We have time. I take her by the hand and beckon to the older children to follow. We walk for a few minutes down the tracks until there's a bend. I stop at a clearing on a gradual slope beside the tracks and flatten the grass with my foot by stamping on it several times. Then I help her to squat. Watching her, listening to the gush of urine, both siblings decide they need to relieve themselves too. They make a game of squatting, one behind the other, and attempt to create a rivulet. Finishing first, Chooti Duwa picks a leaf and uses the stem to divert their collective output in a jagged path down to the tracks. They shout and laugh together as they follow their stream until it is absorbed into the red earth and disappears. They pick a few more leaves and mark the place where it ran dry, memorializing the spot like a grave. Finally I, too, squat at a little distance and pee while Loku Duwa keeps watch. Even my urine feels hot as it comes out.

But it is as if the walking has revived them; their steps are light as they go back to where the others are, balancing on the smooth metal of the tracks, the littlest behind her brother, Loku Duwa alone. After a few steps I join this age-old game, my arms spread out, teetering now to one side, now to the other as I try not to fall off. What is it about us human beings that compels us to do this? The children look back at me and giggle. I smile, sheepishly. A few of the people hear the children's voices and glance back at us and then at one another. Let them think what they wish. I am free.

As we draw nearer, I hear fragments of conversation.

". . . probably dead by now . . ."

". . . in the basket . . ."

". . . two others . . . nearby . . ."

I realize what those looks meant: they were not judging me; they were simply asking me to hurry, wordlessly telling me that I was missing the story. I glance back at the children. They are still playing but safe. They chase one another up and down the tracks; my Raji tries to knock his sisters off balance by rushing up, tickling them, making them laugh.

"Don't go beyond the bend!" I shout, then turn my attention back to the crowd. A newcomer from the area tells me that the police believe the bomb was planted in the basket of an old man selling buns and rolls. "The old man was still alive when they pulled him out," he says, "but he was severely burned, along with two others with whom he had been talking."

"How do they know?" I ask, drawing the fall of my sari over my upper body to settle the hairs that have stood on end from my wrists to my upper arms. I could have been standing by that basket when it exploded. What would have happened to my children then?

"They can't be sure, but they found bits of the charred basket closest to the explosion," the young man says. "There were no other bags or boxes or anything else that could have contained a bomb to be seen, they say. They have a bomb expert there. That's how they know."

"And the old man told them he had left the basket to give some food to somebody," says another.

"He hadn't got back to it when it exploded. He was on his way back, but he stopped to talk to an older couple. They were not near the basket, but they were near enough. They've been taken to the hospital." The white-haired woman who says this clucks her tongue and shakes her head. She wipes her eyes surreptitiously with the side of her index finger, as if afraid to show that she is scared or that she is upset.

"Did he say to whom he gave the food?" I ask this, trying to sound as if the answer is not important, as if I am merely curious about the details.

"No, he didn't say much. Even that part they gathered from the few words he did say. He was nearly unconscious."

"Maybe he was lying," says the young mother, suspicious of the world now that she has something to protect from it.

"Yes," agrees the father, taking the baby from her, full of wisdom about the world now that he has contributed to it with a child. "Maybe he *was* the bomber. Maybe he was a terrorist."

"Probably a Tamil," says someone else nearby.

I do not cry easily. I cried for days when my mother died. I cried when I heard of my father's suicide, knowing that there was nobody left to affirm the source of my pride: that long-ago upbringing, a parental blessing for a good life. I cried the first few times my husband beat me. Since then I have found that swallowing that salt water brings me strength. But this journey has tested me. It forced those tears from my body when I saw the dead mother and her children. And now, I feel them rise again. How vile that these people who know nothing, who never spoke to that man, feel they have the right to judge him.

"He was not a bomber or a terrorist," I say, my voice trembling despite my effort to keep it steady. "You should be ashamed of yourselves for saying such things about him."

"How do you know?" someone asks me, some man in the crowd,

and the voice is dismissive of me. As if I am foolish and ill informed. As if it is presumptuous of me to even speak, let alone have an opinion.

"How do I know? I know because he came to give some bread to me and my children because they were hungry. It was his goodness that saved him from dying with his basket. He was a poor, old man."

The reaction is instantaneous. It is as if I am bathed in some kind of contagious misfortune or have been found to have poisoned a common well. One by one they look at me and back away. I don't understand at first, and then I do. They blame me. They blame me for the untended basket, for the opportunity for someone to place a bomb among bread rolls covered in plastic. I want to protest, to insist that some karma brought me and that old man together, to save my children from hunger, to save him from death. I want to say that people who plant bombs would find a way to do it no matter what. That perhaps *they* would be dead now had the bomb been elsewhere. But I realize it is of no use. They blame me. I stare at them, one at a time, and maybe they can feel the curse that I put upon them with my furious eyes; they avert their gaze and clump together. Even the policeman. At least I am not surprised by that.

I turn to my children. Loku Putha must have heard the commotion, because he has stopped walking and stands, wobbling slightly with one foot on the surface of the track. He has taken his sandals off and wears them on his hands, the toe loops snug between his index and middle fingers. The others have done the same. They are all barefoot. The girls come to a stop behind him. There is no use in lingering here. If we stay, there will only be more of this kind of ignorance and accusations, and nothing will change. By nightfall, when those who are familiar with these parts have left, accepting the generosity of nearby strangers, we will still be here, or worse, at the mercy of the constables at some police station. The solace that I had counted on earlier, that fortitude in the face of shared misfortune, would be gone along with daylight, and what would I do then? No, my first responsibility is to take my children to a safer place, not to clear up misunderstandings or worry about people who want to invite the wrath of the gods with bombs.

"Come," I say, walking up to them, "we're leaving this place."

"Where are we going?" Loku Putha asks, still not moving, still on that one foot.

"We're going to get to the road and walk home."

"All the way to the sea?" Chooti Duwa asks. She takes my hand and traces her own eyebrows with the tip of my index finger. It is one of the tricks I use to soothe her when she is crying, and it touches me, her unconscious request for comfort.

"No, not there, to the new home," Loku Duwa tells her and turns to me. "Right?"

"Yes," I tell them. I bend down and kiss Chooti Duwa on each closed eye as a payment for letting go of my hand. "But first, wait here. I'm going to try to get our bags."

I turn around and walk past the crowd, and this time not even the policeman attempts to stop me. The closer I get the more smoke there is, and I hold the edge of my sari over my nose and mouth, squinting to keep the smoke out of my eyes as best as I can. I see the stack of bags on the side. There are two policemen dressed in bulky armor made of stretchy plastic, going through each bag. The first policeman has equipment strapped over his shoulder and below his hips, large, unwieldy boxes with tubes attached to a long pole. At the end of the pole are two circles, one inside the other. He brushes the rings over and along the sides of each bag. As he moves on to the next bag, the second policeman opens the one behind and goes through the belongings inside. I am amazed at how many bags and boxes there are; there were so few passengers left on the train by the time we had to get off. I search for our bags and see that they are among those with which they have finished.

"Sir," I say, approaching the two policemen, "please, sir, could I take my bags?"

They look at me, then at each other, unsure of what to do.

"We're not done yet," the first policeman says.

"Did that other police rālahamy tell you to come here?" the second one asks.

"Please, sir, I am a widow traveling alone with my three children, and we have a long way to go to get home. We are innocent people."

"Where are your bags?" the second policeman asks.

I point to our nylon bag, my mother's market bag, and my brown handbag. He separates them. Set apart, they look menacing somehow. Even I feel afraid of touching them.

"You can take them now," the second policeman says, as I hesitate. "They're safe. We checked."

I shake my head in gratitude. "Thank you, sir. May the blessings of the Buddha be upon you both," I say.

The first thing I do is take that piece of paper with the name and phone number out from inside my blouse and put it into my coin purse. Then I put my handbag over my shoulder and pick up the two bags. I walk past the front of the train, past the others, who stare at me and my bags. I can feel their stares on the back of my neck as I continue on down the tracks, the children beside me. I hope I give an impression of resourcefulness. I hope they feel less sure than they were before, less comfortable, less fortunate than I. And though I know it is sinful to wish such things upon fellow human beings, I am beyond being concerned about the checks and balances of karma. From what has transpired in my life, and what I have seen this day, it is a miracle I have not abandoned my faith in prayer altogether. I lift my head even higher, though it is hard to do with the weight of the big bag, into which I put everything that was worth carrying with us.

"Amma, give me the small bag," Loku Duwa says.

"I can help you carry the heavy one," Loku Putha says. I set it down, and then he and I pick up one handle each. The load feels so much lighter. I take Chooti Duwa's hand in my free one.

"Do you know the way, Amma?" Loku Duwa asks, looking up at me, playing with the edge of her collar. I want to take her hand and put it down, to make her stop fiddling like that, dirtying her dress, which is already looking grimy, but I have no free hands left. I sigh instead.

"Amma knows everything," the little one says, skipping to keep up with my pace.

I do not know the way. I know how to walk to the house from the train station in Ohiya, or at least I think I will remember when I get there, but not by road. Yet we cannot possibly walk all the way on the railway tracks. If we can somehow find the road, we can probably ask somebody to help us find the way.

"Loku Putha, see if there is an easy path to get to the road," I tell him, after we have walked far enough to put several bends in the tracks behind us. I balance on the rails and watch him, the bags at our feet, the girls, too, with their faces upturned as we wait to see what he might be able to find. I am glad that he has proved to be responsible enough to be trusted alone, young enough to be as sure-footed as he is. I have thought a lot about my children, learned a lot about them during this journey of ours, difficult though it has been. Loku Putha slips a few times as he clambers up the side of the hill, but I am confident that he can make it to the top, and I am proved right when he disappears from view.

After a few minutes, the girls get tired of watching for him. They wander away to examine the area immediately around us, the foliage, the dried mud. I watch her as Loku Duwa opens each of our bottles and confirms that they are empty, pressing her eye to the opening and then shaking the last drops into her mouth, her head flung back. When I look down, I see that Chooti Duwa is hacking with a stone at the side of a huge, red-brown anthill that seems to grow out of the side of the mountain. It has two uneven round holes. Snakes.

"Stop that!" I tell her.

"Why?" she asks, still carving out a picture of some sort on the side of the anthill.

"Because that's where snakes live," I tell her.

"Can I look inside, Amma? To see if there is a snake?"

"No! Just get up and come here."

She drops her stone reluctantly but continues to squat next to the anthill. I keep watching her to make sure that she doesn't put her face up to one of the holes or, worse, put her hand down it to see if she can feel a snake. I can tell that she wants to by the way she sits. Her age and lack of experience make her unafraid, of unexplained journeys, of derailments on account of bombs, of snakes. She gives up when she sees that I will not look away. She stands and dusts her palms on the edge of her dress. Red dirt flies off her hands and settles on the dress, and now it is filthy. I sigh. I open my bag and take out the dress that the pregnant girl gave me. I take off the dress Chooti Duwa is wearing, shake it to get rid of the dirt, and stuff it into the bag. I put her in the new white one. It is a little large for her, but at least it is clean, and she looks sweet in it. The only clean one in our group.

"Amma bought me a new dress!" she tells her older sister in a singsong.

"It's not new. Someone gave it to me to give to you," I say, smoothing the skirt.

"It is new. It is a new dress for me," she insists.

"Promise me that you will never put your hand into an anthill like that," I say to her, holding her chin in my hand and forcing her to look at me. "Chooti Duwa, promise me. It is not a joke. Snakes are dangerous and many of them are poisonous and you are too small to know the difference."

She looks defiant. "Snakes are beautiful."

"Where have you seen snakes?"

"At school, in the teacher's book."

"Snakes in books are beautiful," I say, stroking the thick hair gathering in waves at the nape of her neck. I should let her grow her hair, now that she is older. I unfasten the two silver-colored hair clips shaped like fish, comb the hair with my fingers, such beautiful hair, like her father's. I put the clips back in so there are no stray strands covering her eyes. "Snakes in real life are poisonous and can kill you."

"There's Aiyya!" Loku Duwa shouts, and we have to abandon the discussion.

I watch my son scramble, then slide down the hill toward us. He's smiling. "I found the road, Amma," he says. "It's not far from here."

"Stay there," I tell him and pick up both bags, hold them for a moment, and then put them down. Of course, I cannot climb the hill with the bags.

"Amma ohoma inna," he yells to me, and we both smile. "Stay there. I'll come down and help you with the bags."

It takes us a long time to climb out of the shallow valley, through which the train tracks meander, to the crest of the hill. First I hoist the little one up so Loku Putha can help her establish her footing.

Then I do the same with Loku Duwa, which requires more effort. Then I throw my handbag up, and the children pass it along to Chooti Duwa, now farthest ahead. Next I heave the heavier bag over to my son, who hugs it, panting, proud of his superior agility. Somehow he seems to be able to manage to climb and haul that bag. For my part, I am forced to hitch my sari up and tie it around me at knee length like a man's sarong so I won't trip. Even then I fail. I take off my slippers and throw them, one at a time, toward the top of the hill, hoping that they will land somewhere in our path. Halfway up I lose the bag I am carrying, and it rolls back toward the tracks.

"You go, Amma. I will climb back down and get it," Loku Putha says.

"We should just leave the bag there," I say in exasperation. "All that's in it are drink bottles and other things we can manage without." But he doesn't listen. By the time I reach the top, where the girls are waiting, he is already halfway down the slope. We are all out of breath, me especially. Still, I shade my eyes with my palm and look around. From this vantage, I can see the road winding through the hills below. I see one of the half buses that serve these parts and a lorry, both traveling away from us. They look like toy vehicles. Far below in the distance, I see a red car coming toward us.

Latha

Latha had never gone anywhere in a car with Daniel, so it seemed all the more egregious that the first time she did so, and in such a clean and nice-smelling car painted in such a bright color, it was in such somber silence.

No, he had never taken her anywhere in his fancy red car. Not even that time not so long ago when she stayed the night. Despite how happy he had said he was that she was able to stay, when she finally arrived, the weekend had not been that different from any other time when she had visited. She had been given tea with which he had served the packet of *Lemon Puff* biscuits she had brought with her, she had looked at books and photographs, she had eaten unfamiliar food, and she had slept with him. On Saturday night she had drunk sweet and heady drinks that had made her feel dizzy, and yes, that had been a departure from the norm. And it had been fun when Daniel played music and made her dance around the living room, even though she hadn't known what he expected her to do, and after a few minutes of holding on to her hands and tugging her this way and that he had eventually given up and sat down. He hadn't been upset, she didn't think, he had just smiled and patted the seat beside him; and for dinner he had served food that had been delivered from outside.

"This is Thai food, Latha-girl," he had said, opening round plastic containers with transparent lids and rectangular boxes made of rigiform and packed with flavored rice with peas and carrots and bits of onion and flaked chili and fat, slobbery noodles unlike the *Harischandra* kind that she cooked at home.

"Thai food," she had repeated, doing what she usually did when she felt something was required of her, verbally, but she wasn't sure what.

"Thai food is from Thailand," Daniel had said, then paused in his serving to point out the two statues he had of the Buddha. "Those are from Thailand, from when I lived there," he had said and sighed. "I liked Thailand a lot," he said, after a long silence that made her think that he would rather be there than here.

She had gazed at those heads again this morning before they left, Daniel opening and closing the door to the house behind her, then opening and closing the door of the car for her. The heads were so different from the Buddha statues in her country. These had crowns, and the tops were almost as high as the heads themselves, with concentric circles that grew smaller and smaller until they tapered off in sharp points. Like the cups of *Angelina* bras. They had given her no solace.

Yes, that night had been different, she thought now, the drinking, the music, the food. But the highlight, the one thing for which she had been truly grateful, was the experience of going to sleep in that colorful bed, cozy under the blankets and safe from the icy, air-conditioned outside, and then waking up with somebody next to her. And for once she had not minded that Daniel was foreign, odd, unknowable, and not Gehan. He was a man, and there was his arm, flung around her body the same way it had been flung in his sleep the night before. She had lain in the meditative quiet of the early morning—having woken at five the way she did at Thara's, an hour earlier than anyone else there, even the houseboy—with a deep sense of pleasure. She had lain there trying to imagine what it would be like to do that every day. To go to sleep with a man and wake up with him. What it would be like to care so little about this moment that she could simply slide away from such an embrace and go to the kitchen and make herself tea, open a window, sit by herself, not wait, as she had done, barely breathing, enjoying every second of that one morning. What would it be like to curse and scream at a man as Thara did so regularly, and still have him come home every night to climb into the same bed?

"Are you okay?" Daniel asked now, next to her, making the humidity and buzz of the city jar against that remembered moment.

She nodded and fiddled with the edge of her blouse.

"It's the best thing," he said. He glanced at her and patted her thigh, then returned his hands to the steering wheel.

Yes, it was the best thing. He had said that several times. He had said it for two whole weeks, until she had agreed. She had agreed because she had seen, finally, that it was the best thing for him, and if that was the case, then there was no option for her but to agree. Agree, not only to his persuasions to rid her body of a second indictment of her character, but also to rid herself of this man, who, she now realized, had been exactly as she had once imagined him to be: like Ajith, just lighter-skinned.

Outside, the city passed by slowly. Daniel was not accustomed to driving his own car and was clearly unhappy about having to do it at all, but alerting the driver to their predicament was out of the question, he had said. He cursed intermittently under his breath, and even though she could see the sources of his irritations—the scooter taxis that veered without warning inches from his elbow; the erratic pedestrians who darted past the hood of the car like the colored fish among the artificial fronds of the fish tank he had installed recently in the dining room; the buses that huffed and snorted their way to the front by sheer dint of overpowering fumes; the wall upon wall of posters protesting this, condemning that, advocating something else over the occasional photographs that still remained of the fallen trade towers by the Colombo harbor that had been blown apart by suicide bombers in February of that year; the way all of it must have reminded him of the chaos that was her country—despite all that, she could not shake the feeling that some of the curses were directed at her. The absence of concern for her sensibilities indicated the presence of antipathy. Simple as that.

Part of her wished that she had never told Daniel she was pregnant; part of her knew there had been no option but to do so. Who else could she have told? How else would she have had a chance to be a mother, a real mother, with a real child, no matter its color? But after a great deal of quiet between tea drinking and hand-holding and little else, he had finally said it.

"I think we should arrange for you to have an abortion."

Abortion. This was a new word in her vocabulary. It sounded so disconnected from the physical process of being pregnant, carrying a child. He had to show her what he meant with his hands, an ugly gesture that looked like he was washing her vagina for her and throwing away the water. He even had a sound, a sibilant hiss, to go with it. In her language, the process was referred to as *nathikireema*, an end to being. How much closer that was to the truth of it all: an end to being.

"It's not so bad," he had said. "It's very quick. You'll be in and out within a few hours. I'll take you myself." She had forced herself to feel better that he hadn't snapped his fingers.

Odd how a man who knew so little about her country, who had treated her like she was an ordinary girl and believed all her little lies and the big ones too, who had seemed so charmed by her and so happy with himself, would know where to go to rip babies out of the bodies of pregnant women. Maybe that was how he remained so happy. He knew how to do away with complications. He lived easily in the web that was her country, moving around it like a spider. No wonder he liked it here. She wished she knew who caught the spiders. Which made her think of God. God, who seemed so real to virtuous people like Leelakka and gave her that look of serenity, that peace which made her voice so soft, her needs so few. No gods for her, Latha thought, for women like her who wanted things from people, from men like Daniel or Ajith or even Gehan.

"We'll be there soon," Daniel said.

Again, she nodded. They had left the Galle Road, with its hubbub and horns, and turned down a residential lane. She didn't recognize the roads, only the feeling of the spaces: it was Colombo 7. Somewhere close to Thara's home and also the Vithanages', surely. She cringed low in her seat. That would be the end of it all, to see Mr. Vithanage now. This would be more than even he could forgive, she was sure of it.

"You don't have to hide. This is a private appointment," Daniel said, smiling at her good-naturedly. "Nobody else will be there."

What was it about men that made them believe they knew what women thought? She had never paid much attention to Daniel, content as he had been with her occasional visits. She had not been attentive to his character, or his misunderstanding of her, except in the last month, when she had needed to gauge the extent of his fondness for her, to evaluate how much his good humor was tied to her arrivals and departures. And he had fared poorly under her scrutiny.

"Is it a doctor?" she asked, finally.

"Absolutely! He's a specialist in doing this, in doing abortions, and he's expecting us. I've already paid for everything. You don't have to worry about a thing. You caught it so early that it's just a womb wash, really. Not a big fuss. That's what the doc said."

She didn't even try to look grateful. It wasn't his fault, really. He could hardly get married to her. But with all the money a foreigner like him must have and the private life he told her he led, surely he could have found a way for her to keep the child. If not with him, then somewhere else? Somewhere she could stay and still remain involved in the lives of her girls, so she could escape being banished as she had been before, for Thara surely would banish her if she knew. And a second child! How could she stand to lose another one? She felt panic rising in her body, and she turned to Daniel and clutched at his sleeve. He swerved the car to the side of the road, scraping the underside against the pavement, and reached past her to open the door. She hung her head out, but all that came out of her was a thin stream of transparent bile. And when she turned back in, there was a quick flash of disgust in his blue eyes before he handed her some tissues from the box between them. It was a look that matched the voice when he had said, "What's the matter? Oh, Jesus. Are you going to be sick?" before he stopped the car.

"Blessed is the fruit of thy womb, Jesus . . . ," she said aloud, after she had wiped her mouth and thrown the crumpled tissue on the floor in flagrant disregard of courtesy.

He laughed. "That's the Hail Mary! I thought you were Buddhist!"

"I am Buddhist," she said. But sometimes Jesus seemed more

accessible to her. To yell at the traffic with, like Daniel did. Or to invoke with words overlaid by implication with a sort of curse in moments such as this: to speak of wombs and fruit and death as the father of her child drove her to wash it out of her body. Womb wash. Wasn't that what he had said? As though she were a vehicle or a vegetable, a pathola perhaps, some sort of watery gourd that had been muddied in the rain. There was nothing clean about what they were going to do to her. She could tell that much from how quickly he had arranged it all. If anything was being washed, it was his hands.

He turned down a gravel path that led to a house hidden behind a wall. The black, wrought-iron gates swung open as if he had uttered some magic words. And again, Daniel grinned at her. "See? I told you they were expecting us."

How important he must be in his world to make arrangements such as these with local doctors. She prayed that the doctor was a woman; then she remembered that Daniel had said *he*. Of course. What woman would build a house like this, with gateposts topped by ugly concrete animals and bright electric lanterns, with money earned through such butchery?

Daniel parked the car and came around to help her out. She didn't need any help walking; it made her feel managed to have him hover there, although she might as well not have made such a point of walking forward by herself for, after that first moment, Daniel seemed to have no problem maintaining a particularly meaningful distance between them.

"Doctor Sir will see you in a moment," a servant man said to Daniel after they had been served tall glasses of passion fruit juice— freshly squeezed, she could tell from the quality of the pulp—on the cool veranda.

There were large palms and thick-leaved begonias around the front that shaded them from the neat gardens beyond. The plants had been recently watered, so that even the slightest breeze that blew through them was refreshingly cool. She shivered suddenly, a living-walking-over-her-grave shudder. Maybe it was just the cold drink. Or what was about to happen to her. She looked at Daniel without seeming to. He sat with his legs crossed, the picture of decency in his khaki longs and maroon cotton shirt, a leather belt. She wondered absently about the ironing. Who ironed those shirts, and how often were they delivered to him? She had visited him a dozen times maybe during the past year and a half, and she had never opened a cupboard. Odd that she had never thought to explore, or even to ask. Looking back, she realized that she had asked so few questions. There was so much more she had hoped to know, things she would need for the life she imagined for herself. But time had stretched out interminably then, the future holding many other hours like those few she had spent in his company.

Daniel looked up at her and smiled. It was more like a grimace. "It's quite hot here, isn't it? Even though we're in the shade." He gripped the edges of his cane chair and pushed himself up, swiveled his head around, and peered through the foliage. "Must be that high wall. It blocks the air." He eased himself back down and tugged at the top of his shirt, trying to cool himself.

Latha didn't feel hot. She felt cold. "Use a magazine to fan," she said.

"Yes, right," he said and looked about for one.

"The newspaper can be used also," she said, eyeing the daily paper beside her with its big red title and slogan. Like it was painted with a thick brush. She was still getting her tongue around the word *circulation* when the doctor came rushing in, preceded by the sound of quick yet authoritative footsteps. He walked straight over to Daniel, who had stood up, and took his hand in both of his, as if he needed to be comforted or reassured or something. He didn't look at Latha, though she had stood up, and after a few moments she sat back down.

"Good morning, Daniel, good morning. Sorry, I was a bit tied up. After a long time, isn't that so? Last time was where? That Super Bowl party at *The Blue*? How are you?"

"Fine, fine, Sarath, you know, the usual work. I was up in Kandy for a couple of weeks, and then I had to go down South."

"South is a bit troublesome these days, no? Better avoid it if you can, too many educated riffraff thinking they know what's what," he said and laughed like this was a huge joke, and it must have been because Daniel joined in.

"Yes, I know what you mean . . . but . . . work's work. I have to go where they tell me to go . . ."

"I say, don't listen to those government buggers telling you to go here and there, Danny boy. You should watch your own back. Tell them you got local information that the South is dangerous!" Still holding one of Daniel's hands in his own, the doctor thumped Daniel on the back like he himself was the Local Information and repeated himself. "The South is dangerous!"

"You crack me up," Daniel said, and they laughed again.

Crack. Me. Up. Crackmeup. It wasn't hard enough of a thumping to break him, surely, but maybe he was feeling breakable too, though he wasn't showing it. That thought didn't last very long, as the two men continued to talk about various things to do with the government and the South that they both seemed to find hilarious. Neither acknowledged her until finally they both, in a moment of agreement whose coming she hadn't been able to gauge, looked over at her, both men still smiling, neither seeing her. It was as if they were frozen, hand in hand, like lovers united against an unpleasant confrontation they were trying to postpone.

"This is . . . this is Latha," Daniel said, finally. "Latha, this is the doctor I told you about." And he gestured from one to the other. It was a proper introduction, and she tried to be gracious about it by nodding. She even attempted to smile.

"Oh, your woman speaks English!" the doctor said, glancing with approval at Daniel. "Good. *Hondha mahaththayek ehenang, ingreesi ugannalath dheela nedha?*"

She disagreed with his pronouncement by staring straight at him. Daniel had not taught her English, and even if he had, that did not make him a good master. To begin with, he was not her master. She didn't work for him.

The doctor looked at Daniel and shook his head slowly, his mouth pulled down in sympathy. "Trouble, I can tell."

Daniel shuffled a little but did not contradict him. "I told her everything will be taken care of."

"Oh yes, Danny boy, leave it to me. It is very good of you to take care of your domestic this way, I must say that. Even bringing her here yourself." He looked approvingly at Daniel for a moment, genuine respect in his eyes, and then glanced over at her, pointed to Daniel, and nodded. "You are very lucky. Most other men . . ." Then he turned back to Daniel. "Anyway, you can wait here, Daniel. Come!" And he beckoned to Latha.

Fifteen minutes by the clock on the wall behind the doctor's head, the one she focused on the whole time she was there, her skirt lifted up, her body gaping open for him. Five before for her to remove her underwear and climb up there and five afterward to absorb the words that it was done. The doctor said what he was doing before he did it. "I will be stretching the cervix," he said before he went between her legs with an instrument he waved so briefly in front of her that she could not describe it after. "This is the tube," he said, and this registered with her: the length, the milky color of it, how harmless it looked. She felt the scraping inside, and she listened to the sound of the second hand ticking and tocking relentlessly, and the doctor's breathing, wheezy through the gauze pad over his mouth and nose. He gave her some moist cloths to wipe herself with, and a large pack of *Free 'N Easy* like the ones she had seen on TV and the ones that Thara used. Then he was gone.

When she came out, an hour after he had walked in front of her, leading her to his examination room—the doctor had said half an hour of rest and then she could go home—Daniel was still sitting there. There was something different about him, though.

"Let's go," he said, and he didn't help her to the car though this time she was dizzy and wished he would. He started the car and reversed without throwing his arm over the back of the seat and turning to look behind him as he had done when he had backed out of the house. When they reached his house, he pulled into the porch and sat silently. Then he turned to her. "The doctor told me your medical history," he said. "This is your second pregnancy."

She didn't say anything. She didn't remember saying that to the doctor, but she must have, she must have said it as she lay there, tears dripping without clamor in two narrow streams toward the pillow.

Daniel shifted his weight in his seat to reach for his purse. The same one he had opened to give her his card at *The Palace of Fashion*. There it was, still smooth and light brown, like her skin. He handed her a sheaf of thousand-rupee notes, all the money that was there. "This is for any medications, or . . . anything . . . you might need," he said. "You should not come here again. I thought you were a decent girl, a good girl."

Decent. Good. What words at a time like this! What words for someone who treated decent girls, good girls, as he had done. Latha wished for the strength to get up and slam the car door in his face the way she had seen Thara do so many times to Gehan. But she felt too weak. She got out of the car slowly, carefully, taking just herself. She left the sanitary pads and the money behind. Daniel said nothing more, but she knew his silence was fleeting. She knew what real silence meant, the kind that was impervious. She touched her earrings.

That night at home she tried to direct the houseboy to complete the daily tasks, and he did so, glancing at her with a concern that she appreciated. The girls, however, clung to her, some primitive instinct making them aware of her state of mind, her private suffering, and persuading them that they should distract her in the ways they knew best.

"Latha, come and play!"

"Latha, braid my hair!"

"Latha, I can't sleep! Pat my bottom so I can sleep!"

Latha this and Latha that until even their parents began to chime in, taking on Madhavi's and Madhayanthi's needs as their own, absorbing them, augmenting them.

"Latha! Bring me some lime juice!"

"Thara! Tell the woman to iron my shirt. I have an early meeting tomorrow."

"Latha! Iron this shirt and come and rub my feet. They're aching from walking around the *Freedom Plaza* all day long with Amma, looking for shoes . . . *Lathaaa!* Where the hell are you? God, this woman is becoming a real burden now. I should have listened when Amma told me how to handle her. Now it's too late, I suppose."

Latha heard that last muttered observation from Thara even as she brought the lime juice, and something in the tone of her voice, the way it reminded her so much of Mrs. Vithanage, made her pause before she entered. And perhaps it was the sadness that poured into her with those words, or the anger that rose up with them, or both, and the loss of blood that had been going on all day, so much so that she had no more dry cloths left and had to rip lengths of rag from her one little girl dress that she had kept for sentimental reasons, and she felt herself beginning to fall and grabbed the curtain, bringing it down with her. She heard the glass shatter and felt the shards enter her in pinpricks wherever they could find her. And between those moments, between the touch of the new curtain with its green on green pattern and the sharpness of the glass, she remembered that long ago she had felt such pain, but not from glass. Something had scratched her then, fingernails from a hand she was trying to hold on to? Thorns on a bush by the road on which she stood? And through that memory came Daniel's words, and she reached once more for the earrings, for a time of pain erased by the presence of her own family, found or otherwise.

Thara was bending over her when she recovered consciousness. She helped Latha up and led her to her room. "Latha? Are you okay? Come, I'll take you to your room. Here, lie down . . . lie down on the bed."

She didn't answer the question about why she felt sick or why she had fainted, but when Thara saw the bloodstains on her skirt, she went away and came back with sanitary pads. "You take the strip off like this and stick it in there," Thara said, demonstrating on some old underwear of her own, perhaps not wanting to violate her privacy by going through Latha's things, or maybe not wanting to touch them. "I'll help you to put this on."

It was awkward to stand, and worse to have Thara see the mess she had made of herself, the blood everywhere, on her skin and down her legs. Latha tried not to feel ashamed, but she did because Thara wrinkled her nose as she tried to clean her up, and finally, after all her efforts seemed to produce little result, she gave up and took Latha, step by careful step, to their bathroom, not the servants' one.

"Latha, sit here," she said, pointing to the commode. "I will have to wash you properly."

Latha sat on the commode and let Thara remove her clothing piece by piece until she was completely naked. She sat there and let Thara rinse her off like she was watering plants, with the handheld shower. At first, Thara sprayed from a distance, as if she did not want to get wet, but little by little she moved closer until Latha felt herself being washed by genuinely kind hands. Hands that cared to put shampoo in her hair, soap on her body, holding her up by her arms while she scrubbed herself between her legs, and even stooping to smear some soap on her feet, which Thara then proceeded to clean with her own, their toes catching and separating and making the suds on their feet bubble. She listened to Thara's voice issuing the same instructions she, Latha, gave to the girls when she washed them—"close your eyes," "open your eyes," "bend forward," "hold the soap"—and it was like a lullaby, so she kept her eyes closed, not caring which way her head was moved, which of her limbs was being scrubbed or rinsed. Nobody had ever washed her before, she knew that. She could not remember hands such as Thara's, which were soft and gentle, or any voice that sounded like hers did just then. It seemed to Latha that Thara washed her more than once, for they were in there a long time before she said that they were done.

Thara wiped her dry with a towel that was hanging there. "Now you must feel better, right, Latha? Do you feel better? Come, here, put these clothes on and I'll take you back to the room," she said and helped Latha to get dressed in the old panties lined with a real sanitary pad, and a nightdress that she pulled over Latha's outstretched arms. Once Latha had lain down, Thara went away again and came back with a *Disprin* dissolved in water, and held it to her mouth so she could drink it. It was sour and acidic and sweet and comforting.

She was not alone so long as she had Thara. If nobody loved her, surely Thara did, for why else would she, this mother who relinquished all care of her own children even when they lay pale and sweaty and recovering from some fever or cold, who never wanted to clean their soft, untarnished bodies, why would Thara do all that she had done for her? For three days, Thara tended to her, more frequently at first and then less, her visits more to check on her progress than to offer solace. But those three days healed Latha in new ways, her body and her mind sealing off the wounds she had received, closing them to thought, to violence, opening her heart once more to the past, to a time of friendship and sisterhood and a world uncomplicated by their love of men.

PART III

Biso

As I watch the red car approach, I wish, briefly, that I had my earrings, something to pawn or exchange for grace in our circumstances.

"Amma, are we going to stop that car?" my son asks, beside me, noting with what rapt attention I have been focusing on the vehicle.

"No, I wasn't thinking of stopping it, but . . . what do you think, Loku Putha? What do you say?" I look down at him, suddenly confident that he will have an answer.

The question makes him look up at me with just a faint touch of anxiety. Is he really being asked to decide? There are rivulets of sweat dripping down the sides of his hairline. I reach over and wipe his face with the edge of my sari pota. He smiles, perhaps remembering that he already helped us climb out of the mess that was the train journey and find our way to solid ground, and one with a vantage at that. When he realizes that, yes, I am asking him for his opinion, he pulls his lower lip in and frowns as he stares down the road.

"I think we should walk for a while and then see," Loku Duwa says. "We should ask someone who lives here. How do we know if those people live here?" She is holding her sister tightly by the hand, so tightly I am not sure if it is out of concern for her younger sibling or to quell some fear inside herself. I want to smooth her brow, erase the furrows, even trust whatever female instinct makes her scared, but I resist. My older daughter is too timid, too fearful, and more pandering would only harm her. How would she ever learn to manage if she found herself in a situation like this, alone with children of her own, if she is allowed to entertain demons as constantly as she demands it? No, I turn away and look at my boy, waiting for his answer.

"Let's stop the car and ask for directions," he decides, glancing from his sister's perturbed face to my resolved one, and, without hesitating for my permission or approval, he raises his arm and waves his hand in the air. It's like the movement of a bird, that hand, the rapidness with which he shakes it. Almost like a tremble.

The car looks so much smaller as it approaches, tiny and rounded like the old ones. There's a V and a W in silver on the front of it. It reminds me of the expensive, dinky cars in the rich shop in Galle with all the imported things, the one that was closed down after the Mathiniya took over the country and made us all wear the same blue and white flowered cloth and buy everything on ration cards. I used to like looking in that window, to see what was in the world even if nobody I knew could afford to go in, even if Siri himself denounced it as being full of unnecessary luxuries. At least it was colorful! Not like the bare storefronts that came after, with only the necessary things, rice, dhal, coconuts, the tins of powdered milk with no labels, the rack upon rack of clay and coal cookers. I am delighted by the look of this car; it has reminded me of a happier time.

It slows down as it nears us, and now we can see the driver, a young man with a mustache, maybe in his twenties, and a foreigner beside him. It is only when it stops and rolls down the window that we see another man in the backseat, a boy, really, or a man who looks like one, fair and thin. He is playing with a toy in his hand that makes faint beeping sounds, and every now and again he exclaims in annoyance or smiles.

The driver looks me up and down, glances at the children and then back at me. He lifts his chin and jerks his head at me. "What's the trouble?"

"Our train," I begin, gesturing down to the tracks even though they cannot see the train from inside their car, "had an accident . . ."

"A bomb blast," my son says, in English, and they all look at him, their eyes alert with interest. He holds the small bag behind his back, arms crossed, and lifts his eyes to mine, shyly, swaying a little from side to side. My heart, I feel it in my heart, a sudden accidental skip of a beat, and regret: I shouldn't have asked him to decide. I see him clearly now, such a little boy, a child. I stroke his head.

"Bomb?" asks the foreigner, frowning. "Where?"

"Down there," I answer him, also in English, feeling proud of ourselves. We are not ordinary people, though we may look it. We are educated, decent. I smile to express cordiality, and then I continue to talk to the driver in our language. "That's the thing, malli. A whole compartment blew up, and we had to get out and wait for the police to clear everything. But I have to get to my aunt's place in Ohiya . . ."

"So what's the trouble? Ohiya is the next town."

"It's just that I only know how to get there from the train station. I don't know how to by the bus road."

"I thought you said this is your aunt's house. Where are you from?"

"Oh, we're from the South. We don't come here much. This is only my second time as an adult, and the children have never been. That's why . . . so . . ." I look up the road as it rises and disappears around the mountain and then back down toward the way the car had come. The half bus has made a turn, and now it looks even smaller than it did before. I look back at the driver. He must be younger than I had imagined, for I see him waver between sympathy for us, who are of his kind, and arrogance because of his status as a driver for these white people. I try to concentrate on the kindness. "Do you know if there is a bus going this way?"

The driver nods and motions to me to wait. Then he rolls up his window and consults with the people in the car. They keep looking back at us, and the foreigner, he seems encouraging, for he smiles often at me. He leans forward quickly, all of a sudden, like he forgot something. He reaches into the cubbyhole and pulls out a packet of chewing gum. He leans past the driver, rolls down the window just a little, and pushes it out to my son, a yellow pack of *Wrigley's Juicy Fruit.*

My mouth waters; I remember when my mother was still alive, my father and she had bought me a pack of that during New Year's time in April. I remember the way the taste had felt, the soft-but-hard package, the way it had a paper cap of its own, the silver-foil-wrapped sticks inside. My mother had had to show me how it opened. The dull cream chewing gum, with its wriggly zigzag pattern, had felt like an unlikely treat in my hand. But the first bite, the way the flavor of something otherworldly took over my mouth! It was as though sweetness was singing from every pore and tooth with my tongue conducting the song. My mother had laughed as she watched me, her head tilted a little, her chin resting in her open palm. She had looked beautiful to me right then: her slim, tall presence, the neat hair pulled back in a bun at the nape of her neck, her cotton sari and her laughter all complemented by that taste.

I hear my son's exasperated voice. "Amma! Can I take the chewing gum?" he asks.

I smile. "Of course. And say thank you to the white uncle." I glance over at my girls, particularly the little one, who seems crestfallen that things have not gone the usual way, with strangers singling *her* out for special favors as the most adorable, as the youngest. "Aiyya will share," I whisper to her.

"Thank you," my son says to the foreigner and grins. Such a grin for the infrequency with which he lets us all see that he has it in him, that boyish delight. Even the foreigner responds through the window he has rolled back up, and although I want to be grateful, I don't like his smile because it reminds me of the way the white people smiled at our children on the beach. Something both covetous and condescending, as if they had the right to either emotion when we can take care of ourselves and have so much to be proud of. I don't like foreigners. They come and go so quickly, and they don't inspire trust. I don't want to be reminded of these seaside concerns. I want to forget that we ever lived in such places, exposed to such people. Now I regret that I let my son accept the sweet.

"Here, the white gentleman said to give you some money to help you on the way," the driver says at last, rolling down the window again. For the third time now we can all feel the gush of cold air as it escapes from the interior of the car and fondles us, briefly, before it is absorbed by the heat around us. It seems to come at us in waves that break in time to the rhythmic turning over of the engine. Brr . . . brrr . . . brr . . . that's how it sounds to me. Like the ocean that I will never set eyes on again. Not I, not my children.

"That's okay. We don't need any money," I tell the driver. "I just wanted to ask the way to Ohiya. Can you get there on this road?"

"Don't be foolish," the driver says, gesticulating with the money, his kind face gone, his own lost dignity rising up before him, perhaps, in the shape of my words. "Take this money. He has plenty more. You're by yourself and you have three children with you." And now he laughs. "Think of it as winning the Mahajana lottery!"

"No, thank you very much, please tell the white gentleman that I am very grateful, but—"

"Malli! Come here and take this money and keep it for your mother," the driver says to my son, trying to woo him by calling him that, little brother. "Come! Come and take this. Put it in your pocket. Keep it for later."

But my son knows better than to go against my sense of pride, I know, even though in his heart he wants very much to protect us with the fistful of money that is being offered for no good reason when we haven't even asked for it. That is the other thing that gives me pause, this offer of money. Why would we need money when we are but a village away from family? No, I have never been under obligation to people, and I won't have my children being so either. I lay my hand on my Loku Putha's shoulder just in case he is tempted to disobey me, and he looks up at my face. I smile to reassure him, maintaining courtesy. My son knows that I have two faces, this one, which I am presenting to strangers who have offended me, and the other, of disdain and indifference, which I show to those about whom I care enough that I want them to know what I think of them. The village people back home, for instance; those people knew exactly what I thought of them even when I was a kind guardian to their children, my children's playmates, or neighbor when neighborliness was called for, during childbirth, after a death.

I lower my head a little so that the foreigner can see my face. "Thank you, sir," I tell him in English, my voice soft. "We are all right. My aunt is in the next village; they will look after us." I shake my head at him and smile as I say all this. It feels important that I let him know that it is not simply pride that keeps me from taking his money, but that I truly have no need for it. As I speak I am aware of the driver's eyes on my face, of my children listening to me. They have rarely heard me speak to people in English. The only time they hear me is when I read my old books to them. When I stop speaking, I realize that my heart is beating fast. As if this foreigner has threatened me with his money, or as if he could. He only nods.

"Then we can't help," says the driver, shifting the gears, and now his voice is kind again, respectful. I have not jeopardized his relationship with these white men by rudeness, and, indeed, perhaps he thinks they will treat him with more regard now that they know that his people aren't all beggars; that in between the ones who ask for school pens and those who spit on the white people, there are multitudes of people like me, who are courteous but in no need of being rescued by them.

"Keep walking down this road," he continues. "It is a little far, but eventually you will come to a crossroads. One side is just a dirt road, no tar. I don't know where that goes. Anyway, there's a thé kadé at that junction. Ask them for directions on how to get to your aunt's place. If nothing else, they'll be able to tell you how to get to the railway station, and you can go from there." He doesn't look at me.

"Thank you," I say, but he has already shut the window. I watch the car hesitate for a moment and then move down the road and away from us, returning to its deep sounding but unhurried pace. Maybe the foreigners don't like speed on these sharp turns.

"Amma! Why didn't you take the money?" my boy asks me, already unwrapping the package of chewing gum. He takes out one piece and breaks it into four, one for each of us, then puts the pack into the pocket of his shorts.

"Do we need money?" I ask him. "We are going to my aunt's house. You don't need to take money when you are going to family for help. Money is not going to persuade them to help us."

"Persuade? Why do we have to persuade them to help us?" he asks. "Then Amma, why did you tell us that they would help us?"

"Can I have more of that toffee he gave?" the little one says.

"Did you swallow it already? Don't swallow it, you fool."

"It's stuck," she says. "In the back."

Loku Putha puts his fingers into his sister's mouth and finds the bit of gum. He peels it off his finger and puts it back in her mouth. "You are supposed to just bite it, like this, see?" My son opens his mouth, sticks his bit of chewing gum between his teeth, and chews ferociously for his sister, with loud smacking sounds. Chooti Duwa laughs. "You can't have any more until that has finished tasting sweet," he tells her. "Then we can add a new bit and the old piece will be tasty again. That way we won't waste it."

"What if they don't help us?" Loku Duwa asks in her timid voice, returning me to our larger concerns.

I am immediately sorry for the words I chose. After all, it is not that they would not help; yes, they would. It is just that I have not visited my aunt in so many years, so many countless, silent years, and I do not know my cousin's situation. What is her husband like? After all, mine had not seemed as bad when I visited with him. And yet even then hers had appeared to me to be ridden with flaws. Perhaps she had looked at mine with the same harsh eyes with which I had viewed hers.

But I have to admit now that in fact our visit had not been greeted with as much hospitality as I had hoped for. They had welcomed us, of course, and served us tea and made a special lunch for us. It had been a good lunch, too, with even a chicken that my cousin's husband had killed to be cooked just for us. Still, that is what they were expected to do by tradition. And we had arrived unannounced, so there was no time for them to prepare a colder reception. But my aunt had remained quiet in the background, and when I worshiped her, she had cried a little and murmured regrets, about my mother, about how she had left, and what she might have done to persuade her to stay. That had surprised me. I had thought that my mother had a good relationship with her sister although they did not visit, and that she had eloped with my father for love. If she had lived, I would have been able to ask her these questions, but when my mother fell ill I was far too young to be concerned about such things. I was still content with the life that was being presented to me by my parents, still unaware of the secrets they might keep.

"People leave home for many reasons, Duwa," my aunt had whispered to me. "They leave because they love the wrong people, or they leave because the right people don't love them," she had continued, and her eyes had welled up again.

I hadn't had the opportunity to ask her anything more, because my cousin and her husband had asked us to stay another day, but when we'd protested and said we didn't want to inconvenience them that long, they had chosen to believe our story, that we had someone else to visit in Nuwara Eliya that day, and they hadn't argued with us as they should have. My husband and I had ended up taking our leave and spending the night on the benches inside the railway station, he smoking to stay warm, and I curled against his bulky frame. Maybe it was that unfortunate visit that had persuaded my husband that I was not worthy of his care; he had seemed less interested in me already by the time we climbed aboard for the long train journey home.

And now here I am again, and not simply with a husband who did not have the kinds of graces my mother's family might have expected but with three children with many needs. It is so much more complicated—marriage, parenthood, family—than children could ever know. Nor should they understand the misgivings, the ruptures, the disappointments that cast their pall over women and men tied irretrievably to each other's fortunes and loss of prospect. I can only hope that they, my children, make unsanctioned unions like I had with Siri and, perhaps, my mother had with my father, for I have come to know that those are the only kind that allow love to take us by her hand, to visit with us for a while. In a way, now that it is over, now that I have my little girl beside me, I am glad that he is dead. Yes, glad that Siri is dead. For how would I have borne the end of that illusion too?

"Amma," she says, as if she hears my thoughts, "Akki says they won't help us!"

"No, I didn't say they won't help us, Nangi. I only asked what if they don't help us," Loku Duwa says, trying to set everything straight.

I look at each of their questioning, troubled faces, imagine how careworn we will seem to my cousin when we arrive. That is good: people always help the destitute. That is the nature of our people. The last time I went I must have seemed prosperous and conceited to them, with all the gifts my husband and I had brought for them and my gold jewelry that he had forced me to wear over my protests. Jealousy or embarrassment may have played a part in the failure of their grace. Now I have nothing, and, if nothing else, they will want to relish that, keep me close to reassure themselves of my fallen fortunes, to content themselves that they have done better, are better. And I will tolerate that for the sake of my children until I can find employment. I can withstand anything at all if it means I do not have to return to my husband.

"They will help us," I say to my children. "I just said that we don't need to take money to them to ask for help. We have our strength and good strong legs and we can walk there, can't we?"

They murmur their agreement, but I know they are tired. Tired of this journey, weary with the idea of a place of rest that they cannot reach no matter how they try, how far we go. And what if they had seen the dead family? Here I am, I can barely keep all my sorrows in check—those that came before our early morning departure, and those that have happened since: the dead family, the burning train, the departure of the one gentleman who had been kind to me on the train, and the pregnant girl. Oh, to have her with me now. A girl of her age, pregnant or not, someone to bridge the years of innocence that separate me and my children.

"Remember how they said there's a tea shop down this road? When we get there, we can rest," I tell them. "We can buy hoppers and hot plain tea and rest our legs."

"Our good, strong legs," Chooti Duwa says, giggling, game again for another adventure, this time with crispy hoppers at the end of it.

"Can I have an egg hopper?" Loku Putha asks. He rarely asks for anything. He rarely expresses a preference. I am relieved by the changes in him, the way he has let down his guard, most of the time anyway, how he lets me know that he has desires and that they are simple ones: for chewing gum, a chocolate, egg hoppers, for a sense of responsibility, and for pride in being able to take care of his mother and sisters as all young boys should.

"You can have two egg hoppers," I tell him. "Three if you like. A whole stack of egg hoppers." They all laugh.

Chooti Duwa says, "We'll tell them to bring only egg hoppers to our table. We'll say we don't want any plain hoppers."

"I want at least one plain hopper to eat with jaggery," her sister says, tentatively, as if she is afraid that her request might be too mundane to be included in this feast.

"Yes, we must have some plain hoppers with jaggery too," I say, smiling at her. "That can be our dessert."

"And plantains," Loku Putha says, his voice trailing off as he looks down the road.

We all follow his gaze. The road is empty, the car long since gone. Nothing else, no other vehicle moves toward us from either direction. Everything feels quiet. We sigh, contemplating the walk, which feels long despite the promise of the food and drink that wait for us at the tea shop.

"Let's go," I say and pick up the heavy bag. "Loku Duwa, could you help me?" She picks up the other handle. It is helpful to have her on the other side of the bag, but not as much as it was when my boy helped me. I am glad that I have one strong child with me, one grown old enough to be useful in that way. The heat scorches the top of my head as we walk. I take the fall of my sari and drape it around my head and the head of my little one, walking right by me. "Hold the other side, Chooti Duwa," I tell her, "and you will have some shade." She treats it like a new game; unburdened by bags and age, she is free to be happy. Loku Duwa looks at me, and I see reproach in her eyes. I try to avoid the judgment, but I can't.

"Loku Putha! Stop and wait a moment!" I call to my son, walking purposefully some distance ahead of us. I open the bag and get his two long-sleeved shirts out. I unbutton them and drape one over my Loku Duwa's head, tying the sleeves over her brow to keep it in place. I call to my son so I can tie the other on his, but he shakes his head.

"It looks silly," he yells back at me. "Nangi looks silly with her head bandaged like that!"

I offer it once more, and argue with him for a few minutes, but he does not relent. I put the shirt back in the bag. We start walking again. It seems even hotter after all that effort. We have not gone too far before we hear a boom in the valley below us. It sounds like thunder, but we know it isn't. Somewhere on that train, there must have been another bomb. Good. I hope those people who judged me realize that the old man was innocent. As innocent as I am of causing things to explode and burn.

Latha

When the school bus exploded, the flames a dull gold behind curtains of soot and smoke, Latha had already picked up the girls with the driver. She still went with the driver to pick up the girls. Thara, with her growing list of associations and committees and clubs, appeared to have meetings with somebody or the other every day. Whether she met Ajith or not, Latha was no longer involved; Thara was out and about under her own steam, with a new group of friends in a city full of clubs and bars and malls and restaurants and foreign things and billboards full of blue-eyed people advertising cell phones and *Pantene* shampoo. Yes, Thara didn't need Latha even to get in touch with Ajith now; in fact she barely needed Latha at all, except on those days when she could not meet him. When that happened, Latha was summoned to rub feet, make telephone calls, squeeze limes. Otherwise, all her time was for the girls.

But now, with the bomb blast so near the school, wedged as it was in the crowded city between the American Center and the Russian Embassy, not to mention the Japanese Consulate, Latha was needed by everybody. By Thara, not to comfort her daughters but to deal with the aftermath of a canceled meeting with Ajith; by Gehan, to ensure that the car came directly from the school to pick him up at work; and, reliably, by the girls, who ran to Latha's room as soon as they reached home and insisted that they be served lunch there by the houseboy, not Latha, to whom they clung, hanging on either arm like refusing-to-be-ripened fruit.

Before everything, nobody went into Latha's room, a converted storeroom really, accessed by the passage between the garage and the kitchen, unless she invited them. The only people she used to invite were the girls, and usually it was to save them from proximity to the quarrels that unfurled without fanfare like tattered flags between their parents. But after that, after the future had been washed out of her body, after those three days of bliss when Thara had bathed her and tended to her as true as any sister at her side, after those days had come and gone as quickly as the city dried up the rains, the fights between Gehan and Thara escalated because of Latha's inattention to them, and the girls came more and more frequently to her room until it seemed it was a mere extension of their own spaces. And among the furnishings in Latha's room, what captivated them the most was her collection of sandals and shoes.

Even today, with the terror they had just barely escaped so fresh in their minds, they discussed her acquisitions between the balls of rice and curry that she was feeding them with her own hand, a special treat, often requested and usually denied in the interest of maturing them.

"Why do you have so many shoes?" Madhayanthi asked her again, as if she divined that the answer Latha gave her the first time, because she had the money to buy them, could not be the whole story; she kept repeating this question, clearly hoping for some new bit of information about Latha's love of footwear.

"Latha hasn't bought any new ones, Nangi," Madhavi observed, sitting on the edge of Latha's bed and watching her sister try on sandals one after another, almost as though she wanted to find one that would fit her nine-year-old feet. "Those won't fit you," she added.

Madhavi sat with her legs crossed, like a lady. Eleven now, tall like Gehan and slender, chaste in all her choices, she was, without a doubt, Latha's favorite. Latha squandered hours on Madhavi's concerns. If she wanted her special cotton-polyester blend uniform washed and ironed before wearing it a second time, it was done; if she wanted a French braid, Latha was on hand to loop the long, thick ropes of hair into its complicated twists in time for her to be ready for school; and if she wanted money, which she seemed to with regularity now, Latha gave it to her. The things Madhavi bought filled Latha with girlish happiness, and she loved looking at the treasures that her older girl, which is how Latha considered her, brought home: stickers that puffed up, pink gum she blew into bubbles that exploded on her face, hair ribbons with edging, an autograph book with space on the cover for a photograph.

Latha gave money to Madhayanthi too, but with a less generous heart, and Madhayanthi knew it. It made her jealous, possessive, and sometimes sharp-tongued. Like now: "You don't need all these shoes, you don't have anywhere special to go wearing them anyway," she said.

"I don't own them because I need them, Chooti Baba, I own them because I like having them. I like buying what I want when I want it. Don't you like buying what you want when you can with your pocket money that Thāththa gives you?" Latha said, and went to wash her hands and put away their empty plates.

"It's silly to buy what you don't need," Madhayanthi said, as soon as Latha returned, a statement that was laughable coming from a girl who owned more glass baubles and hair ornaments than her entire class of girlfriends combined.

Latha, however, didn't laugh. She shrugged. She refused to be moved by Madhayanthi's running commentary on her doings. Instead she smiled at Madhavi and stroked her hair. "Loku Baba, what is happening with the debate tournament?" she asked her.

"We're winning. Today we won two debates. Tomorrow we will have another one." She thought a moment, then frowned. "Although, maybe we won't have school tomorrow because of the bomb and everything. What do you think?"

Latha sighed, concerned more with a small blemish that had appeared on Madhavi's forehead than with the reality of bombs. She didn't know, of course, but she also didn't care very much either way. Bombs went off these days, it seemed, without rhyme or reason, killing people she didn't know. Yes, she did feel sorry for the living when the dead—a student going to her A/L examination, a father of three, and so on—were described on the television, but there was something surmountable about bombs and their aftermath. There was something insurmountable about not having family to lose. She stared at the girls and wondered how she would feel if they were lost to her. At first it made no impression on her, that thought, given that they were sitting there, pretty and well-fed, cocooned in her room with its assortment of colorful decorations bought at church fairs and Sunday markets, her simple bedding, her rows of sandals, but then something changed in the air. A picture of an empty room, empty of these two girls. And the pain that rose up within her took Latha by surprise and she cried out to the gods, *Deiyyo!* that it should never come to pass.

"What, Latha? What?" Madhavi asked, concerned. She stood up and put her palms on either side of Latha's face. Madhayanthi dropped the sandal in her hand and rushed to join her sister and clutch at Latha, looking over her shoulder to see what terrible thing might have lurked behind her.

"Nothing, petiyo, nothing," she said, holding the girls close to her body, grateful for their soft solidity. "Nothing at all. I thought . . . I saw . . . a cockroach . . ."

Of course, that was enough. The girls screamed and leaped onto her bed, fearful yet laughing, and Gehan came stalking in, uninvited, to see what was going on.

"What's the matter? What is happening here, Latha?" he asked. He asked the question, but his eyes were glancing around the room, taking it in: the pile of sandals along the wall, where Madhayanthi had made her usual mess, the simple table where Latha had a kerosene *kuppi* lamp, which she liked to light at night. She liked the way it made her room seem mysterious and refugelike, that wavering lamplight, as if hideous crimes were being perpetrated outside, as if she was lying low in a safe house. She liked to read by it, glancing over whatever came her way, usually the children's textbooks and the ones they borrowed from their friends, comic books like *Tintin,* and *Amar Chitra Katha,* and others by Enid Blyton, books with words that she didn't fully understand but that she enjoyed sounding out, sometimes with help from Madhavi, words like *Mar-ple, dis-trust-ing, bar-na-cle, sus-pi-cious,* and so on. In fact, there was one open to a page right now: *Astérix and Cleopatra*. Latha was glad it was there even though she had never read it. Madhavi had borrowed it and had been reading it earlier in the afternoon. Still, it showed that she was no ordinary servant woman, and he should be reminded of that.

She crossed her arms and waited as his eyes rested on the book, then continued their journey, across her walls, hung not with pictures of useless film stars but with watercolor paintings of the hill country that she had saved from a fancy calendar Thara had got from a director of the Tourist Board one Christmas, and that she had paid to have framed behind thin glass, in Wellawatte, passing up new sandals in favor of this preference; her neatly made bed, the corners creased at each visible edge, the woven mat beside it; the Buddha statue and the tray before it, brushed clean and waiting for the evening's flowers, the incense ready, no dust in sight. Even the open windows were dressed with a bit of bargain lace. She was glad that she had replaced the old mosquito coils with a repaired net over her bed, one of the family ones that Thara had thrown out. Latha had always disliked the reedy, acidic smell of the coil smoke, the way it clogged up her throat and got into her clothes, and at night when she went to sleep, the net draping to the ground from above her head made her feel hot but grand. She hoped he could see that, too, how grand she felt in her own room.

Gehan's eyes returned to the cause of his intrusion: his daughters. They lingered on the three faces, the younger ones frozen midgiggle, waiting to be chastised, their hands on Latha's shoulders, balancing, and the older face gazing with such pride and composure at his own.

"Don't make so much noise . . . I'm trying to get some work done. Latha . . . get the children to take a nap; they should rest after all the troubles of this afternoon."

"Take a nap?" Madhayanthi snorted, after her father was safely out of earshot. "We haven't taken a nap for five years now!"

"He's right, you should rest for a little bit," Latha said, feeling tired now the way she did whenever she had to interact with Gehan, all the unsaid words and unmet needs rising up all over again. "I'll come and wait with you till you fall asleep."

"Can we sleep here?" Madhavi asked.

"No, you have to sleep in your own room."

"But yours is more comfortable," Madhayanthi whined, flopping down on the neat bed and burrowing into the pillow. "It smells better."

"Your pillows would smell better too if you washed more often," Madhavi said and ran out of the room before Madhayanthi could respond, barely missing the pillow that she threw. "You can't get me!" she yelled.

And they were gone, leaving behind that same odd absence again that Latha knew they would leave permanently someday, now that she had thought about it, had let it enter her consciousness. She neatened up her room, straightening the sandals on their shelf, pulling the sheets tight on her bed. Perhaps she should write to Leela again, she thought. Maybe she would reply this time.

She did write to Leela, but not right away. She wrote because Gehan whipped the houseboy. And the reason that moved her so greatly was that she had taken the girls to Galle Face that evening and thought she had lost them forever. One minute they had been standing beside her, the next they were gone. She had torn around the green looking for them, her insides churning with fear, with grief, but they hadn't been lost, they had been standing close by, watching a magician performing tricks on a raised stage. She had grabbed their hands and scolded them and then pressed them to her body, dwelling within loss and keeping until her whole being seemed ready to explode.

And right in the wake of that, the whole matter with the houseboy. It wasn't his fault, really. How could he—who was not sent to school as she had been in the Vithanages' house, Thara announcing that he was too stupid to benefit from school and saying screw the government, which couldn't make her send him—how could this boy know the things that children find out only from one another? About how to fly a kite, for instance, or play marbles, like the other boys did. But most of all, how would he know how to watch his step around girls, particularly those who could not, would never belong to him?

Madhavi came of age. It happened in Latha's room, and without the hysteria that had accompanied her mother's advent into puberty.

"Latha, I've got my period," she said, and Latha felt a stab of pain in her side, so she laughed and clapped and rubbed their foreheads and noses together and planted breathed-in kisses on Madhavi's cheeks and pretended to be thrilled.

Madhavi agreed to observe her first period in the traditional way but insisted that her solitary time should be spent in Latha's room while she was confined to the house. The houseboy, invisible to everybody except when something went wrong, was doing his usual chores, which included sweeping the house and cleaning the family bathroom and kitchen, and, on his way out of the kitchen that Saturday, day three of Madhavi's confinement, he saw her through the bars on the window in Latha's room. It was a window that she usually left closed since it offered no vista other than the corridor, but since Madhavi had taken up residence there, she had forced it open, mostly to entertain herself by booing at and scaring her sister when she came by to see her.

And so, in order to banish whatever ill had been ensured for Madhavi's future because she had been seen by a boy while observing her period of seclusion, the houseboy was whipped by Gehan. His screams were terrible; Latha knew the lashes that fell upon the boy, free to run but too scared to do so, came from some deep, vengeful place in Gehan's heart, some anger at somebody else, something—at his daughter for growing up, at his wife for her caste, at Latha for setting up a room truly her own, at the way the women in the house twined together, at the way they had space in their world for the houseboy but not for him.

"Stop it!" she screamed at Gehan. "*Deiyyané* mahaththaya, please stop it!"

And she could not be sure whether it was accidental or whether he meant it, for the belt, looping above his head like an airborne reptile, came down on her body. Once, yes, but it was enough. It stopped both her and Gehan, the rage draining from his face, she struck dumb. She turned away and gathered the houseboy to her, where he fell, broken and sobbing, murmuring "Amma, Amma, Amma," even though he was an orphan, an orphan who had been brought to them by somebody on some estate somewhere, another anonymous donation to the Vithanage-Perera families, like she had been. A child when he came, a child now, and from that time, her child.

So she went back to explain to Madhavi that she should return to her room, but she didn't have to. Madhavi had been removed forcibly by her parents and sent, crying, to her own room, where she waited, Latha knew, for her to come and make things better again. Instead, Latha helped the houseboy in and laid him down on her bed, which he filled with his body grown gangly over the thirteen years of his life, and she cleaned the stripes, some smaller, some like bands around his back and legs. She cleaned them with *Dettol*, hushing him when he winced. She got *Cicatrin* powder and covered the soft oozes with it. There were no bandages in the house, so she tore up the rest of the white little girl dress and wrapped those strips around the wounds. And since he was lying on her bed and she liked it to be clean, she washed his dirt-caked feet, bringing basin after basin of water into the room and scrubbing them till they were as spotless, though not as soft, as hers. Then she went to the kitchen to make koththamalli.

Something in the aroma of the coriander seeds, popping and dancing over the high heat, and the sweetness added on by the ginger she threw into the water, cleared her head. It was like the whole house was being fumigated of old ideas, old hopes. It was such a strong sensation that she grabbed a tea cloth and held her own head over the steam, inhaling and inhaling the sharp scents, as if her whole body could be cleansed by the strength of this one simmering pot. Of everything that was leaving her, the hardest to let go was her bond with Thara, the sense she had that they were united in some way, tied together even though she had glimpsed it only in flashes in the years after her return from the convent. So she forced herself to stay under the cloth, the heat burning her nostrils until she could be rid of that last illusion, and though she couldn't be sure that it had left her entirely, when she pulled her head back out, the pores of her face open, perspiration beading on her upper lip, her brow, she felt renewed.

When the brew was ready, boiled down to a single cup, she strained it into a glass, put a spoonful of sugar into it, and took it to the boy along with a dissolved *Disprin* in an old cup. She watched him drink it and then told him to lie down and go to sleep. Then she got dressed, put on her best shoes, and went out to buy him a pair of DSI sandals for his own. On her way out she threw his old rubber slippers, held together between the toes by a rusted safety pin, in the kitchen dustbin.

"Podian will be sleeping on the floor in my room until he gets better," she told Thara later that night. "Whatever happens, someone needs to look after him after all."

Thara pursed her mouth and looked away. How thick her neck had become, like her mother's, except with much less poise. Latha felt pity for her, for the way her transgressions kept her away from her children, for the lack of courage to stand up to a man who beat her or to go to the man she loved, for not remembering their friendship enough to at least go and look at Podian's wounds. Latha felt sorry that what kindness Thara had to offer had been used up over her, with those few days of care. It made Thara seem barren, that lack in her psyche, which had only a finite amount of goodwill to bring to the world.

Which is why Latha wrote to Leela. To tell her about Podian, who had no family and who had been ordered about all his life, certainly ever since Latha met him. She wrote about what it felt like when she moved into the new house, Gehan bringing his servants, first one houseboy, then this second one, Thara bringing hers. *We were like the dowry, I suppose,* she wrote, *except we couldn't be put in the bank or marked off with barbed wire or pawned.* She smiled as she wrote that, anticipating a smile when Leela heard those words read out to her by someone at the convent, even though it wasn't funny. It was the truth. *Now we are three,* she wrote: *Leelakka, Latha Nangi, and Podian.*

But after she had sealed the letter and walked down to the sub–post office run out of a house behind the *New Eros Theater,* which showed only Tamil films that Podian longed to see and had never been allowed to, she walked home musing over those words. They were three, but they were really five. Somewhere in the country were two children, hers and Leela's, two daughters without the benefit of her resourcefulness or Leela's kindness. In a few years, wherever she was, her daughter would be as old as Latha had been when she had given birth to her, alone except for the waiting nuns. Her daughter would be fourteen years old now, only a little older than Madhavi, the daughter she had been given to love. So Latha went to the temple on the way home, in the middle of the hot day, and poured oil into five lamps, one for each of them. She lit incense and waved them over the lamps until the smoke from the fire and that from the incense mingled and floated above her head. And though she was not given to asking for things, or praying for them, that day she did. She hoped that something in all their characters would see them through life, together or apart. She hoped that their daughters were part of their own families, not serving those to which they would never belong. Then she stood there for a long time, trying to put her finger on why she always felt a sense of foreboding when she stood before a real shrine in a temple, why the way the air moved around her head, the stillness, and the sensation of inevitability disturbed her. So she brought her palms together again and stayed that way, reciting every fragment she knew: precepts, prayers, sutras, and even, at the very end, tagged on like a small decoration, the Our Father and the Hail Mary she had been taught at the convent.

And after all that she went home to tend to Madhavi, to tell her stories about how things were when she was a little girl, growing up with her mother at the Vithanages', about how Thara came of age and how she bathed her.

"I can't imagine it," Madhavi said. "I can't picture you bathing Amma, Latha."

"I did. She wouldn't have anybody else come near her."

"Can you bathe me too?"

Latha gazed at the child before her. Madhavi was sweeter than any child she had met. She had grown from being a serious-faced little girl with strangely adult cares and worries into a serene-eyed eleven-year-old. Everything about her was simple, which only accentuated how truly lovely she was. Latha felt she had played a role in that transformation, in drawing out and discarding the fears and nurturing the inner calm that Madhavi now possessed. She would have liked to bathe this girl, the one who was closest to her heart, but she knew better. "I don't think so, petiyo," she said. "I think Amma has made plans for you. Or if not her, then your grandmother would have."

She was right and wrong. Thara had made plans, and Mrs. Vithanage had endorsed them, but Madhavi suddenly proved to be just as obdurate as her mother had been, and no amount of cajoling or threats could convince her that anybody but Latha should bathe her.

And so Latha did. She woke up early, boiled the water, carried it in, prepared the herbs and flowers, and washed the child. This time Latha's admiration was wrapped in her recognition of her innocence, and that misted her eyes and made her get soap in Madhavi's so that she ran around the bathroom hopping her reed-thin body up and down on both feet and turning around in circles shouting, *"Ahh! Ahh! Wash it out! Latha, wash it out! Auw auw auw!"* and that made Latha laugh. So it was a happy morning, a happy girl stepping out toward her mother and grandmother, who waited, one with a coconut and the other with a carved knife, safe in the knowledge that she, Latha, stood behind.

Latha took Madhavi to the shops one afternoon that week and bought her a new pair of shoes, with a heel on them. It was a pair that Madhavi had been hoping for, to wear with the baggy jeans and hooded shirts that were all the rage among the girls at her school. And Latha bought her a bar of chocolate from Podian, who had, of his own accord, given her ten rupees for it, understanding at last that something of significance had taken place in Madhavi's life, and finding generosity now that he had someone to emulate.

And perhaps that was why Madhavi came into her room one night before going to bed, dressed in her baby blue pajamas, her hair in two long braids, and worshiped Latha.

"What is it that you are doing Madhavi baba?" Latha asked, backing away, alarmed.

"My Buddhism teacher said that it was better to worship the servants who work in our houses than the politicians and people that we are supposed to at the prize givings and other events at school. She said the servants actually do something for us. So that's what I'm going to do from now on. I'm going to worship you, Latha."

Politics, Latha thought. What right had that teacher to insert politics into her class? Still, it was the first time anybody had ever worshiped her, and if that was Madhavi, well, it wasn't so bad after all. She had looked after this girl for almost twelve years, watched her, fed her, protected her, and taught her. Yes, it was all right. So she let the girl bow before her, and she laid her hand on Madhavi's head and blessed her.

Biso

The children look over their shoulders at the sound of the explosion, but they don't stop walking. It is as if this too is now just old experience to them. I am amazed at their resilience. It must be their youth, for I feel my heart thudding in my chest in time to our steps. There's a small temple on the side of the road when we take the next bend, walking single file just in case some vehicle comes speeding by, a silly thought, I know, on a mountain like this, where the air is so quiet that an engine can be heard miles away.

"Let's stop here and light a lamp for the people on the train," I call out to my boy, who has already passed it by. It's not a real temple, just a little white-tiled ledge set into the earth in the shade of a Bo tree. There's a spring nearby, and two old clay pots. I put our bags down and fill the pots so each of the children can water the tree. Then we find an unlit lamp and pour the oil out of another that has gone out into ours. I tear a strip of cloth from an old underskirt, and the little one helps me make a wick, standing opposite me and twisting the cloth in reverse to my direction. She puts her finger in the middle and I let mine go, watching her delight as our separate parts wind around each other in a loving embrace. It is peaceful, standing there shoulder to shoulder before our lamp, under that tree. I feel grateful.

We recite Pansil, and then I bless each of them, my fingers grazing the smoke from our lamp before I place my warm, hopeful palms on each of their heads. Chooti Duwa imitates me, gathering something—I don't know what she imagines she is gathering—from the air around her and blessing us with a pouring motion over each of our faces, bent low to receive her piety. The older children laugh.

"Amma, can we wash here?" my son asks.

"I suppose it is okay, if we make sure that the water runs away from the Bo tree," I tell him.

The water is cold, very cold, on our skin, but it feels good to wash ourselves, finally. Wash the dust, the tiredness, the anxiety, everything, and then to wipe it all away with our towel. I drape the towel around Loku Putha's shoulders.

"It will keep you cool for a while, and it will dry it out too."

"Aiyya is a rack," Loku Duwa says.

"Aiyya looks like an old man," the little one says. "He looks like the old man who gave us bread."

Loku Putha smiles but doesn't argue, happy to be within our happiness. I let each of them drink a fistful of water from the stream to quench their thirst, trusting that they will not fall sick.

"Let's get going now," I say, though I don't want to leave the shade of the tree or the coolness of the water. I don't want to pick up the bags or keep walking.

"How far do we have to go?" Mala asks.

I look ahead to where the road takes a turn around the mountain and goes who knows where; the world seems to end where my line of vision does, a sudden, precipitous termination to the forward motion of our life. "I don't know, Loku Duwa," I tell her, "but it can't be far."

"I'm tired of this trip," Chooti Duwa says, and none of us responds, seconding her statement with our silence. I pick up the big bag, and Loku Duwa reluctantly takes the other side. After a few turns, Loku Putha walks back to where we are and squats beside the little one. Wordlessly, she climbs up on his back and puts her arms around his neck. He holds on to the feet she has wrapped around his waist and struggles to his feet. He continues to walk, still ahead of us but slower now. I am happy for my Chooti Duwa, that he is there to take care of her in this way. And happy for him that he knows to be mindful of her.

At each turn we expect to see the thé kadé that the driver told us about. Each time, we are disappointed: vistas drop and rise to our right, and the thick foliage, some with thorny flowers, crowds us to our left, short, sturdy bark glistening with numerous greens, but ahead of us there is nothing but the road, hot and unending. Nineteen such turns before the mountain begins to gain ground with the road beside us so that I no longer feel the need to watch my children quite so closely, afraid that their feet might slip and they themselves be lost in the tumbling forests beneath. Now the road is sheltered on both sides.

At the twenty-seventh turn we see it: the shop, a portion of it beside the road, the rest stuck in the earth behind, like an inverted *L*. It sits at the end of this stretch of road. I wish it were brighter, painted in some fresh color, this beacon of ours. But it is dark and old, part stone, part brick, part wattle and daub; something that seems to have risen from the unseen ground and clawed its way up onto the road, where it stakes the barest of claims upon the progress implied by broken granite and rolled tar.

"Amma, there it is!" Loku Putha says, pointing at the shack. "It doesn't look like it sells egg hoppers," he adds, a little sadly.

"We'll see, you never know. They might make some just for us."

"I can see plantains!" Chooti Duwa says, contented, at least for now, by that prospect. "I hope they are seeni kesel. I don't want any other kind."

"You always want sugary things," Loku Putha says to her, putting her down and stretching his shoulders, "even with your plantains! You'll get worms soon, and then you'll see. Ambul kesel is better for you. I hope they're ambul."

"I won't get worms," Chooti Duwa says, unperturbed. "I never get worms." It is the gift of a youngest child, this conviction that ordinary difficulties will pass her by, and I am glad she has that. I secretly hope that the shop sells sugar plantains, a little bonus for my baby, who has traveled so far without complaint. And ambul too, for my Loku Putha, who has done so much to help me and his sisters.

"Let's get there and see what they sell," Loku Duwa says, practical. Loku Putha takes the towel off his shoulders and carries it in his hand. He gets there first, Chooti Duwa close behind; my Loku Duwa keeps pace with me. By the time I get there, the owner has come out. He gestures with his head toward my son and speaks in the gurgling, curved-jaw speech of a betel chewer.

"This son of yours doesn't say much," he says, teasing my boy.

I smile. "My Loku Putha is tired, isn't that so? And hungry."

I follow the man's gaze toward the shady interior of his shop, and it takes a few moments for my eyes to adjust to the darkness within and the one glass cupboard that sits next to his counter. Arrayed on the topmost shelf is an assortment of chocolates, their wrappers dusty, their faces pressed against the glass, a clear indication that the inventory is both low and old. A short pile of steamed bread leans against one corner on the second shelf; next to it are two round cutlets on an enamel plate. Besides those, there are two plates of string hoppers and two bowls each of sambol, kiri-hodi, and fish in a heavily peppered brown gravy on the third shelf, and, on the last, four plain hoppers. I look back at him. He is an older man, closer to sixty than fifty, though who knows how the chilly up-country life weathers a person. I wonder if there is a wife or a daughter somewhere in the house.

"We have been walking for a long time," I say, "and the children . . . I was hoping that there would be some food for them here."

He shrugs and gestures with his hand toward the display of food, his mouth turned down in regret. He picks up a tin and spits out a stream of red juice. "This is what we have left from the morning." His voice is clear and sounds heartlessly matter-of-fact now that his mouth is free from spit.

The children look at the food, Loku Duwa biting the fingernail on her left thumb, anxious and hungry and disappointed, but not as much as Loku Putha, who looks like he might cry. My Chooti Duwa is in imminent danger of actually doing so. The plantains are neither the sweet kind nor the sour kind; they are the long, pasty aanamaalu. The man must feel sorry for me, for he says, "We don't sell lunch here. Nobody comes this way at that time, but my family, we'll be eating soon. I can ask my daughter-in-law to cook some extra rice for you as well. The children might like hot food. You can sit there and wait while I go and ask what is available."

"Thank you," I say, sinking down onto the smooth bench on his veranda. The children join me, casting their belongings to the ground, glad for the rest. They look haggard again, the wash back at the Bo tree having completely evaporated off their skins, off their minds. Off mine, too.

"Here," the man says, coming into view in the relatively bright light of the veranda, and holding out a comb of sugar plantains that he has brought from inside. "Give the children some of these while they wait. They must be hungry."

Chooti Duwa beams at him and helps herself to the fruit without waiting for my permission, and the others follow her lead. I am too tired to reprimand them, mother them, coach them on proper behavior; I just murmur my thanks and take one and hold it in my hand, too tired to peel it or eat.

"Where are you coming from?" the man asks.

"We are traveling from Matara," I tell him. "It's a long way, I know, but I didn't expect it to be this long for us. We had to get to Colombo and then switch trains from there. Our second train had trouble on the tracks, and then it got stopped, a long way back it seems now, somewhere after Pattipola—"

"*Deiyyo sākki!* Were you on the train with the bomb?" I nod, and he calls out loudly to someone in the house below. "Sumana!"

Sumana, when she comes, is about my age, though her manner is that of an older woman. She is fair-skinned and homely. She wears a long skirt like a sarong and a blouse with a cardigan over it. She looks intently at me. She must be the daughter-in-law, for, right behind her, is a formidable woman who is clearly the lawmaker in the house. The storekeeper's wife is round-faced with a trickle of tiny warts between her left ear and her throat, and she is three times as large as he is, the way wives are supposed to be in these parts. She stands there with her hands on her hips, the fingers twitching compulsively. Their poverty is visible. Sumana's ill-fitting clothes, the way the colors don't suit her, and the fact that the older woman's sari blouse is held together by safety pins and worn on the outside at that, a clear sign that she has little to hide or be ashamed of; impoverishment has blighted her all her life.

"This is my son's mother, Dayawathi," he tells me, "and this is our daughter-in-law." He turns back to them. "These people were on that train we heard about on the radio," he tells them, and they are instantly kinder, our fate their excuse to take care of us. They both start talking at once, overlapping each other's sentences yet neither seeming to care.

"You must eat with us . . . so far to walk . . . where are you going?"

"How frightened you must be . . . I would be terrified."

"I heard it was old JVP people . . . but some others said Tamils . . . do you know?"

"Children had died . . . how many children? . . . did your children see?"

I can barely keep up with their observations and questions, so I give up trying. I nod or shake my head and shrug when appropriate and leave them to tell my story. My children stare at them, openmouthed, as if learning about all this for the first time; it certainly sounds more important in their voices, the event that we have survived.

"Leave them alone now, they should rest a little. Sumana, break a bottle of *Portello* for them," the man tells the younger woman. The children perk up when the drink is mentioned, but I am only reminded of the half-eaten meal beside those dead bodies. *Portello,* too sweet like new love and dark purple like bad blood. When Sumana returns with a tray of cloudy glasses and the bottle of lukewarm *Portello,* it feels ominous. I want to refuse, but I cannot; I watch the children drink and feel nauseated, the bile rising up to my throat. I stagger to the corner of the house and retch over the side of their half wall.

"Better stay here today. You can't travel like this. You are sick, and the children are tired," the older woman says, and her voice is both comfort and temptation.

Before I can argue, the children start to beg: "Nangi and Chooti Nangi are tired, Amma," my son says, "they can't walk any more today." He curls his toes as he says this, and I feel like weeping for him, for those weary feet. Theirs, yes, but mostly his oldest-child feet, the uncomplaining ones.

"Are you sure you don't mind?" I ask the man, Veere's Father. That, Sumana tells me, is what she calls her father-in-law, ever reminded of his importance and contribution to and role in her life. I ask repeatedly over the next hour, making the customary protestations, feigning polite reluctance, gauging the strength of their offer. But it stands. They are good people. We stay.

The meal they serve is simple: rice with white leek and potato curry, a spicy tinned fish curry, and sambol. The children are delighted, and so am I. It feels good to be inside a home, at a table with hot food and more plantains and plain tea with ginger to follow. Afterward, I help them wash the blackened pots in the equally blackened sink, its cracked concrete crevices packed as if by intention with years of dirt and grease. Still, I am warmed by the sight of the ineffectual bar of *Sunlight* soap. I imagine that people of our means will always buy those hard yellow cakes with dogged determination; it is as though we imagine faith and loyalty alone would transform it from a rudimentary lard-based block into billowing suds that make everything in our lives sparkle. I imagine it now, that possible transformation, as I scrub and scrub with the wad of coconut fiber in my hands, the thick soap oily and useless. These things are the same everywhere. We are the same, our people, up-country or from the South, down to the calendars we leave on the walls, long after their years have passed, as our simple decorations, our paintings.

There is no way to stave off the "father of your children" questions, and by evening I have told Dayawathi the entire story of our journey. I tell her of the abuse, but not about the infidelity, for she would not sympathize. Women who are loyal to good husbands never understand, and the others, tied for unexamined reasons to some variety of louse, feel only hatred toward people like myself, we who choose, we who don't live by those rules of propriety that are established for us by men: For the sake of. For the sake of the children, the parents, our honor, our appearances that fool nobody. All one earns by living that way is pity, and of all the emotions I wish to arouse in another human being, pity is the least of them.

"Are you still feeling sick?" she asks, and I realize that I have spat on the ground.

"No, no, something was caught in my throat, nendé," I say, shaking my head. Sumana brings me a glass of water and returns to watching the children. She holds my Chooti Duwa in her lap as she shows them how to play a game with a fistful of seeds, tossing them up and throwing them down. I observe her for a while. The old woman reads my thoughts.

"We don't have any grandchildren yet," she says. "My son has gone to the Arab countries, to Jordan, to earn something for them. He is the one that sent money for our radio. Otherwise, we wouldn't know half the things that are going on even in our parts, let alone in the rest of the country. Not many people from our area go abroad, only a wife from one other family who went at the same time, but my son is headstrong and he heard about it from a friend in Colombo. There's an agency there, and he found a way to go. They, my daughter-in-law and my son, want to move to the city, to Nuwara Eliya. They say there is work there. They don't want to tend our vegetables and mind the store." She shrugs, disappointed and judged.

"This is a peaceful place," I say, noting how neatly they have laid out terraced vegetable beds behind their house, a garden that was invisible from the road. It is not large, but it is sufficient. I would live in such a place. I try to imagine what it would be like. The children going off to school, myself at home alone. How clean the store would be, how I would dust those chocolates, cook better food, perhaps buy some tables so people can sit to eat, not hunch over handheld plates on the benches lining the veranda. I would put in a window, get some light inside . . .

"Where are you going to from here then?" she asks.

No, the store cannot be mine. I have somewhere to go. "I'm going to my aunt's house. I hope she is still in good health, and that there will be room for us there."

"We would let you stay, but we find it difficult to manage as it is," she tells me, a real apology in her eyes. "People have moved away. Few stayed nearby. And even most of them go to the town for what they want. Only the old-timers on their way to the milk factory each morning and the occasional car stop here. People like you . . ." Her voice trails off again. There's a mix of apology and resignation and resentment, too, in her voice. For the inability to join that movement headed somewhere else.

"Don't worry about us," I tell her. "We will be all right. It is good of you to allow us to rest here for the day."

"Well, you can stay till tomorrow and then you can get an early start. That way you will be at your aunt's house by afternoon. The station is not that far from here. Our son's father can show you the way."

I am grateful that she makes this offer. Having had the opportunity to take my mind off the journey, the getting-there, having been allowed to let the children roam free and to unburden some of my story to this older woman, I feel too tired to move. I am so exhausted by what I have managed to accomplish—the escape, the difficult journey, getting my children to safety through all of it—that her kindness is almost dangerous. It is the type of goodwill that convinces me that everything is well, that I can relax, hand over the care of my children to good strangers like her. Perhaps, I tell myself, just for a few hours I can give in to that relief. Surely I have earned that respite.

Dinner is bread warmed over the fire and leftover sambol tempered with a new onion. It is more than enough for me and for the children. My Loku Duwa in particular seems very happy, blossoming even, with her conversation about the gardens, what she has found there, the size of the vegetables. She has always been domestic by nature, and I am glad to listen to her. Hearing her talk, I permit myself to imagine a future for her, to picture her grown up, a nurse or a lady doctor who comes home to a well-managed home, a loyal husband at her side.

"Big! The carrots are so big!" my Loku Duwa says, making me smile.

"And the other vegetables too, everything is bigger and brighter than what we have in our village." That is my Loku Putha.

"But they don't have fish," Chooti Duwa says, claiming a little something for us.

"That's true, duwa, we don't get much fish," the old woman tells her. "It's expensive. That's why we rely on the tins of *Jack Mackerel* that we buy from town."

"We only buy tinned fish for special occasions!" Chooti Duwa counters. "Amma makes cutlets with tinned fish and potatoes. Even potatoes we don't buy them much there. Amma says potatoes are not as good as dhal. That's why."

They all laugh. "We do get some river fish," the old man says, "but not much. Mostly it's vegetables."

It is safe talk. The kind I am not accustomed to: conversations about food, the sources of sustenance, the prices of things. In our household, the sea-fish-flavored dinner was eaten fast and in silence, and any statement cast out on a brittle raft, expecting to be hit by lightning, sunk. This conversation is like the ones I remember from when I was a child, between two cordial, if not overtly affectionate, parents, and a single, beloved daughter, safe in a well-lit home, free from fear. And yet, the children talk as though this was the norm. How quickly they adapt, how deftly they leave behind the scars that I continue to carry.

Tomorrow, when we wake up, I will do the same. I will leave everything behind, buried somewhere beside the road, and I will be like my children, rejuvenated, flawless, new.

Latha

Podian's wounds had taken a long time to heal and left behind a smooth collection of scars. When she ran her palm over his back, they felt like fish bones. One of the lacerations had required a visit to the clinic at the top of the road. Latha had taken him. Afterward, she had paid for the small tube of orange gel that had to be bought from the fancy *Crescent Pharmacy* full of western medicine, a place she had never before set foot in, and when they came home, she had done the applications. And maybe it was only gratitude, but after that, Podian decided that he would be her servant too. Now, he made her the morning and evening cups of tea, and when he was sent to the store, he came back with a *Delta* toffee or sometimes, usually after he got paid his hundred rupees a month, 250 grams of chocolate biscuits, at seven rupees and fifty cents, that sometimes smelled of kerosene, wrapped up in a newspaper for her.

"Akka, I bought some biscuits for you to eat with your tea," he had said the first time.

"Why did you waste your money on me? You must learn to save it for something useful for yourself," she had said, cuffing him lightly on the side of his head.

And he had remained silent, his eyes cast down, communicating two things: first, that she was worth his money, and, second, that his gift to her was a gift to himself.

"Here, you have some too then," she had said, and he had smiled as if it had been she who had bought a present for him, his uneven teeth covered in flecks of sweet brown crumbs.

And maybe what Gehan noticed was not Podian's reverence toward Latha, who was, after all, more than twice his age, but his gender. The fact of Podian, a boy, and his attention to Latha, a youthful woman, the way women remained when they had no husbands and children around to be assessed by, must have begun to creep into his consciousness and disturb his sleep, for he began to spend more time at home, and most of that time in Latha's sight.

And who could blame her if, in the quiet house, its moneyed mistress out on her own rendezvous, its children safe at school, Latha would begin to dream that all of it belonged to her? The house, and everything inside it, particularly its owner, whom she had, in fact, once almost owned, and then lost to the girl who had needed him then?

She had been good, she told herself, as she dressed with increased attention to how the newly fashionable synthetic fabrics draped and hugged her curves. She had done right by Thara. She had been loyal, she had helped her cope with this lesser marriage, lesser future, she had found Ajith for her, and lied for them both. She had protected Thara's children, caring for them as though they were her own daughters. In fact, the girls *were* her daughters, the things she knew about them, the way they came to her, even their resentments of her ministrations, these were the stuff of mother-daughter relationships. And she had played that role and still allowed Thara to wear the title: mother. And all she was doing was pretending, after all. No more.

But she dressed just a little more sleekly when she went to drop the girls at school, Gehan in the front seat, Madhayanthi and Madhavi beside her, Madhavi still holding her hand through the whole drive, just as she had done as a baby.

She held his gaze just a little longer when their eyes met in the rearview mirror, in which he always checked his hair before he got down at his Duplication Road office, wondering if he noticed the kohl rims of her eyes, which she made up just for this morning drive and wiped off as soon as she got home and before Thara could wake up and notice.

She leaned just a little lower when she served him his tea.

And more than once on the sudden afternoons when he was home, her hair would come loose from the bun she had tied and fall down the side of her face.

And on one of those occasions, when both things happened at the same time, Gehan put aside the newspaper he was pretending to read, pushed away the cup of tea, and touched her.

And she did not move.

"Forgive me," he said, after a long moment. "Latha."

And she knew that he could not be apologizing, that he was only saying what he thought he should so they could begin speaking to each other again, she knew, she knew, but she turned away from the truth and simply shrugged and said what he needed to hear. "It was a long time ago, and we were very young, sir."

"You don't have to call me sir," he said, and his voice was low and full of that long ago; full also of trust, which made her feel the past more forcefully than his words.

She shrugged again, but she smiled just a little. She had never called him by his name even when they had been children, meeting for the first time or during any of their walks to school, or any of the clandestine arrangements where all they had done was walk, and once or twice hold hands. No, not in all the four and a half years of her innocence, when she had imagined a perfect future with herself and her boy, Gehan, at the center of it, had she ever uttered his name in his presence. She had referred to him by name only in the notes she had written to him in school. Somehow, those syllables had never made it to her tongue; they had stayed locked in her heart. Perhaps some greater wisdom had warned her that saying them aloud was not going to be her lot in life.

She was still standing there, half tilted forward, his hand on her arm, when she heard the gate open: Podian was back with the evening's bread. She straightened up at the same time that Gehan, clearly oblivious to Podian's return, removed his hand from her arm and caressed the loops of hair that reached to her hips, so it felt as though he had wrenched it. She winced, and turned away, rewrapping her hair into its bun. Even the gesture felt madam-like. She let an enormous smile spread across her face, unwitnessed by either Gehan, who had picked up his newspaper again, or Podian, who had just come in and was removing his sandals by the door.

And that smile, secret and wide, was like a gate through which an even larger, uncontainable, and incautious joy escaped, pushing down on her past like a rocket off a launching pad. That day, when Thara, relaxed in the way she was on those evenings when Gehan was making his weekly visit to his parents with the girls, asked Latha to make her a glass of lime juice, Latha volunteered to rub her feet.

"Your hands feel so good, Latha," Thara said, sighing with pleasure and leaning back against the plump pillows on her bed. "Even Ajith's hands are not so strong. And Gehan? My god. His hands are like steamed bread! There's nothing there. Not even like a man's." She started laughing. "I thank my lucky stars that after I got my tubes tied he's not even interested in the other stuff. He's much more likable from a distance."

Latha bent her head and kneaded Thara's calves with greater intensity. It was true that Gehan's hand had felt unsure and vaguely feminine. But she had always liked that about him. He had never been handsome or particularly brilliant the way Ajith had been, talking all the time, commenting on this and that, but his hands had seemed connected to his emotions, extensions of them, not mere tools to grab and grope with. Yes, of the three men she had experienced—Gehan, Daniel, and Ajith—even though she had not actually known Gehan the same way, physically, she had found the other two lacking. Ajith had been competent, Daniel had been awkward, but both had seemed furious and swift. It was not how she imagined things would be with Gehan. The leg beneath her palms jerked toward her face.

"Why are you stroking my leg and not massaging? Stop daydreaming! What are you thinking about? Must be some man, the way you are doing that!" And Thara shrieked again with laughter, communicating the improbability of the thought.

Latha laughed along. "Don't be silly," she said, looking Thara full in the face. "Why would I be interested in men at my age?"

"Well, I'm still interested in men, and I'm the same age," Thara said.

"Not men, one man, only Ajith Sir," Latha said, having learned that this was the way to distract Thara, by talking about Ajith.

Thara sighed her contented agreement. "Yes, only him. If only my life had gone differently, we would have had sons, Latha. Imagine? You could be looking after my sons."

Sons? Why would anybody want sons? And why would . . . "Why would you have sons and not daughters?" Latha asked, horrified and curious at the same time.

"Daughters are pests. Haven't you noticed ours? One of these days they will start up with some boy or other and I'll be putting out fires this way and that. Gives me a headache even to think of it. Thank goodness you're there to keep them under control and at least watch where the hell they are going and what they are doing. I would have given up long ago if I had to do all this on my own."

"But still, how would you have sons?" Latha persisted, pushing aside her other observation: Thara did very little on her own, and in fact did nothing at all with her daughters.

"Ajith says that Gehan is not manly enough. That's why we had two daughters."

Latha snorted. "That's stupid talk. We learned about all this in grade eight, don't you remember? You don't get boys or girls because of the virility of the father!"

Latha frowned. "Ajith studied in America. He knows a lot more than the goday schoolteachers here. Anyway, what would *you* know about these things?"

And Latha knew she had embarked on a new phase in her life, because something inside her body beamed at that remark. More than you, Thara, she wanted to say, fleetingly glad that even Ajith, whom Thara thought so highly of, would count her as his first experience of intimacy and furthermore, that she, Latha, had found him so disappointing sexually. So she shrugged and said magnanimously, "You're right. What would I know?"

There was a little silence after that as both women turned inward to the sound of the fan whirring overhead. Then Thara spoke again.

"Not that you are unattractive, Latha. That's not what I meant."

"I know."

"You are quite attractive," Thara continued, sitting up a little and staring at Latha, and as her eyes moved over Latha's body, her voice became slightly flavored with alarm. "Some might think even prettier than me. If only you weren't just a servant woman, you might have been able to make a good catch."

"*Aiyyo,* I'm too old for all that now," Latha said. "Let's talk about something else. How are your parents these days? Is Mr. Vithanage still taking his walks every morning?"

"No, no, I really mean it." Thara stood up, all of a sudden alert and motivated. "Look, nobody's home. I'll dress you up like I used to do when we were small. You'll see."

And no amount of protesting could dissuade Thara from her entertainment. She had decided to amuse herself this way and Latha might just as well have been a life-size, fully mature doll.

"Which sari shall I put you in? Hmmm . . . ," Thara said, while Latha stood behind and watched Thara slide her fingers up and down over the twin stacks of saris in her almirah. Why she had so many Latha had never quite understood, given that she wore them only to weddings, official functions related to Gehan's work, or the children's annual concerts. The rest of the time Thara wore blue jeans and short corduroy skirts, usually both in sizes too small for her ample hips, and long kurta tops in, admittedly, heavenly colors from a shop whose bags announced it as a place called *Barefoot,* with price tags that indicated that one had to be quite well shod in order to afford anything from it. Latha, for one, could probably never acquire a single thing from such a store, not even if she saved her salary for a year.

"*Aney,* Thara Madam, this is really not necessary," Latha tried again, though this time, after seeing all those saris, she was hopeful that Thara would persist with her plan.

"This one," Thara said, drawing out a purple sari. It was rather plain. "No, don't look disappointed, look at the palu!" and she swung the sari open onto the bed. And indeed, once the yards of cloth had flown up with their magical swishing sound, releasing the fragrance of luxury, and come fluttering down again to the bed, Latha saw that there was nothing to be disappointed about. The fall of the sari was embellished with hand-done lime green and gold paisley embroidery intricately twisting in and out of a black grid. The pattern continued on the top and bottom edges all along the six full yards of the sari in a three-inch square border, each square of it embroidered with a single dot, first in green, the next in gold. It was quite magnificent.

"I've never seen you wear this," said Latha, made slightly timid by the spectacle of the sari and its colors.

"Yes, it's one of those that Gehan bought for me when we got married, and I never quite liked it. It's a little too garish for me, but with your color it should look nice. Let's dress you." She picked up the sari and flapped it about and then exclaimed, *"Aiyyo!* It has no blouse! I never got one made because I didn't like it. Look, the blouse allowance is still attached."

Indeed, it was. Latha looked at the blouse piece, at once attached to and separated from the sari by a thin row of half-unpicked threads, and felt despondent. Nevermind, it had been a nice thought.

"Wait," Thara said, "we'll cut it out and just tie it around you. I don't care for it anyway."

And that was what she did. She made Latha stand still, stripped to her underwear and a borrowed underskirt, her feet wedged into Thara's gold stiletto-heeled sari shoes, while she draped and pinned the rectangle of cloth around her chest, commenting all the while on Latha's figure, the firmness of her unnursed breasts, the plunging, front-fastening purple bra she was wearing, exclaiming at the fact that even Latha, a mere servant, had taken to shaving her underarms. Latha endured all this without fuss. She had worn a sari only once before, and that had been at Thara's wedding. It had been a simple nylon sari handed down to her by some unknown relative claimed by the Vithanages. Not a real sari like this one, rustling, silk, endowed with proud colors. Thara dressed her in a Gujarati style that, she told Latha, was the rage these days. The pleats fanned out between her legs when she walked, and the fall came tipping over her shoulder, cascading to the floor in front of her body with the palu revealed in all its glory.

"Do you have a comb?" Thara asked and didn't wait for an answer. "Podian!" she yelled and sent the boy scurrying to Latha's room to fetch her comb. "What are you staring at? Grinning like an idiot? Go! Go and do something useful in the kitchen," she said, shooing Podian away when she noticed him peering at them from behind the curtain even after she had dismissed him. First she tried to pull Latha's hair up in a bun, and, when that didn't work, not being accustomed to combing any hair but her own, she told Latha it looked better loose and let it go. Then she applied a maroon lipstick with her fingers, choosing one after rejecting a dozen others and flinging them half-open to the bed, where, Latha couldn't help hoping, they wouldn't stain the white sheets; it would be terrible to try to get such stains off, even in the washing machine.

"Look in the mirror now, Latha," she said.

What Latha saw in the mirror was not Latha the servant but Latha the mistress of the house. She stood up straight and moved her body this way and that, taking in the sight. She looked like the women she saw on TV, the ones in the Indian films that she now watched with Podian late on Friday nights, the ones who knew how to sing and dance and shimmy their shoulders and always got caught in the rain in plain sight of handsome men. Yes, she was beautiful. And Thara, standing a full four inches shorter beside her, barefoot and ordinary in sweatpants and a baggy shirt, her hair uncombed after her stop at the new gym she had joined, could not quite compare. But the way Thara was looking at her, her eyes shining with goodwill and humor, a slight pride in her achievement tightening the corners of her smile, made Latha want to weep. It was too late now for her to step back to the place she had once inhabited, uncomplaining if not exactly retiring, leaving Gehan safe with his unused loyalty to his wife by law. It was much too late for this sudden kindness from Thara, for this moment from the past now that the past had returned to her through the most improbable of people, Gehan, and for that Latha was truly sorry.

"Let's take this off now before sir gets home," Latha said, tugging at the pleats tucked into her underskirt without much enthusiasm.

"No! Stop! Let's take pictures before we put it all away," Thara said. "This is the most fun we have had together since we went shopping for curtains for this stupid old house of Gehan's!"

Do this, hold up your hair, sit here, lift your shoulders, lie down. It was almost as though Thara wanted to apologize to Latha for having mocked her earlier, or perhaps for never having allowed her to display her beauty, by finding the perfect pose, the one that she could hold up and say, "Look! Look here! You are beautiful." And Latha complied. She did as she was told, and the pleasure she felt in this late-bloomed, borrowed-feather loveliness mixed so efficiently with the feelings she was trying to recapture for her lost friend who had drifted off to the scent of coriander and ginger that, unknown to her, the camera caught Latha in a particularly wistful radiance. And so taken was Thara with her activity, so enamored with this forbidden enjoyment of a servant, and their rekindling of a preadult girlhood, that she shot almost an entire roll of film and still would not let Latha undress. Which is how Gehan, having returned with two sleeping girls and come in before them to put away the usual food-based gifts from his parents before going out to waken and coax his daughters in, and having come upstairs to discover the origin of the unusual sounds of mirth that were floating from his own bedroom, managed to witness the cruel beauty of love shared between the two women in his world, the wrong one and the wrong one, and the relative value of each to the fulfillment of his life.

Biso

It is far too early when I wake up. It is still dark, the outside illuminated by what must be moonlight. The room itself feels anxious, as though it is waiting for something, and perhaps it is this disturbance in the air that has woken me.

Around me, on the floor, I sense my sleeping children. When my eyes accustom themselves to the dark light, I can make out the bodies of my daughters, dressed, still, in the clothes we came in. They are motionless but noisy, their full natures revealed in the artlessness of sleep. I gaze at the girls, the way each of them rests, one, my Loku Duwa, on her belly, curled in, fearful of the world, the other on her back, fearless and inviting. They are both wrong. They should be cautious yet open, confident of their strength yet wary of strangers. I know they are young and that time may change these things about them, but character is like a second, hidden skin: what you are born with is what you have. I wish I could realign them somehow, fix this, change that, mix them up. I turn them both so they face each other; now they are halves, and I comfort myself with this small intervention in the course of their lives.

Loku Putha is gone. I am so absorbed in my contemplation of my incorrectly arranged daughters that it takes me a while to notice my son's absence. He was sleeping on the other side of Loku Duwa, his head facing the same direction as mine was, her feet between our two faces. That's how we had gone to sleep, like the miniature fish in a flat tin box that one of the Irish nuns at the convent had once shown me; *These are herring,* she had said and explained that the name on the box, "sardines," came from a Mediterranean island called Sardinia, where every eating house serves them. I remembered the nuns last night as we lay down, end to end, taking up no more space than two adults would on the thin mattress that Sumana dusted out for us.

I get up with some difficulty, easing myself from the floor, registering the aches that have crept up my back as I slept. The house is quiet, but I can hear insect sounds outside. Small ones, like crickets and fruit bats. Perhaps he, too, could not sleep. The back door is pulled shut, but it is not latched. The smooth, long beam that serves as a barricade—against what? I had wanted to ask, as I watched Sumana slide it into place the night before but didn't, knowing that such visual reminders are necessary to guard against both what comes in and what might go out—is leaning against the wall. Outside, the air is so cold my body folds into itself.

He is standing at the top of the dirt steps leading down to the vegetable garden. He is looking at something I cannot see from where I stand, and I am about to call his name when the moon slides out from behind a cloud and he is in silhouette. He is peeing, the urine arching the way it does without effort for little boys. It makes a quick moonlit fountain full of separate particles, and he wiggles his hips, writing something in the air. It makes me smile, the way my son looks: like a small child, unburdened in every way, safe even among strangers in this unfamiliar darkness. When he finishes, he shakes off the last of it and pulls up his shorts. He continues to stand, suddenly feeling the cold, it seems, for he shivers and clutches his elbows. I want to stay there, watching him, but I know this time is precious to him. He is gaining something from his solitude, strength, perhaps, or vision or a dream. So I leave him and go inside.

I must have been more tired than I thought, or fallen into a far deeper sleep than I intended to, for when I wake up for the second time, it is to the sound of shrieking. The girls are screaming.

Chooti Duwa: "Aiyya! *Aiyya!*"

Loku Duwa: "Amma! *Amma!*"

And a mix of other voices. In the time it takes me to get up, untuck the fall of my sari from my waist and draw it over my left shoulder, and scoop my braid into a bun, I have heard what has transpired: my son has fallen down the hill below the vegetable garden. He had been trying to reach a moon moth perched on a dewy plant and slipped.

"Amma!" he sobs from the ledge below, where he lies looking as though all that he has hurt is his sense of himself. "My leg hurts . . . my leg . . . awww . . ." And in his wet voice there is an unmistakable slurry of pain, thick and desperate.

"Don't move, putha," I say, as calm as I can manage to be with an injured child I cannot comfort or even reach to touch. "Our nice seeya is coming, and he will get you out of there, my sweet son, my fair-skinned one, don't cry . . ." I can't stop myself from uttering the words that only make him cry more because this is all I can do from where I stand, hunched over the unsteady earth that has already betrayed him. And I know it helps him, this crying and crying unlike any grief he has ever expressed. Years of it come out of his body as he lies there, stroking his own leg, his eyes only on my face, crying.

It takes a long time for Veere's Father to get my boy up from where he is. First he has to enlist the help of a faraway neighbor's teenage son, left alone at home. They construct a sort of stretcher with a long stick and the handle of an *ekel* broom looped with three sarongs. The neighbor's son slides down to where my child lies, and the old man follows after, more slowly, grasping at roots and bushes as he goes. It is not that far, this distance that my son has fallen, yet he seems so badly and so invisibly hurt. I whisper prayers to myself as I watch them lift him onto the stretcher and struggle every inch of the way up the slope. Sumana and Dayawathi stand behind me, each with her arms around one of my daughters, protecting them from the sight, from my concern, from their brother's pain. When they get halfway up, Veere's Father says something to the teenager, and they stop.

"Get that for the child," he tells the young man, pointing to the moth.

"It's dead now," the boy says.

"I know," he says, "but only recently. If you reach out you can pick the leaf he is lying on."

"Don't!" I yell to the teenager. "You might drop my son!" But he has already reached past my boy and picked the leaf. He deposits it on Loku Putha's stomach.

Loku Putha stops crying. When they get up to the top and lay the stretcher down, he won't let them take the moth away. "I want to keep the moth!" he says, protecting the carcass with his fingers knitted around it. I have never seen one so close, and I, like my son, am struck by its beauty. It is several inches across, with a delicately curved tail that parts decorously at the bottom like a young dancer's feet. Each purple-edged wing is translucent, milky like moonlight, yet tinged with pale green, like morning grass. This one has four unseeing eyes drawn on the back of its body.

"Can I keep this moth?" he asks me.

I stroke the damp hair off his forehead and nod. I turn to Dayawathi. "Do you have something . . ."

"I already sent Sumana to get a plastic bag for him," she says, and her smile, though barely apparent, is kind.

As soon as the moth is taken away from him by Sumana, lifted along with its leaf and placed inside a clear plastic sleeve that must once have covered an English-language greeting card, it is as though a spell has been broken. The pain returns, and with greater intensity. His leg is broken; this much is clear from the way his left leg looks shorter, and from the heat around the swelling on the shin.

"I will make a poultice for him," Dayawathi says and walks away.

"Let's take him inside," Veere's Father says and picks up his end of the stretcher. The teenager picks up the other side and they go in, taking the steps through the vegetable garden carefully, talking to each other. I am left alone to follow. Alone except for a daughter on either side, one hand to hold in each of mine. I feel judged, as though it is I who pushed him, I who had raised my son to desire something he should have left alone.

"Will Aiyya's leg get better? Will he be able to walk?"

"Yes, Chooti Duwa, we have to get him to a doctor . . ." I trail off, feeling hopeless.

"How will we do that? Where's the hospital?" Loku Duwa asks.

"That seeya will tell us," I say, trying to sound reassuring, knowledgeable.

"What if it is far away? Too far to walk? Can they carry him all that way?" my little one asks and doesn't wait for the answer. "They can't carry our aiyya that far. See? That seeya can't breathe from all that work, and he only carried Aiyya this short way!" She looks back at where her brother had been lying and traces the path to the back door of the house with an open palm, showing me the evidence of our collective helplessness. Perhaps it is her voice, the way it is pitched, high and upward arching with every statement, the way small children speak, afraid to lose their audience, afraid that the importance of their words might escape an adult's mind, but whatever it is, it makes my eyes well up.

"I'll find a way," I say. "Go and clean yourselves up for the day at the tap." I watch the girls go around the side of the house to the washing area, Chooti Duwa in front, Loku Duwa behind. I go inside. They have laid my son down on the mattress, and his face is scrunched in pain.

"Duwa, give him this," Dayawathi says, following me in and giving me a tin cup with about an inch of dark oil flecked with white in it.

"What is it?" I ask, cautious.

She just gestures toward him with her head. "It will make the pain go away."

"Will it make him sleep?" I ask, smelling the liquid. It is not unpleasant, but it is strong, like crushed sweet herbs and something else, something bitter like the taste of the powder inside the antibiotics I once took after a nail from a boat gouged the side of my leg as I stood there with Siri. I hesitate, not wanting to put the cup to his mouth.

"It will be like he's sleeping," she says. "We can give him something else later. Right now he should have something to help him become numb, to not feel the pain."

"Here's the poultice," Sumana says and waits, without asking, for her mother-in-law to step aside.

I put the drink down and try to apply the poultice to my son's leg.

The scream that comes from him brings the girls running back, their faces wet. I am afraid to touch his leg to remove the steaming-hot, garlic-steeped bread, soggy in the long strip of cloth. I can barely think with the sound of his screams. I grab the cup and hold it to my son's lips, cradling his head in my arm. "Drink this, Putha, drink it quickly. It will make the pain go away." He swallows it in a gulp, and Dayawathi is on hand with a glass of water.

"Rinse the rest out and make him drink it," she says, and I do. I am willing to do anything she tells me so long as my son stops screaming. He does as he is asked, and I lay him back down, loathe to remove my arm from under his head but knowing I should let him rest. I stroke his hair, his arm, whatever I can, trying to make him stop whimpering until, at last, only the tears are left, dripping silently from the corners of his eyes, and, minutes later, not even those. He has fallen asleep.

I clean myself at the tap outside; I wash my hands and feet and face. I ask Dayawathi for some oil, and I make a wick out of a strip of old cloth from the underskirt I had torn for this same purpose when we were still on the road. This time, my little one does not volunteer to help, and the wick is made quickly and efficiently, though, I feel, with less faith and delight held within it. I light the lamp underneath the family's pictures of the Buddha and stand there, waiting for some relevant prayer to come to me. I wait, but there is no prayer I can think of for my circumstance. I can think only of the story of Kisa Gothami and her dead son, and the Buddha's request that she find mustard seeds from a house that had withstood no death; I picture her running from door to door in her fruitless search, until at last her footsteps cease and she returns to acknowledge the lesson of impermanence. But my son is alive! He is only damaged, he can be mended, I know this. But what prayer? What prayer?

"Don't cry, Amma," Chooti Duwa says, startling me. She begins to recite Pansil. I want to tell her those words are useless. I want to tell her there must be some prayer that will bring grace to us, but her voice stops me. It is sweet and innocent and full of belief. So I join her in uttering the precepts, vowing to show compassion toward living things, to refrain from taking that which is not given, to abstain from sexual misconduct, to devote myself to truth and clarity in thought and expression, to refuse to imbibe drinks that would impair my judgment.

Loku Duwa joins us in the middle of our chanting, and when we are done she hands me a flower. I don't know what it is called, but it is large and purple with soft, lush petals that look like a child's drawing, so perfectly pointed and shaped, so neatly arranged, I am shocked that she has picked it, but when I turn around to see if anybody has noticed, I find that both Dayawathi and Sumana are standing behind us.

"It's okay," Dayawathi says, gesturing with her head toward the shrine. I place the flower next to the lamp. I let her lead us in the familiar meditation:

Pujemi Buddham kusumena 'nena
puñena 'metena ca hotu mokkham
Puppham milayati yatha idam me
kayo tatha yati vinasabahavam.

I close my eyes as I make the offering, and I want to release myself into this simple prayer about the ending of all life or, if nothing else, at least the already fading life of the flower we have placed before us. I want to be at peace, but it eludes me. What I see when I close my eyes is the flower, radiant in its purple color and unpicked; the moth, not dead but alive, returning again and again to that same plant; and my son, whole and striding before me, helping me show us the way forward, flagging down a car with a driver whose help I should have accepted.

And just as the last words are uttered, we all hear the sound of a car pulling up, drowning whatever private hopes we had taken out to gaze at in that moment, sending all of them and us scattering.

When I finally make it up the stairs to the storefront, I see the driver of the red car. "This boy stopped us," he says, gesturing toward the teenager. "We were on our way back to Thalawakele. What has happened?"

"Her son fell, and he has broken his leg . . ."

"... can't walk ..."

"... We can't carry him to the hospital ..."

"... can you take him to the hospital?"

"... trying to get a moon moth!"

"... mother was still sleeping ..."

"I need to get my child to the nearest hospital," I say, breaking through the other voices with the greater authority I can claim by my ownership of both the victim and the crime of negligence. "I will give you whatever I have if you can get us there." I slip my bangles off my wrists and hold them out. The driver doesn't look at them, and finally I put them back on.

I don't like the way the driver looks me up and down. He clucks his tongue and speaks disparagingly to me now, unlike before. "I told you to take the money, and you didn't want to, foolish woman. This is what happens when people think too highly of themselves. Now see? Now you have to beg."

I know he is disappointed that I am no different than he is, that I have not lived up to the regard he found for me when we last parted company. Then, I had spoken graciously and with unhurried polite-ness. Now, I am needy and clamoring for him to advocate on my be-half with white people. I want to tell him that the money would not have helped. Money does not have wheels or an interior or anything that we could have used. But I must remain silent for the sake of my child, so I bow my head and look contrite.

"You will be blessed if you can just get me to the hospital," I tell him again, this time infusing my voice with the deference he is demanding of me, for having let him down, this boy. How glad I am that my mother is dead, that she has not had to see me come to this, to beg from *Suddhas*.

"I'll go and ask the white gentlemen," he says and walks out.

I follow him. We all follow him, and I wish the others, even my own daughters, had not. I have seen our people through the eyes of foreigners when I lived by the sea. The way we cluster together, as if becoming larger would make us as wealthy or more deserving of the sweets and rupees they sometimes fling at us, more worthy of the gifts their children hold out, the ugly white plastic dolls with their yellow hair and unblinking blue eyes that stare and stare at ours. I have always believed that we are more worthy than they, and of better things than what they bring to us. I try to shake off the others and stride ahead a little, purposefully. I alone will do the negotiating. I know how.

The driver, who has got back into the car, is listening to the foreigners discuss my request. He looks straight ahead. The two foreigners stop talking and look at me. I don't like the way they look at me, but I am willing. I am willing to do anything they want if they will help me do right by my son. The older man smiles encouragingly, and I lower my eyes and then look back at them again, wordlessly saying what they must want to hear: *Yes, Yes! I will! I am not one of those women, but I will do this for my son!* They speak to the driver, and now it is his turn to stare at me. I don't know what they have said to him, but he looks at me differently now, sympathy and disgust and self-loathing all rolled into one, and finally another emotion taking over: blame. He is blaming me. He seems angry when he gets out of the car, and I back away a little.

"The gentlemen can only take your son with them," he says, "because there is no room in this car for more than that. You can see for yourself. The old *Suddha* can barely fit into the front seat."

"Malli." I call him this, hoping that this time, too, it will help a better nature to come forth. "I beg of you. I cannot send my son alone to a hospital, even if you are a good man, and they are good people . . ." I glance over at the older foreigner, who is watching me, his head lowered so he can see through the short three-cornered pane of glass on the window.

"That is their offer," the driver says. "They are already going out of their way to help. We will have to go to Hatton to find a hospital. Take it or leave it. You are in no position to be demanding anything. We have other things to do today without having to stand here negotiating with the likes of you," he concludes and spits to one side.

How does he know to do this? To remind me of the filth I left behind, to make me feel more vulnerable and weaker than I already am? I go to the car and open the door on the driver's side. I put my palms together and bring them to my forehead. "Please, sir, I will do anything. Please let me come with my son, sir. He is only nine years old, and he will be frightened to go alone, sir."

They look again at each other. The younger one is protesting, and they argue with each other in another language and I understand only one word. It is one that I have heard often by the boats when foreigners like them came to watch the catch being pulled in by the men and older boys: *Junge.* Boy.

Veere's Father and Dayawathi and even Sumana have come forward and are encouraging me to send my son with the foreigners, though I don't want to listen to them. What do they know of white people? I try to tell them to be quiet, but they don't seem to hear me.

"Duwa," Veere's Father says, "the little one will be all right. Better anyway to send with foreigners. The hospital will even take more notice, don't you think?"

I hear Sumana now. "That is it. They will rush baba to emergency. That's what he needs, isn't it? He needs an operation right away. Our local dispensary can't do those things. He has to get to the big hospital."

"Just think, duwa, we were standing there, all of us, asking for help from the gods, and this car came just in time, didn't it?" Dayawathi adds. "Like our prayers were answered. It is your good fortune that they arrived. If not, how are we to get Putha to the hospital?"

Veere's Father steps in front of me and looks into my eyes as he speaks. "And anyway, the driver is a local boy, and he will be like an older brother. I am sure he will take care of our Putha and see that he gets help fast. He's the driver after all. He can drive quickly to the hospital."

"The longer you delay, the worse it is," Dayawathi says, placing her hand on my back. "The kasāya that I made for him will wear off soon, and he will wake up in so much pain. We must act quickly and get him out of here and to the hospital. That is the most important thing, isn't it, duwa? That he gets to the hospital?"

That word, *daughter,* hearing it from these two old people breaks down some of my misgivings. Aren't they like my own parents? Wouldn't my own parents have given me the same advice? They have been so kind to me, to my children, taking no payment, offering us not only food but their home. I feel torn. What they say makes sense. They are good people. But I am his mother. Should I not listen to how I feel? It is *my* son who is injured, not theirs. And how can I send him alone?

I turn back to the foreigners. "Please, sir," I begin again, but the older man waves his hand at me. He is annoyed, and so I remain silent, looking instead at how red his face has become, how the sweat glistens on his hairline from the single open door that has let the heat flow into his previously cold car. I look again at the younger man, the boy, and I want to like him, he looks so much like a girl. He is thin and long-faced, and his hair is like my son's, sticking up and falling over at the same time. I almost smile, but he looks at me just then, and his eyes, as blue as the lotuses, are full of contempt for me. I take a step back. And right then, as if to rescue me from my shame, I hear my older daughter.

"Amma, I can go with Aiyya to the hospital. They will be able to fit me in because I'm small, not like you," she says.

I look down at my daughter and realize that my palms are still clasped, vainly, as if I had been at a temple and the temple had been blown up and left me standing there. It is hard to take them apart, but I do, to hold her face in them. She is suddenly sweeter to me, my Loku Duwa, suddenly more beautiful than she has ever seemed, as if she is, truly, a decoration like the necklace for which she is named, my Mala Devi, little goddess. My heart clenches with regret at how easily I had passed over this daughter in favor of the one who came to me through love, not duty. I smooth her hair back and absentmind-edly take her plaits in my hand, feeling their weight, remembering how I combed her hair the night before, parting it in the middle into two sections, dividing each section into threes and braiding them. They look like the wicks we made for our lamp. I remember what I had been thinking of now, as I stood before that lamp. I had been thinking about this car, about the driver, the offer they had made earlier, how I had refused them. Dayawathi is right. What else could it mean but that the gods looked down on me and saw fit to send me my deliverance?

Her words cut through my thoughts. "I can go, Amma, I can. I'm old enough. I can look after him."

"No, duwa," I say, but I smile at her. "I must go with him. I can't send him alone."

"He won't be alone. He will be with me!" she says, and her mouth trembles. As if in answer, my boy shouts from inside the house. A scream of pain that makes everybody stop talking. The driver spits again and strides over to the car. He bends down and says something to the foreigners in their language, making sharp gestures toward us. The foreigners look at each other and come to some agreement. Then the driver speaks to me, looking now and again at my daughter.

"They will allow you to send your daughter with the boy. They can manage that. They will not take you."

I want to protest, but she is already bounding away from us, into the store and down the stairs, and all I can hear is her voice raised in disproportionate elation. "Aiyya! I'm going to take you to the hospital! Don't worry! I'm coming with you to the hospital!" The children are mine and no longer mine, growing into strengths I could not have imagined, surviving tragedies they should not have been exposed to. No longer Loku Putha, Loku Duwa, Chooti Duwa, they are themselves, unrelated to me, and I have done all this to them. It is my fault that they have grown up so fast.

I look back at the men in the car, and they are both nodding at me, as though encouraging me to nod, too, in agreement. The older man has his eyebrows raised, adding a question. Is this acceptable to me? Is it? It is not, I want to say, but it has to be, for while I am still standing there everybody but Dayawathi has gone inside to get my little boy ready to go to the hospital. I bow my head in thanks and let Dayawathi lead me downstairs. I follow the sounds of my son's screams, wiping my face so I can join mine to the other voices offering solace to him: *Hush, hush, be courageous like a good boy, your sister will come with you.*

Latha

"I better take the girl with me to the market," Gehan said one Sunday morning, gathering his car keys and slipping his purse into his pocket.

"What girl?" Thara asked.

"Latha. Who else?" he asked, looking around the house as if for another female servant he had missed.

"Girl?" Thara laughed. "Far from a girl, haven't you noticed? Probably got some gray hairs too by now!" She tossed her own head, recently streaked with burgundy highlights to cover the few strands of white she had discovered one evening, going to Latha for confirmation and solace.

"Latha! Is it true that I have gray hairs?" she had asked, wailed, really. "All my friends were laughing at lunch today. Nobody else has them! I'm too young!"

Latha had examined the bowed head carefully and pronounced the verdict: "Yes."

"*Aiyyo!* What am I going to do?"

"You can only see them if you look hard, so don't worry about it," Latha had said. "There's probably a gray hair or two on my head, surely, and have you even noticed them?"

"Well, I'm always out there for people to see. You just stay home and nobody gets close enough to look, so no wonder you don't care," Thara had said, making it sound like an accusation, something Latha had brought upon herself, this staying at home.

"No," Gehan said, seemingly distracted with counting his money. "I haven't been looking at her head for gray hairs, so I don't know. I just need some help at the market."

"So why not take the boy?" Thara said, though she didn't seem particularly concerned either way.

"Podian is a pest, always looking here and there. And he is slow. And a fool. He never understands any instructions," he said and then raised his voice. "Latha!"

"My god. Who would have thought your mother herself picked out such a gem for her son!" Thara said, pouncing on the opportunity to remind Gehan of the fact that the only proper servant they had was the one *her* mother had trained and provided: Latha. The comment fell to no great effect on Gehan's long-abused shoulders. "And to think you'd admit it even at this late stage," she added, to even less success.

Latha had always been ready for the outside world, for which she had once dressed smartly yet much more casually, a certain alertness to possibilities lightening her gait. After the hard disappointment with Daniel, she had almost given it up, particularly when she saw on television that even her childhood heroine, Princess Diana, had got nothing for her effort and heartbreak but a horrific death, and in a lonely tunnel at that. For a while, Latha had taken that as a personal message to her from the gods that their kind of enterprise was not going to be rewarded in this life. But, in the end, she had decided that living without intention and assurance of good fortune was like being dead anyway, so, after she had recovered and mourned the poor princess by lighting a lamp for her at the temple for seven days in a row, she had deliberately worn all her best clothes, day after day, even when she hadn't felt like it, even when she wasn't going out of the house, until she recaptured her former optimism.

And now, she was just as ready for the world inside her home, and with even greater expectation, and in the call from Gehan to join him on the marketing expedition, alone, the two worlds blended delightfully together. She unhooked the two cane baskets from their perch above the rice bin and went out, pausing to remove her *Bata* house slippers and put on her sandals by the front door, freshly energized by the sweetly reminiscent sight of Gehan's narrow body clothed in his usual weekend wear of blue-checked, untucked, short-sleeved shirt and khaki trousers. A body that she now looked at without fear, indeed, with the fondness of ownership, as he stood with his back to her, turning the key in the car door on the driver's side.

Thara wandered to the front door just as Latha finished buckling her sandals. "Make sure you don't let him buy from the Vatti-Amma. God knows where she brings those leaves from. Probably from that filthy sewer behind her house."

Latha waved her head sideways in agreement but pursed her lips. What would Thara know about any kind of vegetable? She had never shopped for anything but cutlery and crockery and draperies and clothes. And everything had to be imported. She didn't even go to *The Palace* now, because everybody who was somebody went to a new place called *Old Dale,* she had told Latha, and taken her there one day to show her a shop filled with people, a lot of them foreigners, buying clothes and sunglasses and handmade things like notepads and coffee mugs and odd-shaped caps with elephants on the front. But after a few minutes she had met a friend who wanted to go to the store café, and Thara had told Latha to go and sit in the car and wait for her, which she had done, but not before touching as many fine, unaffordable, and completely useless things as she could on her way out.

"And don't get goday stuff. Buy some up-country cabbage at least!" Thara yelled before Latha could get into the car.

So, okay, Thara did know something about vegetables. She did shop for food, but only at the fancy supermarket that had opened up inside the *Majestic City,* and that too only because she felt guilty on her way back home from seeing Ajith at the *Hotel Renuka,* where they now had a regular room, Thara had confided in her, or from his rented room on School Lane, where the De Sarem family turned a blind eye to their doings and to which Latha had once brought steamy hot packets of *lampreis* from *Green Cabin* for them, which Ajith took from her dressed only in a towel. Yes, Thara shopped for food some-times. She bought things with labels like *Pastene* and *Ketchup* and *Fruit*

Cocktail in Syrup in a tin, all of which were inferior to the *Harischan-dra* noodles and the *MD* tomato sauce and the baskets of bright and flavorful fruits that Latha herself fetched from the local markets. But now was not the time to reveal any of these disparaging thoughts, so Latha contented herself with the pursed mouth.

The pursed mouth and, later, the fact that Gehan drove not to the market but to the same *Hotel Renuka,* where, for the first time in her life, Latha experienced sex with a man who was her peer, his marriage up and her fallen fortunes abandoned outside the door. And, as she had imagined, Gehan was unlike either Ajith or Daniel. He was unhurried and present with her, with Latha, not another woman, not a notion of who she was but herself. But before all that, before the closing of the shades and the lighting of the lamps and the drawing down of the improbably heavy embroidered bedcovers in the air-conditioned room, he gave her a gift.

"Madam . . . Thara . . . madam doesn't know I took these," he said, handing her a package.

They had just walked into the room and shut the door, and Latha's body was adjusting to the way privacy felt. It was unlike the privacy at Daniel's house, which had felt more like a museum. This was different. This was a refuge. And with every second that passed, the mad beating of her heart—which had begun when she realized where they had parked, and what that meant, and the quick rush of self-recognition, which reminded her of her inferior status as a servant, not a lady like Thara, and which had swelled out of her body and into her throat and out of her alarmed eyes as Gehan checked in and walked without saying a word to her to the lift—subsided. It subsided the way the house she cared for subsided at night, taking its sounds and tucking them away to relinquish the space to her. And lately, not just to her but to her thoughts of herself and Gehan as she lay under that mosquito net, thoughts so explosive and improbable that she had sometimes had to hold her breath, afraid that one of the five sleeping bodies in the house, Thara, especially, but any of the others really, would hear them and cry out.

It took her a few moments to look down at what Gehan had given her: it was a sheaf of photographs. They were the pictures that Thara had taken. Latha gazed and gazed at them. She had never seen a photograph of herself. Not even at Thara's wedding had there been one taken of her. And in all the years that she had looked after the girls, whenever the camera had been brought out, she had always been asked to hand over the children and move out of the frame. And now, here were twenty-one photographs of her. They seemed to be of someone else, some mythical creature that lived inside her, someone younger, more free, unnaturally blessed.

"How did you know she took these pictures?" she asked, still staring at them.

"I came back home when she was still photographing you," he said, taking the bundle back and looking through each one, his finger caressing the corners so slowly that Latha felt a rush of anticipating warmth deep within her that made it hard to listen to what he was saying. "The children had fallen asleep, and I came in to put away the foodstuffs from my mother. I watched you for a while." As he described what he had seen, he sounded so sad that Latha put her hand between his shoulder blades. And something about that gesture effectively ended whatever misguided mores had tethered them in two adjacent but opposite-facing places. Gehan embraced her, and she embraced him back.

"I should never have agreed to the marriage, I should never have agreed," he said somewhere over her head, the rest coming in a rush, two decades condensed into a few sentences. "When I heard about what was happening, what you were doing, from Ajith . . . I felt nothing but rage. And then you went away and Ajith refused to marry her. I felt sorry for Thara. I thought she and I shared a common pain even if I could not speak about it with her. Even though she could never know that I had lost something too."

"It wasn't the driver," she said abruptly, wanting to make sure that he hadn't buried that bit of knowledge, allowed a lie to sprout and grow between them, "it was Ajith." She moved away from him and went to stand at the window.

"I know," he said, following her. "I know it was. I knew from before. Ajith told me. My parents would not have allowed it, between us, you know, but I had plans to find a way. I had thought of getting work abroad, in the Middle East even, I didn't care. But Ajith, he took that dream from me. I haven't spoken to him since."

And she understood then where the rage had come from. How foul she must have seemed to him, to betray both him and her friend. But, in that room, alone with Gehan again, she did not regret what she had done. She tried to feel something like that, to feel bad, but she did not. It shouldn't matter. Why should it? She and Thara had been friends before the boys had come along. They had a bond that shouldn't be allowed to break because of what she had done. And it hadn't, had it? She had found Ajith, given him back to Thara. She had given up her baby. What more could she do? She gazed at the strip of ocean that was visible beyond the farthest buildings, wondering what to say.

"I had a child while I was at the convent," she said, at last. "They took her from me. I have paid for my part in all of this. I think I have paid more than everybody else."

"Why did you do it, Latha?" he asked. "You were always so good to Thara. That is what I could not understand. Why would you take Ajith from her? Surely you could not have loved him?"

Had he not heard what she said? Why had it broken him to know that she had gone to Ajith? Ajith had always looked down on him. Why had that been excusable until her actions made everything unforgivable? And still, she wanted to avoid blaming him, not only for the question he was asking but for the one he hadn't asked, about what it must have been like to lose a child. And maybe she wanted that not because he was deserving of her forgiveness but because she wanted to forgive herself, for having once been young. She wanted to be with him, to have this future, which, though unlike any future she had once imagined for them, complete with a wedding and a poruwa and faithfulness, was still better than not ever having the chance to be together at all.

"I didn't intend to hurt Thara," she said. "It wasn't her. It was her mother. I was angry at Vithanage Madam. I wasn't thinking. I should have . . ." She trailed off into silence. She had wanted to prove that she was not just a proper servant, that she was as good as they were, better, that she could get one of them, one of their kind, and Ajith was the only one she knew. But she couldn't say that aloud, not to

Gehan, who wasn't part of that world. It would only crush him. All he would hear was that she had once thought Ajith had something he did not, something for which it was worth risking everything. He wouldn't understand that it had nothing to do with Ajith.

"What are you thinking about?" he asked.

"The past," she said. "The past is called that because it is over."

He said nothing, and a small disquiet unfurled inside her body and flashed across her mind, a sharp and piercing hurt. It was the memory of Gehan at the Vithanages' dining table when she had first met him on her return after the baby, how callous he had seemed to her then, talking loudly about his wedding preparations, never once even looking at her. She wanted to stay with that thought, to listen to what it might have to tell her, but here he was, holding her like she had never been held by anybody in all her life. How soothing it was to stay there, to believe that the past had come and gone, leaving no lasting imprint in their lives. How comforting to set aside her watchfulness for a while, not to hope but to have.

So she did. And everything changed.

Who would have thought that a house with such bitterness hid so many spaces that could generate euphoria in the minds and bodies of two people? For a while, it seemed, the whole house was refreshed by her secret union with Gehan. Those two ancestral armchairs, each in turn, served a finer purpose for them in the smallest hours of the morning while the house slept. The half walls around the wraparound veranda offered themselves up, mute participants in their while-coming-and-going trysts in the dead of night. And once, on a night of passion intensified by the complete terror of being discovered, he had joined her in her bed, the repaired net around them following their movements and leaving Latha with the sensation during all the nights that followed that she was never again alone in it. Even the kitchen sink complied, wet against her belly when his arms slipped around her waist and his face sank into her freshly washed, dried-in-the-sun hair. Fleetingly, yes, but endless in the way those moments stayed on her mind, slowed her movements, and delighted her heart.

"Latha," he would call to her, "could you make me some tea?"

And there was a delicious thrill that crept up her spine when he said her name with Thara in the house, wrapped as it was with the danger of being found out and, she had to admit it, the insolence of carrying on in this way right under Thara's nose.

"I'm coming," she would say and arrive with the required lowering of her head, her hands firm on each side of the tray, but her fingers soft around the fine porcelain cups she held out, wordless utterances melting in her eyes.

"Mahaththaya has really taken to drinking tea these days, hasn't he?" Thara said one evening. "Gehan, better stop drinking so much tea. Once in a while, at least in the evenings, wouldn't it be better to invite some of our friends over for a proper drink?" They were sitting side by side on the veranda. Thara was reading a book, and Gehan was making notes on a stack of papers in his lap.

"I gave up drinking several years ago," he said, cocking his head to the side and looking Thara full in her face while Latha stood at hand, waiting for the right moment to set the tray down on the side table and pour the cup of tea for Gehan the way she had learned to do: fingertips on the lid as she poured the fragrant amber brew from the swanlike spout of Thara's wedding tea service.

Thara raised her eyebrows. She had taken to plucking her eyebrows at the same time as she had got the burgundy hair. It made her face more severe, the way those sharply defined brows drew attention to the harshness of her appearance, magnified all the more by the tight ponytail that left not tendrils but a frizz over the entirety of her head. *Sunsilk, Sunsilk,* Latha thought. She should use *Sunsilk Egg Protein.*

"Really? Hmmm," Thara said. "I hadn't noticed."

"You don't notice much," Gehan said, still looking at his wife but in a way that communicated to Latha that he was really looking at her, offering his face up for her to look at. So she looked at it, the beloved ordinariness of it. If he had no driver and no car, if he sat on a bus, would she be able to tell him apart from all the other men who went about by public transport? Which reminded her that the only times she had ever ridden a bus in her life had been to deliver food to Thara and Ajith and to try to run away with the girls and the houseboy somewhere south; Gehan had never asked her to take public transport anywhere for any reason, not even when the driver was on leave. Yes, she thought, she would be able to tell him apart. Not because he looked any different, because he didn't—with his thick head of common, wavy hair, the clean-shaven face but for a thin mustache over his weak and effeminate mouth, his height unblessed by a corresponding broadness to his shoulders—but because he felt different. Something in him was the same as what was in her, and those things, unnameable, intangible, would arch toward each other the way they were doing now in this room with his wife between them.

"Well, we haven't invited anybody to this house for years, so what is there to notice? If we had people here more often, maybe there would be something worth looking at!" Thara retorted, not losing a beat.

"What do you want to have for dinner?" Latha asked, hoping to avoid an escalation. There had been such an absence of conflict in the house ever since Gehan had spoken to her that first time, each of them, Thara and Gehan, seeming to turn away at the last instance from the usual confrontations, that she was loathe to have it return.

"Cook anything you want. I don't care," Thara said. "I'm going out to *Banana Leaf* with some friends."

"Ask the children, Latha," Gehan said, turning his eyes slowly to meet hers. "Maybe they care."

Thara pressed her lips together and looked away at the insinuation. Latha backed out of the room with one last glance at Gehan and went to the kitchen to cook noodles. That's what the children liked. Madhayanthi smelled the garlic and ginger frying and came running to the back door, taking in great gulps of air and yelling for her sister.

"Ooooh! Noodles! Akki! We're having noodles!"

"Are you going to make salmon curry to eat with that?" Madhavi asked, tripping over herself in her rubber slippers, which were wedge-heeled according to the latest fashion and whose height she was practicing getting used to.

"Yes, Loku Baba, do you want to watch? You should start learning how to cook now that you're a big girl," she said and chucked Madhavi under her chin.

Madhavi was a proper young girl now; she stood up straight, wore a real bra, and even knotted her hair on occasion. At the last wedding the family had attended, she had gone in sari. Both girls had. They had looked so different to Latha, like ladies. Ladies who would grow up and make marriages and have homes of their own. Who would look after them then? Whom would she tend to besides Podian? It had taken all her effort to step away from those thoughts, to tuck a pleat in here, a stray hair there, rub soft powder into their supple skins, attach thin, real gold chains with gold pendants of their names written in Sinhala script (Gehan's choice) around each slender neck, and simply enjoy gazing at her girls, at who they had become, who they might yet be. At times like these, though, when they came rushing into her kitchen screaming like urchins, she could pretend that their leaving was a long way from coming. She could pretend that there was still a lot more to do in order to raise them right, in order to teach them how to go about in the world.

"I don't want to peel or cut onions," Madhayanthi said, wrinkling her nose and pouting, managing to look disgusted and beautiful in her tiny denim shorts and tank top.

"I'll do it," Madhavi said, taking the five small red onions from Latha's hand. Madhavi no longer wore shorts; everything she wore had to be below the knees, a self-imposed virtuousness having taken her over the day she had her coming-of-age celebration.

"Podian, go and sweep the outside," Latha said, reminding him as she had taken to doing that he should not be found anywhere near the girls; it was her way of protecting him. She felt a quick twinge of guilt that she had forgiven Gehan for Podian too, and she frowned.

"Latha, why are you angry?" Madhavi asked her. "Don't you like Podian?"

"Of course I like him. Podian is a good boy. He just sometimes forgets to do his work, that is all," she said. She pried three cloves of garlic from a bulb and put them in front of Madhayanthi. "You can peel and cut these," she said.

"You're just trying to get us to do your work," she protested, but set herself to the task. After a few moments she looked up. "Latha, do you know that Soma still cuts onions and chilies on the floor?" Madhayanthi said. "Can I try?"

"No, Chooti Baba," Latha said.

"Soma taught me how the last time we were there," Madhavi said. "She said I'm old enough to learn it. See? I'll show you." She took out a knife, turned it blade side up, and squatted quickly on the floor, gripping the handle with her toes, trying to keep it steady as she held an onion over the sharp edge.

Latha sighed, bent down, and took the knife away from Madhavi. "I said no, and that means no to both of you, I don't care how old you are," she said, firmly. "That's the old-fashioned way. You don't need to learn to cut like that. You'll only end up slicing your fingers. You can stand and cut on the board, like me."

Madhavi shrugged and began chopping the onions. Latha watched the girls work. Madhayanthi was in her kitchen now only because Madhavi was there. She wanted everything her sister had, every part of what her sister did. Latha sighed. What would it have been like to grow up in the same house with an older sister? she wondered. With a sister like Leelakka. A sister and a brother. Podian. She would be the middle child, cared for by one sibling and taking care of another. Where would they have lived? She sighed again. Whose children . . .

"Latha is thinking of boys!" Madhayanthi exclaimed in a sing-song voice, giggling into her shoulder.

"Nangi! Don't talk of things you don't know," Madhavi said, but she was smiling.

"What boys for me? I'm an old woman now!" Latha said, turning away from them, suddenly afraid and ashamed.

"You're not old! I heard the paper man ask Podian about you," Madhayanthi said. "He told Podian that your face was just like some Indian film star called Maduri. And he said that if you were Indian you would be in a film too."

"Stupid paper man. I should tell Podian to stop talking to that crazy man. Maduri indeed. *Kolang.*"

"What is nonsense?" Thara asked. Latha hadn't noticed her come into the kitchen. She stood by the door, leaning casually against the frame, taking in the scene. What it must have looked like to her, Latha didn't know, but she wasn't about to alert her to anything they had discussed.

"Nothing," Latha said.

"Latha is like an Indian movie star," Madhayanthi said, looking from her mother to Latha, "someone called Maduri." Her childish face was alight with that inner power that Latha hated to name, knowing too well how easy it was to abuse it once it was acquired: the power to start fires whose strength she could not gauge nor understand how to put out.

"The paper man is interested in Latha, Amma," Madhayanthi continued.

Thara stared at Latha until she looked up at her. "Is it true, Latha? Now the paper man is interested in you? First Podian, now the paper man?"

How could she say such a thing, about a boy who was like her brother! "Madhayanthi baba was just making it up," Latha said, shaking her head and trying to look as elderly and unworthy and unwomanly as she could. She looked at Madhavi. "Wasn't she, Loku Baba?"

Madhavi, glancing from Latha's face to her mother's, chose to come to Latha's rescue. "Yes, Nangi is always telling lies. She's always creating problems wherever she goes! Even for me at school—"

Madhayanthi glared at her. "Maybe I should tell Amma who sent you a no—"

Madhavi dropped her knife and clapped her palm over her sister's mouth. They disintegrated together, laughing and screaming, one trying to be heard, the other trying to drown her sister out. Latha watched them with amusement in her eyes until she realized that Thara was still standing there, still watching her.

"She's growing up, our Madhavi baba," she said, trying to change Thara's mind about whatever it was she was struggling to remember, or trying to say.

"She's only a little older than we were when we met Ajith," Thara said, and something crept into her eyes, something that harkened back to that past and brought it, complete, into the present where they stood, each in her own world. "Ajith and Gehan," she said.

Latha picked up the abandoned onions and garlic and added them to the saucepan, where they sizzled with her green chilies: mouthwateringly pungent and furious.

"Ajith *and* Gehan," Thara repeated, wonder in her voice.

Biso

I don't want them to, but they insist, so I must let them.

"It's just something to cheer him up when you get there," Dayawathi says. "The foreigners say there is no time to feed the children."

She pronounces the word with a *p* and the native plural, *la: porinersla*. I want to correct her. At least say she should use the clearer word, *suddho:* white men. Instead I say, "He likes dried fish," trying to be grateful to Dayawathi and Sumana, who have taken on the role of relatives, fussing over my son, doing their best to smooth the way for him, pushing what is possible within their poverty to the absolute limit. The smell of the frying onions and green chilies makes me feel ill. It is too lush and alive and only reminds me of how broken he is, my son.

I am nothing but a spectator. Everybody else seems to know exactly what to do. All I feel is that I should not permit this. I should keep him with me. But here beside me is Dayawathi, stroking my arm and murmuring that I should not be afraid, everything is as it should be, my son will get help soon. And there is Sumana, smiling and telling my little one to stay away from the stove so the oil won't get on her baby skin. That's what she's calling it, baby skin. And the old man, I don't know where he is. I can hear his voice somewhere, and he sounds authoritative and worthy of trust. I should be glad, yes, I should. My son will get help. I have been lucky each time on this journey, haven't I? I have known what to do, what to keep from my children, what to share, what to escape from. I knew to accept the old couple's hospitality, to stay here and rest. They are older than I am. I should listen to them.

I wish I had more time to gather my thoughts, to fully examine my fears. But by the time I go down to the back room, the driver and the teenager and Veere's Father have already lifted my son onto the stretcher and are bringing him up the stairs. His eyes are squinted tight, and the smallest of tears escape from them, the concentrated tears that come from real pain. I step backward against the wall and stroke his head as they pass by.

My Loku Duwa follows them with a pink siri-siri bag. She has changed out of her old dress and is wearing her good one, the dress I had the tailor make for her last year to wear to important functions, like prize givings and concerts at the school. It is the slightest bit too tight for her, the puffed sleeves pinching against her upper arms. The hem, too, is a little short. I want to stop her, to ask her to get back into the old dress, but no, she should wear this one, a clean one, to go with her brother. At least it is made out of good material, and it is a good color for her, that mauve.

"Amma, I'm taking his shirt and the blue school shorts and the small towel," she says, sounding competent and in control.

"Amma! Aiyya has to take his moon moth!" the little one yells from below.

"*Hanh! Hanh!* All right, all right," I say to both my girls. I hurry them, though what I want is for everything to slow down. Chooti Duwa runs up with the plastic-wrapped dead creature and pushes past me. I follow them upstairs to where they have set the stretcher down to make room in the car for my son. I am glad for this pause; everything seems too fast, too much out of my control.

"Chooti Nangi brought my moon moth," Loku Putha says with a wheeze, trying to smile at his sister, and then he closes his eyes again, holding in the pain. Such concern, such love that flows between siblings when the thought of defeat draws near, everything sweetened by the horrific possibility of never again. I want to reassure them both, to say, "This is temporary, your brother will walk again," but they don't need my promises. Instead, I hold my lips between my teeth so I won't cry and watch them communicate with each other in this way that they are doing, without words.

When the back door of the car is opened, it looks so small inside. Pain rushes through the marrow of my bones as I imagine my son having to curl and bend to fit in there. "Please . . . ," I say again, but the driver intervenes.

"Move aside now, we have to get this boy into the car, and you are blocking the way. Move! Move!"

Loku Putha opens his eyes and looks at me. "Amma, you will come quickly to the hospital, won't you? You must promise me, Amma. I don't want to go inside the hospital without you." And this time the tears are the slow-moving ones of loss.

"I will, I will, my son, my golden son, my Loku Putha," I promise, grasping his hand and kissing the fingers, though I know I cannot reach the hospital before they do. "Putha, Nangi will be there, and you stay together. She will look after you till I can come. Tell the doctor that your mother is coming. Tell the doctor that we are at this shop—" I look back, but there is no name written over the store, nothing to identify it by. "Tell them your mother's name, Biso, Biso Menike Samarakoon, make sure to give the whole name, and that I am coming."

"Now enough! See how you're upsetting this boy?" the driver says. I look up at him and see that the two foreigners have got down and are pacing on the other side of the car, discussing something in low voices that sometimes seem angry, sometimes pleading.

"Is that boy his son?" I ask the driver.

The driver looks at the two men and then back at Loku Putha. "Yes, they are father and son," he says, but he's lying. I can tell because he doesn't look at me when he speaks.

"Why are you lying?" I ask.

Veere's Father hushes me. "Don't ask all these questions, duwa. It doesn't matter. They don't matter, nor even who they are. The only thing we need to worry about is getting our Raji Putha to the hospital. That is all, isn't that so?"

The driver nods. "Yes, listen to what this uncle is saying."

But I ask again, as if it makes a difference, "Why are you lying?"

And now it is Dayawathi who tries to soothe me with her mother's voice and care. "They must be. Only parents talk like that to their children, shouting at them. Don't you know? Isn't that how you talk to your son and daughters when they don't want to listen?" She smiles. "This driver *unnahe* has been traveling all this time with them. I am sure he knows everything about them. All their troubles too. Even though they are *suddho,* I am sure they have the same kinds of problems we do with our children."

And now the driver says something else. "Listen, I don't want to get in the way of anything, I just do what I am told to do. This is my first hire in months! The *suddho* don't come to the country much now that the Mathiniya has taken over everything, all the corporations and all. I picked these people up in Nuwara Eliya. And I don't know if they are father and son," he says, "and I don't care if they are father and son, and neither should you. They are going to help *your* son. That's all that should matter. That's all I am trying to arrange for you."

He sounds kind, and I know he is right, that there aren't as many foreigners coming to our country now, but I feel that he is keeping something from me. I want to press him further, but then my boy, my baby boy, screams again as they try to lift him off the stretcher, and my heart tears open and I cannot think. The driver puts him back down and says something to the young boy, and he gets in. Then it is Loku Duwa's turn. She smiles encouragingly at me, as if she has taken her brother's place as the child in charge during emergencies. She gets into the car with great care, smoothing her skirt under her as she does so, the way she has been taught to do in school. She straightens her dress over her knees and puts the siri-siri bag near her feet. Then she looks out and grins at me again.

"May the blessings of the Triple Gem . . . ," I begin, but the words are swallowed along with my fears and my desperation. I say them again and again to myself, murmuring all kinds of prayers, snatches of one thing and another until there is nothing left that I remember except a fragmant of a hymn I learned as a child with the nuns, which I repeat now to myself, *help us in all times of sorrow virgin help us help we pray.* And once more I think of the pregnant girl, which reminds me of our journey.

"Stop! Wait!" I yell and run back inside the house to find the name and number for the man we met. Near the entrance to the store is a long coil of rope with a flickering ember at its edge and a stack of small squares of paper, torn from school notebooks and skewered untidily onto a wire, for the *beedi* smokers to light up. I tear a piece off, find a corner, and copy the information down onto it. I call my Loku Duwa back and put the piece of paper into the pocket of her dress. "Keep this just in case," I tell her and bend down and kiss her head. Her braids still have the yellow bands I put on to match her other dress. Maybe she should wrap the purple ribbons that go with this dress around those. I am about to suggest it when she asks me about the paper.

"What is it, Amma? What is this paper?"

"The name for that gentleman on the train. You won't need it, but it's good to have somebody's name in case they ask."

"In case who asks?" she inquires, shielding her squinting eyes with her palm against the glare of the late morning sun.

"The doctors or nurses or anybody. Just keep it. Even the foreigners. You can tell them, too, that this is your uncle from Colombo. I don't want them to think we are homeless like the *ahiguntakayo.* We are better than that."

She shrugs and shakes her head. She goes to the car and then runs back to me and wraps her arms around my waist, burying her face in my belly. I can feel her cool cheek against my bare midriff.

"Amma is warm," she says. "Amma might be getting fever. You should ask that seeya for a *Disprin,*" she finishes, and she runs to the car.

Dayawathi comes up right on her heels and gives my son another dose of the kasāya she had made earlier. It is good that she does this, to bring the numbness back, because they are unconcerned with his pain and take no care. They lift him into the car so swiftly and I am too agitated to beg them to be careful; I simply want his pain to end. I want them to get to the hospital as fast as they can, I want him to stay, I want to go, I want to make him believe that it is all right to go with strangers, I want to reverse time, I want, I want . . . When they are done he lies with his head in his sister's lap, her arms cradling his face; his right foot is firm on the floor, but his left is bent and laid on the lap of the young boy. At least I can be proud that I have always taught my children to maintain clean feet. My son's slipperless foot is scrubbed clean; they are the feet of a decent boy. I kiss it once more before the driver starts the car and I must shut the door.

Even my kiss causes him pain. He winces. "Come quickly," he says between clenched teeth. I note with relief that already his eyes are beginning to droop. Silently I give thanks to Dayawathi for her native skill.

"Yes, Loku Putha, I will come soon," I tell him, and then I turn to my daughter. "Duwa, Mala, go safely and take care of your brother," I say and close the door as gently as I can. The car pulls away while my hand is still on the door. And already the other two women and even my youngest are inside, cooking. The air feels dry and cold around me, and the road dusty and uninviting.

"Sumana and Veere's Mother will finish getting the food ready for you to take," Veere's Father says beside me, rubbing one forearm with the palm of his other hand. "Don't worry now. Putha will be all right. They're foreigners, after all. They will admit him before all the other patients. It is good that you sent him."

I say nothing, trying to hold on to the sense of what he is saying. It is true. Then he says, "You will have to get going quickly to make it to Hatton and meet them." I am startled out of my inner worries and brought face-to-face with a new one.

"Hatton . . . yes . . . How will I get there?" I ask him, feeling utterly helpless. "I cannot walk all the way to Hatton. Is there a bus that will come this way?"

"Usually there's a bus, but there has been a partial strike locally so we can't tell when the next bus will come . . . Putha?" He looks over at the teenager, who is still standing there after all the commotion of the morning.

"All right, uncle, I will go and come," he says, before Veere's Father can even finish, and disappears around the corner of the house.

"Where is he going?" I ask. "Do they have a vehicle?"

Veere's Father shakes his head. "But they have a bicycle. Maybe he can take you at least part of the way, until you can find a proper vehicle. Maybe there will be some others on the road who might be able to help you. These days are not so good for traveling anywhere, even up in our hills there is all kinds of trouble. Didn't used to be that way, but now . . . Anyway, come, let's go inside and get things ready to take."

Dayawathi urges me to change into a better sari. My little one takes my orange sari out of the bag; it's her favorite of all my clothes. I used to entertain her for hours as a baby, showing her the tiny pink and green and white flowers on it. It is not the one I would have chosen, it is made of a synthetic fabric, but I change anyway, because it makes her happy as she watches me, coming near to feel the silky cloth against her face.

After what seems a long time, the teenager returns, wheeling a bicycle, and there is space only for me and a single bag, or me and my little one. I refuse to leave my Chooti Duwa behind, and as it is, the boy is going to have to struggle to get us any distance. I have to leave our bags behind.

"It's a good thing you will be going downhill, not up. At least that will make it easier," Veere's Father tells the boy.

"Putha, you will be blessed many times for all you have done for us," I say to the teenager, noticing his youth for the first time. His trousers stop a few inches short of his ankles, like he has outgrown them too suddenly for his mother to replace them. He must be about seventeen years old, a faint fuzz growing on his upper lip and his eyes still respectful and full of innocence. Had he not been around, how would the old man have got my little boy up to the house from where he had fallen? How would we ever have found a way to get him to the hospital? Even if they had stopped as they did, I am sure those foreigners would not have wanted to sweat that much. And they wouldn't have wanted to waste their time. I should be grateful.

"It's nothing," he says and tries to deflect my attention away from him. "Malli was in a lot of pain. We should go soon."

"I can walk part of the way if you can just carry my little one," I tell him.

"I can walk also," Chooti Duwa says, looking up at the boy.

"No, no, baba, I can double your amma on the bar, and you can sit on the back, on the bike rack," he tells her.

Her face brightens. "Then I can see everything!"

"Maybe she would be safer on the bar, Putha," I suggest, but he points out that I would be too heavy on the back.

Inside the house the old couple and their daughter-in-law bustle around, getting things ready for us. Sumana is warming a large, flat leaf over the stove, and the woody fragrance caresses my nostrils and reminds me of our hopeful beginning. How long ago was that? Three mornings ago, just two nights; and yet it feels to me as though we have traveled for a week, each day of that week a year or more, a lifetime. I smell the leaf, the dried fish that Sumana and Dayawathi are nestling into the warm white rice, and I see a woman standing there, a woman who is not me. That woman is strong and proud and full of courage, glad to be free at last. That woman's body is lean and tall. She is capable, trustworthy. I am no longer that woman. I am fretful and helpless, and my mind is laced with the scenes from our journey. I am plagued by the way the gods have turned away from me and from my children, and these things thicken my movements and my brain. How can I think? Tell me. If there is somebody out there who could remain calm in the face of a life like mine, in days such as these last three have been, show them to me, and I would kneel at their feet, for they would not be of this world.

"Amma?" my little one says beside me, looking concerned. "Don't cry. This aiyya will take us to the hospital."

I wipe my face, ashamed that I have forced adult concerns upon my children, on all of them. First my son, then my older daughter, and now the baby. I stroke her face and smile. "I'm not crying. The smoke was in my eyes," I tell her.

When it is time to go, I feel as though I am leaving parents, not strangers. So I get down on my knees, touch my head to the ground, and worship each of the old people, Veere's Father first, then Dayawathi. They put their palms over my head and bless me.

"Go now. We'll be here, you can come and see us on your way back, we will keep your things safe here," Dayawathi tells me. "Go quickly. Putha is waiting."

I nod my head in agreement. I don't know when I will come back this way. How long will my son have to stay in the hospital for his leg? I shrug inwardly and sigh. Never mind; I will have to find a way to return to these good people, to bring them something better than what I have: starving children, injuries, foreigners, and mounting obligations toward their one neighbor on this lonely road.

"I'll go and come back," I say and walk over to the boy, who is waiting, his foot braced against the first step into the store.

"You get on, and then I'll put the little one onto the back," Sumana says.

I sit sideways on the cushion the boy has improvised from a towel and look back to make sure that the little one is all right. Sumana has picked her up and is trying to put her onto the rack, but she can't let go.

"Can't you leave her here with us, aunty?" Sumana whispers, a deep longing clouding her eyes. "I can look after her till you get back. She doesn't need to go to the hospital after all. It might be easier if you go alone."

I know that longing. And I know no mother who would abandon her child into such desire. I feel sorry for her, I want to wish her happiness or say something else that is kind, but the words will not be spoken.

"I can't leave her, duwa," I say. "She's too little to be away from me."

Sumana lowers her eyes. She settles my daughter on the bike rack, tells her to be careful not to get her feet caught in the spokes, and presses a few sweets into her palm. Then she lets her go.

"Hold that aiyya tightly with both your arms now, okay?" she says to my Chooti Duwa. "The road is bumpy sometimes, and you can fall if you are not holding on properly, petiyo." She takes my daughter's arms and wraps them around the boy's waist. "There, like that. Now you'll be safe." She steps away from us and waves. "Come and see me, baba," she says, trying to smile.

"I'll come as quickly as I can, and I'll bring my aiyya and my akki and everybody!" Chooti Duwa says, and her happy, childish voice, raised and sweet, lifts all our hearts. Even the boy laughs.

At first it is almost pleasant, riding on the bicycle. The boy is not tired, and I am moving forward, toward my children, not standing still, and this one fact brings me small, intermittent waves of comfort. The road, too, seems easy, and for a long time the boy barely has to pedal. We reach and pass the sanctuary where we lit the lamp, and we pass the place where the train must have been; the smell of burnt steel and foliage still drifts up from the valley where the tracks lie, hidden from our view. If I am silent for too long my children crowd into my mind—my girl, too young to take care of her brother, and my little boy, his face full of pain—and I have to close my eyes and pretend they are with me again, whole again, just my children, traveling safely within my care. Such thoughts, so different from my reality, from theirs, make me feel weak and desperate and I grip the handlebars so tight that a few times the bicycle swerves to the side and the boy has to work hard to regain control. So I apologize and keep on talking, discussing the things we had passed on our way to the shop just the day before, trying to make it seem as though this is just an ordinary day, a day in which such conversations are possible, a day of which I am still in control, untroubled by the visions of my broken journey.

We stop once to drink from a spout on the side of the road. "Is this water safe to drink, Amma?" Chooti Duwa asks, looking doubt-fully at the crude, hewn-out thrust of bamboo that delivers the ice-cold water to us and probably thinking about all the pots of boiled water that I bottled for them back home.

"Yes, Nangi," the boy answers. "These waters come from the mountains. This is very clean. Much cleaner than the water in our houses even, I would say. Taste it and see. I'm sure you have not tasted water like this anywhere!" he says proudly.

She puts a palm full into her mouth and agrees, nodding her head. "But then why are they wasting it and letting it run down the mountain?"

"It's not wasting. Lots of people come and get water from here," he tells her. And as if on cue a group of three women with two children, both boys, come around the corner carrying buckets and pots. "See? People come and get water from here for drinking and cooking."

But after that rest, we all grow quiet. Chooti Duwa is tired, and I feel bruised from the endless bumping. With long stretches of flat road, the boy has to pedal. But the darkness of my predicament, my children's, seeps once more into that quiet and I am too terrified of the silence to keep moving within it.

"Putha, we'll stop here and walk for a bit," I say, and he stops almost immediately.

"Just for a little bit, nendé, if you don't mind."

"I don't mind. Come, Chooti Duwa, we'll walk for a bit."

She gets down, but after a few steps, she bursts into tears. "I'm hot!"

"I know, it's hot. But we have to get to Aiyya. He's waiting and Akki is waiting, so we should try to keep walking, petiyo, just a little longer," I say, even though I don't know how much farther it is. She wants to sit under a tree by the side of the road, and I agree, noting the relief on the boy's face. He's a child too, after all, though he is taller than I am. I try to fan both her and myself with the fall of my sari, to get rid of some of the sweat trickling between my breasts and making patterns on my belly.

All I want is to hold on to my strength until I can get to the hospital. There is still so much to be done for my son: I will have to find a proper doctor, someone to perform an operation on his leg, and where will I get the money to pay for it all? Next to me, my little one starts to play with my bangles; she takes them off and puts them on her own thin wrists and shakes them up and down her arm. They go all the way, almost up to her armpit, she is so thin, and they make a pleasing sound. Perhaps I will be able to pawn them at the hospital.

It almost hits us as we sit there, a motorbike that comes careening around the last bend and toward the next, where we are sitting. The driver stops in front of us, and we all get to our feet. The man gestures to us, and the boy steps forward. I hang back with my little one.

"What is it?" I ask, worried that he brings some bad news.

"Veere Aiyya's father told me that you need to get to Hatton. You can't go on this bicycle. Malli, you go back. I'll take them from here. Hurry up! Climb on! Don't stand there, get on the bike!"

I run to the motorbike, dragging my girl with me, and I shout my thanks over my shoulder: "Putha, I am eternally grateful to you for your help. Go back safely now. I will go with this aiyya to the hospital. Tell them I'll come and see them soon."

"Give that handbag and the parcel to me," the driver says, and stacks them inside a basket tied to the front of the motorbike.

Luck. It has found us. He had only stopped by the store to deliver a letter from their son, who is in Jordan and had sent it through this man's wife, who had just returned from the Middle East. It is so comfortable on the seat of that motorbike after everything. It is hard not to relax just a little bit, my baby's cheek pressed to my chest, her back against the man, her legs twined around my waist, her eyelids fluttering open and shut against the wind that is suddenly cool now that we are moving so fast, and speed, speed! toward where we need to go.

"Malli, how long will it take to get to Hatton?" I ask.

"We can get there in about an hour and a half," he says, glancing at me in the side mirror. Although we have to shout above the roar of the engine and make eye contact in the mirror, we talk companionably. The little one falls asleep. I am glad to be in the company of another adult, the way it absolves me of having to be responsible for topics of conversation. I am grateful, too, to be spared my own thoughts by the sound of his voice, and I give myself fully to his concerns. I listen as he tells me about the possibility of unrest on the plantations, the foreigners who are trying to take over the bigger estates, the explosion on the train; most of all he talks about his wife. How they made the decision for her to go, what it cost to send her, the sale of the small plot of land that had belonged to his father to buy her ticket, and the way her departure had clouded their young children's lives. And had it been worth it?

"She sent back a lot of money," he says. "After one year we have paid back most of our debts. Even this motorbike I bought mostly with the money she sent from there; the bank gave me the rest. It is one of the only ones in these parts, a *Honda*. A *suddha* had got it from Japan and I bought from him after he had used it for only a few years. I don't think they have even in Colombo yet motorbikes like this. And now nobody is going to be importing anything with this government. Anyway, it is a good thing because now I can earn money for the family this way. I load all the vegetables and take them to the markets. It is much easier. Even though life was not easy for her there, she has done her best to make it better for us."

He is a heavyset man, with rounded shoulders and a matching belly, and a face creased by a well-maintained beard. A capable man, someone who could do heavy work if he felt inclined. I want to think less of him, but I resist. Who knows what ails such men and their families?

"Will she go back again, now that she is home?" I ask.

He turns the corners of his mouth down: regret and inevitability. "Thing is that her sisters need to get married too. She's the eldest in the family. I can't pay for everything with this bike and our vegetables. So . . . *we* don't want her to go," he says, and he slashes the air diagonally with his right palm to emphasize his feelings. "*I* don't want her to go, and the little ones don't want her to either. They cry all the time when we talk about it. But . . . family . . . what to do when the family needs something . . . That is why Veere Aiyya also went to Jordan. Same time as my wife. To help the family." And he looks carefully at me in the mirror to see if any trace of judgment has taken over my face.

"That is it," I say to assuage his guilt. "When family needs something, we have to come forward and do it."

And we are both silent, thinking of family. We remain that way until we reach the hospital, when I have to wake up my baby, collect her package of rice and curry and my handbag, and thank him for his help. I am so relieved to have reached our destination—this hospital where my children wait for me, and I am so anxious to go to them, that I barely listen to what he has to say and, instead, murmur my thanks repeatedly.

"Akka, I have to get back to Ohiya, but I will come here again tomorrow," he says. "If you wait by this door around ten in the morning, I will come, and I will bring some food for you too. Or if you call the temple they can get a message to Veere's Father. I don't have the number, but someone here should know. It's a big temple. Oh, and another thing. Veere Aiyya's father said he has some relatives not far from the hospital, and he said he will come back with me to take you there after he sorts out some things at the store. They will help you. Don't worry."

I thank him again and run up the wide red steps so fast that Chooti Duwa, struggling to keep up, slips and falls on the fresh polish. I stop and help her up with one hand, my feet barely hesitating. The security guard tries to stop me, but I don't listen and he is not concerned with the likes of me, a little girl in one hand, clearly a mother. I beg and plead my way to the front of the queue and peer through the hole cut in the glass front where the receptionist sits.

"My son was admitted here this morning," I tell her. "Raji Samarakoon. Raji Asoka. He had a broken leg. Two foreigners brought him in a red car. Just this morning. He fell—"

"We didn't have any foreigners coming here today," she tells me.

"They came," I tell her, pointing at the thick ledger before her, its yellow pages full of potential, "foreigners. They were foreigners, so might have just written down their names only, not my son's name. Just look there, carefully, please, duwa, they came just this morning, look for foreign names. They had a driver with them too. And my other daughter. A little girl, about as high as my chest, she was wearing a nice light purple dress with pleats and pockets, a little too tight for her—"

"I told you nobody came here this morning. We don't have anybody called Raji Samarakoon, and we don't have any foreigners."

"Can you ask somebody else? Another lady nurse might have been here . . . maybe they checked him in. Maybe they went directly to operating? Because of the foreigners?"

"There is nobody else to ask. I'm the one here. Who is the next person in queue?" she asks, looking past me.

And she will not speak to me again. The people in the line look at me with sympathy. A few offer words they hope are comforting but are not: maybe they took him to a different hospital, maybe they got lost, maybe they registered him under a different name because they can't pronounce our local names.

I go to the security guard. "*Aney malli,* could you tell me if a red car came with a little boy and a girl, about as high as my chest, like this one, she was carrying a bag . . . My boy was in a lot of pain. He had a moon moth in a bag. He was bringing that to the hospital. You would have remembered. He couldn't walk, so the hospital would have had to bring a stretcher to get him out. The driver was one of us . . ."

He shakes his head, looking carefully at me and at my little one beside me and shifting from side to side as if he regrets that he cannot say otherwise. "Nobody came in a red car," he says. "I have been on duty since seven this morning."

No. I shake my head. No. They cannot be right. I run past the queue, past the receptionist, to the place where the patients are. The waiting room is full, but my children are not there. Beyond that I push through a door with big red letters saying on one half, EMER, and on the other, GENCY. They swing shut behind me, and the nurses inside look up at the sound. They come quickly toward me.

"You can't come here! Who are you? What are you doing?"

The quietness of that place tells me he is not here. My son is not here. They have taken him. And they have taken my girl too. I shake my head again and again, no, no, no. Nurses gather around me. I hear them talk about foreigners. Foreigners who take over the country. Foreigners who force themselves on servant girls. Foreigners who steal children who live by the oceans, near the hotels. Steal them. For ugly pictures. For bad things. Bad things. My children. My children. My children.

Latha

With one casual conversation between her daughters, Thara had acknowledged what she had refused to see all those years ago: that in all the times Latha had accompanied Thara to her meetings with Ajith as a child, being her excuse, giving her cover, there had been two other children with nothing to do but spend that time with each other: Gehan and Latha. And the more that Thara remembered, the steadier she became. She left the house less, and when she was home, she paid more attention to whatever Latha did.

"We seem to have dried fish every day," she observed one Saturday afternoon, looking up from the array of dishes that Latha herself, not Podian, had laid out on the table. Latha had resumed this duty, now that she wanted to be near, not avoid, Gehan. Besides, she liked to be sure that his glass of water came to the table dry, not wet the way Podian brought it in his clumsy manner. The family had just come into the dining room to have lunch when Thara made the remark. Latha knew what she was implying, that the fish was being cooked because Karāwa caste Gehan enjoyed it.

"Not always. Sometimes we have fresh fish," Latha said, trying to make it seem as though they were, truly, discussing menus.

"But even then, small fish that you have to fry with those long chilies."

"Fish is less expensive than meat so—"

"Fresh fish is not less expensive—"

"Arlis Appu gives me a good price. We have been buying from him for years now. Even after some of the others down this road stopped opening their doors when he comes by with the catch, because they all go to the big supermarkets and buy old fish," Latha said, her head to the side, eyes aimed at something halfway between Thara and the floor, trying to chalk something up for herself in Gehan's presence, but not too much. Besides, "malu" had been one of the first words Madhavi had learned as a baby, from the fishmonger who came up the street, his two wooden disks piled with fish and swinging from the dipping pole over his shoulder, and that cry, *Mālu! Mālu! Mālu! Thoramālu, Balamālu, Kumbalava, Karalla, Hurulla, Mālu!* No, she would not banish that man from her door.

"Maybe the fishmonger is like the paper man," Thara said, still standing by her chair. Gehan had sat down and was serving himself rice and, Latha noticed with satisfaction, a generous portion of the dried fish. Thara continued, "Maybe you are not buying but rather selling something for that good price."

Latha looked directly at Thara, the fake humility gone in an instant. "I stay here, I look after the children. I am not out in the streets causing people to talk scandalously about this household," she said, holding Thara's gaze, hoping that the children hadn't heard between the clattering of spoons and plates and their own conversations.

Thara lowered her own eyes. She was about to sit, but she glanced over at Gehan first and saw that he was looking at Latha. "From now on," she said, her voice sweet and malicious, "I want you to buy fish from the supermarket, and we will have only respectable fish like seer, the way we used to in my parents' house."

"I like dried fish," Gehan said.

"We like dried fish too!" Madhavi said. "It makes everything taste better."

Latha smiled at Madhavi, at the way she had mimicked an old radio advertisement for a Japanese flavor enhancer called *Ajinomoto*, something she herself had taught the child. She softened. "Thara Madam, I can buy seer for you and make dried fish for the children," she offered. And Gehan.

"Go and bring me some peeled onions and green chilies to eat my lunch with," Thara snapped. "This food is tasteless."

She had said it without having put a single grain of rice in her mouth, and it made Latha angry. She sent Podian back with the bowl containing one green chili and one onion, neither washed.

She was glad that Gehan had spoken up. He had sided with her, if not directly then at least by inference. And for her part she was not sorry that she had called attention to Thara's behavior, even if only between the two of them. It was the kind of thing that was probably an open secret in her circles; Latha knew at least two other friends whom Thara brought home sometimes when Gehan was not there, who were having affairs of their own. She had heard Thara on the phone with their husbands more than once, lying on their behalf, telling the men that their wives were with her when they were not. It was a solid criticism, that Thara was the one who was behaving inappropriately, and one that Latha felt could be safely leveled against a married woman, and she contented herself with this line of reasoning for a few days while Thara and she circled each other in an uneasy truce. Until the next time Gehan took the girls to visit his parents and they were alone.

"Latha? Bring me a cup of tea," Thara said, and when Latha had prepared it and sent it through Podian instead, he was sent back to ask her to come.

"Is the tea not good?" she asked, trying to sound concerned but sounding petulant instead. "I used *Lakspray*."

"I suppose he doesn't like the imported milk either now?" Thara asked.

Latha gazed at her. Thara looked better now. Perhaps it was the gym, or the fact that she had started to eat less. She had lost a little weight, enough that she had a proper figure again. Latha tucked a stray tendril behind her ear in self-defense; of the remark, of Thara's improving looks. It was true. Gehan had steadily demanded one change after another until the only products Latha brought into the house were local brands: *Maliban, Harischandra, Kandos, Lakspray, Marketing Department, Astra, Sathosa, Elephant House,* and *Sri Lanka Leather Corporation* shoes. Even the girls were dressed only in clothes made from *Veytex,* the textile mills shop in Wellawatte with its walls of amazing prints and bold colors. The only foreign thing Latha bought now was *Marmite* and, occasionally, *Kraft* cheese in a round blue tin from England. Because those weren't available here, and even Gehan was not yet persuaded by *Kotmale* cheese, which, he had confided to her, still felt and tasted like soap. He had been lying on his back when he told her that. He had been laughing in the aftermath of the silly conversations that often followed their sexual engage-ments at the *Janaki Hotel,* which, Latha had told him, being farther from their home, would be safer, because she couldn't tell him that the *Renuka* was where Ajith and Thara went. The memory of that afternoon made Latha feel panic and power, both of which made her quiet.

"Why aren't you saying anything? Am I right?"

Latha tried. "*Lakspray* is less expensive and creamier. You have to use less to make the tea taste good," she said.

"Sit down," Thara said, indicating the floor at the foot of the bed where Latha usually crouched to massage her feet. Latha sat and put her hands on the smooth legs that jutted out from Thara's shorts. "No, I don't want you to massage my feet. I want you to listen to me." Thara's voice was soft, dangerous, with the kind of depth a voice gains when it conceals rage.

"The only reason I am not married to Ajith is because of what you did." She stopped and waited for her words to sink in. Latha's body tensed. She knew then? She knew that Latha had seduced her boyfriend? Carried his child? Set a little girl adrift somewhere? Ajith had told her?

"Baba . . . ," she began, fifteen again, then, "Madam . . ."

"Don't talk. Listen. If you had kept your legs together and been a proper servant like my mother trained you to be, the driver would not have done what he did. And you wouldn't have got yourself preg-nant and had to be sent away, and my poor, decent father wouldn't have been suspected of fucking the servant girl. And if those things had not happened, Ajith's family would have agreed to our mar-riage."

Latha froze. There it was again: a proper servant. That was all they had expected of her. Despite her education, regardless of it, and her looks, she was supposed to be no more, no less. Servant. A role, she understood now with bitter regret, that had been the very thing that had protected her from Thara all these years; the thing that had concealed her intentions, her desires, her womanliness, her very soul from Thara. And there she sat, Thara, once her friend, now just another woman who had so casually indulged herself in all those things and more besides, not answerable to anybody. What made it possible for Thara and so impossible for her?

Latha lifted her head. "If I had been allowed to be a proper human being, I would not be a servant in your house. I would be living in a house of my own with a husband of my own. With children who came from me and belong to me."

Thara spat. And it did not matter that she had lost weight or colored her hair or polished her nails; she looked hideous. "Human being? You owe my parents your life. If we hadn't looked after you, who would? You would have walked the streets. We fed you. We clothed you. We sent you to school. Servant? What servant? You lived like a lady in that house. You didn't even have to cook! Old Soma did all the work. I am ashamed to say that I once thought you were like me. You are nothing like me. You are a common whore, just like my mother said. Just like Gehan's mother said."

"I wasn't paid," Latha said, but her voice was low from the tears she was willing to stay inside, inside, not one should fall.

"What? What did you say? We pay you good money!"

"I wasn't paid!" Latha said, standing up. "I worked for your family and they did not pay me. All I asked for was a pair of sandals." She pointed to her feet. "I asked Vithanage Madam for some money to buy a pair of sandals! But she wouldn't let me have them. She didn't think I was good enough to even have a pair of new shoes!" And saying those words again, she could feel everything she had felt that day, the longing to look pretty, the way she had believed that she was only asking for what she owned already, her money that she had earned, the way she had wanted so much to make her clean feet look decent in real shoes, to hide the fact that she was a servant.

Thara, who had risen with her, sat back down. "Sandals? What are you talking about? You have a room full of sandals! Why, even Madhayanthi is always talking about them!"

Latha did not trust herself to speak. She simply stood there, swallowing the salty water that rose up from somewhere deep within and filled her mouth over and over again. She could not tell if Thara was doing the same, only that she, too, was silent.

"You ruined my life, Latha," Thara said, eventually. "This is not the way my life was going to turn out. I was going to finish school, go to university, be a lawyer. You knew that. You knew what plans I had. And Ajith and I were going to get married and have children together. Instead, look at me now." Thara began to cry, and Latha forgot herself again as she watched the sad woman on the bed, her heart alternately expanding and hardening with everything Thara said. "I am here in this place, no proper education to speak of, no job, married to that idiot and with two children who belong to him. Yes, to him. You can think the worst of me if you want to for saying that. Those children have never felt like they belonged to me. And what about Ajith? A good man like that, not married because I'm the one he wants. People talk about him. They say he likes boys . . ." She spat again and said no more.

"Thara Baba, don't cry now," Latha said, feeling sorry for Thara, a wife and a mother with neither husband nor children she could bring herself to love. How much worse was that than her circumstance? At least she was a woman whose only challenge was how many she could love: Leelakka and Podian and her girls and Gehan. And Thara. She loved Thara despite everything. For the years they had spent orbiting the neighborhood hand in hand, one way of looking at the world, one world to look at. And for a moment she felt again that, if there had been no Gehan, no Ajith, no men at all, it would not have mattered if they could have continued that way. She and Thara, loyal to each other, picking flowers, staging their small insurrections, growing up.

"All I have is the time I spend with Ajith. That is all."

"Forgive me for saying anything, Thara Baba," Latha said. And she wanted to say more, and perhaps Thara did too, but they both heard the sound of the car in the quietness between them. Gehan was returning and no more could be said.

For a few months after that, they were, indeed, good to each other. Latha cooked dried fish only thrice a week, every other day, favoring Thara's preferences over Gehan's. She bought seer fish and even chicken sometimes from the supermarket. Thara joined in the cooking on the weekends, and they made old recipes, the birthday-party-only food that everybody craved the rest of the year: Chinese rolls and patties and cutlets stuffed with their savory fillings and served with chili sauce. They went to *Veytex* together to buy new lengths of fabric for the girls and for themselves, and Latha shared in Thara's excitement when they stepped into the *Majestic City* and shopped for the foreign food that Gehan hated. They ate lunch together once, Latha moving her chair so that she faced away from Thara, perching on the edge of her seat and continuing to clutch the bags so people could tell they were not friends on equal footing but rather had an understanding that, by its very tolerance, favored one over the other. And when a few young men whistled at them, Thara laughed and acknowledged that it was Latha they had been looking at, not her.

It was like the time before the end of flower picking. It could not last. Not in a house with so much to hide and so many being loved by the wrong people. And the end, when it did arrive, came about because Latha, newly and completely loved, was filled with generosity and suggested to Gehan that he make peace with the Vithanages and invite them to his home for a meal. And because he was happy and fulfilled, with his wife for appearances' sake and his woman to love, he did. It might have been all right if they had been free to come right away, but by the time all the negotiations had been done, and all the arrangements made, Latha had confirmed, without medical assistance but by practice, that she was pregnant, at the age of thirty-three, for the third time. And because she had hope, this time, to keep this child, a perfect one with two parents who had come together in love, she bloomed.

"Latha, I wish my skin was like your skin," Madhavi said, peering at an adolescent blemish on her cheek.

"Latha, I wish I had never breast-fed. Then my breasts would look like yours," Thara said, peering down the top of her dress as Latha sat on the hiramané and scraped coconuts, the white flakes falling onto the rising mound beneath.

"Akka, you look especially happy these days," Podian said, bringing her chocolate biscuits twice in a single week.

"*Renu Renu mal mité renu . . . ,*" the paper man sang as he handed her the daily paper, making her smile, his own smile broadening in turn, the song getting louder as he cycled to the next house.

So it was only natural that, by the time the Vithanages arrived, Latha's pregnancy, though not obvious, was abundantly clear to Thara's mother.

How much better if she had stayed hidden in the kitchen and kept away from the reconciliations going on at the front of the house. Thara smiling, Gehan welcoming his estranged in-laws on bended knee right there on the floor that Latha herself had forced Podian to polish not once but twice with coconut refuse laced with kerosene to keep away the ants, and then again with red *Cardinal* polish. But no, she had to watch. She had to see how the years had changed the old couple, whether they had been mellowed or embittered by their differences with Gehan.

Well, she saw all right. There they stood, their faces decked with hope, the gladness banishing whatever traces of regret remained. They both kissed Gehan, embracing the son-in-law they had, finally relinquishing the kind of son-in-law they had hoped to have. Mrs. Vithanage in a baby blue sari—Gehan would approve, Latha thought, of a sari purchased at the *Lanka Handloom Emporium*—and Mr. Vithanage in a matching light blue shirt. Both of them were more gray-haired than black, and Mr. Vithanage stooped just a little, as if he were trying to catch himself from falling down. Mrs. Vithanage stood as she always had, straight and solidly, her body balanced perfectly over her two feet. The girls too, dressed up for the occasion in their idea of good clothes—blue jeans and bright store-bought T-shirts, long hair brushed to shining by Latha—were delighted. And in that colorful scene, with all the tangled joys that were being created, Latha saw there was no space for her. But she parted the deep green curtain that hung between the living room and the pantry and peered out anyway. She and Podian, one on either side.

"Latha, *kohomada?*" Mr. Vithanage said. "After a long time, isn't that so?"

Mrs. Vithanage turned to look, and the expression on her face, witnessed only by Latha, since she was the only one who was looking at Mrs. Vithanage, the others all staring at her like they had just remembered she lived in the house with them, left her in no doubt that the old lady had seen what even Gehan, with his palms on her naked body, had missed.

Latha smiled with genuine happiness at Mr. Vithanage, if for no other reason than that she was not sure when that opportunity would be hers again. She smiled at him for not having been unkind to her, for being bullied by his wife, for having noticed her and spoken to her, for having brought her into this family, which had, in turn, led her to Gehan. When he turned to Madhavi to ask about her studies, Latha dropped the curtain and went back into the kitchen.

Biso

Where is my son? Where is my girl? Who will help me? I want to scream these questions, but the words will not come. Why didn't I keep him with me? I knew it. I knew it was the wrong thing to do and I let myself be persuaded. How could I have listened to two old people who have never been anywhere? How could I, who have known foreigners, known what they are like, who have always been suspicious of them, how could I have trusted them with my own children?

One of the nurses kneels beside me. She looks too young to be working. "Ammé, come, the police want to talk to you," she says.

"The police? Do you think they will help me, child? They only help rich people. They must be here for something else. They will never help somebody like me. I know the police. They never do what is right for us. Please, duwa, find somebody to help me. I have to get my children back. My son needs a doctor!"

She takes my arm and lifts me to my feet. "No, come with me. These are good policemen. Come, I will take you there and we will go and try to explain what happened."

I want to trust her. I must. Maybe I am wrong. Maybe the police here are different and they will help. I have been wrong about so many things. But I cannot forget how they sided with the foreigners any time somebody complained back at the hotels. Always the *suddhas'* side. That was the side they were on. And even though these are up-country policemen, they might be the same. Still, I go with her. I have to. There is nobody else to go to for help now.

The constable in the admissions room looks disapprovingly at me. A group forms around us while I stand, clutching a useless parcel of food, still hot, hugging it to my chest as though it is a poultice to drain a poison out of me, or a bandage to stop my heart from bleeding to death. Oh, I can feel it in my very bones, this flame that is lapping at my heart: my children are lost for good. They are gone from me. And it is my fault. I have lost them. I have lost them.

"Ammé," he begins; I can see in his eyes that I am common now, in the way I look, my concerns, the impossibility of recourse. "We have put out a police alert for a red car with foreigners and two of our children. When did you last see your son?"

"Son and daughter," I correct him, and in saying those words aloud, I make my loss unalterably true. I feel as though my legs will give way under me as I say those words, but I cannot let them. I must keep standing up; I have to find my children somehow.

He sighs. "Yes, son and daughter. When did you see them last?"

"I last saw them when I gave them to the foreign men," I tell him. "They were so clean . . ."

People stir around us. "What are you saying? You didn't give them away to the foreign men, correct? They took them from you?"

"Yes, yes, they took them afterward. But first, I was the one who asked if they could take my children, not me, I didn't want to, but Veere's Father, the people we were staying with, they asked if the foreigners could take them, my children . . ." People start crowding forward and talking loudly. I can't think. They are accusing me of selling my children. "No!" I say. "No! I didn't sell them! I only asked the foreigners to take them—"

"So then why are you asking us to find them? If you gave them?" The constable interrupts me in a loud voice. "Why are you wasting our time like this?"

"Please, rālahamy, my children are lost!"

"But you wanted to lose them, right? You sold them. That's what you said just now. You said you gave your children to the foreigners."

I shake my head. "I shouldn't have let them go, but I did. I thought they would help us. I had a bad feeling about them, about those foreigners, but I let them take my children because the driver said they were a father and a son. I didn't think a father and a son would do such a thing. Would steal my children! I put them in the car and sent them away with the foreigners because my son . . . my son . . . he was injured . . . his leg was broken. He was in so much pain, and I thought that they would get him here fast . . . They wouldn't take me, and I had to find another way to get here. I came as fast as I could. You must believe me. Please help me, rālahamy . . . I couldn't come any faster . . . I promised him but I couldn't . . ." My body starts heaving despite my best effort to keep it still.

The policeman stares at me. "You must stop crying and listen to me now. Listen. Try to stop crying. Crying is not going to help . . . Nurse, help her."

The nurse gives me a handkerchief. I wipe my face. I wipe it, but the tears won't stop. I press the cloth into my eyes until all I see is red. He is right. I do not deserve the solace of tears, no. My guilt should stay trapped inside me, it should burn me from within like the fires of hell.

"Do you remember me?" the policeman asks when I look up again. I feel my mouth trembling, but my face is dry. "I was one of the policemen at the bomb site. You came and asked to take your bags," the policeman says. "You had all your children with you. I recognize you because of this one." He points to Chooti Duwa. "I remember her very well because she was the youngest child there, except for that baby."

I had forgotten her. Where had she been all this time? Her face is tear-streaked, and her eyes are edged with fear. She tries to put her hand through the bend of my elbow, but I hold myself tight because I am afraid to feel that childish touch. If I do, I will come undone, and who will find my children then? Her hand slips away.

"Yes, this one stayed with me," I tell him. "My daughter didn't, my older one. She wanted to go with her brother and I let her. I was foolish. I should have known. Please forgive me. Can you find them?"

The policeman gestures to a row of chairs and sits down next to me. *"Yanna! Yanna!"* he yells at the spectators around us. "Why are you all crowding here? There's nothing to see. Give these people some room to breathe!" They back away in a single movement, glancing at one another, and inch back again. Like flies at an open plate of rice. Shoo. Return. Shoo. Return.

"You have to tell me the truth now. Otherwise I cannot find your children for you," he says. "Tell me the truth. When did you meet these foreigners?"

I want to be helpful, I must tell the truth. I want to make sure they have all the information. Everything. "I refused money," I tell him, because I want him to know I am not of that stock. I would not take money from foreigners for any reason. I would never sell my children! "We met them yesterday. They offered us money, but I said no . . ."

"Did they offer money for your children?"

"No! I don't know why they wanted to give me money. I was on my way to my aunt's house. I didn't know the way, sir, from where the train had stopped. I had to get to Ohiya. I asked them the way."

"Why did you think foreigners would know the way to Ohiya? Couldn't you ask one of us?" His voice is scornful.

"I didn't know they were foreigners."

And now he laughs at me. "Didn't you see their white skin?"

He looks around at the crowd for their approval, and they smile spitefully at me. Why are they treating me like this? Perhaps they, too, are scared of people like him, of the police, or his scorn. But I have lost my children! Don't they have any sympathy for me? I want to tell the nurse that this policeman is not going to help me, that she must get someone else to find my children. I look around for her, but she is nowhere to be found. I turn back to the policeman and try again.

"Sir, my son and I stopped the car when it was coming. We didn't know there were foreigners inside it. The driver was one of us. He told us how to get to a tea shop. But the foreigners wanted to give us money. They gave my son a packet of chewing gum. That's all we took from them, nothing else, not one cent. Then they left."

"Did they take your children with them when they left after offering you the money?"

"No, they didn't. I kept my children with me. We kept on walking till we got to the shop."

The policeman sighs. "I don't know what you are saying. First you say you gave your children to the foreigners. Then you say they gave you money. Then you say they didn't take your children. How do you expect me to help you? I can't even believe anything you say! You sound like a madwoman!" He turns to the crowds. "She sounds like those madwomen who walk about at the bus halts and talk rubbish!"

"My children are gone, sir. I didn't sell them! Please believe me. I only asked the foreigners to help them . . ."

"Amma had to get my aiyya to the hospital, and the *sudhu* māmas would not let her come with him. So then my akki said she would go. And they found room for her. Because they said she was small. That's what the driver uncle said. And then . . . and then . . . it was because my aiyya had to get the moon moth for me, but after he fell down I didn't want to keep it. So he took it. I gave it to him. I didn't want to keep it . . ."

I look closely at my daughter. Her eyes are large and slanting. Where did she get that slant? Were her father's eyes slanted that way? I don't remember. And her skin is like a *Delta* toffee, firm and light brown. Whose skin is that? My arms are darker. Had I once been fair-skinned too? I think of Siri's skin, but he is covered in blood. Like the family on the tracks is covered in blood. And now my Loku Putha . . .

"They will be covered in blood! Blood!" I scream, the tears beginning again. I press my fingers to my mouth, ashamed of my outburst. More people crowd in. I wait until I can control my voice. "Why won't you listen to me?" I ask the policeman. "I'm trying to tell you what happened, and you are not listening to me! Listen to me! Listen to me! My children are lost!" I know that I am screaming now, screaming at this policeman, but I cannot stop. The nurse comes back and puts her arm around my shoulder and hushes me. I shake my head. "Dirt from the road and the train got on all my clean children because of me. And now the gods have punished me. They have taken them from me."

"We were going from our house to another house in the mountains. That's why," my little girl says now. She is trying her best to help me.

"Where were you going, baba?" the policeman asks her. He takes her hand and draws her near. He strokes her head. Dirty man. I pull her away.

"I don't know," she says, shaking me off, discarding me.

"Where were you taking the children?" the policeman asks me.

"I told you I was taking them to my aunt's house. That's where I was trying to go. To Ohiya. Then my son had an accident, and the foreigners offered to take him to the hospital. They told me, the driver told me, that they would take my son to the hospital." I am no longer screaming or crying. There is no use. He is unmoved.

"Did they tell you the name of the hospital?"

"They said they had to go to Hatton, I think, to find a hospital."

"Did they say this hospital? Do you even know the name of this hospital? Tell me then, if you know. Tell me."

I stare at him. It is useless. Nothing I say will make any difference to this man. He doesn't want to help me. He doesn't believe me. He wants to punish me for having left the train site. He wants to make an example out of me. He doesn't care about my children. Or me.

The policeman stands. "I can't help you if you won't tell the truth. If you had not left the station when I told everybody to stay there, these things would not have happened. But you fought with the people there and you left. Didn't I tell you to stay? I know I did." He turns to the other people there and talks to them about me, and they murmur as a group, commiserating with him. That is all right. I forgive him for that, for enlisting strangers against me; isn't that what I have done too?

"Yes, she was very headstrong. She fought with all the others there too. I *told* her to stay there. But she wouldn't listen. I was still getting the details down, of the other passengers, and she took her bags and those three children and she left. Now see what has happened? Now she has lost her children. I don't know whether she gave them away or sold them or they were kidnapped. We are never going to be able to find out. And by now it's too late anyway, even if they did take her children. This is what happens when people don't co-operate. It's a good lesson for everybody." The people around him agree with him; every single one of them, it seems, believes that I am somehow at fault.

He turns back to me. "We are the police, after all. We are here to help you." And now, to the nurse, "Nurse, see if you can get her to talk. Otherwise I will have to go back to the station and write an independent report of this. I can only hope that they find these foreigners from the alert we sent out. Of course now I'm not so sure that we should be harassing them. Sounds like this was an agreement and now she's regretting it and making a fuss about it." He mutters the last words to the crowds, but I hear him: "Might end up having to arrest her."

He shuts his notebook. It doesn't make much of a sound, but there is finality in his gesture. He is right: I am responsible for what has happened. There is no forgiveness for me. I own all my crimes. My journey to safety was a journey toward endings. Had I not seen it along the way? I had chosen to ignore each intimation of what lay in wait for me, for my beloved children. I had spent innumerable hours asking for help from deities, but I had missed the signs that the gods had strewn in my path. How could I have held on to hope so strongly that it blinded me to what they were saying? *No, you will not reach your destination! Go back! Go back!* That was their message, and I had not heard it. I deserve their justice. I let their verdict wash over me, and it is unlike any pain that I have ever known, a thousand sharp knives scraping my body from the inside out.

Somebody puts a cup of tea in my hands. It is plain and sweet and very hot. I pour it into the saucer and blow ripples across the surface for a few seconds; then I sip the tea from the edge. I notice that my little girl is doing the same beside me. I feel my strength returning. My mind is clearer now. The nurse comes back before we are done.

"Ammé, I want you to rest here for a while. After that the con-stable sir will come and talk to you again, do you understand?"

"I don't need to rest, duwa, tea is enough. But I am very grateful

to you for all this concern. Now I must go. I have to go." I pour the
rest of the tea back into the cup and put it down on the floor under
my chair. I stand up.

"These are police orders. You have to give them a statement. In
any case, where can you go in your condition? Do you know anybody
here?"

"Amma and I, we don't know anybody," the girl says to the nurse
before I can answer. "We live near the sea."

"Then it is best that you stay. I will find a bed for you."

"No, please, let me go now." I start to walk away, but she grips
my elbow.

"You have to stay here or go with the police. The chief doctor is
trying to do you a favor. Which do you prefer? The hospital or the
police station?" she asks. Her tone is no longer gentle.

My daughter whimpers beside me. "Amma, don't go with the
police. Police people are bad people."

I touch her face. "There's nothing to worry about, my little one.
I won't let the police or the nurse or anybody take you away," I say,
and she presses against me.

"I must go and see if there is a bed available," the nurse says. She
looks at her watch. It has a gold, oval face and a thin, dark brown
strap. My mother had a watch like that. I don't remember who got
that wristwatch when she died. It wasn't me. Maybe it was burned
with her. My mother's body went up in flames. What was it that
killed my mother? All I see is the smoke of her funeral pyre. "It won't
take long. Baba, can you look after your amma until I come back?"
she asks, and my little girl nods.

"Don't ask her to do anything," I tell the nurse. "She's too small.
What does she know?" But she pays no attention. She gives my
daughter a piece of paper and a pen to draw with. When we are
seated again, she leaves.

People take turns staring at us from a little distance. One woman
with a child about my Loku Duwa's age comes over and strokes my
Chooti Duwa's face. She tells me that I should go to the temple and
do a pooja for my children, to ask the gods to help me find them.
Another woman sits down next to me and tells me that the police

will never help, that I should call the government agent. A few people talk about us as if we are not there, and almost everybody with a child holds their son or daughter close to them as they pass by us. I say nothing to anybody. I cannot absorb anything more. Not advice, not kindness, not even disregard; all I can do is sit and dwell on the fate of my poor children.

The gate to the hospital is visible from here. Beyond that is a row of low buildings, and through an arched opening I see rows and rows of white nurses' uniforms drying in the sun. From this distance, they look like the flags that mark the road to a funeral. They sway in the breeze, and I find that I am rocking myself, forward and back, the way I used to do to put my children to sleep, long ago, when they were infants. And now my daughter lays her head in my lap. I feel the heat of tears soaking through my sari. I stroke her head, over and over. Because she is here, because that is what good mothers do. I cannot comfort her with words, for what would I say? There is nothing left but this child. How safe is she with me? I must protect her somehow, but I do not know how.

After a while, she stops crying and sits up. She begins to draw. I watch as her picture takes shape: an ocean with coconut trees and the shape of a Dagaba with a house in the corner and a very small, smiling sun, whose rays come all the way and touch the sand. It is a last communication from the gods. Looking at that picture, seeing what it is she associates with happiness, I know what I must do. I must keep her away from that place, from me. I stand up.

"Come," I say, "let us go."

"Where, Amma? Where are we going?"

I say it gently. "I am taking you to a nice place."

"But I thought you said we had to go very far to get to your aunt's house. And Aiyya and Akki are lost . . ."

"Shh. Yes, that's too far, I should have known it. See all the trouble we have had trying to get there? We won't go there. This new place is not so far."

She looks reluctant, but she stands up. "Nurse Aunty told us to stay here till she comes back. She said Police Uncle will help us to find Aiyya and—"

"No, no, we don't need to wait. I will leave her a note." I write in English on the back of her drawing: *Dear Lady Nurse, Thank you for your help. Now I am going. Yours sincerely, Mrs. Biso Menike.* Then I show it to my girl; even though she cannot read my writing, at least she can see that I have written something important in English. "See? Now she will know what we did."

I take her hand, and we walk outside. The day is bright and hot, and I shade my eyes. In which direction should I go? I feel unsteady on my feet, my body weighed down by my losses. Two vendors sell *Elephant House* drinks, *Necto* and *Orange Barley* and *Cream Soda*, and foreign fruits, grapes and apples, and newspapers from their stalls by the gate. I wish I had time to buy my daughter something special, some taste that would soften the hardships of this day; her hand in mine is so small. Among the people coming in and going out of the hospital, I and my sorrow are invisible. As I stand, an older woman pauses and looks straight at me and then at my daughter. Her scrutiny strengthens my resolve. I straighten my spine and walk faster.

"Don't pull, Amma, you're hurting my hand. I am coming," my little one says, her voice trembling.

I stop. I take her chin in my palms and stroke her cheeks with my thumbs, marveling at the strength and softness of children's faces. "My Chooti Duwa, don't cry. Amma will get you something to eat as we go, okay?" I pick her up and rock her in my arms for a few moments, then I put her down again.

I pull my sari pota over my head, and we walk more slowly toward the stall to the right side of the gate. The vendor asks for three rupees for a single apple. I must have left my handbag somewhere, because what I have with me is a parcel of food and my coin purse. When I look in there, all I have is one two-rupee note, the slip of paper the gentleman on the train gave me, and thirty cents. I shake my purse over his hand and beg him for the apple. He complains over the coins and shoves the paper back to me. He gives me an apple, a smaller one, but at least it is red and ripe.

When I give it to my little girl, she beams. "It smells nice," she says, her eyes shut, breathing the scent of the fruit. "Amma, do you want to smell?" she asks, but I shake my head. Why smell it? My own mother had bought me an apple once when I was sick, an apple and ten grapes. I can still remember how it all felt in my mouth, the crisp bite of the apple and then the gush of flavor, and the grapes, cool and sweet. No, my sweet little one, she should enjoy this apple all by herself. She chews it happily as we walk, and I try to concentrate only on the way she looks, happy to enjoy her treat. If I think of my lost children, I will do this little one harm as well; I will make some bad judgment the way I did with them, and she, too, will be lost. I must make sure that she will be safe.

Outside the hospital gates, there is a row of cars of various sizes and makes for hire. The drivers stand as if by prior agreement, perched against the hood of each car, one leg propped on the front bumper, each one picking at a tooth or biting a nail, bored. I go up to the oldest one.

"You can't pick one from the middle," a young man yells at me. "We are in order here! You must go to the first one!"

I ignore the commotion around me. I ignore my child's tugs on my sleeve, her murmurs of concern. "How far is it from here to the convent near the railway station?" I ask the old man.

"From here it is about ten minutes by hiring car. If you wait for a bus of course it will be longer, and you have to walk from the stop. That is if a bus even comes. With the strike . . ."

"How much?"

He looks from me to my Chooti Duwa. "About two rupees. But you have to go with that blue car," he says, spitting some bark out of his mouth and gesturing with his head to the man at the front of the line.

I don't want to go with a young man when I don't have any money to give him, but what else can I do? They all watch me walk with my daughter to the first car.

"Take us to the Hatton convent near the railway station."

"Five rupees," he says dismissively.

"Get in," I tell my daughter, without even looking at the man.

He smiles at one of the other men and gets into the front seat. "You visiting somebody at the convent, or were you visiting one of the estate patients from there?" he asks after we are settled into our seat. I don't say anything, and he sucks at his back teeth in reply to my silence. "Hmmm. Must be another one of the girls with no father, then. They are regulars at the hospital. They all come from the cities. How many of those children are working at the bungalows around here now only the gods know." And he sucks his teeth again. Such disgusting manners. It is too bad that we have to travel with a man like this.

"Amma, what is the convent?" my Chooti Duwa asks.

"That's where we are going, petiyo," I tell her, keeping my voice low, my face close to hers, murmuring against her ear. "Remember that nice akki we met on the train?"

"I remember the uncle. He gave us money."

"There was a girl, a good girl. She will be at the convent."

"What is her name?"

I don't remember. We had shared so much, and yet I had not asked for her name. Perhaps the nuns will recognize me. "She is a good girl," I repeat, "a really good girl. I am sure she will be happy to see us again. I gave her my earrings, don't you remember? You asked me why. She is staying at a convent called St. Bernardine. Isn't that a nice name?"

She fondles my bare ear. "Are my Mala Akki and my Raji Aiyya, are they there too? Is that why we're going there?"

"No, shh, they are not there. Don't talk about them. Now why are you crying? Don't cry now, don't cry."

"Is that your daughter?" the driver asks me, his eyes on my baby. I fold her to me so he cannot see her. What liberties his sort takes with people like me.

"What business is it of yours whose daughter? Your job is to drive!"

"Not my concern who she is, but I am not getting mixed up in any strange business. There have been plenty of stories about children from other places. We have all heard. Don't think we don't know these things just because we're from up-country. You people from the low-lying areas come here to hide all your sins. Don't we know it."

"Shut your mouth! Can't you see you're upsetting my daughter? Just keep your opinions to yourself. I have a lot of things to do now, a lot of things to think about."

"Would have been better if you had thought earlier, from the looks of it. Up to no good, I can tell. *Chih!* I should have refused this hire."

I ignore him and talk to her instead. "See, petiyo? See how we are getting closer to the convent? See that sign? Look how they have planted beautiful flowers all along the road. Don't worry, my little one. I'm going to make sure that everything is done right this time."

The road is like a lullaby. It rocks us back and forth in its curves. I feel like I am drugged, numb to everything but this moment of quiet, this moment of holding my daughter, her damp face drying in the flower-decked breeze that visits us through the open window. The driver drops us off at the gate, and I ask him to wait. We have to walk up four more bends to get to the top. I take Chooti Duwa's hand and start climbing. At the end of the last turn I see it: my refuge. The convent is stone. I had not pictured it being made of stone. I had imagined it to be made of brick, with white paint. But the stone makes me hopeful. This building, with its high center and low bordering walls, with all this apparent abundance of space, of growing things, will stay still, keep its secrets, be unassailable. I will leave her here. It will be a fine gift to her, yes it will. After all my guarantees, at least this one will be true. This place will keep her safe from me.

Latha

The meal Latha prepared had been delicious, full of the flavors she had learned to create with the use of smell and intuition, elevating traditional dishes to culinary art. Moreover, the food had been suffused with the inimitable essence of goodwill, served at the perfect temperature, neither too hot nor already cooling, the curries reaching just so up the sides of dishes wiped clean of stray drips.

But none of it, not the food, or the good plates with the trailing vine pattern that Latha had learned to tolerate, taken out of the teak and glass display closet and warmed, or the plantain leaves heated and placed over the plates for a special touch and, secretly, to please Gehan, or the expensive table linens, or the cut-glass vase of fragrant pink dahlias and white orchids that Thara had brought home in an arrangement from the flower shop, or, at the very least, the auspicious occasion of this reunion could prevent the fallout.

"Latha, go and bring my camera from the almirah," Thara said, after everybody had been served and they were about to begin eating. "I want you to take a picture of all of us at this table after all this time."

"No need right now, Thara," Gehan said. "Let's enjoy the food that Latha has cooked before it gets cold."

"This will only take a few seconds. Latha, quickly! Go upstairs and get my camera. I think it's with my good saris."

Latha went to bring the camera, which was, like Thara had said, nestled among Thara's manipuris and silks and hand-loomed cotton saris. It sat, in fact, on top of the hastily folded deep purple silk sari in which Thara had dressed her. That sari, its color, the memory of why it had been so swiftly taken off her, their intimate evening ending with the sound of Gehan's return, and the way the actual photographs had made her feel, who had handed them to her, made Latha hesitate. Downstairs, she could hear Gehan still trying to dissuade Thara from trying to take a photograph. Perhaps she could hide it. She reached out to take the camera and stuff it somewhere else, buy Gehan a little time. Under Thara's shoes, maybe?

"Latha! What is taking so long?" Thara came into the room. "What are you doing staring at the camera instead of bringing it to me, you silly woman? Give that to me. Honestly, I don't know how I've put up with you this long. You have become just as foolish as that mad Podian. Two imbeciles. That's what I have." And she laughed.

Latha listened to Thara's heeled shoes going down the staircase. She didn't follow her. She took the purple sari and folded it neatly. The blouse allowance slid out from the folds. She picked that up and tried to smooth it without much success: it was far too crinkled from the twisting and tying that Thara had done to create a blouse for her. She was still standing there holding the sari when the fight erupted.

"There's no film in here! Where's the roll of film that was in here?"

"Maybe you didn't put any film in, duwa," Mr. Vithanage said soothingly.

"I bloody well had film in here. I know I did. Someone took the film out. Who touched my camera?" Thara's voice rose. Latha listened to the tremulous high notes that took flight from among the usual tones of Thara's voice, like miniature birds scared from their nest by some hostile creature. That voice was directed only partially to the girls, Latha could tell. If Thara had truly suspected them, her voice would have grown deeper with the assurance of nothing changing. Latha turned to look at herself in the long mirror. She held the sari up to her face, admired herself fleetingly, then pressed her nose into its folds, breathing in the scent of something lovely and sweet, a blend of Thara's fragrances, of unused things, and of her own jasmine soap and her sweat. It was the smell of irretrievable time, falling back from her even as she tried to inhale it into her very bones and keep it.

"I took the film out, Thara," Gehan said clearly. "I took it to be developed."

"Why did you take it out when it was not finished yet?"

"I finished the rest of it. I took some shots of the garden," he said. "Of the garden and the house. There weren't many left anyway."

Latha went out onto the landing and descended reluctantly, and so slowly that her feet were soundless on the stairs. Something told her this would be the last time she went down that staircase, and she couldn't yet tell whether that would be a good thing or whether it would be something terrible.

"Since when have you started being interested in photography?" Thara asked and, after a moment or two, asked again. "Why aren't you saying anything? Since when? I'm always the one taking photographs. This is my camera. Why all of a sudden have you got interested in my camera?"

Latha entertained the thought of telling them. But what could she say? That he had given her the photographs? That she was grateful to have some pictures of herself? That he had only been doing her a favor?

Mr. Vithanage spoke again. His voice had changed over the years, grown even more resigned, but with a small amount of gaining strength, like contentment or acquiescence to the order of things and a determination to inhabit his lot fully. "It doesn't matter, does it? We can take a picture another time. Come now, let's eat. I'm hungry. The children look hungry too, aren't you, darlings? Put the camera away."

And it might have all subsided there, except that he chose to push his advantage, having been able to get that much out without interruption and, perhaps, feeling that he was, finally, the peacemaker he had always aspired to be. Or maybe he spoke only because Thara had not yet sat down, was still lingering by her chair, camera in hand, as if she needed a better reason to give up and rejoin them.

"You must have picked up the photos, no, Gehan Putha?" Mr.

Vithanage said. "Why don't you give Thara the photographs and we can all get back to dinner."

"Yes. Did you pick up the photographs?" Thara asked. "The last pictures I took on this were of no use to anybody. They were of Latha."

Standing on the bottom step, Latha willed Gehan to lie. To say anything but the truth.

"Latha?" Mrs. Vithanage joined in. "Why Latha? Since when are you taking photographs of the servants? Thara, you really must remember how to keep them in their place. God, never in my day would the servants have even been in the same room with the family—"

"Where are the photographs?" Thara persisted, ignoring her mother. Her voice shook. She was asking the question because she had to now, not because she wanted the answer.

He was going to tell them. Latha knew it by the fact that he hadn't responded to Thara's question right away. She knew that lies sprang quickly to lips; the truth was what got caught up in people's throats, as if it wanted to give them one last chance to save themselves from what was sure to follow. She took that last step and came into the room. They all turned to look at her. She stood there before them with the sari still clutched to her chest.

"What are you doing with my sari?" Thara said, an exasperated shriek, really. "Go and put it back!"

Latha shook her head. "Please, Thara Madam, let me take this sari with me. I will give you money for it. I have enough to pay for it."

"Take it? Where? Where are you trying to go?"

Mrs. Vithanage rose to her feet. "I might have known it. The little . . ." She trailed away and yelled for Podian, who came scuttling to her side, his brows knit, his fearful eyes lighting on Latha's face and then fleeing just as swiftly to Mrs. Vithanage. "Take the children to our house with the driver and then ask him to come back. Old Soma will look after them," she told him.

"But, Āchchi, I don't want to go anywhere. I want this food. I'm hungry," Madhayanthi whined.

"I don't want to go either," Madhavi murmured, but with less force.

"Take them and go!" Mrs. Vithanage said again to Podian.

"You can't boss us!" Madhayanthi said.

"Amma, what are you doing? Why are you sending them to Soma?" Thara asked, turning from Latha to the girls. "Sit down and finish your dinner," she told them.

"I gave the photographs to Latha," Gehan said, softly, getting the words in before Mrs. Vithanage could respond.

"What? First you take my camera and then you give the photographs to the damn servant woman? What is the matter with you?" Thara frowned at him, but in her accusation Latha could feel the pulse of postponement. Thara was simply trying to avoid the future that was barreling toward her like a derailed train, with all its sharp edges and bulging suitcases full of secrets, of tired families and things gone wrong, the entire unmanageable weight of it. Or perhaps she was a Vithanage after all. Maybe she would find a way to deflect all of it or, at the very least, ignore it. "What is the matter with you, Gehan?" she yelled, pushing at his shoulder when he said nothing.

"You don't know anything, do you?" Mrs. Vithanage said. "To think that I raised such a foolish child! Blind as a bat, that's what you are."

"You keep out of it, Amma," Gehan said. "This is between Thara and me."

Mrs. Vithanage snorted. "If it had been between Thara and you, we wouldn't be facing this situation, would we?"

"This is not the time to discuss anything," Mr. Vithanage said, staring at his plate. "There are children here; can you not see that there are children here?"

Mrs. Vithanage made a dismissive gesture with her hands. "You are the cause of all this, Mohan, bringing that creature into our home—"

"She is not a creature, Wimala, she was a child," he said.

"A monster! She—"

"Thara Baba . . . ," Latha began, but she couldn't continue. The scream that came out of Thara's mouth soaked up every word, every sound, even the smell from the curries laid out, and all the human beings around the table seemed to have surrendered their strength to that cry. She picked up her plate and flung it to the ground, and Latha found something uplifting in that sound, the brittle smashing sound and the small pieces flying everywhere. Mr. Vithanage, Gehan, and the girls all got to their feet and backed away from the table. Madhavi began to cry.

"You . . . *ruined* . . . my . . . *life* . . . you . . . *whore* . . . you . . . *bitch* . . . you . . ." Thara lunged around the table, smashing one plate after another, gasping out the words with each plate that she flung to the ground, her voice, robbed of its power by her scream, almost a whisper now. Mr. Vithanage tried to hold on to his daughter when she reached his side of the table, but she shook herself free. Latha must have fallen into a trance because she didn't see Mrs. Vithanage coming until she grabbed hold of her hair and wrenched her head backward.

"It wasn't enough for you to destroy my family's reputation once, you had to do it again, didn't you?" She began to drag Latha toward the front door, alternately twisting her head back and forth and beating her wherever she could. "Get out of this house! Get out! Get out!"

"Let her go!" Gehan yelled, a voice nobody had ever heard before. He strode up to Mrs. Vithanage and, after a tussle, pulled Latha away from her. She thought he was going to hold her, but he didn't. He merely set her aside, apart, like a piece of a puzzle he couldn't quite fit into an otherwise still manageable picture.

Mrs. Vithanage spat. "You common thug, putting your hands on me like that. You are unfit to be in our household, do you know that? Even today, I wasn't going to come here except that Mohan begged me to do this. How humiliated I have been . . ." Tears began to fall down Mrs. Vithanage's face, something Latha had witnessed only once before; and then, too, she had been the cause.

Latha staggered back, and they both turned to look at her.

"Latha," Gehan said, "are you hurt?"

". . . talking to her like she's one of us . . . ," Mrs. Vithanage said, bitterly.

"She's a human being!" Gehan said. "Do you think your family is the only one that has been hurt in all of this? You talk about your family as if they are something special. You are not special. You are no better than any other family!"

"We are better than yours; that much I can tell. Some filth that came crawling into my house through the back door—"

"Filth knows how to find other filth, I suppose," he said.

"Do you know she's pregnant?" Mrs. Vithanage asked, and the question managed to cut through the din of Thara's smashing and breaking plates and dishes and the almost musical clatter of silverware flung to the polished cement floor. Into the noise came the larger one of absolute silence.

"Pregnant?" Gehan said, turning to Latha again. "You're pregnant?" he asked.

She nodded. "I was going to tell—"

"I didn't know—" He stopped. He took a step back from both Latha and Mrs. Vithanage and ran both his hands through his hair.

There was a further silence as everybody waited for what would come next. Nobody was looking at Thara, but it was clear it was her turn to speak. Latha was not surprised by what she said. She was a Vithanage, after all, Thara was. That was what her sinews were made of, the Vithanage Way, something tensile and adaptable, a way of realigning, redefining, retelling that made the world livable.

"Podian?" Thara said. "You couldn't leave Podian alone, could you? You couldn't have raised your skirt—"

"Come, Duwa, there is no need to talk like this in front of—" Mr. Vithanage said.

". . . with the newspaperman or the fishmonger, you had to pick a boy young enough to be your son. Have you no shame? Not one bit of shame after all these years that we have looked after you?"

Latha stared at Gehan, but he said nothing. He simply stood there, shaking his head. His eyes were turned away from her, his body facing his family. She was outside that circle, no matter that she could sense in the curve of his back some sympathy for her, a forlorn wish for a different outcome, tenderness even. But he was not a strong man; he had never been one. Were there strong men in the world? If there were, she had not met them. No, all she had met had been men who ruled small worlds from their perches upon the backs of strong women. Or who, like Mr. Vithanage, were beaten by one. All she knew were men who had used her or permitted her to use them. But he had loved her, Gehan had, hadn't he?

The words escaped from her. "Gehan Sir, he is the father of my child."

"Who?" Thara asked, her eyes glinting. She hesitated for only a moment before she continued. "Gehan? You have the nerve to accuse my Gehan?" She strode up to Latha and slapped her. "This man who has tolerated so much from my family, who married me when nobody else wanted to, who has stood by me through all the abuse I pile on him? You think you can point a finger at my good, decent husband now, you common tart? You think you can do this too?"

Latha could see what was happening. There she stood, Thara, giving away for free the love she did not feel for Gehan, not because she wanted him but because she hated her, Latha. Thara was lifting Gehan up, placing him high, excusing, forgiving, elevating him in the eyes of her parents, sowing doubt, reaping loyalty in a single statement of deceit. It made Latha stumble for the first time in her life; that Thara, whose girlish precociousness had been lost when she lost Ajith and returned to her only as bitterness toward Gehan, had taken that rage and transformed it into this performance, into uttering such a preposterous lie.

"He is the father of my child," Latha repeated, against her better judgment, knowing that only he could redeem her now. "Tell her you are the father of my child!" she said to Gehan, her voice rising. "Tell her! Tell her!" But Gehan would not look at her. She fell to the floor and kissed his feet, more out of despair than out of hope, and still he stood. "You should have been my husband," she pleaded. "You told me this. You said you should not have married her . . . You said this to me every time . . . every time we were together. You told me you had been wrong to marry her!"

He did not move, and she stayed there, holding those feet she had first noticed so long ago, their shabby lower-class wear and tear, the way they had never matched hers. They had not changed, those feet, and now she took stock of them, refusing to let go even when he tried to lift her off with hands that were neither kind nor cruel, simply impassive, refusing even when Thara hurled more bile at her, even when Mrs. Vithanage joined in, even when she kicked her in the ribs. She stayed there until Thara dragged Podian, crying and pleading, into the room by his ear, screaming at him to confess that he had "fucked this bitch." Then, in one swift movement, Latha stood up.

"*Oyay balli*," she said to Thara. "You're the bitch who is married to him and has spent the last twelve years fucking Ajith."

And not Mrs. Vithanage's flailing blows at her head or Mr. Vithanage's pleading or Thara's horror could stop her from telling them everything, from the first meeting she had orchestrated to the meetings at the De Sarems' house, to their room at the hotel, and to the lie after lie after lie she had told for Thara.

"Stop!" Gehan said at last. "Stop it! Why are you telling all these stories? In front of my children! Latha, you are not a bad woman, you don't have to make up lies."

"They are not lies, and you know they are not," she said, her voice cold.

Gehan stared at her for a long moment. In the background there was only the sound of the girls crying, and Podian too, whimpering like a child, in sight but beyond their reach. Then, Gehan went up to Thara and put his arm around her.

"She is lying, Thara, I know that. I don't believe what she's saying." He turned her face to his with his palm and spoke so clearly it was like he was reciting something memorized by heart. "She is lying because you know it was Ajith who made Latha pregnant the first time. You would never go with a man like that. I am not the person you would have chosen, but you knew what he did. You would never have forgiven him for that."

And there, revealed to Latha, was Gehan's price, repaying Thara for her deceit with some of his own. That he believed her, knew that what she had said was true, was unimportant to him right then. This was a negotiation to decide who owed what, and to whom. He was going to make Ajith pay through Thara for what he, Gehan, had lost, twice now, to the same man. That was that he was thinking of, not her, Latha, not how he felt about her or their unborn baby. And by giving Thara that reason for why he did not believe Latha, and using it to tell his wife about Ajith and how he had once betrayed her, Gehan was felling both Thara and her family, severing everything, exposing all the lies, laying waste to the whole of it. Something in him wanted that just as furiously as she had wanted her own revenge so many years ago.

She listened and she knew, Latha did, that, when all was said and done, when spite and revenge had fizzled out, as they always did—didn't she know it?—he would want to return to her, later, when his life with Thara had coalesced into a meaningless series of smaller wounds, inflicted ritually and relentlessly. But it would be too late.

Thara cried out. The pain in her voice was palpable. Latha looked from Thara to Gehan, wondering if now, hearing his wife's hurt, watching her break, he felt adequately rewarded for what he was losing. Still standing within the safety of Gehan's arms, Thara turned to her mother. "You told me it was the driver, Amma, that's what you told me! You told me that our reputation had been damaged and that's why his family didn't want to marry into ours. You didn't tell me it was him."

"I am not the one for you to blame, Thara, she is!" Mrs. Vithanage pointed to Latha.

Thara turned to her. "You forgot everything, didn't you? You forgot how I treated you, how you were like a sister to me. You forgot how I stood up to Gehan's parents, to Gehan, for you. I kept you here when nobody wanted you to stay. I trusted you with my children—"

"You kept me because I was a way for you to show how little you thought of your husband," Latha said. "You needed my help in carrying on your affair." She was playing Gehan's game, but she knew that her fires weren't the kind to be put out. What did it matter that they had once been friends? No, this room had no space for love that was not made impure by secrecy. These people did not know how to keep love, and now, neither did she. She would set it ablaze and watch. "And you didn't just trust me with your children. You didn't have time for them. You *gave* them to me! You don't know them. You told me they weren't yours. You wanted sons, you said, you wanted sons with Ajith." Latha went up to the girls and took them from Mr. Vithanage, who let them pass from his arms and into hers. He looked like he might faint. "These poor girls, look at them now. Soon they will leave this house, and you gave them nothing!"

"You get out of my house," Thara said. All that was left in her voice was hatred.

The girls clung to Latha. "Don't go, Latha," Madhavi said. "I don't want you to go. Please stay here with us. Amma, please let Latha stay."

"Get out," Thara repeated.

"Thāththa! Tell Latha to stay!" Madhavi cried, holding on to Latha's waist.

"Madhavi," Thara said, striding up to where they stood and disentangling her daughter from Latha's body, her fingernails drawing blood on both her daughter's hand and Latha's as she struggled to separate them. "Let her go. She is a serpent. You are old enough to understand what she has done—"

"I hate you! *Latha* is the one who has looked after us! *She's* the one who has helped me and listened to me. *She's* the one who bathed me. *She's* the one who gives me money when I want some. You didn't even buy me a present, and *she* bought me shoes!" Madhavi sobbed, pushing past her mother and going back to her grandfather.

"Where is she supposed to go?" Mr. Vithanage asked Thara. "She doesn't have anybody in this world."

"This is what we should have done the first time," Mrs. Vithanage said.

"She can learn what it is like to live without anybody," Thara said. "I'm not having her in this house."

"I have lived without anybody all my life in your houses," Latha said. "I know just what that is like." She turned away from them and tried to speak to Madhavi, but when she touched the child, Madhavi flinched away from her and pressed into her grandfather's arms. Latha didn't even try with Madhayanthi. She stood there for a moment, then walked deliberately to the opposite side of the table. She swept to the ground everything that was still remaining on it, sending curries and glasses of water and the cut-glass bowl full of bought flowers in the middle sliding across the table and through the open space between the dining room and the sitting room beyond. She went to the dining room cabinet and pulled out whatever was left of the wedding dishes and smashed those too. "Now all your bad karma is gone," she said. "You can start again."

On her way out, she picked up the purple sari from the chair onto which she had flung it. Back in her room, she threw everything she owned into two suitcases—the one she had brought back from the convent, and another she had bought not long ago to use as a storage space. She put her books, her pictures, and all of her best shoes into one bag, wrapping each pair carefully in a piece of clothing. She put the rest of her clothes in the other, along with her Buddha statues, which she wrapped in her blouses. Into her brown handbag, she put her passbook with the careful numbers of her bank deposits recorded in a blue *Pilot* pen. She took three of the photographs. The rest she tore into pieces and left on her table. She lit a match to the sari and sat down on the edge of her bed to watch it curl and burn, slowly, like a long tale unfolding inexorably, meticulously, and without fuss, turning its beauty to ash.

Biso

She won't let go of me, this girl. "Go!" I tell her. "Go inside and ring the bell. When the nuns come, tell them that they have to keep you here."

"I don't want to go inside, Amma! Amma, come with me!" she begs. "I don't want to go alone!"

"I can't come," I tell her. Then I add the lie she needs to hear. "I have to go and see your brother and sister. Tell them inside that your big sister is already here; your mother dropped her off to the nun at the station just yesterday morning. See this dress you are wearing? That's your big sister's dress. She'll recognize it as soon as she sees you. Tell her I gave it to you already, before you got big. Go!" I push her, but she hangs on to my hand, her eyes terrified.

"Amma, don't leave me here. I'm scared. Stay with me. We can both stay here."

"Then how will I go and find Aiyya and Akki? You tell me that. Your akki was very brave and went with him to keep your aiyya safe. Isn't that good? Now you must be good too. Like your akki, okay?"

She begins to cry loudly. "Then I will call the taxi uncle to take us back to the hospital," she says and starts to walk down the road. I grab her hand and bring her back to face me.

"Shh! Don't make a noise," I whisper to her. "I don't have money for the taxi uncle. I have to walk. I am going to walk. It is too far for you to go, my little one. That is why I have brought you here. To

354

be safe. Now I want you to go inside. Let go of my hand, child, let go!" I shake her off me, but she keeps grabbing at other parts of my body. I slap her face, hard. See what she made me do now. I want to cry, but I must not. No, no, I must show her how to be unafraid. How to turn around and find a better place for herself.

"I . . . want . . . to . . . go . . . home . . . ," she sobs; big, heaving sobs that tell me how frightened she is, how much she wants to convince me that I am wrong. "I . . . want . . . the . . . sea . . ." I want to comfort her, but I know I should not. I have made up my mind, and this time I know that I am right. I want her to be strong. My Loku Duwa was right. I have spoiled this one. Yes, my big girl was better served by my neglect. I am glad they are together, my Loku Putha and she. For better or worse, together. She will be able to look after him.

"Be strong!" I tell her, firmly. But then I relent. I go to take her face in my hands, but she flinches from me. I drop them to my sides. Yes, I have no right to feel that soft skin in my palms, or trace that heart shape again. I have no right at all. I should be going. I turn and walk away.

"Amma! Amma! *Come back!*" she cries. "Amma, don't leave me!"

I stamp my foot at her. "Shh! I told you not to make a noise. Wait until I am gone, and then ring that bell. That is all you have to do, child." I go back to her and sit her down on the top steps. "Here, take this parcel of food. Take this, and you can tell the nuns you have to eat it as soon as you get inside, while it is still warm, okay?" I stroke her head. She has stopped crying. Even her eyes have settled down. She takes the parcel. "Now I have to go. Don't worry about anything. Things will be all right."

This time she makes no sound. She just sits there, looking up at me. What a picture. She sits with her knees drawn up to her face, her chin resting on them. She is clutching the parcel of food to her chest with one hand, and I can imagine the soft heat making its way slowly through her white dress to her bare skin. I remember that particular bolt of skin, how small it once was, holding all of her inside a length only thirteen inches long. Small, she used to be. Her whole body curling toward itself, only the head even then tilting backward. As if her thoughts were heavy, or she wished to be warned of what was coming at her from the places she could not yet see with her newborn eyes. She seems to have resigned herself to staying there, on that step, forever. There she sits, my last child, the only one left to take care of. But I'm choosing how to lose this one. This is my only good decision. This is what the gods wanted from me. Their price. And I will pay it.

"Chooti Duwa, my little one, keep this," I tell her. I take her right hand and press my coin purse into it. It is made of some kind of fur, and she rubs her face on it. "Inside this is the name of the uncle we met on the train. You can tell the nuns that he will know what to do with you. If they need money, he will give it to them. You tell them that. Tell them . . . tell them . . . that you don't have a mother . . . that you are an orphan. That is what you will have to say so they will look after you. Don't shake your head. Yes, it's not true. It is not true at all. You have me. You will always have your amma. But you need to say that to them. No mother. No mother. Will you remember? No mother."

"Don't cry, Amma," she says, which is when I realize that I am crying. I wipe my face with the edge of my sari pota. It's not good to cry. I must show her that this is a good place, that I am glad to be leaving her here. I try to smile, but I must have failed because she repeats herself. "Don't cry. It doesn't matter. I will stay here and be good and wait for you to come back, Amma. I will do everything right. Don't cry."

And I cannot resist it, so I take her face into my hands and feel its weight for a moment. So delicate, so perfect. I kiss the top of her head. "May the blessings of the Triple Gem be with you, my daughter," I whisper these words over and over. Then I walk, run down the road. I don't look back at her. I run, and I cannot stop myself from weeping.

"What are you crying about?" the taxi driver asks when I come around the last corner. "Where's that child?"

I walk past him, sobbing harder than I ever have in my life. Lost now, all lost.

"Wait! Where are you going? I have to get paid. Where's my money?"

"I have no money. I have no children."

"You have to pay me!" he shouts.

"With what? With this?" I take the fall of my sari off my shoulder, and he stares at me.

"Stop that! You madwoman. Only I would get stuck with a madwoman. Put your clothes back on. What are you doing?"

I fling the pota back over my shoulder. It is half undone, my sari. I am undone. The taxi is alongside me now, the driver staring at me.

"I'm going to the railway station," I tell him. "It must not be far from here."

"It's not far if you go from behind the convent, but it is far on this road." He indicates the convent with his head. "If you go to the back, there's a path down to the station from there."

"Then I will go that way." I start walking back the way I have come.

"Wait, where are you trying to get to? Maybe I can help you."

I laugh. Help me? Who can help me? "Go back safely, Malli, I will find my way." I don't hear his engine start up until I am almost back at the front steps of the convent. But then I hear voices, so I stop and peer through the ferns along the road. It's a nun, a different one from the nun who met that girl at the station. This one is tall and thin and very fair. She looks like a foreigner, but she can't be, can she? Talking in our language the way she is doing? Probably a Lansi nun.

"Child, what are you doing here?"

Chooti Duwa stands up. She is so small. Far too small to have been left alone like that, on the steps of a building made of stone. How could I have done that? How could I? Bad mother, who doesn't deserve such a beautiful child. It is right that I should not have her. That I should have handed her over to better people.

"My . . . sister is inside," she says, clutching her parcel in one hand like a talisman.

"What is your sister's name?"

"Mala Akki," she says, and she begins to cry. My heart. I clutch at the branches in front of me and hold on so I won't be tempted to go to her. I bite my tongue until I taste the blood in my mouth.

"Where's your mother? How did you get here?" The nun looks down the road, but I am safely hidden from view. "Who brought you here?"

"Taxi uncle," she says.

"What is his name?"

"My aiyya's name is Raji Asoka. They got lost. Foreigners came and took them," she says now and cries even louder.

The nun takes her face in her hands. What gentle hands they seem, the way they tilt a little girl's chin upward to look at her, as if she would like to hear the truth but would love her anyway if she lied. "What are you talking about, baba? What foreigners? Where do you live?"

"I'm from the ocean. Near the fishing boats. But my aiyya fell after we came on the train and the bomb blast. And my akki went with him and they got stolen. That's what the policeman said."

The nun smoothes the back of her skirt and sits down on a chair. She draws my girl toward her, her arms around her. "And your father and mother, where are they?"

She looks down the path. "I don't have a mother," she says after a few moments. She says it. And when she looks back at the nun, she is not crying anymore. She has put her parcel of food down on the ground, and she is playing with the rosary around the nun's neck. It is a bright blue rosary, and I can see it from where I stand.

"No mother . . . ?"

No. The child shakes her head. She shakes it slowly, from side to side, in big movements. Then she gives the purse to the nun. "Train uncle will tell you everything. Train uncle will give you money to keep me," she says.

The nun takes the purse and shakes her head like this is not unexpected. She unfolds the paper inside and stares at it. She presses her lips together and looks across the gardens. I am sure she can see me, but she must not because she puts the paper back into the purse and stands up. "What is your name?"

"Latha Kumari, but my aiyya and akki call me Chooti Nangi, and my amma calls me Chooti Duwa, and sometimes, when she loves me, she calls me her pet, she calls me petiyo."

"Come then, Latha, let us go inside. We don't have room for grown children, but you can stay with the younger nuns at the sister house until we can find your uncle."

My little girl yanks free from the nun's hand at the last instance.

She comes back to the top of the steps and peers down the road, standing on tiptoe, bowing her head, trying to see through all the foliage between her and the bends in the road. No, don't come down here, child. This is the last thing I can do, and I have done it. Someone at this place will give you comfort and safety and a quiet life. Someone inside this building will do that for you. Go! Go with the nun! And still she stands and stands and stares down this road. The nun comes back to her and puts her arm around her. The girl won't go with her. The nun takes off her rosary and gives it to her, and at last she stops looking for me. She holds the bright blue beads in one hand and pours them into the other, back and forth, back and forth. She is still doing that when she goes in with the fair-skinned nun.

I don't know how long I wait, gazing at those steps. They are empty the way only things that contained too much can be. They are bathed in sunlight, and some of the flowers on either side have lost petals along the far edges. There's nothing on them. But a few moments ago they held everything. I look at it until my eyes hurt, but nothing changes. Nobody comes back out, and nobody comes up to the door from the road behind me. At last I hear a bell ringing inside. It is a loud, heavy sound, not the kind of peal I imagined I might hear in this place. It sounds dark and foreboding.

I shake my head. I must not dwell on such things, I must not imagine the worst, only the best for that child. That is my work now, to let her be. I make my way around the side of the convent wall until I see the path.

It is narrow, barely wide enough for my feet, and yet it is so smooth, so well-worn. It is as if nobody walks side by side on this trail, only in single file, one of them in charge, another clearly having given up control over the journey. Well, I walk alone, nobody behind, nobody in front.

The grass is thick with nidikumbha. I am hypnotized by the way they close and close and close before me, going to sleep the instant any part of my body or my clothes grazes their leaves. Like the eyelids of sleeping children. Only the powder-puff flowers, bright pink and tiny, remain erect and facing the sun.

I stumble on a root and fall. I feel a hundred pinpricks upon my exposed arms, on the side of my face, and deep into each palm. I close them tighter over the nettles, but there is only so far they can go, weak things. I sit up and open my hands. Like the beads to a broken necklace, these bits of blood. I rub them together, touch my face. I grind my palms into the skin. My palms are smeared now, but not thick like paint; it is just a brush of red and sweat and green things. Salty and grainy like the earth, on my swollen tongue. Around me there is only the sound of afternoon insects. Nothing that I can recognize as being of my kind.

I crawl for a little while. On my hands and knees, I am almost lower than the nearest plants, like an animal; a light-colored, four-legged creature. This is madness, and I am not mad. I stand up. I am empty-handed, and now, you, O gods, you who have taken everything, I have no more to hold or give or take or lose but myself. I rub the edge of my sari pota in my sweat and clean myself as best as I can. My face and hands will not get clean. Each new bit of cloth I use is smeared with just as much red and brown. Never mind. I will go like this. I cannot undo what has been done or reclaim what is now lost. I am on this path out of choice. I chose this. I chose Siri. Where is he now? Everybody lost and dead because of me, but not her. Not my last one. She is safe.

There it is. I can hear it coming, though it is so faint. Far away, somewhere in the distance, the high-low blast from the train. My answer, my hope. I walk faster, but I trip again, and so I stop and take off my slippers. Barefoot, it is easy to run downhill. After a minute or two, it is almost like flying. Nothing catches at me, no leaves, branches, stones, nothing at all. Only the breeze, and even that is on my back, pushing me forward, a blessing, an affirmation of intentions. I run until the path spits me onto the platform. That is how it is, the path and the platform almost one road, except that one tapers off in dust, the other picks up in concrete. I feel the change on the soles of my feet, abrasive and cold.

"Sir," I say to the stationmaster, who is standing there like he had never moved.

He steps back and flings up his hand as if to deflect an assault. "What? What? Where are you running to?"

"Sir, I am trying to catch the train."

"Are you from the convent? Did they send you to meet someone off the train?"

I suppose I do not look like the woman he met here before. Why would he remember? "Yes. I came from there. I need to fix a tear in my sari, sir. Do you have a box of matches? I can hold it to the flame and fix it; it's just some kind of nylon . . ."

"The train is coming soon." He checks his watch and glances down the tracks. "It will be here in a few minutes. You might miss it."

"Please, sir, I cannot go like this. Can I use the lavatory to fix my sari?"

He clucks and takes out a key from his pocket. "Here, be quick! You don't have much time at all."

"Sir, matches?"

He looks doubtfully at me. I look down and away from his feet. He shrugs and gives me a box of *Elephant* matches and looks away. It feels solid in my hand, a full box. I go into the station and to the bathroom at the back. I can barely see my face in the mirror, but I wash it with ice-cold water from the tap. Why shouldn't I clean myself up? I undo my sari and drape it again, my pleats neat, the wrap ending straight along the side of my body, the fall touching the ground. This is how my mother wore her sari. This is the way good women wear their saris. And I am not a bad woman.

I light the matches one after another. First the edge of the fall, then in a circle around the hem. Then the pleats that offset my waist. The fall burns slowly; it is still damp from tears and the plants and whatever is left of the blood of small wounds, but those things are no match for the fire. By the time I open the door and step around the back of the building toward the tracks, I can feel the flames reach tender parts of my body, my midriff, my ankles, the nape of my neck. This pain is bearable. This one I can tolerate. Nobody will need to light a pyre for me.

I walk along the tracks toward the sound of the approaching train. I hear the stationmaster from a distance now, and I begin to run, burning faster as I go. I picture them beside me, running, and I make them stop, grateful that they listen, this time they listen: Not you, Loku Putha, not you either, Loku Duwa. Nobody for me. None of you must come with me. Kumari. My Latha Kumari. My Chooti Duwa. Petiyo. No! Stop here! Go back! I close my eyes and let my feet take me toward the train. I will not think of them, no. These are not tears. Nothing will put out this fire. I will remember nothing. I am already dead.

Latha

The smell of smoke must have brought Mr. Vithanage into the room, she thought, for the first thing he did when he came in was to throw the purple silk to the ground and stamp all over it. She continued to pack, ignoring him until she couldn't anymore. He would not stop stamping on the sari with his feeble feet, like a child throwing a tantrum. But when she turned to look, she could see that it was not age that was making his feet lack the punch the job required. It was sorrow. The old man was actually crying, mopping at his face with a gray handkerchief.

Latha had never seen a man cry. She had seen Podian cry, but that was more like bawling, and in any case he was a boy, and, being slow in the head as he was, he would remain a boy. She had seen Thara cry, but those tears had seemed like whining to Latha. The only tears she had truly wanted to wipe dry, or whose unchecked pain she had felt in her very body, had been Madhavi's. Even Madhayanthi she had treated with some skepticism, her artful, careful eruptions so patently full of some ulterior design. But what could she do with old Mr. Vithanage?

"Mahaththaya," she said, "sit down, sit here," and she dragged over the chair from her table and helped him to sit down, wondering if he might have a heart attack from all the emotion swirling around the usually easygoing man, or at the very least from his own exertions over the sari. She put out the small flames that she had created with a few strong stamps from her own feet. It wasn't that hard. The sari was a heavy natural silk and did not burn easily.

Behind her, Mr. Vithanage blew his nose loudly, signaling recovery. She turned. He looked around the room and made a vague gesture with his hand to encompass everything in her space, including herself. Then he blew his nose again. "Latha, child, this is, all this . . . it is my doing."

"Sir, I will leave as soon as I finish packing. Then you won't have to blame yourself. And nobody will be able to blame me anymore for the things that have happened in this household." She emptied everything out of her bags and began repacking them neatly.

"Where are you going?"

"I am going to the convent," she said. "To where Leelakka is."

"Who? Who is that? Leelakka?"

"My sister."

Mr. Vithanage stopped blowing his nose. "You found your older sister?"

"Yes, when I went . . . When Vithanage Madam sent me to the convent, I met her there. Her name is Leela. We agreed. We promised."

"Does she know where your brother is?"

"Brother?"

"Yes, your older brother?"

Latha sat on the edge of her bed, still holding on to a sandal. It was a dark brown sandal with a silver buckle. She had bought it recently, and Gehan had been with her. He had taken her to the place where he went to get his shoes made, and he had seen her admiring it and offered to buy the pair for her. She was so glad she had said no, she could pay for them herself.

"I opened my purse and bought my shoes with my own money," she said to Mr. Vithanage, holding out the sandal for him to look at. "See? This is made of real leather. It says 'genuine leather' inside. Made at the *Leather Corporation*. This is very good quality. These kinds of shoes won't break, and that's why I didn't mind paying extra for them."

Mr. Vithanage took the sandal from her and examined it all

over. Strange how quiet the room seemed right then. Outside there were voices, Mrs. Vithanage's and Thara's, and every now and again Gehan's, but they were the kind that were used to fill uncomfortable space. The girls must have gone to their room, and yes, she could hear Podian clearing things, scraping, sweeping, rinsing, restoring. Inside her space there was the smell of singed fabric. She pushed at the sari with her foot. How powerful it had once felt to her, this same silk.

"Do you remember your brother?" Mr. Vithanage asked gently, giving the sandal back to her. "Do you remember anything at all?"

"She is not a real sister, she is someone I met there," Latha said, wanting very much to say it differently, to claim Leela as a blood relative. She shrugged. "But she said we could be sisters. I asked her, actually; I wanted someone for me. She said yes. She didn't have any family either."

Mr. Vithanage raised his eyebrows and blew his nose again, so vigorously this time that his head shook. He put his handkerchief away in his pocket. "Do you remember anything about the convent? How you got there?"

She shook her head.

"Do you remember when I came to get you?"

Again, she shook her head.

"You don't remember riding in the train with me? The noise in the tunnels? The chocolate?"

Chocolate! She remembered that. "*Cracker Jack* chocolate!" she said, smiling. "I remember, Vithanage mahaththaya, you bought me that. A whole one." Then she frowned. "Then you gave me money, didn't you?"

"No, Latha, I didn't give you money then. That was two different times. I . . . I knew your mother," he said. And there before her was a picture of Mr. Vithanage with her mother, some lovely creature whom he had loved and discarded like Gehan had discarded her, a woman whose daughter he had forced her to abandon.

"You are all the same." She spat and stood up. "Your kind—"

Mr. Vithanage looked mortified. "No! Not like that. I didn't know your mother like that! Stop . . . child, sit, please sit!" He clasped at his chest and coughed vigorously and then pounded his brow gently with his fist. She would have offered him water from her glass, it was sitting right there on the table, but that would have been insulting. So she sat down again and waited for his troubles to subside.

"I met your mother," he said, finally, "on the train up-country. I was going to visit my friend in Pattipola. I take the train once or twice a year, and one day I met your mother."

What did she want to know anyway about a mother? And a mother known to the Vithanages at that. Something vile must have clung to her, too, to allow her to let a daughter become what she had permitted Latha to become. And yet, "What was she like?" Latha asked, cautiously.

"She was, or she seemed to me to have been, an honorable woman," Mr. Vithanage said. "She was clearly from a respectable family, and she took good care of her children. Your father, too; he sounded like he had been an intelligent man. He had worked hard to try to change our country for the better, she told me. He had connections at the universities, and he was going to work for the government. He gave his life for his principles." He looked searchingly at Latha like he was testing her, or expecting her to pounce on him. "You were one of three children," he said at last. "You were the youngest."

Three children. Three. Herself and two others. Siblings. A brother and a sister. She tried to say the words to herself, silently, testing their merit. Aiyya, Akki, Aiyya, Akki, Aiyya, Akki . . . "Raji Aiyya . . . Mala Akki . . . ," she said suddenly, aloud. The names felt like sharp glass, except that, after the cut, there was only cool comfort, the soothing flow of blood.

"Yes," he said.

"They got lost," she said suddenly and closed her mouth with the palm of her hand, trying to take it back, that information that she had not known she had.

He held out his hands, palms up. "I don't know what happened to them."

"They got lost," she said again, feeling the knowledge seep out of some secret place and permeate her being, bringing pieces of memory with it, the smell of things: antiseptic and oils and rich soil, the sensation of some fragile dead thing, large and beautiful in her hands, the color red, the sound of explosions, the voices of strangers, soft, plump arms holding her and letting her go, the crisscross press of a bicycle rack against her bottom, the warmth of food against her chest, sharp fingers against her cheek, warm ones cupping her face, prayers, blue beads.

"The foreigners took them. My mother left me to go and find them, she said. She said she would come back."

"Your mother committed suicide," he said and waited a moment to see if that had any effect on her. It didn't. "She set herself on fire and threw herself in front of a train."

Latha stared at him. She tried to picture that, but all she could see was a ball of fire rolling like a wheel toward a train. "Where is my brother? And my sister, where is she?"

He shrugged. "I don't know," he said. "The nuns said that some old couple had come to the convent saying they knew your mother, and they wanted to take you with them, but they couldn't give any information that was useful and they were very poor, so they were sent away. I meant to try to find out about your brother and sister. When I came for you, the nuns told me that you had mentioned foreigners. But the police, even my friends in the government, couldn't do anything. They said it was useless to try to chase down foreigners . . ." He had been talking to his shoes, and he stopped and looked up at her, his face heavy with regret. "But I should have tried harder. If I had tried harder back then, when I first heard about you . . ."

"How did you know where to find me?"

"The nuns called. They had my name and number. I had written it down for your mother in case she needed help. I told you I was struck by her. She seemed so competent and gentle. I cannot believe . . . I intended only to give the nuns some money to look after you, to bring you up as a lay novice there."

Latha listened to Mr. Vithanage tell her how he couldn't bear to leave her. How they had called his house in Colombo and Mrs. Vithanage had contacted him in Pattipola. How he had gone to the convent right away, and how, when he realized that she was the same age as his own daughter, and that she had no mother or any family left, he had felt compelled to take her with him. He had thought that this was what the gods wanted from him. It was fate that he had changed compartments, gone to the one in which her mother had been. He had seen how her mother had seemed to care especially for her. Back then he had fought for her, having not even asked Mrs. Vithanage before he returned to Colombo, bringing her with him. He had not allowed his wife to talk him out of keeping her. He had meant to look after her only until she came of age, he said, until she could be married off. He had planned to tell her all this at that time.

"But after all that happened, you know, with . . . with . . . Ajith . . . we had to send you back to the convent, and then you were too old to be married, not good enough, that's what they said. Thara wanted to keep you for herself, to help her cope with . . . Gehan, I suppose, and help her raise her girls." She had grown up beyond his reach, become a young woman so fast, almost overnight, and he could no longer intervene in the direction of her life, he told her. That was why she'd had to stay with Thara.

Latha wanted to sit there and listen to him for a long time. To have the story of her life repeated to her, with new details to fill up and color the blank spaces, and to make it seem as though life had once been full of other possibilities, full of other people who had loved her and only her. But she wouldn't ask him for that. She did not want to give any of them, even Mr. Vithanage, the opportunity to refuse her anything ever again. So she simply sat and listened so long as he kept talking.

Podian came into the room. "Mahaththaya, Vithanage Madam wants you to come. She wants to go home now."

"Tell madam that I will go home after I have settled this," he said. Podian glanced at Latha, at the open half-packed suitcases, and backed away.

"You may not remember, Latha, but we tried to take you back to the nuns when you were very small, I don't remember how old now, but by that time it was hopeless. Thara would not let me leave you there. So we went to the Hakgala gardens instead and to the Diyaluma Falls and pretended it was an up-country trip. Thara got attached to you. You were . . . her friend."

"And now she can't wait to get rid of me," Latha said.

"We all pay for what we have done," Mr. Vithanage said, nodding.

"I have lost two children who should have been born to me, and two who came to me from the gods. Those children, those girls, they were my gift for staying here. But even they have finished with me. It is all right. We all pay. So must they."

"I no longer know where you could go to," he said after a long silence. "I don't know where they scattered your mother's remains. Even that, I didn't find out."

Amma. She hardly knew how to say that word without it being a reference to someone else's mother. What did she need of a mother's ashes now? Of a grave site? What would she do with one? No, it was better that she had never remembered the woman who had left her at that convent to find her own way. If this was where that path had led her, she would keep going forward, taking only herself.

"I have no use for the past," she said.

She got up and finished packing while he continued to sit there, in a not uncompanionable silence. She left some things: the sheets, the towel she had been using, shoes that Madhayanthi had broken when she played with them, old clothes, the string of twine behind the door on which she dried her underwear, the old mat she had once slept on, and also other bits of things that did not pack well, like oil and half-opened packets of shampoo. She took everything out of the suitcases and repacked them twice.

Her journey was deliberate. She was not running away and she was not being thrown out; she had a destination and an intention. When she was done, she swept the room and put all the dust and the ash and the destroyed sari into the wastepaper basket by the door. Then she took a fresh set of clothes and went to the servants' bathroom to wash and change.

When she returned to the room, Mr. Vithanage was still sitting there. She had combed and knotted her hair and dressed herself in the one sari that she owned, the one she had permitted Gehan to buy for her and, even then, only because it had been given to her as a gift. Had she been there, she would have paid for it herself. It was red and white cotton, hand-loomed. She wore it like the Southerners did, not like the Vithanages.

Mr. Vithanage sat there watching her put on her fine brown leather shoes and slide two thin bangles on, one on each wrist. Gold. Real gold bangles that she had got made at the jewelry store only this last year. She had traded in her star-shaped child earrings and Thara's little-girl bangles to do it, melting those down and paying only a little more for these two new bangles. They were like the two of them, she thought, herself and Thara, blended together, created out of the past but inhabiting a new incarnation. She touched her earrings to make sure they were there.

When he saw that she was ready, Mr. Vithanage got up and took one of her bags. Then he stepped out of the room, leaving her to follow.

"Where do you think you're going now?" Mrs. Vithanage asked in exasperation when Latha and Mr. Vithanage came out. "Stop it!" she said and tried to grab his hand when he didn't answer her. "Stop it! Where are you going with this creature?"

"I am going to take her wherever she wants to go," he said.

"She can go by herself," she said.

"I brought her into this situation—"

"Situation? We were not a situation, we were a family!"

"I will get her out of it," he finished.

Latha kept on walking. How serene she felt. How disinterested now in the people who stood about her. All the years she had thought she was in control, she had been fooling herself. She had been exactly what they had wanted her to be: a servant. Serving them, serving herself to them, something that they packed along with other necessities, like rice and salt and dhal. There to trim the beginnings and endings of their days, there to embellish their lies, there to blame their half-truths on. Present every waking moment to wash them of guilt and innocence.

And what had they known of her? What had she known of herself, if in an hour she could have uncovered so much? Yes, this at last was peace, to know herself, to guide her body through such waters, to be able to hold her head above the tide of their deceit and abuse. They shed off her. First Mrs. Vithanage, then Thara, then Gehan, then Mr. Vithanage, and last the girls. Last of all, Madhavi. Virtue consisted mostly of avoiding temptation, and Madhavi was that temptation, carrying her unloved self in her lovely form like poison, willing Latha to look at her, to fulfill a need. But no, she was, beautiful as she was, adored as she was, simply another Thara reborn, and there was no room in Latha's life for such insatiable, blind need.

"Latha!" Thara said, her voice tearful, followed by full-blown sobbing.

"Latha!" Gehan said and turned around as he caught the echo in Madhavi's voice. "Latha!"

Madhayanthi said nothing, but she took her older sister's hand.

Mr. Vithanage put the suitcases into the dickey. He opened the front passenger door for Latha, shut it firmly behind her, and tapped the door several times. The car was still reversing when Podian came into view, dressed in his one good pair of longs and short-sleeved shirt, a siri-siri bag of belongings in his hand. He put up his palm, looking directly at Mr. Vithanage. Mr. Vithanage stopped the car and rolled down the window.

"Get in," he said, ignoring the new commotion this caused on the steps of the veranda. Podian opened the back door and climbed in. He caught Latha's glance in the rearview mirror and gave her a weak smile.

The station felt crowded and familiar to her. Mr. Vithanage stood by as she bought tickets to Hatton for herself and for Podian. He bought a platform ticket for himself and waited while they had their bags opened and checked by the police. They called her lady, *nona*, when it was Latha's turn. Podian they referred to as malli, and their voices were not unkind.

"You don't have to stay," she told Mr. Vithanage. "We will be all right."

"I know," he said. But he didn't move. They waited in silence until the train arrived. And after they had boarded, and he had helped hoist the suitcases in and wedged them in the overhead racks and said good-bye and left, he came back to their window with a bag of oranges. "You might feel sick on the train," he said. "The night mail train won't get there till early morning."

"Thank you," Latha said, acknowledging the gesture with a real smile.

"If they . . . if the nuns . . . don't allow you to stay, give them my number and ask them to call me," he said, pressing a piece of paper into her palm. He held her hand in both of his for a moment and then dropped it.

The horn blew, and the train jerked forward and then rolled backward. Mr. Vithanage took out his handkerchief and wiped his entire face. He tried to speak but didn't seem able to. Latha felt sorry for him. She took an orange out of the paper bag and lobbed it gently at him. He caught it but lost his handkerchief in the process. He laughed and waved at her with the orange. She stared at him until the train had left the station and he was out of sight, then she unfurled her palm and let the piece of paper with his name blow out and join the accumulating litter beside the tracks.

"Akka, where are we going?" Podian asked.

"We are going up-country to get Leelakka, then we will come back south," she said. "I know how to live in the city. I have money. I will take care of you."

He nodded and settled into the cushioned seat of their booth. She took stock of him. He was thin but strong, everything seemingly gone toward building muscle. Yes, he was not smart, but there would be a job for him, and she to make sure it was good work. She slipped her hand underneath her sari pota and stroked her smooth belly between the waistband of her sari blouse and the top of her pleats.

"We will be a proper family," she said. "I will see to that."

Acknowledgments

This book is the work of many hands.

I am indebted to Michael Collier and to the Bread Loaf Writers' Conference, where my writing life received its first, profoundly transformative, affirmation.

I thank my teachers Percival Everett, Lynn Freed, Ashley Halpé, Charmaine Scharenguivel, Ursula Hegi, Nihal Fernando, Margot Livesey, Carole Anne Taylor, and the late Jean Pinto and Rehana Mohideen. Some example of the wisdom they imparted is, hopefully, to be found within these pages. Their kindness and affection abide with me. This book began in Lynn Freed's workshop and evolved in sight of her passionate contribution to the literature of home; I am tremendously grateful to her.

I am blessed to have Julie Barer and Emily Bestler as my agent and editor. Their love for their work, their enthusiasm for mine, and their commitment to retaining the integrity of the story I wanted to tell is the stuff of dreams. I am thankful to Kate Barker, Heleen Booth, and Mariagiulia Castagnone for taking a chance on a new author.

I owe a special debt of gratitude to Mary Akers, Charles Baxter, Amaud Jamal Johnson, Charles Rice Gonzalez, Rishi Reddi, and Paul Yoon, talented and big-hearted people who provided a steadying hand.

Lisa Erickson, Rebecca Green, and Dorian Karchmar read the

earliest versions of this work, which my dear friend Sara Taddeo made possible for me to write. Without the goodwill of the people of Maine, particularly those in Waterville, who supported the many projects in which I was involved, I would not have found the courage to stay the course.

Were it not for my brother Arjuna's brave conduct of his life, I might never have been inspired to write my first, unpublished novel, and through it, find my way to this one.

This book's sense of place and history comes from my brother Malinda, who, with unstinting patience and love, offered his guidance during countless hours when my day was already his night.

Thank you most of all to my girls, Duránya, Hasadrī, and Kisārā, who learned young how to let me go and the joy of a creative life; and to Mark, who separates the grain from the chaff and continues to affirm despite the imbalance. They are the true loves of my life.

I remain grateful to Latha, who was once a friend.

ml

FREEMAN   Freeman, Ru.

A disobedient girl.

DATE			

BAKER & TAYLOR

OCT 2009